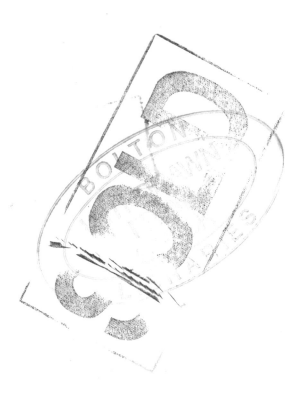

BOLTON LIBRARIES

BT 096 0419 7

Son of Thomas

Son of Thomas

Sarah Shears

BOLTON PUBLIC LIBRARIES

PIATKUS

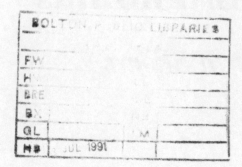

BOLTON PUBLIC LIBRARIES

FW		
H		
BRE		
BX		
GL		M	
HB	JUL 1991		

0960497.

14912484

Copyright © 1991 by Sarah Shears

First published in Great Britain by
Judy Piatkus (Publishers) Ltd of
5 Windmill Street, London W1

British Library Cataloguing in Publication Data

Shears, Sarah
    Son of Thomas.
    I. Title
    823 [F]

    ISBN 0-7499-0063-6

Phototypeset in Compugraphic Times 11/12pt by
Action Typesetting Limited, Gloucester
Printed and bound in Great Britain by
Mackays of Chatham PLC, Chatham, Kent

Part One

Chapter One

Subaltern Thomas Cartwright would never forget that night – the night he galloped back across the barren Punjab plain, sweating and fearful, facing a court martial. Three days and three nights absent without leave. It was a very serious offence. Yet he had no recollection of those three days and nights. He had drunk himself into a stupor on the strong native liquor the girl had purchased at his command. His only vague memory was the stink of his own vomit, and the soothing voice of the girl.

'I am here, Sahib. I am your slave.'

Back to the garrison. Back to face his punishment as a soldier of the Queen. Back to his adored young wife, Rosalind. He had hardly given a thought to the girl. He couldn't even remember why she was there. She was so small and light against his chest. A native servant had no status. They were back in the compound behind the trees, where the native servants had their quarters, when the shot rang out and the girl's body slumped.

'I take her, Sahib.' It was no sniper's bullet that had killed her. It was her own father, the bearer, the man they called 'Boy'.

'I take her, Sahib,' he had repeated in his calm, quiet voice, and reached up his skinny arms to receive the limp bundle. Then he was gone. It was all over in a matter of seconds, and only the warm blood on his clenched hand to prove it was not a dream.

When he had calmed Jason, and wiped away the blood on a soiled handkerchief smelling of vomit, he dropped it

3

in the long grass and led the horse through the trees into the moonlit garden.

Rosalind was hunched in a lounge chair on the back verandah. She lifted a tear-wet face and gasped, 'Thomas! I thought ... They said ...' and stumbled to her feet. Only then, as the flimsy negligee fell away from her naked body had he realized she was carrying his child. He could not remember when they had last slept together. Too much whisky and too much lusting after the fascinating Isabella Foster-Clarke.

Shamed by his neglect after only a few months of marriage, he had scolded her gently: 'Have I not told you, my sweet, never to listen to gossip?' Then he had taken her in his arms and promised his guilty conscience he would be faithful, from henceforth, according to their marriage vows, 'Till death us do part.'

Colonel Maitland regarded his son-in-law with the critical eyes of a commanding officer, and the suppressed anger of a doting father. His lovely daughter had married this handsome subaltern only a few months after he had joined the regiment, 'still wet behind the ears', a Sandhurst cadet with all the dash and charm of youth, combined with a loyalty and dedication inherited from a parent who had died gallantly some twenty-five years ago, at this same garrison. Stiff as a ramrod the young officer stood before him, and he was duty bound to hand him over to the guard. There could be no favouritism, and Thomas would not expect it.

Torn between his duty to the regiment and his love for Rosalind, his only child, it was the kind of situation he would prefer to shelve, but it had to be faced. For an officer to be absent without leave for three days and three nights was a very serious offence, punishable by a court martial, and a court martial almost invariably concluded with the culprit being dismissed the service.

The Colonel sighed. To punish Thomas was to punish Rosalind. She was a daughter of the regiment. Born to the sound of the bugle, the tramp of Army boots, the neighing of horses, the raucous voices of sergeants, and scarlet uniforms. They were two of a kind, for Thomas had also been spoiled, from babyhood, by that doting grandmother who

4

had attended the big military wedding at Aldershot. As for Rosalind, he had never denied her anything. A motherless child, especially a girl, is a big responsibility for a man.

'Stand easy!' he barked irritably. 'Now, what have you to say for yourself? Such conduct is inexcusable, but you are entitled to a hearing.'

'Thank you, Sir.' Thomas stood at ease, but his heart was hammering. His whole future was at stake, and he knew it. To be dismissed the service was a terrible disgrace. He would never live it down. It must not happen. He couldn't bear it! He squared his shoulders, and told his story, truthfully and convincingly, while his commanding officer listened, absorbed, to the tale of a small boy growing up in the image of his father — the handsome hero in the silver frame on the nursery mantelpiece. Proudly the boy had followed in his father's footsteps, through prep school, public school and Sandhurst, to join his father's old regiment. That photograph was still there, but the proud image was shattered for ever when a native servant revealed the truth.

'He asked me whether I had visited my father's grave in the military cemetery. I told him I had not yet done so, but intended to do so in the near future. I knew, of course, he had served my father and that he had loved him, so I was not unduly surprised by the question.'

Thomas's voice was husky with emotion as he continued the story. 'He then told me, "Sahib, you will not find your father's grave in an honourable place, with those who died for their Queen and country. He lies in a corner, beside a memsahib who was not your mother. He lay with her, Sahib, many moons, and when he found she lay also with another officer, Sahib, he killed the memsahib with his bare hands, and shot himself in the garden of her bungalow".'

Thomas paused, his young face strained and pale, his blue eyes misted with tears. 'I swore at him, Sir. I told him he was a liar. "Go and see, Sahib. I speak the truth," he answered me. And I went, that same night, and found those two graves, marked only by plain wooden crosses, untended, bare of flowers — and the shame lay heavy on my shoulders. I am his son, born in the same image, his shame is my shame. I drank and drank of that strong native liquor. I remember only that I fed and watered my horse, Jason. That is all I remember of those three days and three nights. You must believe me, Sir.'

'I do believe you, my boy. Sit down.'

And Thomas collapsed on the nearest chair, and buried his head in his hands.

The Colonel studied that bowed head. As a father-figure to his young officers, he had often to listen to problems of a domestic nature, and help solve them with sensible advice and warm sympathy. But this was a problem he had never encountered in all his years as a commanding officer. He was profoundly touched by such a confession. But discipline must be maintained. It was a decision that he alone could make. His heart ached for Thomas, so shattered by this cruel blow to his young pride. To have built up a hero's image over the years only to have it shattered at the start of his army career was a tragedy. He cleared his mind of sentiment, and of the picture of his beloved child sent back to England with a husband stripped of his scarlet uniform and stripped of his pride. Sympathy must not be allowed to interfere in his decision. Duty and loyalty were the key words. The regiment was his first loyalty, and duty an essential part of that loyalty.

All about them the garrison went about its normal routine. It was a world apart, remote as an ocean liner on the high seas. Men died on the Frontier, women died in childbirth, children died of fever and all were buried in that military cemetery where English roses bloomed, and green mounds were kept watered by a small native boy with a large watering can. The Colonel attended all funerals, but he had not seen the two isolated graves, as Thomas had described them.

When he spoke, his voice was the voice of the father-figure, infinitely kind and understanding, not the stern disciplinarian. 'What have you told Rosalind?' he asked.

Thomas lifted his head. He seemed to have aged ten years in those few anguished moments. The careless, golden youth was gone for ever. The man who stared from dull eyes was haunted by the ghost of a hero who had existed only in the imagination.

'I told her I had been on a secret mission to the Frontier, Sir.'

'That was sensible. There is no need for her to be told the truth.'

'No, Sir.'

'Am I right in assuming that only three people are aware of the actual reason for your absence – you, myself, and the native servant?'

'That is so.'

'Is he trustworthy? Is he likely to speak of this matter to the other servants?'

'I would trust him with my life. As for talking of confidential matters to the other servants, that he would never do, for he considers himself superior. That would be beneath his dignity. Boy is a very dignified person.'

'Boy? My sister has spoken of him, when she kept house for you during those weeks Rosalind was recovering from the measles. There was a daughter he had trained to wait on the memsahibs. What became of her? Is she still maiding Rosalind?'

'She died, quite recently. She was only ill for a few days. Some kind of fever. Boy sent his sister, quite an old woman, but actually more useful than the girl. She has been in service as an Ayah to several army families, I understand.'

Thomas had every reason to withhold the truth, and Boy's conscience was clear. A father must have obedience. She was promised in marriage to a farmer. It had been a mistake to teach her the ways of the English memsahibs. The silly child had fallen in love with the beautiful young Sahib, and run away with him. Did she suppose, in her ignorance, that an English Sahib would lie with a native servant? She must have been mad. He was shamed by such a dishonourable daughter. So he killed her, and his beloved young Sahib was back where he belonged. It was the Will of Allah.

'Rosalind is expecting a child. The doctor has confirmed it, only an hour ago,' Thomas said, surprisingly.

'That is splendid news. Congratulations, my boy.' They shook hands gravely.

'I had noticed she was getting a little plump, but attributed it to all the tea-parties and too many of those fancy cakes. She doesn't get the exercise to which she has been accustomed. A quiet game of croquet is all very well, but she misses the

7

riding and the dancing. The doctor knows best about such matters, so we must abide by his advice.'

The Colonel stroked his Vandyke beard thoughtfully. 'I have no doubt you will think of something to amuse her, my boy, during the tedious period of pregnancy, other than the croquet and tea parties.'

'I shall do my best, Sir.'

'Perhaps you could teach her to play chess?'

Thomas's mouth twitched with amusement. Rosalind and chess were about as far removed as Rosalind and Charles Dickens. Anything of a serious nature was boring to his adorable little wife. Surely her father should know her pretty head was stuffed with such petty decisions as whether to wear the garnet necklace or the pearls with her new afternoon tea-gown − whether to adopt the new hair-style that was all the rage among the young wives − whether to place a definite order with Hatchards of Piccadilly for the latest title by her favourite romantic novelist. Both men knew they were going to need all their patience and tolerance in the weeks ahead. The Colonel was wishing his adored child might have been spared such a traumatic experience for at least another twelve months. But these virile young subalterns, straight from Sandhurst, were all alike, and could not control their passions. Rosalind a mother at the tender age of eighteen? It was inconceivable.

'I shall take the greatest care of her, Sir.' Thomas interrupted his anxious thoughts.

'It's your company she will need, my boy, during the next few months. Then the baby will occupy much of her time, I daresay.'

It was wishful thinking. They both knew the infant would be handed over to the Ayah, who would cherish her 'Baba' with all her native patience and loving care until the regiment was drafted back to Aldershot. The baby would be a plaything, to dangle on her lap and show off to the other young mothers. There was so much the Colonel could have said to the young officer, but he kept silent. Fate had dealt him a cruel blow, and he would not add to his distress. The fact remained, Thomas had been neglectful. He had spent too much time in the Mess,

8

and his close association with Isabella Foster-Clarke was no secret.

So they parted and went their separate ways, both knowing they had skirted a dangerous topic.

The Colonel's sister limped painfully up the steps of the bungalow and was greeted by Boy, in a starched white coat and white trousers. He salaamed respectfully.

'Good morning, Memsahib.'

'Good morning, Boy.'

He liked the Colonel's Memsahib. She was one of the few English memsahibs who had taken the trouble to learn enough Hindustani to converse with the servants. The young Memsahib would not bother, so Boy had to act as interpreter. The Ayah spoke a little English, but only what was actually required in the nature of her duties.

The Ayah was overjoyed at the news of the new baba expected later in the year. It was her life. For the first three years she would carry the child on her hip, unless she was commanded to put it down, but the memsahibs were usually too much occupied with their own pleasures, and seldom interfered in the nursery routine. The children became difficult to manage as they grew older. They slapped and kicked, threw their food on the floor, and would not do as she asked. They called her rude names, and said she had a smell, but she washed herself all over every day, and put on a clean sari. She was humble and apologetic, but the children had no use for her in that last year before the regiment was drafted back to Aldershot.

'Allah is good, Memsahib. Allah has blessed the seed in your womb. The seed is fertile,' she told Rosalind, when Boy had imparted the news.

'It has nothing to do with Allah. And I wish you would not speak of my womb as though it were a piece of soil. I find it singularly indelicate,' her young mistress answered, haughtily.

'Very good, Memsahib.' Ayah salaamed respectfully and withdrew as silently as she had entered. Her brother had warned her that the young memsahib behaved like a spoilt child, and that much patience was required. Ayah was not unduly surprised, and patience was a virtue she had been practising for many long years.

'She turns a deaf ear when it suits her,' Rosalind complained to Aunt Millie.

'She hears, my dear, but she does not always comprehend your meaning, so she keeps silent.'

'Stupid woman! I wish I had brought Lizzie. First I had to endure that silly girl, sly as a little fox. Now this old woman, so humble and obliging! I declare I could scream.'

'An Ayah is only at her best with a child in her arms. They are all alike, these native women who serve the army families. You will see for yourself how loving and devoted an Ayah can be.'

Rosalind sighed, and changed the subject. 'Thomas has promised me a nice holiday in the Murree Hills. He says he will ask for compassionate leave, so that he can accompany me. I wish it was all over and done with, then I could enjoy myself again. It's all so tedious. I am bored to distraction.'

Auntie Millie was fond of her young niece, but there were times when she wished her brother had not spoiled the child so ridiculously. She also wished that Thomas had seen fit to control his passions in the marriage bed. It was too soon. Rosalind had barely recovered from the measles, and her heart was weakened. She could die. So many young wives died in childbirth. Rosalind's own mother had died. For eighteen years Auntie Millie had travelled around, at home and abroad with the regiment, the Colonel, his motherless child and a succession of nursemaids and governesses, none of whom ever had any control over the wilful little girl. Would there ever come a time when she could stay quietly at home and enjoy her retirement? She was remembering the fright Rosalind had given them when the naughty girl took an overdose of laudanum and nearly died, because her doting papa had not listened to her passionate declaration of love for the young subaltern from Sandhurst. She had her way. The engagement was announced, and the wedding followed a few months later.

'I have thought of something, dear, that should amuse you and at the same time provide us both with the means to visit the native market,' Auntie Millie told her niece.

10

Rosalind had the grace to look interested. The native market had been out of bounds, but she knew several of her friends bought materials there and visited the native dressmaker. It would be fun. Thomas would be cross, but she would blame Auntie Millie.

'I have seen that odious woman, Mrs Foster-Clarke, driving her own pony-trap, similar to the one we had in Singapore. Rumour has it that she has broken her ankle and cannot ride her horse. Be that as it may, we will ask your Papa to make enquiries about where you could get one. Her husband would know, would he not, since he would be the one to pay for it?'

Rosalind clapped her hands, like a child who has been promised a new toy.

'I think it would be the greatest fun. I shall ask Papa to order it this very day.'

'It may take a little time.'

'Not if I tell him it is just what I need to cheer me up. He was saying, only yesterday, he wished he could think of something to amuse me other than the croquet. And here it is! How clever of you, Auntie Millie, to think of such a device. I declare I can hardly wait.'

'Do not excite yourself, child or the doctor will blame me if your temperature is up again when he calls later.'

'But I *am* excited. I feel better already. My spirits flag when there is nothing nice to which I can look forward. I cannot help myself.'

'There is the baby.'

'Oh, *that*. I would sooner forget it until it actually arrives. Shall I tell you what Ayah had the effrontery to say to me? She said Allah had blessed the seed in my womb, and it was fertile. Was it not indelicate for a native servant to mention my womb? As for the seed, I cannot conceive what the woman is talking about. But they are all alike, these ignorant natives. Thomas dotes on Boy. I cannot understand why he is so well disposed to the fellow. A servant is a servant. Do you find him so very special?'

'He is certainly superior, and the other servants obey him.' Auntie Millie sighed with relief. To have to explain about the seed would have been so very embarrassing for an

11

unmarried lady. Fortunately, Rosalind's mind always hopped from one topic of conversation to another, so anything of an embarrassing nature could be avoided. But to dismiss the baby in such a casually indifferent way was shameful in an expectant mother. It was all too obvious that her niece hadn't the slightest interest in the unborn child. Would she respond to the infant when she held it in her arms? That was a question that could only be answered later.

It was not necessary for Boy to be told to make fresh tea for the Colonel's Memsahib, and he served it with his usual respectful salaam, together with the Huntley & Palmers ginger biscuits her sister sent from England in a sealed tin. After 25 years of faithful service to the English families, Boy was still amazed at their insistence on everything British made, even the biscuits. His young Memsahib drank only fruit juice now she was pregnant, and did not enquire the source of the little fancy cakes of which she was so fond. He bought them in the market, and he was quite sure it would not occur to the proprietor of the stall to wash his hands after he had relieved himself in the dust.

'Sahib has sent a message that he will be home early tonight, Memsahib,' he told his young mistress.

She squealed with delight, but it was the Colonel's Memsahib who thanked him.

'You are looking very beautiful tonight, my sweet,' was her husband's greeting when he arrived soon after sundown, and bent to kiss the flushed cheek.

Rosalind wrinkled her nose and complained, 'You have been drinking that horrid whisky again.'

'One must be sociable. As I have explained, sweetheart, it is customary for men to have a drink together in the Mess at the end of a working day. It's relaxing.'

'You could drink fruit juice to please me, could you not, since I find the whisky smell so very distasteful?'

'They do not serve fruit juice in the Mess. Fruit juice is for ladies and children. Whisky is for men.'

'So you say, but it does not signify. If you love me, you should wish to please me.'

'I *do* love you. Haven't I told you so a million times?' He sat down, pulled her onto his knees and kissed her pouting mouth. 'Tell me what you have been doing with yourself all day,' he coaxed.

She stroked his cheek affectionately. This was a good moment to ask a favour. She had discovered, in these early months of marriage, that one must be clever in choosing the right moment. She had made the mistake soon after they were married of chattering about domestic matters at the breakfast table. Now she breakfasted in bed to avoid a scene.

'Auntie Millie has been here for most of the day,' she told him. 'We played a game of croquet before lunch, and I won. After the siesta, she read to me from a novel by Mrs Henry Wood till teatime. She had the pleasantest suggestion for my entertainment. You will never guess, so I will tell you. That odious woman, Mrs Foster-Clarke, is riding around in a pony-trap with a broken ankle. Why should we not have a similar contraption?'

Thomas knew about the broken ankle, and had called to offer his sympathy. He writhed under the implication that his fascinating ex-mistress was an 'odious woman'. Since he was still on his best behaviour, following that affair of being absent without leave and narrowly escaping a court martial, he had not been invited to spend the evening with Isabella. It was not in his nature to eat humble pie or to repent of his misdeeds. Life was a challenge, and should be lived dangerously. It was a man's world, and when a wife held the reins too tightly, a husband had every reason to find his pleasures elsewhere. Isabella excited him as his adorable Rosalind would never excite him. Isabella reminded him of his Aunt Kate. She wore the same French perfume and used the same tricks. When he arrived for a chota peg, he would find her in the bath. And there is no better place to enjoy a romp than in the bath!

'You are not listening,' Rosalind complained.

'I have heard every word,' he lied.

'Then you agree it is an excellent plan?'

'Indubitably,' he said, with casual disregard of its nature.

'It is just a matter of acquiring the pony and trap, and Papa will know best how to set about it, will he not? Darling, it will be the greatest fun. I have always wanted to explore the native market.'

13

'The native market?' Thomas removed the clinging arms from around his neck, and his eyes were dangerously bright. 'The native market is out of bounds.'

'But that is the reason for the pony-trap. You were not listening! Now you are going to spoil it.' She began to cry.

Thomas could not bear to see her tears. She always got what she wanted in the end, he thought irritably.

'*If* we can get the pony-trap, and *if* you promise not to get out of it, and if Boy drives the wretched conveyance, then I will ask permission for you and Auntie Millie to visit the native market,' he grumbled.

'Thank you, darling. You are so good to me.' She dried her tears.

'Then you can be good to me. That is a fair exchange, is it not? I want to make love to you.'

She slid off his knees and asked, tremulously, 'Have you forgotten what the doctor said?'

'Damn and blast the doctor! Do we have to live our lives in fear and trembling of what might happen if we ignore his advice?'

'Pray do not use such offensive language.'

'Offensive? I could tell you of several offensive words beginning with 'b' if you care to listen?'

'No, I should not.'

'Then am I not allowed to make love to my own wife without the doctor's sanction?'

'Thomas, I do declare you can be so very provoking. It is not me we are considering. It is your child.'

'*My* child? Ha! Ha! This is interesting. So you had no part in it? So you were not aware I had taken you, and we two were joined together as one, according to our marriage vows? Have you forgotten the trauma of our wedding night, or shall I jog your memory? You refused me, your own newly-wed husband, and I rushed out of the room and into the street in torment, straight into the arms of a prostitute who was waiting for a customer. I was sorely tempted, for my loins were aching with desire, and I had already erected.'

'Stop! Stop!' Rosalind cried, piteously, covering her ears. But Thomas pulled her hands away, and she stood there, wringing her hands, shivering with the memory of that unforgettable night.

'I told the woman I had changed my mind, and I gave her a sovereign when her charge was a shilling. *One shilling*, my sweet. Can you believe that? To prostitute yourself for every Tom or Harry. The pity of it. So I gave her a sovereign, and she bit it to see if it was fake. Then I came back to you, my adorable little wife, on her wedding night, and found you sobbing in the marriage bed. I took you in my arms and was ashamed. Yet what had I done? Only expected what every man expects on his wedding night. With my body I thee worship, I had sworn, and it was true. But how could I worship you my sweet, when you pushed me away?'

'It was not you, Thomas. It was that ugly thing. I did not know it was there. I had never seen a naked man, or a naked woman. Young ladies are taught to be modest, and to cover their private parts. It was a shock when you lifted my nightgown. And you cannot conceive what I suffered when I touched that ugly thing. I was near to swooning.'

'And you still think it ugly?'

'Yes. I cannot help myself.'

'That is a pity, for we cannot enjoy the perfect union of man and wife while you consider the very means of that union repulsive. You say you love me, sweetheart, when what you mean is cuddles and kisses. For a man it is something more, much more. It is the absolute ecstasy, and the profound satisfaction of intercourse. If you could forget the ugliness of the penis, we could enjoy such rapture together.'

'Is that what it is called? I do declare I have never heard the word.'

Thomas yelled with laughter. 'Isn't that priceless! What shall I do with you? Come to bed, my adorable innocent.'

'You will not mind if I close my eyes?'

'I mind only that you open your legs,' he chuckled, and swung her into his arms.

'Must you be quite so vulgar, Subaltern Cartwright?' she chided.

'No, Ma'am. I shall conduct myself with the utmost propriety,' he teased – and pushed open the bedroom door.

*

15

'I wish you had not mentioned this foolish escapade to the child. It is unlike you, Millie, to be so indiscreet,' the Colonel chided his sister the following day.

'My dear brother. I am at my wits' end to think of something fresh to amuse her. She is bored with the croquet and she tires so easily when I suggest a walk. The doctor said to keep her occupied and cheerful. That is all very well, but he does not say how it should be done. Thomas has given his consent, providing we take Boy with us to drive the conveyance, and to barter with the shopkeepers should we wish to purchase anything.'

'You know how I dislike circumventing army regulations, and the native market is out of bounds for the officers' wives and children.'

'Then why has Foster-Clarke's wife been seen in the market? Boy tells me he has seen her several times of late in the pony-trap.'

'Drat that woman! If her husband were not one of my best officers, I should feel inclined to have him transferred to another regiment, but I cannot spare him. His knowledge of the movements of the frontier tribesmen is invaluable. No other officer has succeeded in penetrating their strongholds. He speaks their dialect fluently, and he is a master of disguise. His own mother would not recognize him. How he comes to be married to such a woman is beyond my comprehension. No, we have to contend with her. There is no alternative.'

'Then the regulation must be lifted, or we shall be accused of favouritism.'

The Colonel sighed. 'I suppose it could be left to the discretion of the husbands. Accompanied by a reliable servant, the wives and children should be safe enough. As for the pony-trap, they probably hired it. Foster-Clarke would not go to the expense of purchasing such a conveyance when his wife will be back on her horse as soon as the ankle has mended.'

'How did the accident occur?'

'She was climbing on a wall and missed her footing.'

'To what purpose should a lady be climbing on a wall?'

'For a bet, so the story goes. There is nothing that woman will not attempt to attract attention to herself.'

'So long as she stays away from Rosalind, that is all I care about. The child has a positive dislike of the woman, and is barely polite when we meet her.'

The Colonel made no comment. Thomas was to blame for his close association with Isabella Foster-Clarke – a dangerous woman, in her mid-thirties, who knew how to attract the young subalterns with their child-wives, just out of the schoolroom, innocent as new-born babes. The grape-vine spread rumours with the speed of a prairie fire, and his handsome son-in-law had not escaped, for all his cleverness. They had been lovers, and could still be lovers, for Isabella Foster-Clarke had the audacity to flaunt all the conventions.

'Then you think the pony-trap is for hire?' his sister was asking.

'I am sure of it, but I will have it confirmed and let you know tomorrow.'

Rosalind was in no mood for a disappointment. The morning sickness left her feeling weak and wretched. The Ayah fussed over her and promised her young Memsahib it would soon be over.

'The pony-trap is for hire,' Auntie Millie explained. 'Mrs Foster-Clarke has the first option, that is to say she has the use of it from 10 o'clock till noon each day. Your Papa has arranged for the trap to be delivered here at 8 o'clock.'

'But I cannot be ready so early when I feel so wretchedly ill. Do you suppose that odious woman would change with us?'

Auntie Millie sighed with exasperation. She, too, was suffering acutely with arthritis, and her joints were stiff and painful, but she was spartan by nature and upbringing, and put up with it. The doctor had prescribed laudanum to ease the pain, but it was kept in a locked cupboard, since that fright they had with Rosalind taking an overdose.

'I will send Boy with a note to the Foster-Clarke's bungalow. There is no harm in suggesting it, since she must know you are expecting a child.' She limped away to the drawing-room, and when she had penned the note, she went in search of Boy.

'I go at once, Memsahib,' said he, obligingly, and she

17

waited on the verandah for his return, watching the garden boy busy with the hose. She knew he crept away as soon as her back was turned, but he was only a child, with a child's mentality. Once again she was spending more time in this household than in her brother's, but they seemed to need her. Everything revolved around Rosalind and the unborn child. Would it be a boy or a girl? Thomas wanted a son. Rosalind had not yet shown the slightest interest in the child she carried. Perhaps it was too soon.

When Boy returned he brought only a verbal message. It was impolite and most improper, but at least it was agreeable.

'Memsahib Foster-Clarke say she go early. It make no trouble. She say to tell you she is much pleased about the baby,' he reported, gravely.

'Did she indeed? Thank you, Boy.'

They exchanged a meaningful smile.

The weeks dragged by. The daily outing in the pony-trap proved an excellent idea, but there still remained much of the day to be planned agreeably. Rosalind tried the patience even of the patient Ayah with her childish whims and fancies. She became so possessive of Thomas, he dreaded the moment he must leave the lively company of his brother officers in the Mess to return to the fretful company of his young wife. If this was the natural state of pregnancy, there would be no more of it, he promised himself, and Auntie Millie was inclined to agree with him.

With Boy to barter for the materials Rosalind chose from the shop in the market, they had no need to set foot in the place. The shopkeeper carried out bales of silk, satin and muslin, and all kinds of trimmings for her inspection. She was much too extravagant and overspent her dress allowance, but she was so pleased with her purchases, Auntie Millie hadn't the heart to upbraid her. With a generous contribution of 200 rupees from the Colonel, however, Thomas was spared the ignominy of having to borrow money to settle his wife's dressmaking bills. The native dressmaker, his sons and grandsons were kept busy all year with orders from the wives of the army officers and high-ranking civil servants.

Few women could resist the colourful selection of materials, and it was such fun to have the little man attend you, at your home, with nothing more than a tape-measure, a notebook and a stubby pencil. Designs were chosen from the English magazines, or copied from favourite gowns. The craft was handed down from father to son, and the grandsons could be seen squatting, cross-legged on the floor, diligently serving their apprenticeship.

When the ban was lifted, and more pony-traps became available for hire, it became an amusing way to pass the time. Whether or not you had money to spend, you were served with dainty cups of tea in your pony-trap. Boredom was a common complaint among the young wives who had nothing else to do but amuse themselves. One English governess would give lessons in the morning to children from several families, while the ayahs took care of the little ones. During the hottest season of the year, the wives and children, with governesses and ayahs, would travel to the Murree Hills, where they enjoyed the invigorating air of a higher altitude, pleasant walks and gardens. For those who wished to get away from the faces they saw every day for nine months of the year, there was Simla. The best accommodation was usually reserved for the wives of senior army officers and civil servants, whose children had already been despatched to boarding schools in England. Boredom also affected the older generation to a lesser degree, for there was money to spend more lavishly on bridge parties and exclusive little dinner parties, and more servants. The snobbery of the senior officers' wives and the strict control of protocol did not concern the young wives, who were not invited anyway, unless it was the occasion of the Queen's Birthday, when the Colonel was host to a formal dinner, and all were seated according to rank. For this occasion, even the youngest wife of the youngest subaltern had to afford a new gown − or die of shame.

Isabella Foster-Clarke was a law unto herself, and her dinner parties always included at least two of the young subalterns, her favourites being Thomas Cartwright and David Jones. That they were sworn enemies, and had, at one time, been rivals for the hand of the Colonel's daughter, was an added attraction, not a deterrent, since it added spice to the evening's entertainment.

Thomas was jealous of the young Welshman, whose singing voice was guaranteed to dispel the boredom of any musical evening. His dark good looks rivalled the fairness of the other. They had nothing in common, these two, but their love for the Colonel's daughter and loyalty to the regiment. Thomas had a light-hearted charm and amusing manner. He was popular and enjoyed his popularity. Since his earliest years, growing up in his grandmother's house, there had always been someone to encourage his self-importance – an adoring Grandmama and sister, a young disciple at prep school and public school, and two loyal friends at Sandhurst. He strode through life with the confident air of a conqueror, and seldom stopped to consider those who were less fortunate. His doting Grandmama had encouraged in his small person an arrogant superiority that his own gentle mother had deplored.

'Give me a child until he is seven, and I will tell you what he will become' a learned Jesuit had once declared, and it was true.

Character was formed in those early years. Only once had Thomas Cartwright experienced the shock of disillusionment. Then he had drunk himself into a stupor rather than face the shameful facts of his father's death. The memory of that barren grave, so far removed from those who had died honourably, still haunted his dreams, but he gave no thought to the young native girl who had shared the purgatory of those three days and nights. Only his own mother and Boy had known the truth about his father. The Colonel of the regiment at the time of the tragedy had long since died, but now his own Colonel had been told the story, in confidence, but Rosalind would never know. It was a cruel blow to his pride. As for Boy, he had kept silent for twenty-five years, and only desperation had prompted him to disclose the truth to his young Sahib, and the conviction that history could be repeating itself. A fascinating Memsahib and too much whisky; the two together had once proved a disaster, and could do so again.

Foster-Clarke Sahib was away again, on one of his

dangerous exploits at the Frontier, and his Memsahib was enjoying her role as a convalescent with her broken ankle. On those early morning drives in the pony-trap, she would invite Subaltern Jones to accompany her, if only to tease his hated rival. David was a silent companion, but his eloquent dark eyes held the admiration to which she was accustomed. It was amusing to play off one against the other, and she had to be amused now that she was deprived of her two favourite pastimes, riding and dancing, until her ankle mended. It pleased her vanity that she still could attract the young subalterns and keep their wives guessing, though David was not yet married. Was he still in love with that silly, empty-headed little creature who kept her husband on such a tight rein because she carried his child? David denied it, but he was a dark horse, and could hide his feelings. Unlike Thomas, the naughty rascal! He would be bringing her flowers as soon as he heard that his rival had been favoured.

The Bearer raised the alarm, one morning, when he found his Memsahib lying, fully clothed, on the sofa. He put down her breakfast tray with hands that trembled, and touched her cheek. It was cold as marble, but her eyes were open, accusing him of something of which he was innocent, as so often in the past. She was a difficult, demanding Memsahib, who treated her servants badly, but to see her lying dead, and he the one to discover the body, was a frightening catastrophe. What if he were accused of her death? They would hang him by the neck as a murderer. A shuddering sigh shook his thin frame as he backed out of the room and hurried in search of the other servants, who came at his bidding because he was the head servant of the household, but they would not enter the room. They huddled in the doorway, peering with frightened eyes at the still form, with the bandaged ankle. An empty glass stood on the table beside the sofa. Their Memsahib drank like a man, the whisky and soda.

'I telephone Doctor Sahib,' the Bearer decided, and drove them back to the kitchen, where they stood waiting silently for further orders.

21

The Doctor spoke sharply to the bearer. 'Speak up, man! What are you saying?'

'Foster-Clarke memsahib, she is dead, Doctor Sahib.'

'All right. All right. I heard you the first time.' Doctor Sahib had little patience with native servants. They were all alike and went to pieces in an emergency, he told his wife as he kissed her goodbye. It was just a habit, but it meant a lot to a woman.

'Supposing one of us should die before we meet again?' she had explained, vaguely. So he dutifully kissed her cheek. Women had strange fancies, especially in pregnancy. He had actually known a woman who fancied nothing but bananas, but after the birth, would probably not eat another banana for the rest of her life! His own dear wife had lost their baby. She was no longer young, but the heart-ache was still there. She waved him away with her patient smile. He was a good husband.

A servant was waiting to take his horse, and he hurried up the steps of the Foster-Clarke bungalow and into the drawing-room, followed by the Bearer. Automatically, he felt for a pulse, and closed the lids over the staring eyes. There were so many questions to ask. There was no sign of a struggle, so how had she died, and why?

He picked up the glass and sniffed. The answer was here. 'Who served the Memsahib with her last drink?' he asked the servant.

'It was me, Doctor Sahib.'

'What time?'

'It was late, Doctor Sahib. The Memsahib go always late to bed.'

'How late? 11? 12?'

'It was after 12 when the Memsahib see her guests to the door, and I clear away empty glasses and make all tidy. Then I pour her drink.'

'And went to bed?'

'That is correct, Doctor Sahib.'

'So you were alone in this room while your mistress was saying farewell to her guests?'

'That is correct, Doctor Sahib.'

'Your mistress has been poisoned.'

22

The servant's eyes bulged with fright. He fell on his knees and pleaded brokenly, 'Not me, Doctor Sahib. I not poison the Memsahib.'

'I am not accusing you, man. Get up. I must see the Colonel Sahib immediately. There will be an inquest and many questions to answer. Nobody is blaming you, but it will be better if you can *prove* your innocence. You understand?'

'Yes, Doctor Sahib.'

'Very well. Close the shutters, fetch a sheet to cover your mistress, and lock the door.'

'Yes, Doctor Sahib.'

'Pull yourself together. *Nobody is blaming you.*'

The distraught servant salaamed respectfully, and watched him ride away.

Before the end of the day, the head servant was taken into custody, weeping bitterly, and protesting his innocence. The other servants were questioned, one by one, by the police inspector, who spoke fluent Hindustani, in the company of the coroner. They all confessed to fear of their late Memsahib, but for Foster-Clarke Sahib a deep respect. Since they were all sent to bed and only the head servant stayed up late to serve the drinks and other refreshments, he alone was responsible, and the others were dismissed to their quarters, where they stayed, huddled together like sheep without a shepherd, doing no work since Captain Foster-Clake had not yet returned from the Frontier.

The Colonel arranged the funeral in the military cemetery, and it was attended by the entire regiment, marching in slow and solemn procession to the haunting 'Funeral March' of Chopin. The coffin was draped with the regimental colours. It was a moving ceremony, and would have delighted the woman who had so often offended those who now honoured her memory.

The two young subalterns for whom she had shown such preference followed the cortège in stunned disbelief. Fortunately, they had not been present on that last evening, so were not questioned. It had been a quiet evening of bridge, and Isabella had won 100 rupees. She had lived extravagantly and was always in debt. Her husband would discover heavy bills to settle with the dressmaker and the wine merchants. The servants had received no wages for three months, so it was not surprising they stole from their mistress, and were sullen in their manner.

She had died alone, and her last moments must have been agonizing. In her flamboyant fashion, she had become the symbol of unconventional behaviour, and the envy of those who dared not risk their reputation. The young wives made no secret of the fact they would shed no tears for that 'odious woman' who had captivated their husbands. But the men who had known and admired her, shared her bed and her favours, were wondering how they could survive another four years on the Frontier without Isabella.

Thomas felt particularly deprived, because he had been a favourite. He needed the excitement and the danger in his private life, to compensate for the exacting demands of his child-wife. There was no pleasure in his home, and even the anticipation of a son and heir had lost its attraction.

Boy served his whisky and soda on the night of the funeral with a grave face, after the young Memsahib had retired to bed. They were both thinking of that other Memsahib, so long ago, who had no lasting tribute, no honourable grave. Yet the two women were similar in their self-indulgence and their disregard of the proprieties that were even more strict in that day and age. Both had died at the hands of an assassin.

'You are sad tonight, Sahib?' Boy asked quietly, as he waited to be dismissed.

'Yes. Who is to blame, Boy? We may never know. They say the bearer has been charged with the murder, but the poor fellow swears he is innocent.'

'He was the last to see her alive, Sahib. He poured the drink.'

'That does not prove he was guilty of poisoning the drink.'

'No, Sahib?'

Black eyes met blue eyes in a meaningful look, and suddenly Thomas was aware of the ugly and shattering truth behind this second tragedy. It was Boy who had waited in the shadows and had crept into the drawing-room that night. It could never be divulged, and the innocent servant would die.

'Thank you, Boy. That will be all for tonight,' said Thomas, quietly.

'Very good, Sahib.' Boy salaamed and went away on silent feet. He felt no remorse. It was the Will of Allah.

Chapter Two

The doctor and the midwife had been in attendance on Rosalind from the early morning of Tuesday till the late evening of Wednesday, when Rosalind was delivered of a son, so puny he was not expected to live.

Thomas has been appalled at her suffering, and her screams had chilled his blood. '*Never, never* again,' he told Auntie Millie. 'This is terrible. You must *do* something.' He acused the doctor of allowing his wife to suffer unnecessarily.

'I shall give her chloroform to assist the birth. This is not uncommon in a first child,' the harassed doctor explained. It was a difficult birth, and he was more anxious than he cared to admit, even to the midwife. 'Why not go to the Mess, my good fellow. You can do no good to your wife, or yourself, by staying here.'

'She is not going to die, is she?'

'No, she is not going to die.'

'I feel such a brute. She is such a child, and so frail.'

'It would have been wiser to wait a year or two, but what has wisdom to do with it? Now, off you go. I don't want a second patient on my hands. You wouldn't be the first husband to collapse during childbirth. We will send a servant to fetch you when it is all over.'

So Thomas went off to the Mess, to be fortified with chota pegs and good-humoured teasing by fellow officers who had all been through it. So he stayed with them, and was persuaded he would find his adorable wife smiling happily and singularly proud of her firstborn.

It was Boy who came to fetch him, his face aglow with

the joyful tidings. 'Allah is good, Sahib. You have a son!' he said.

'Congratulations! Another one for the regiment! Fill up the glasses, steward. We must drink the health of the son of Thomas.' It was Foster-Clarke, the senior officer present, who proposed the toast. Back from the Frontier, he had received the news of his wife's death with calm acceptance of the tragedy. They had lived their separate lives for so long, he could not pretend to grief he did not feel. The servants were back in the bungalow, the senior being appointed bearer, and life went on. They serve their Sahib with smiling faces and grateful hearts, for he had paid their wages and thanked them for their loyalty. After a decent interval, he would marry a young governess who would adore her husband and bear his children.

Back at the bungalow, Thomas found the Colonel sitting by the bedside of his exhausted daughter, full of praise for her brave performance, but there was no sign of the child.

'Where is my son?' he asked, as he bent to kiss her pouting mouth.

The 'Ayah has taken him to the nursery. I do not care for him. I do declare he is not even pretty,' she complained peevishly.

'Who wants a pretty boy, my sweet? I am sure he will grow up to be a most handsome fellow,' he teased, and hurried to the nursery, where Ayah was cradling the infant in her arms and Aunt Millie was fussing over a bottle. Ayah unfolded the shawl and he looked at the face of his son. Rosalind was right. He was not pretty. In fact, he was the ugliest scrap of humanity he had ever seen. A smudge of dark hair and dark eyes, too big for the tiny face.

'He is rather small, is he not?' he ventured.

'He will grow. You will see,' Auntie Millie promised, as proud as a hen with one precious chick.

'But he is dark, and we are both so fair.'

'It does not signify.'

'I thought you said all new-born babies had blue eyes?'

'So I did, but this little one is unique, aren't you, my precious?' And she handed the bottle to Ayah, and stood back, lost in wonder at the suckling child. 'It is a miracle he is alive. He was scarcely breathing, and blue in the face, but Ayah knew it was only warmth he needed,' said that good woman.

'Thank you, Ayah,' said Thomas, and went away. Saddling Jason, he galloped for miles across the moonlit plain, and gradually his sagging spirits revived, and he could think more hopefully of the future, and that tiny scrap of humanity born of their union. Auntie Millie could be right about his growth, but she could not change his darkness. There was something alien about the child. Thomas had no sense of parenthood, no sense of love, but that would come later. It *must*. It would be unnatural not to love the child they had conceived, but it was not surprising that Rosalind had handed him over to Auntie Millie and Ayah. The poor girl was exhausted from her ordeal. His son would get plenty of loving care from these two women, and would not miss his mother at this early stage of his life. Surely one pair of arms was as good as another to a young child?

'My son.' He tasted the words on his tongue, but they had no flavour. They were meaningless. He pulled Jason to a halt and sat there, bathed in moonlight, remembering the night they had galloped back to the garrison, haunted by the memory of a fallen idol and a barren grave in a military cemetery. Fate had usually favoured him, but not always of late, and he was much disturbed by the implication that he was no longer the favourite of the gods. First there had been the measles epidemic on the voyage, and Rosalind had succumbed to the malady and was isolated. To be separated from his young wife so soon after marriage was a cruel punishment. When at last they were settled in the bungalow, he had been warned that her heart had been weakened, and she changed from an adorable companion to a fretful, complaining wife. 'Could he be blamed for seeking his pleasure elsewhere?' he asked himself. A man could not wait for ever to satisfy the demands of the flesh. He had not loved Isabella, but they were two of a kind, self-indulgent and unrepentant. Then came the shock of Boy's disclosure. True he had escaped a court martial, but he had to lie to his fellow officers, and keep on lying, for they were curious about his absence during those three days and nights.

28

Hardly had he recovered from one blow when fate dealt another. Isabella was dead. It was still inconceivable. No woman had been more alive, or more satisfying to the senses. But fate had not finished with him. His son was so puny he could still die, and there would never be another. He had sworn a solemn oath, and Rosalind would keep him to his promise. A man needs a son to grow in his image, to follow in his footsteps − prep school, public school, Sandhurst. But he knew in his heart it was wishful thinking, and that this son of his would never serve his Queen and Country.

Enveloped in a wave of self-pity, he sat motionless till Jason moved restlessly, and he spoke his thoughts to the horse, as he was accustomed.

'Well, my beauty, you have not been supplanted. Rosalind was right when she accused me of favouring my horse before my wife. The regiment is my first love, then you, my beauty. That is how it will be, whatever fate has in store for us. Come, let us go back.'

And they moved as one, the man and the horse, across the moonlit plain.

'Why not take a month's compassionate leave, my boy? Rosalind needs to recuperate in the invigorating air of the Murree Hills, and it will be good for the child,' the Colonel suggested.

It was not so much a suggestion as a command, and Thomas had no choice but to obey. Boy had trained another servant girl to replace his daughter as personal maid to the young Memsahib, for Ayah had her Baba and was not expected to do anything more. Under the strict supervision of Auntie Millie, the old woman fed and nursed, bathed and dressed the child with a loving heart and gentle hands. Even in his infancy, the baby seemed to recognize the touch of those small, dark hands, and his fretful wailing would cease when she picked him up and cradled him in her arms. He spewed out his milk on Ayah's shoulder when she lifted him to pat his back, for the first week or so, till she remembered a baby food called Cow & Gate and that seemed to suit him. He had to be fed every three hours, day and night, and Ayah slept on a mat outside the nursery, with

29

the door open, as was customary. Her sleep was so light, she knew the moment her Baba awakened, and slipped like a shadow across the threshold.

He had been christened Paul by the army chaplain. Auntie Millie was his godmother, and she had chosen his name because neither of his parents had any preference. Rosalind had not yet changed in her attitude towards the child, and had not held him in her arms. She turned a deaf ear to his fretful wailing.

'I do declare, he is nothing but a cuckoo in the nest,' she told Auntie Millie. 'And why does he not smile?'

'It is too early yet and anyway the poor mite's little stomach is so uncomfortable, but now we have put him on the Cow & Gate, he has ceased to vomit.'

'Pray do not mention it. Remember my condition,' her niece reminded her peevishly, and reached for another fondant.

Neither the mother nor the child was strong enough to travel for another month, and Rosalind enjoyed her role as an exhausted mother who had nearly died in childbirth.

'This lassitude is not uncommon in young mothers with their first babies. We must be patient, my dear fellow.' The doctor's sensible advice was becoming a little tedious, and the thought of spending yet another month in the Murree Hills, dancing attendance on a semi-invalid, for so Rosalind saw herself, was a gloomy prospect. The grape-vine spread a rumour that the Cartwright child was almost as dark as a native, and the mother's condition was a direct result of shock. Be that as it may, there was one person who found the infant son of his rival of the greatest interest.

Only once, in the absence of Thomas and the slight indisposition of Auntie Millie, had David spent an hour or so in the company of his adored Rosalind, but she had finally succumbed to his gentle persuasion. He had no intention of claiming the child, or shattering Cartwright's ego, but it gave him immense satisfaction that it was *his* child she had carried in her womb for those nine long months, and *his* child that Ayah held up for his inspection when he stopped by to deliver the small teddybear he had bought in the market.

'*He* like it, Sahib, see, he smile for you,' the old woman told him.

For David Jones it was a wonderful moment, even more wonderful than the moment of intercourse, and his romantic Welsh heart was touched with emotion.

'He is adorable,' he told Ayah, his own sad, dark eyes reflected in the child's.'

And Ayah read his secret in those two pairs of eyes, and kept it, as only a native servant knows how.

'Of course, Paul is like Mama. Why have I not seen it before, my sweet?' Thomas exclaimed, as he stood watching Ayah spreading a rug on the lawn, with the baby hanging over her shoulder.

This was their second week at the hill station, and already there was a marked improvement in the health of both mother and child. They had brought Boy because Thomas felt such an affinity with the loyal head servant, he liked to have him around. With Boy to valet him, keep his uniforms in immaculate condition, serve drinks, and order the servants, Auntie Millie to supervise the household, and Ayah in constant attendance on little Paul, the young parents were relieved of worry and responsibility. Two servants and the garden boy had been left behind to spring-clean the bungalow, and apply fresh paint wherever Boy had indicated.

When Thomas remarked on the child's likeness to his own mother with such obvious satisfaction, Rosalind bestirred herself to answer, as calmly as her racing heart would allow. 'How clever of you, darling. Now I do see it for myself. Your Mama will be happy, will she not?'

'Indeed she will, but alas she will not make his acquaintance until he is four years of age, when the regiment returns to Aldershot.'

'That is not such a bad thing. His looks may have improved. They could hardly get worse. I do declare he is quite the plainest child, and it gives me no pleasure to have him shown to other mothers with adorable infants of which to be proud. Sometimes I wish there had been no child to upset our contentment, for we were happy enough, my darling, were we not?'

31

'Indeed we were, my sweet, but a man needs a son.'

'Now you have seen a likeness to your dear Mama, his darkness does not bother you?'

'No, it does not, for Mama has a very agreeable countenance, as you have observed.'

'Yes, indeed.'

'Would a quiet little canter amuse you this morning? Jason has already enjoyed a good gallop, and can be persuaded to behave like a gentleman, if the pace is somewhat tedious. What do you say, sweetheart? You are looking better than I have seen you for quite some time, with colour in your cheeks, and a sparkle in those lovely blue eyes.'

'You flatter me, Sir!'

'It is true, my love. It's this wonderful air.'

Rosalind could have told him that her blushes had nothing in common with the bracing air. A guilty conscience had delayed her recovery. Now that Thomas had discovered a family likeness in the child, she could put her mind at ease, and calm her ragged nerves. Thomas need never know of that one lapse. Such wanton foolishness and ignorance! Only once had David entered her, and so gently she had hardly been aware of The Thing, and certainly had not seen it. To plant a seed that made a child was monstrous. Would there ever come a time when she would not be reminded of breaking her marriage vows? As the boy grew into manhood, would the likeness be more marked? Would David claim his son and shatter their marriage? Such questions could only be answered in the future, and it was not her nature to worry. It had been a disquieting few weeks since Ayah had shown her the child, and she had feared for her own security and happiness. She loved Thomas. Of course she loved him. She would quiet her conscience this very day by surprising him with her willingness for love-making in the marriage bed. She would pretend her revulsion of The Thing had been completely overcome. He was missing that odious woman. As if she didn't know! Men were sly creatures, given to deceit and flattery. They took what they wanted and were not obliged to pay the cost. It was most unfair. Auntie Millie had declared it was a man's world and that woman had been subject to man since the time of Adam and Eve.

Such nonsense! That was all very well for the wives of the rank and file, but not for the Colonel's daughter.

She was no fool, for all her ignorance of the facts of life, and Thomas was not a saint. Indeed, now that she was in a fit state to think coherently, there was really no need for her to have felt so guilty in the first place. Thomas had been unfaithful to their marriage vows a number of times, while she had been unfaithful but once. So there it was. She was guilty of nothing more than a trifling indiscretion.

'What are you thinking about, my sweet?' Thomas was asking as they climbed the hill in companionable silence.

'I was thinking we could share the marriage bed again, now that I am so much recovered, could we not?'

Thomas pulled on the reins, and both horses were halted. 'You mean it, sweetheart? I would not wish to have you so soon after your terrible ordeal.'

'It was indeed a calamity, but since you have promised me I shall never again have to endure such agony, you may take me whenever it pleases you.'

'My love, I am profoundly touched. Indeed, I cannot wait. Shall we turn back?'

'If it pleases you, my lord,' she teased.

Thomas yelled with laughter, and saw her, once again, as the most desirable of women in his small world. It was like a second honeymoon, and infinitely more enjoyable for Thomas, who was so self-assured he had no difficulty in convincing himself that his adorable young wife had indeed conquered her aversion to that proud manly organ.

'If you could bring yourself to hold it, my love, I should be the happiest man alive,' said he, when he had finished caressing every sensitive part of her naked body.

'That is singularly selfish of you, my darling. Pray do not spoil our delight in each other with such an ugly thought.'

'Very well, my sweet.'

A secret smile played about his lips. There were other ways of making love of which his innocent litle darling had no conception, such as kissing her soft breasts until the nipples hardened, and kissing what she still insisted were 'her private parts'. By the time he had finished with her, nothing would be private!

'Open your legs a little wider, my love!' he coaxed.

Her body stiffened. Surely this was a liberty no wife should allow?

Thomas raised his head from her thighs to plead, 'Relax, my sweet.' He was enjoying every sensuous second, but his fair Rosalind had no defence against such tormenting sensuality. Her back arched, and her body trembled.

'Take me! Take me!' she sobbed.

Still a moment longer, to teach her who was master, and to feel her quivering flesh. When he entered her, and her wet thighs widened to receive him, he knew for certain he would never again have to seek elsewhere for his pleasure. It was here, in the marriage bed, and had been here all the time.

Back at the garrison, Thomas was immediately confronted with the urgent need to send more men to the Frontier. A number of officers, including Thomas, had orders to select and train a small company of men, and make their separate ways under cover of darkness, across the plain. It was the kind of foray that Thomas enjoyed. Excitement and danger held a challenge that every soldier welcomed after a long spell of enforced marches, mock battles and parades.

The men he chose had been bored and restless, and welcomed an opportunity to show those native devils on the Frontier they meant business. Natives, whether wild or domesticated, were regarded by the rank and file as scum, and were treated with contempt. The soldiers hadn't the intelligence to discriminate between savage tribesmen and loyal servants, yet few could compare with Boy for loyalty and faithfulness. They were the dregs of humanity, seeking to escape the poverty and misery of the teeming cities, and criminals evading the law. The majority of the sergeants had been promoted from the ranks for their brutish discipline. Very rarely was a man singled out by an officer for his natural tendency to rise above his fellows. Such a man was Sergeant Jock Macpherson, a sturdy Scot from the slums of Glasgow, who feared neither man nor beast, but surprisingly feared the God of his fathers as a just and merciful Deity who dealt out rewards and punishments accordingly.

Jock had married a young woman from his own crowded

alley, who worked as a nurse in the hospital, and was often called upon to deliver a child. Maggie was always clean, and that in itself was a miracle. And Maggie was a cheery coul. Her merry laugh and her buxom bosom appealed to the sturdy young Scot, and after he had signed on for the Queen's shilling, he sought her out to ask, with blunt directness, 'Will ye no marry me now, Woman?'

'Aye, indeed I will, for I like ye fine,' Maggie answered with promptness in case he changed his mind!

After their marriage, they left behind them the slums of Glasgow for ever, and exchanged one rough and ragged world for another. The garrison at Aldershot was no place for decent citizens to wander after nightfall, and the crowded barracks, swarming with barefoot children and blowzy women, fighting each other for a few square yards of space, disgusted Jock and Maggie. They had accepted the poor conditions of their own folk, but this lot were strangers. Their speech and their habits were alien, and Jock was soon involved in a fight with a brutish sergeant who had nearly killed a young private with a savage blow from the butt of his rifle. Jock was tough, and when his temper was aroused, he used his fists. The streets of his home town had been a good training ground for the army, and Jock suffered nothing more serious than a black eye and a bloody nose before he sent his adversary sprawling and groaning from a savage blow on his jaw. A senior officer had witnessed the fight and noted the contrast in the two men, the one hitting out wildly, above and below the belt, and the other aiming his blows to the head, a clean fighter and a man worth watching. Six months later, when Jock Macpherson was promoted to sergeant, Maggie had already established herself as a competent midwife. They were allotted a sparsely furnished hut a short distance from the crowded barracks. It was their first glimpse of paradise in a harsh world. In his world of men, Jock was feared and respected. In her world of women, Maggie was accepted as an authority on childbirth, even by the army doctor, who was glad to be relieved of a job he found distasteful.

On several occasions, before they left England, Maggie had been called to the bedside of an officer's wife when the doctor was not available, so her reputation was already established when she boarded the troopship at Southampton. It was there that she made the acquaintance of the Colonel's pampered daughter and the other young wives, but newly-wed, and suffering the pangs both of seasickness and homesickness.

'The army is no a fit place for these soft wee lassies,' she told Jock.

The measles epidemic spread quickly among the officers' children, and added to the misery, but it was nothing to the misery the families of the rank and file were suffering in the crowded, stinking hold. Thomas had no direct contact with the wives and children of his own company, and detailed Sergeant Macpherson to supervise the daily rations of food and water. He was more concerned with Jason, who found the rolling deck a hazardous place for exercise. The grooms had to share the quarters of their restless charges.

'You don't care for it, my beauty. Neither do I, but I promise you a good gallop as soon as we disembark,' Thomas comforted.

The stewards had been grateful for a little practical help, and Maggie soon discovered she had a stomach for the rolling and tossing on the high seas. No stranger to the smell of vomit, she changed nightgowns and sheets, and sponged sticky hands and faces with a cheerfulness that went unnoticed by the suffering women and children, but would long be remembered by anxious husbands and fathers, many of whom were seen hanging grey-faced over the rails as the troopship plunged its way through the Bay of Biscay, and round the Rock of Gibraltar. Neither Jock nor Thomas was afflicted with seasickness, and this in itself served to bring them in closer contact than would normally be possible between an officer and his sergeant.

Jock's sturdy gait and curly red head had a way of appearing in the most unlikely places, and when he disclosed that he slept more comfortably on a bale of straw, in the well-deck where the horses were quartered, than in his hammock, Thomas saw no reason to report such a misdemeanour to a senior officer.

'You like horses, Sergeant Macpherson?' he asked.

'Aye, I do, Sir, though I've no had the pleasure of riding.'

36

'You shall. When we set foot on Indian soil. I shall make it my business to find you a mount.'

'Thank you, Sir,' said Jock, surprised and pleased by such an offer. His healthy countenance and bright blue eyes contrasted noticeably with the poor wretches, with their weak stomachs and unhealthy pallor, he had perforce to shape into a semblance of disciplined order before they disembarked. A born leader, Thomas was thinking, as he watched his company of undisciplined, uncouth individuals being moulded into a combat unit by the fiery little sergeant with a voice like a foghorn.

'Poor devil,' he thought compassionately, when a man broke ranks and made a dash for the rail, but Macpherson had only contempt for such weakness.

From different backgrounds, and from different classes of society, the two men had much in common − their love of horses, their loyalty to the regiment, and a challenging out-look on life. Their friendship was strengthened by Maggie's devotion to Rosalind during that traumatic voyage, when she could have died from the combined effects of seasickness and measles. Maggie was always careful not to offend the Colonel's sister, a rather formidable lady, who exacted her full measure of respect from lesser mortals in the hierarchy of army protocol. Maggie was polite but never subservient. She knew her worth, and when she was called upon to deliver a child, that child was her chief concern, and every mother of equal value, regardless of class or creed.

So it was Maggie who, some months later, shared the anxious vigil with the army docotr, turned the child in the womb, and delivered it safely while the doctor held a chlo-roform mask over the anguished face. Little Paul Cartwright was in no mood to thank her for such a rude awakening!

For the first two years of his life, the child was aware of his mother as a vague figure who drifted in and out of the nursery in a rustle of petticoats, leaving behind a faint perfume, and of his father as a stern, uniformed figure, of whom he was afraid. The fear increased from the morning of his third birthday, when Ayah presented him, bathed and dressed, in a tussore silk frock, to his parents, carried as always on her hip.

'Put him down! He is not a baby. He is a big boy,' barked his irritated Papa. 'And take off that frock. At three years old a boy should be breeched.'

'Yes, Sahib,' Ayah answered dutifully, and stood the child on his feet. He was such a little fellow, and his dark eyes flooded with tears. His small world had been filled with the quiet voices of Ayah and Boy, and the native servants who adored him, and Auntie Millie who called him her little treasure. From now on he would be obliged to take his place, as an officer's son, in a much bigger world.

Hiding his face in Ayah's soft sari, he could smell the familiar musky smell of her thin body, as her hand caressed his dark head. His beautiful Mama was nibbling a slice of toast, spread with English marmalade.

'Come, my darling, sit on the bed and tell Mama if you liked your present,' she coaxed.

Ayah picked him up and sat him on the edge of the bed.

'Have you lost your tongue, Paul? Your Mama asked you a question,' Thomas reminded his small son. Standing on the other side of the bed, sipping the strong black coffee Rosalind had poured from the silver coffee pot, he looked immensely tall and stern.

'Thank you, Mama,' he whispered, still hugging the little teddybear that he carried everywhere, and held close to his cheek while he slept.

'Did you like the big red engine, my darling? I do declare it was the biggest and most expensive toy in the bazaar,' said Rosalind. Trying to coax a smile from that grave little face was disconcerting, and she sighed.

'Your Papa has a very special present for you,' she hinted, and Paul looked about the room and could see nothing that could be meant for a little boy.

'You won't find it indoors. It has four legs and a long, bushy tail. I give you three guesses.' Thomas could hardly wait to see his son in the saddle, and the little Welsh pony was just right for a boy's first mount, in his opinion.

Paul looked puzzled, but was spared the trouble of guessing when Auntie Millie appeared in the doorway, holding out a parcel. He slid off the bed and ran to her.

'Happy birthday, Paulie.' She hugged and kissed him

affectionately. He sat on the floor to open the parcel and exclaimed, in delighted surprise, 'An efalump!' His rare smile shone through the sadness of those huge dark eyes, transforming his small, pallid face.

'Say elephant.' His father's voice interrupted the blissful moment.

'Efalump,' the child repeated, and Thomas jeered.

'Let him alone. He is only a baby.' Apart from Rosalind, the Colonel's sister was the only person who dared speak her mind.

'At three years of age all baby things should be put away, and I would remind you, Ma'am, with due respect, not to interfere. It is never too early for an officer's son to learn obedience. In future, Paul, you will keep those toys for the nursery. Today, because it is your birthday, you may please yourself. Do you understand me?'

'Yes, Papa,' whispered the child. The smile was gone, and the light extinguished, as quickly as a candle is snuffed. Only Auntie Millie and Ayah had seen the transformation.

Wearing his first pair of breeches, a silk shirt, and a tiny pair of boots, already purchased for this important occasion, Paul was taken by the hand and led down the steps of the back verandah where a groom stood holding the pony. Ayah stood aside, clutching the teddybear and the elephant. She hardly recognized her Baba in the new clothes that seemed to swamp his small person. Her eyes were troubled. He was afraid of big horses. This was a little horse, but he would still be afraid. If only the Sahib would wait another year. They would be back in England, and she would not have to witness his fear. But then he would be gone from her for ever, and she loved him the best of all her babas, because he was so small, and because of the sadness in his dark eyes that was there from the day he was born, when she held him in her arms for the very first time. It seemed the child had come into the world in sorrow, not in joy. He was such a gentle little boy, and so sensitive he could not bear a cross word to be spoken. The Sahib would speak his mind. It was his right and privilege to do so, but Ayah feared greatly for her little one as he was lifted into the saddle.

They were all watching. His Mama on the verandah, in a silk negligee, with Auntie Millie. His Papa on the steps, and Boy and the servants peering through the windows. The groom had his instructions. He was to take Master Paul on a leading rein six time round the edge of the lawn, morning and evening. When he was well balanced in the saddle, the leading rein was to be removed, and he would ride alone until such time as he was considered to be ready to join the other young children in the paddock.

Paul listened to his father's voice, and held back the tears that trembled on his long lashes, instinctively aware that tears would only make the matter worse. This was not only his first riding lesson, but his first lesson in obedience.

'Head up! Back straight!' Thomas barked impatiently.

Auntie Millie clucked and shook her head. What had he expected? Even in the short time they had spent together in the past three years, Thomas should have realized the child had none of his character or his qualities. Paul would never satisfy his father, no matter how hard he tried, and never make a leader. Leaders were born not made, as the Colonel could have reminded his son-in-law. In a way it was a tragedy, for his fellow officers would watch the nervous little boy on his first pony with lifted brows and shrugged shoulders. As for Subaltern Jones, his heart ached with pity for his small son that morning, watching from a safe distance, conquering the urge to lift him down and cradle him in his arms. Cartwright would never see Paul in uniform, of that he was certain. What would become of this child who had grown from the seed he had planted in the womb of his lovely Rosalind? It was a question that often troubled him. It was not a firm hand but a gentle hand that would best guide the child into the future. Would he find such a hand in England?

Even the garden boy had sense to realize the Sahib's son

would never join that splendid company of officers in their scarlet uniforms. Treading a path round the edge of the lawn would mean there would be less grass for his to water and more time to sleep! Allah was good to a garden boy, who had no status at all.

'He has courage, the little one,' Boy told Ayah as they stood watching the small figure on the shaggy pony a week or so later, with the groom clapping his hands to the rhythm of the trotting hooves. The Sahib had taken his Memsahib to a dinner party. The Colonel was celebrating his 60th birthday. Senior officers and their wives would be present. Auntie Millie was back in charge of the household and hostess to her brother. She had anticipated a pleasant retirement on their return to England, but it seemed unlikely, since she could not leave Paul to the care of servants, and Rosalind was once again enjoying a round of social engagements with her old craving for gaiety and excitement, and had little time to spare for her small son.

Paul breakfasted with Ayah, but the rest of the morning was spent in the company of the other officers' young children, the grooms and governesses who were paid to train and teach them. After lunch and siesta, he was back with the children for playtime. It was all part of his education, but it was all too sudden and frightening for an only child to find himself one of a group. Paul was the youngest of the group, and consequently bullied by sturdy four- and five-year-olds. The regiment was the focal point of their education, and the other little boys were proud and eager to learn the rudiments of such an exciting and honourable profession. Both boys and girls started morning lessons with a governess at the age of four, and every little girl was taught to play the pianoforte, to stitch a neat sampler, to curtsy prettily, and to behave in a ladylike manner in the drawing-room.

As for Paul, he could spell out his name with the wooden blocks, count up to 100, recite the alphabet, and other small accomplishments three months later, for he was determined not to be left behind. Competition was encouraged, both in work and play, and it was necessary to behave like a little gentleman when you were defeated in a game of musical chairs or hide-and-seek. Table manners were corrected when he joined his parents occasionally for an evening meal. It was a shock to discover that he was expected to eat every scrap of food on his plate, for there was no Ayah to scrape up what was left into her own obliging mouth.

'Eat up that meat and vegetable, or you get no ice-cream,' Thomas threatened.

Those were the nights when Ayah was disturbed from a fitful sleep on her doormat, with her Baba vomiting food he could not digest.

'To make a man of him, must the child be sick?' she asked Boy.

'The Sahib must be obeyed,' he answered her.

'If the Memsahib had eyes to see the food is too rich for his small stomach, then the Sahib would also see, for he listens to the voice of his Memsahib.'

'That is true. But this young Memsahib has no deep love for her child. Once, long ago, another Memsahib loved her children first and her Sahib second. That, too, was a mistake. Now that Memsahib awaits her grandson in England, and all will be made plain. Allah is good. He knows the little one's need, and he will provide when the time is ripe.'

'You are wise, my brother, and you speak the truth always.' Ayah was comforted, and went back to her nursery where a teddybear and an elephant regarded her with reproachful eyes.

It was not the scarlet uniforms or the horses, or the marching men on the parade ground that appealed to Paul, but the regimental band that led the parade to church on Sunday, and played patriotic tunes on the Queen's birthday and other important occasions.

When he was three years of age, he accompanied his Mama and Auntie Millie to church, and sat quiet as a mouse, listening to the age-old pattern of morning service conducted by the chaplain. The words of the Scriptures left a lasting impression on his mind, and the hymns, accompanied by the band and sung with such heartiness by several 100 men, brought a lump to his throat and tears to his eyes. By standing on the pew, he could pick out his Papa's distinguished figure, his hair shining like a cap of gold on his handsome head, and his back as straight as a ramrod. 'What is a ramrod?' he asked, for he was constantly asking questions now that his mind was open to receive the answers.

During the sermon, he was lifted down to sit between the two ladies, both in their best gowns, hats and gloves, and smelling of scent. But there was a difference between lavender water and French perfume, as distinctive as between the gowns and the hats. His Mama wore pretty colours. Auntie Millie wore grey. His Mama had a tiny waist. He had seen his Papa measuring it with his hands. It was a loving gesture, and when they kissed, as they did often enough because, as Ayah had explained, they had much love for one another, he felt sad that kisses for little boys were so very different. Just the touch of her cool lips on his cheek from Mama, and a pat on the head from Papa when he was in a good mood. He tried so hard to please, but his Papa was not deceived by his firm hold of the reins, and neither was the pony. The fear was there, and they both recognized it.

Thomas had expected his small son to take to the saddle as a duck to water, because of his own passionate love for Jason. Watching other little boys trotting so happily and confidently on their ponies, he was disappointed and angry at Paul's poor performance. He *must*, he *would* make a horseman of his son. It was never too early to start, he insisted, but Auntie Millie had grave doubts. Thomas was a fool. He expected too much of Paul, and his standards were too rigid.

There were no riding lessons on Sunday, and no games, so it became a very special day for the child, and when he saw the white linen tunic with the scarlet sash, and the straw hat with the scarlet ribbon laid out ready, he ate all his porridge, though usually Ayah obligingly ate half. 'Porridge was good for boys. They grew big and strong if they ate their porridge,' according to Papa.

The Colonel, at the head of the procession, wore his dress uniform with medals and gold braid, and his sword. He rode a white horse. His officers also wore their dress uniforms, with swords, but no gold braid, and their horses were black. The rank and file marched ten abreast, and the ladies and children followed in their carriages. It was a spendid sight, but the small boy, sitting so sedately in the carriage between the two ladies, felt none of the pride and pleasure that Thomas was feeling. He was waiting for the hushed moment in church, when the chaplain's resonant voice would intone, 'Dearly beloved brethren', and the service would begin. Beloved. That word belonged to his beautiful Mama. So who were the brethren? Mama came to church to be admired and envied, so they said. It seemed a funny reason to Paul.

'My sweet, may I remind you, yet again, your extravagance will soon put me in the hands of the moneylenders. Was it really necessary to order another new gown for the wedding of a very junior subaltern?' Thomas was asking, reasonably enough, as Rosalind paraded before him. A new hat had been delivered from the milliner, together with a dainty parasol. The ensemble was intended to steal the limelight from the rather plain little bride, and the expense would be justified.

'I do declare you are becoming positively cheese-paring, Lieutenant Cartwright, since your promotion. It does you no credit, Sir!' was the answer he received.

He sighed. 'The promotion affords but a trifling increase in pay, as I have explained. With all my heart I wish I could increase your dress allowance, but I cannot do so until I have paid these outstanding bills for dressmaking and millinery.'

'You would deprive me of my little pleasure, yet you continue to indulge your thirst for whisky. Your outstanding account with the wine merchant for the past three months far exceeds the cost of my new gowns and hats.'

Thomas flushed angrily. 'The fellow has no right to present his bill to anyone but myself. He can wait a bit longer for his impudence. And you, Madam, will kindly refrain from further extravagance until such time as I am solvent.'

'It does not signify. I shall ask Papa for a small loan.'

'You will *not* ask your Papa. Do you wish to embarrass me still further?'

'I was not aware that I had embarrassed you.'

'Did you, or did you not, mention the fact of Paul's education and the consequent expense?'

'Do not harangue me, Sir. He is my Papa, not yours, and he proposed it, not I. A child's grandfather should be permitted to pay the cost of his education if it gives him pleasure. If it displeases you, then you must speak to Papa. I thought only to spare you expense.'

'It so happens that when my son is ready to start on his formal education, I shall be in the happy position to afford the best schools in the country. Ah, that surprises you, Madam, does it not? You may recall the big drapery store in the High Street at Worthing, Thomas Brent & Son? It was established by my great-grandfather, Thomas the First. Thomas the Second, Grandmama's husband, was tragically killed, leaving her with six young daughters. Now I happen to be Thomas the Third, and heir to the property. When I attain the age of twenty-five, I shall be the legal owner of Thomas Brent & Son, and you, Madam, will have no further cause to accuse me of cheese-paring.'

Rosalind squealed excitedly, and flung herself into his arms. 'Why was I not told? Really, my darling, are you not the most provoking of husbands? Here I am, anticipating improverished circumstances on our arrival in England, and I am presented with a fortune!'

'Impoverished? Who mentioned such dire straits? Not I. As for a fortune, we must see what has accumulated in the five years. Grandmama watches expenditure at The Haven very closely, for she has a head for figures.'

'Shall we be living in Worthing when you inherit the store?'

'Certainly not. We shall be back with the regiment in Aldershot.'

'That is excellent news. With no regiment and no garrison, I should find it a singularly dull place.'

'Just a short visit. Nothing more, I promise you.'

'I do love you so terribly much.'

'Do I not deserve a kiss, or perhaps a little more than a kiss?'

45

'Lock the door, my darling, and unhook me,' Rosalind invited.

Six months later, when the main topic of conversation in the Mess and in the drawing-room was the regiment's return to Aldershot, Paul's world was shattered by the sudden death of Ayah. She had not crept into the nursery with his fruit juice and biscuit, or laid out his clean clothes. They enjoyed the early morning before the rest of the household was astir, and took a little walk to meet other ayahs and their young charges, all bowling wooden hoops. Their favourite walk, in the tree-lined avenue, was planted with lilac, laburnum and pink cherry blossom by an army of natives on the special occasion of the Queen's enthronement as Empress of India. It was the month of May, and all were flowering, as they would be in England. To the sensitive little boy, they were more beautiful than scarlet uniforms and prancing horses, and the scent of the lilac sweeter than the lavender water and the French perfume worn by the two ladies in church on Sunday morning.

He was thinking about the pleasant walk they would take together and wishing Ayah would hurry, for he was wide awake and ready for a new day. Teddybear and Elephant spent all day on his cot because he was not allowed to be seen with them, but he had explained to them that it was not his fault. So they waited patiently for the night, when they cuddled down together, and Paul forgot the harsh discipline of the day in the comfort of their furry bodies.

Now he put them aside, climbed out of his cot, and went to wake Ayah. She was curled on the mat, her wrinkled face calm in her last long sleep.

'Ayah, wake up!' he said, authoritatively, for there were times when even a little boy remembered he was an officer's son, and spoke with the voice of a Sahib. 'Wake up!' He shook her thin shoulders, and touched her cheek with his warm hand. It was cold − cold as the marble floor on which he pushed the big red engine to please his Mama.

'Do you not care for the toy, my darling?' she had asked, and he had lied, and would go on lying for years about this and that, and still not please her.

46

Now he knelt on the floor and pleaded, 'Ayah, please wake up,' forgetting he was an officer's son, and remembering that he loved this old woman best in all the world, and if she would not speak, his day could not begin. Her hand lay stretched on the mat, so small and thin, like the claw of a little bird. He lifted it gently, and held it to his cheek, and shivered at its coldness. It did not occur to him to disturb his parents, but he ran to find Boy, across the garden and the compound to the servants' quarters, a tiny, barefoot figure in a white nightshirt.

'Boy! Boy!' he called anxiously, and Boy appeared, fully dressed, and snatched him up.

'What has happened, Baba Sahib?' he asked, in his quiet voice.

'Speak to Ayah. She will listen to you. She will not wake for me,' Paul pleaded.

With a silent prayer to Allah, Boy hurried to the house and stood looking down on the crumpled figure. Death was no stranger to native servants, and he knew he was looking on death. His heart ached for the child.

'She is tired. She wishes to sleep much time,' he said.

'When will she wake up?'

'When she is rested she will wake.'

'In time for tea? Ayah likes her cup of tea.'

'Yes, she will wake to drink tea.' He was dismayed by the lie on his lips for he had never before lied to the child. But it was too late, and the truth would be told with a bluntness that was normal in the Sahib's relationship to his son.

'Come, little one. I will help you to dress.' He led the child back to the nursery.

'First I have my fruit juice and two biscuits,' Paul reminded him.

'Very good, Baba Sahib.' Boy salaamed and went away.

'Ayah is tired. She wishes to sleep much time,' Paul explained, gravely, to Teddybear and Elephant.

So Boy took over the duties of Ayah that morning, served the Baba Sahib with his fruit juice and biscuits, washed his face and hands, and dressed him in clean clothes. When he knelt on the floor to fasten the child's sandals and looked into those dark, sad eyes, he remembered the words his sister

47

had spoken. 'He is born of sorrow, not of joy, the little one.' It was true, for he rarely smiled, and laughter was never heard on his lips. Boy was so troubled by the lie he had told, he even put the child's tunic on back to front and was scolded for his foolishness. Yet the truth would be cruel when it was told. Who would look after the child in the land of the Great Queen across the sea? Who would bath him and dress him, and eat half his porridge?

In six months Baba Sahib would be gone, and Boy forgotten, but not Ayah. She would live long in his memory. The Sahib would not forget Boy, and for that his heart was glad. He, Boy, had saved him from the fate of his father so that he was still a splendid young Sahib, not lying in a dishonourable grave in a military cemetery; such memsahibs deserved to die for their wickedness. Now all was well, and they were like children in their pleasure. Their small quarrels were the quarrels of children, quickly over, and forgotten, in the marriage bed.

'I take you walk, Baba Sahib?' he asked, deferentially, squatting on his heels when he had brushed the little cap of hair, black as a raven's wing.

'Yes, we will walk in the avenue where the lilac is sweet.'

'Very good, Baba Sahib.' He took the child's hand, and they stepped carefully over Ayah.

'Where is your Ayah?' Richard Forsyth demanded, bowling his hoop with a stick he often used on the buttocks of his own tormented Ayah.

'She is tired. She will wake to drink tea,' said Paul.

'Try pinching her. She will wake quickly enough. All ayahs are lazy,' he said, with the arrogance of an only adored son in a family of girls.

'I do not pinch my Ayah. I love her,' Paul answered truthfully.

'Well, you cannot take her with you to England, so what will you do?'

'I – don't – know.'

'I will tell you. There will be a kindergarten where you will be whipped if you do not learn your lessons, and where you will be made to stand in a corner, with your hands on your head if you so much as open your mouth to say "boo"!' He ran off, whacking the hoop with his stick. His ayah raised her eyes to heaven and wailed, 'He will be the death of me, that one!' and hurried after her charge.

'Is it true that I must leave Ayah behind?' Paul asked Boy.

'Yes, it is true.'

'Are you coming to England with us?'

'No, I am not coming and Ayah is not.'

'I don't understand. You belong to us, Boy, you and Ayah.'

'Only for five years. That is the way of things for a native servant. Another regiment, another Sahib and Memsahib, and we start all over again. It is the Will of Allah, Baba Sahib.'

'I shall speak to Papa.'

Boy made no answer. The little one had much to learn. Even an officer Sahib has to bend to the Will of Allah.

When they got back to the house there was no sign of Ayah or the mat on which they had left her sleeping.

'Ayah is awake!' Paul exclaimed, and rushed into the nursery. 'Where are you? If you are playing hide-and-seek, I shall find you!' It was a game they often played together when he was very small, but not since he was breeched. He rushed about, peering into cupboards, the clothes closet, under the cot and behind the curtains while Boy hovered in the doorway, wringing his hands. 'She is not here. Help me to find her,' said the child.

Then the bedroom door opened, and his Papa stood there, draped in the yellow silk dressing-gown, swarming with green dragons, an exotic garment that made him appear like a Chinese mandarin.

'What is all the fuss about?' he demanded of his small son. 'First we are disturbed by the wailing of the servants, now it is you.'

'Ayah has gone, Papa. We left her sleeping on her mat, and when we came back she had gone.'

'They have taken her to the servants' quarters.'

'Is she sick?'

'No, she is dead.'

'What is dead, Papa?' asked the child, who had been spared

the knowledge of death and the departing of a loved one.

Thomas was getting into deep water. 'Your Mama will explain,' he said, giving the child a gentle push into the bedroom.

The door closed. Boy hovered outside, expecting to hear the little one cry out, but there was no crying, only the voice of the Memsahib, and when it stopped, the door opened and the child stood there, wide-eyed with shock, but still no tears.

'Ayah is not going to wake up to drink her tea at 4 o'clock. She will never wake up. Never, never, never!' He choked on a sob, dry-eyed, in an anguish too deep for tears.

Boy scooped him up in his arms and carried him down the steps into the garden. He knew now what he must do, even without the Sahib's command. 'Give the Baba Sahib the hose to water the lawn, and watch over him or your life will be worthless,' he instructed the garden boy.

'Where do you go?' quavered the boy, greatly fearing the head servant.

'I go to fetch Colonel Sahib's Memsahib.' And Boy was gone, fleet of foot, in spite of his grey head and advancing years, his dark eyes flooded with tears.

Back in the bedroom, they were blaming each other for a situation for which they were totally unprepared. They had had little direct contact with the old woman in the past three-and-a-half years, for her duties were confined solely to the care of the child. Even when she slept so lightly, on her mat, and heard footsteps, she would scramble to her feet, salaam respectfully, and lie down again.

'He is such a strange child. I do declare it is quite beyond me to understand what he is thinking, for he reveals nothing,' Rosalind complained. 'What more could I do than explain, as gently as possible, that his Ayah had gone to Heaven to live with Jesus.'

'It confused him, my sweet. Ayah would not wish to live with Jesus. It is Allah. She speaks always to Allah.'

'He answered you truthfully enough.'

'My darling, you cannot boast that you were more successful. He naturally thought his clever Papa had only to give the word of command and Ayah would be brought back.'

Thomas sighed impatiently. 'It had to happen sooner or later since we could not take her to England, and I cannot spare Boy to look after him. So what do we do with him now?'

'He could stay with the Forsyths or the Kingsley-Browns. They have an Ayah and an English governess.'

'With other children he is shy and withdrawn. He is not a good mixer. In fact, he is nothing but a cuckoo in the nest, my love, as we both know.'

'That is true,' Rosalind agreed.

In less than an hour, to the great relief of the garden boy, the Colonel's Memsahib was seen approaching, followed by Boy, carrying the valise. 'Paulie!' she cried, and opened her arms. He flung down the hose and rushed into them, sobbing distraughtly.

'Hush, my treasure, I am here,' she comforted.

'Ayah has gone away. She is never coming back.'

'Then we must manage without her, mustn't we? You will be brave, and Ayah will be happy in her Heaven.'

'Is there a Heaven for ayahs?'

'Most certainly there is a Heaven for ayahs.'

'With Allah?'

'With Allah. Isn't that so, Boy?'

'That is correct, Memsahib.'

'You see, Paulie, my treasure, it is really a blessing in disguise, because we could not take her with us to England, and she has been spared all the grief of parting. She had no pain, only a great weariness, so she slept.'

'Papa said she is dead.'

'That is true, for the last long sleep is death.'

'I don't want to go to sleep and not wake up. You won't let me, will you?' The dark, imploring eyes, wet with tears, tore at her heart, and she held him close.

'Have no fear. I am staying here, and you shall share my bed. Boy will wake us at 6 o'clock, with tea and fruit juice.'

'And biscuits?'

'And biscuits.'

Paul lifted his hand to stroke her thin, pallid cheek. Her hair was grey, like Ayah's. A new fear troubled him now. 'Have you got a great weariness, Auntie Millie?'

'Not at all. I am strong as an ox,' declared that good woman.

'I am glad, for you will not go to sleep and not wake up.'

'Heaven forbid! Now let us talk of other matters, and you shall tell me what you would most like to do today.'

'May I be excused, Memsahib? I have to serve breakfast,' Boy interrupted, politely.

'Yes, indeed you may. We shall sit here, on this bench, a while longer, and then we shall eat our breakfast on the verandah, shall we not, Paulie?'

'Must I have porridge? It makes me feel quite sick.'

'Then we shall not have porridge.'

'Thank you. You see, to tell you the truth, Ayah would oblige me by eating half.'

'Well, you may depend on it, I should not be so obliging, for I cannot abide porridge!'

Boy hurried indoors with the valise. The guest room was always ready, and the Colonel's Memsahib a most welcome guest, for she made no trouble. He was so grateful for her kind understanding of such a difficult problem. He would have gone on his knees and kissed her feet, but English memsahibs wore shoes and stockings, and their long skirts swept the ground. A native servant in sari and sandals was so much more comfortable.

When he passed the nursery, he remembered that his sister lay at peace, on his own cot, and when he had served breakfast, he would see about the burial. Only six more months to serve his splendid young Sahib and the beautiful little Memsahib. Then they would be gone. Joy and sorrow, and more of sorrow than joy. This was his life.

'Did you fetch the Colonel's Memsahib, Boy?' Thomas demanded.

'Yes, Sahib.'

'Without my permission?'

'Yes, Sahib.'

'I find that singularly impertinent.'

'Yes, Sahib.'

'Stop repeating "Yes, Sahib". You are not a parrot!

occasion, two were missing – the old woman, who had served the English memsahibs and their children many long years, and the young girl whose life had been cut short by a bullet from her father's gun. Boy was sad at the parting as he stood there, waiting to be dismissed for the last time.

As far as the eye could see, through the sprawling garrison town that would soon be empty of all but the servants and overseers until another regiment arrived from England, a long line of ox wagons, piled high with the families of the rank and file and the baggage, stood waiting the order to move off.

Ahead of the wagons, the sergeants bellowed orders to the men who would march in neat columns till nightfall, when they would disperse to assemble another town of tents under a starlit sky. Behind the lines of horsemen and the marching columns, the camels plodded slowly with their laden baskets carrying the wives and children of the officers. It would be an uncomfortable journey, and many would be ill en route, but it was the only way to convey so many people across country to the port of embarkation.

After hours of waiting, and much confusion, Paul found himself in a basket, clutching Teddybear and Elephant, with the horrid Forsyth boy and a cage of white mice that would soon be let out to run amok over both children. But Boy's sad heart would be gladdened when his splendid, tall Sahib leaned from the saddle to shake his hand.

'Thank you, Boy, for *everything*,' he said, with much sincerity. They both knew that 'everything' included not only the normal duties of a head servant, but much more. On two occasions, his loyalty and devotion had been proved to the utmost; and he had killed. Yet he had no regrets as he looked up into the face he had loved before all others. He took the Sahib's hand and raised it to his lips, then stepped back.

'It was a pleasure, Sahib,' he said, and salaamed respectfully for the last time.

As Thomas rode away to join his fellow officers, the regimental band at the head of the long cavalcade played 'Soldiers of the Queen', and Boy's dark eyes flooded with tears. The proud moment had passed. He was old, and tired, and all his strength exhausted. He stood there until the last of the ox wagons had rumbled away in a cloud of dust, and nothing remained but the stench of dung.

Then he walked slowly across the garden and the compound to the deserted servants' quarters, stretched out on his cot, and died.

Chapter Three

'Thomas is back! He is back at Aldershot!' Amelia spoke from the comfortable depths of the big marriage bed in which her six daughters had been conceived and born. Her eyes were as blue as her grandson's, and her fair skin flushed.

'You would think it was her lover she was expecting,' Norah was thinking, as she placed the little silver tray on the flowered quilt. The dainty china tea-set was never used at any other time, and the tin of *petit beurre* biscuits on the bedside table was never empty.

On this bleak winter morning, she had torn open the telegram and read the brief message – 'Arrived safely. All well. Expect us short visit Monday 25th. Love, Thomas.'

Norah's homely face shone with pleasure. Five years was a long time. The Haven had not been the same since Thomas went away. It was not that they saw a lot of him since he had grown to manhood, but there was always the possibility that a telegram might announce his arrival. After he had married the Colonel's daughter and the regiment had sailed for India, that hope was abandoned. His doting grandmother had penned a regular weekly letter, but had received a poor response for her pains. Her daughter-in-law wrote a childish missive, from time to time, and Thomas sent a cable for her birthday that arrived a week early or a week late. She always excused him and pretended not to mind, for she seldom allowed her calm features to betray her real feelings.

But Amelia Brent was a passionate woman at heart and she had ruled her six young daughters with a firm hand, after the tragic death of their father. It could be said, with truth, that

57

she had loved only two souls in her life-time − her husband and her grandson, though she would have vehemently denied it. She had explained Norah's exact status to the little boy:

'She is neither family nor servant, my darling, but a most useful person to have around the place.'

It did not bother Norah to be so humbled, for she was born into a poor family, and had none of the advantages of the Brent sisters. Apprenticed to a dressmaker at an early age, it was Bertha, the plainest of the sisters, with a quick temper and a sharp tongue, who had rescued her from the dreary establishment in a back street and brought her to the comfortable, upper-class residence in Richmond Road.

'I note the naughty boy takes care to mention it will only be a short visit,' Amelia was saying, without rancour.

'How he loves to tease,' Norah agreed, but then she seldom disagreed with this formidable little lady. She knew her place, and had no pride. A big, strong woman, her homely countenance shone with good humour, and a recent application of yellow soap. In that feminine boudoir, with its pretty drapes and white carpet, Norah was not seen at her best. But in the big basement kitchen, with the wholesome smell of baking, she was in her right element. Norah was paid no wages, but received her board and lodging in return for her services. That had been agreed upon before she ever set foot in the place.

'Then I shall give her half-a-sovereign from my own monthly allowance,' Bertha had decided.

'Be that as it may, I still consider she has the best of the bargain.' Amelia always had the last word.

That was all of twenty-five years ago, and she had to admit Norah had been a good investment.

They would kill the fatted calf for the homecoming of this adored grandson, and his own mother, a gentle, unobtrusive creature, would have little to say on the nature of the celebration. Ellen was the eldest of the six daughters, and she had spent much of the time since her son went away in keeping house for her own elder daughter, Prue, and mothering the delicate little girl for whom Prue had little affection. Ellen was a woman who had loved her children with such maternal devotion that it could be truthfully said she had driven her husband, unwittingly, into the arms of another man's wife and to the tragedy in that same garrison town on the North West Frontier. She carried the blemish of that tragedy in her dark, expressive eyes, and in the hidden depths of her saddened heart.

Amelia, in her joy at the birth of a grandson, had practically taken over his education, and almost ignored the existence of the two little girls who were born in India. Thomas had been received like a little prince by his doting grandmother, who had waited in vain for a son, and had to 'make do' with six girls. Ellen had neither the strength nor the personality to assert her authority in her mother's house. Like Norah, she was all too aware of her status, as a widow with two young children and a third on the way, returning to the parental home some four years after leaving it, with nothing but a small pension. She was not surprised, therefore, that the telegram had been addressed to Amelia, but welcomed the news of her son's safe arrival with a thankful heart. To have her son grow from childhood in the image of his father, and to follow the footsteps of that father into his father's old regiment had been a heart-breaking experience for Ellen, for she could foresee another tragedy, and a smiliar fate awaiting the handsome, self-indulgent son of Jonathan. But it had not happened. Her prayers had been answered, and he was safely home, and moreover, had brought her first grandson. There had been no photographs of the child, only a vague reference to his darkness in one of the few letters she had received from Rosalind.

'I do declare he is a droll little fellow,' she had written, in her childish scrawl.

It would seem, therefore, that Paul was not a pretty child, and they had naturally expected a golden-haired cherub. Poor little boy. She wondered whether he would care for the shabby old rocking horse, or the lead soldiers that had been such favourites with Thomas. She remembered the occasion of his third birthday, when he was breeched, and his Grandmama had bought the rocking-horse because she knew it would be the biggest and most expensive present. Thomas had been over the moon with excitement that day, and neither of his sisters was allowed to ride the splendid horse.

'Watch me! Watch me!' he had cried.

'I am watching you, my darling,' his proud Grandmama replied, again and again, while his own mother stood aside, comforting his sister Prue, who was not a favourite. Such a mistake to spoil a boy child and to start a feud between brother and sister. Ellen sighed, in retrospect, as she climbed the stairs to her own apartment on the top floor.

It was rather short notice, but Amelia wasted no time and spared no expense in summoning the family to The Haven for the homecoming celebration. Telegrams were despatched forthwith, and Bertha was instructed to take them to the post office, grumbling, as usual, that she had more important things to be doing.

'As if anything could be of greater importance than the homecoming of Thomas.' Amelia stated, surprised at such an attitude.

'You will expect the house to be clean and shining from top to bottom, and I have only one pair of hands,' Bertha retorted, sulkily.

'Then get Mabel to help. I will pay her sixpence for every extra hour that she works.'

'Mabel has never done anything more than the rough. That is to say, the scrubbing, black-leading the kitchen stove, and the family wash.'

'Really, Bertha, must you be so provoking? This is an occasion for much rejoicing, and all I am asking is that you walk to the post office to send these telegrams.'

Since Amelia was comfortably installed in the morning-room, reading the *Morning Post*, it may be wondered why she could not personally take a walk to the post office, but for all her grumbling, Bertha would not dare to suggest it. Mother was not expected to lift a finger, yet she had not hesitated to dismiss the cook and the housemaid the day following her husband's funeral, and to distribute the household chores among her astonished daughters.

'What is Ellen about that she cannot take a walk to the post office?' Bertha was still hovering.

'Need you ask? She was away, soon after breakfast, to take Victoria to the convent.'

'But the child is surely not more than four years of age?'

'That is so, but they have a kindgergarten at the convent.'

'What is her own mother about that she cannot take her child to school?'

'I am given to understand she is suffering from nervous exhaustion. I have never know a time when Prudence was not suffering from something or other. Ellen made a fool of the child from the day they arrived here from India. Such tantrums deserved only a good spanking in my opinion.'

'Yet Bella was never any trouble.'

'Arabella had a happy nature, indeed she still has, or she could not abide the privations of the Stepney Mission. Now we are wasting time with all this chattering. Off you go! There's a good girl.'

Bertha pulled a face as she closed the door. Mother was incorrigible. A good girl indeed! Girlhood was long since past, and best forgotten. She had always been the odd one. She would not have cared for a husband. Norah put up with her sharp tongue and her quick temper. Norah was her best beloved.

'That will be five shillings, if you please, Miss,' said the counter clerk.

Bertha handed over the money Amelia had taken from her housekeeping purse. 'See they are despatched immediately,' she told the clerk, haughtily.

'All our telegrams are despatched immediately Miss. That is what you are paying for, is it not?' said he, with a twinkle in his eye that was wasted on Bertha. 'A sourpuss, that one,' he reflected; as she walked away.

There had not been such a week of cleaning and polishing, washing of curtains and airing of beds since last spring-cleaning. Overworked little Mabel was so hustled and bustled by the bossy Miss Bertha, she burst into tears when she was expected to help spring-clean the drawing-room in mid-winter.

'But it ain't the proper time, Miss, an' I 'as ter scrub the basement steps an' sweep out the conservatory, an' polish the front gate, which is all extra from what I does most weeks.'

'Of course it's extra, but you are being paid an extra

sixpence an hour, are you not?' snapped Bertha, irritably, for she was trying to ignore a nagging headache, and there was still so much to be done.

'I got only one pair of 'ands, Miss, an' I don't see me way clear to 'elp with the drawing-room,' Mabel muttered rebelliously.

To upset Mabel would be the last straw, so Bertha capitulated and went in search of Ellen. Climbing three flights of stairs to the top floor, she was gasping for breath and even more worried when she found her sister already dressed to go out.

'Ellen, you've *got* to help! Mother wants the drawing-room spring-cleaned, and Mabel is being contrary,' she blurted out.

Ellen hesitated for only a moment. She was not paid an allowance, and lived very frugally on a small army pension, but Bertha was obviously at her wits' end. 'Of course I will help. I will collect Vicky and bring her along. She will play quite happily with Bella's old dolls while we work. Cheer up, dear. You and I together will soon get it done.'

Bertha managed a wan smile, and wished she had Ellen's calm nature.

'Don't start till I get back,' she had called out as she hurried away.

Back in the basement, Bertha found Norah mixing the ingredients for more mincemeat. Mince-pies were definitely on the menu, and all the mincemeat had been used up for the Christmas baking.

'Why do I get in such a panic where there is no need?' she asked that good woman.

'You worry too much, darling. Now sit down quietly till Ellen comes back and drink a cup of tea,' she said, sensibly. Her homely face was flushed and sweating, her hair screwed into a bun, her apron stained, but for Bertha she was the essence of lovely womanhood, and the smile they exchanged held the secret of their happy relationship that not even Amelia had discovered in all of twenty-five years.

In the small morning-room that had once been a private sanctum in the days when her girls had a nursemaid and a governess, Amelia was comfortably installed while her

62

daughters cleaned the drawing-room. Norah had lit the fire soon after breakfast, and it was nearly time for her hot chocolate.

'You may leave Victoria with me, if she is good,' she told Ellen. 'Bring a little mug of hot chocolate and two extra biscuits, if you please.'

But Vicky was too much in awe of her grandmama to be anything but good, and amused herself giving sips of her hot chocolate to the dolls that Ellen had carried down from the old nursery. She was an imaginative little girl, accustomed to playing quietly while her poor Mama suffered with a headache, and that was almost every day. Her small world, in the flat on the top floor of the big store in the High Street, was enlivened by the two people she loved best — her dearest Papa and Nana, her devoted grandmother. Going to the convent had been a frightening experience, with so many children and so much noise, but it pleased Papa that she was mixing with other children. She had few treats, and was not at all spoilt, but Mama complained she felt neglected when she and Papa took a little walk to the park Wednesday afternoon, when the store was closed. So Nana would sit with her, and talk about the old days, when she lived in India.

Amelia regarded the small girl with the severity that had so estranged her from her own six young daughters. Another girl in the family had hardly warranted a christening mug, and she had seen the child but a few times in the four years since her birth.

'She is actually your great-grandmama, but she does not care for the great — it makes her feel old,' Ellen had explained.

'Thank you, Norah,' said Grandmama graciously, when the hot chocolate and biscuits had been served.

'You're welcome.' Norah's smile was warm and kind, and Vicky would have liked to stay with her in the kitchen.

'Why is Norah not Auntie Norah?' she asked, in the way of a four-year-old who like to know what is what.

'Because she is not an Auntie. Norah is neither family nor servant,' Amelia replied, not for the first time.

'Is she a Sister?'

'A sister? Ah, you mean like the Sisters at the convent?'

63

'Yes.'

'No, Norah is not a Catholic, for which I am heartily thankful, for she would spend too much time in church and neglect her duties. Be sure to remind them, Victoria, that you are an Anglican if they should want to take you to Mass.'

'Yes, Grandmama.' (What is Anglican?)

'You always agree with Grandmama because it saves a lot of argument,' Nana had also explained.

'Would you like me to tell you a Hail Mary?' Vicky asked politely.

'No, I would not, Miss!'

'Is it wicked?'

'It is Popery.' (What is Popery?)

'Mary is the mother of Jesus.'

'We all know that, child, but we do not say our prayers to her. We pray to God.'

'Why?'

'Why? Well, because He *is* God.'

'Is God the Papa of Jesus?'

'Well, yes.'

'I expect He loves Jesus as much as my Papa loves me.'

'I am sure He does.' Amelia was getting into deep water. It was always a mistake to start a religious conversation with a child.

'I do not love my Mama,' Vicky pronounced with childish candour.

'That does not surprise me. Your Mama is not a lovable person.'

'Sister Anne-Marie said it was wicked not to love your own mother. She made me stand in the corner.'

'A singularly stupid punishment in my opinion.'

'I wet my drawers.'

Amelia's mouth twitched with amusement. 'Did you now? What happened then?'

'I cried, and Ursula Green took me to the lavatory and took off my wet drawers.'

'And?'

'I had to sit on my bare bottom. It was cold. Nana was cross when she came to fetch me home. She told Sister

64

Anne-Marie it must not happen again because I have a weak bladder, and I should get my death of cold. What is a bladder, Grandmama?'

'Young ladies do not speak of private parts. Modesty is one of the first lessons a little girl should learn.'

'Yes, Grandmama.' (What is modesty?)

Amelia quickly changed the subject. 'You will soon have your little cousin here. You will like that, will you not?'

'Shall I? Vicky asked, doubtfully.

'Of course you will, child.'

'Grandmama?'

'Yes, child?'

'May I be excused?'

'Indeed you may. Quickly now. Leave the dolls.'

Outside the closed door the child hesitated for a moment, trying to make up her mind. There were two lavatories at The Haven, and both were equally enjoyable. The upstairs lavatory had a high seat, smelling pleasantly of beeswax polish, and soft lavatory paper. When you had finished, you stood on the seat and pulled the chain. The outside lavatory was reached through the drawing-room and the conservatory, and across the back yard. It was really Mabel's lavatory, but she didn't mind sharing it in an emergency, and with Vicky's weak bladder, nobody bothered to ask. It was a dear little lavatory, with a scrubbed seat, and it smelled pleasantly of tar and yellow soap. A neat little packet of newspaper squares hung from a nail in the wall, and when you were finished, you left it there.

Mabel was sweeping out the conservatory as Vicky dashed past. ''ullo, duckie. You got took short again?' she chuckled. They liked each other, these two. Mabel was not a lady, but it didn't signify, Nana had explained.

'Can I help you, Mabel?' Vicky asked, back in the conservatory.'

'Best ask yer Nana, 'adn't yer, duckie?'

Vicky nodded and disappeared through the glass-panelled door into the drawing-room. Nana was sprinkling tea-leaves over the carpet, and Auntie Bertha dusting down the walls with a feather brush. Both occupations appealed very strongly to the child, who was never allowed to help at home because

Mrs Jones was paid to do it. On the other hand, she did not like to offend Mabel, for she was a kind child.

'What is it, darling?' asked Nana, anxiously (that bladder was quite a problem).

'When I have helped Mabel, can I help you, Nana?'

'Yes, of course you may.'

'Why are you putting tea-leaves on the carpet?'

'To collect the dust.'

'Why is Auntie Bertha sweeping the walls?'

'To get rid of the cobwebs, Miss!' Bertha answered sharply, for she was not very fond of children and still held to the opinion they should be seen and not heard.

'How did the cobwebs get there?' asked Vicky, quite undaunted. (Auntie Bertha has a sharp tongue but a kind heart.)

'Spiders.'

Vicky shuddered. There were spiders in the lavatory at the convent.

'Why did God make spiders?' she really wanted to know.

'To eat the flies,' snapped Bertha.

'Poor flies. Why did God bother to make them if they have to be eaten up by the spiders?'

'Better ask Him, for they are nothing but a nuisance anyway.'

Mabel put her head round the door. 'You coming duckie?'

'Shut the door. There's a draught,' barked Bertha, in self-defence. 'Questions, questions. I don't know how you put up with it, Ellen.'

'How else can an intelligent child learn, dear?'

'She seems to have quite an obsession with God. Is that the convent training?'

'Poor mite. She gets a bit confused. The convent all the week and St Matthew's on Sunday.'

'Then why send her to the convent?'

'Bella was happy there. Prue was miserable, poor darling, but she was missing India. The Sisters are qualified teachers, and they do concentrate on such subjects as music, painting, and needlework, all very useful.'

'Not a lot of use to Bella in that East End Mission. She

is probably scrubbing floors and making suet puddings.'

'Whatever she is doing, she is happy, bless her heart. I still miss her. But she was ready for marriage, and Roderic is such a dear boy.' Ellen had stopped sprinkling tea-leaves. Her dark eyes reflected her thoughts. 'Do you suppose Thomas and Rosalind will let me have little Paul for a holiday in the summer? I could take both children to the beach. They would love it.'

'So would you,' Bertha teased.

'It's something I always wanted to do when my two girls were small, but Prue did not care for it, so we always went to the park with hoops, and the dolls' bassinet.'

'More fool you! That child had her own way over everything. And look at the result. A poor creature, always ailing. I pity that poor man. Basil used to be quite a lively card in the old days, when he was courting Kate. She led him a fine old dance, didn't she? Couldn't wait to get a betrothal ring on her finger, then off to London with Charles. I always knew she would disgrace the family.'

'But it left him free to marry Lucy.'

'And a lot of good that did the poor man, with Lucy dying in childbirth a year or so later. Then he married your Prue, young enough to be his daughter. He must be wishing he remained a bachelor.'

'But he has Vicky. They are very close. Too close, perhaps. I wish Prue were not so jealous.' Ellen sighed. It was wishful thinking. Prue had always been jealous of Thomas; now it was Vicky. How could a mother be jealous of her own daughter? It was not natural. 'Oh, Bertha, I wish we could put back the clock,' she said. 'The Haven was such a happy place once upon a time.'

'Not for me it wasn't, till I met Norah. I was always odd one out.'

It was true, but she had only herself to blame. As Mother would say, 'Bertha is her own worst enemy.'

Amelia clucked at the discarded dolls, and wondered if the child was using the bladder problem as a means of escape. 'May I be excused?' had been a favourite trick with Kate as a small girl, but then Kate had been as full of tricks as a monkey, and was still playing tricks on that nice husband

67

of hers. Charles was a gentleman. He actually kissed her hand. You would have thought Kate would have behaved herself, having acquired a husband who was a Member of Parliament, with a fine house in Onslow Square, London, but something had gone disastrously wrong with that marriage, as any fool could see. A divorce would have ruined Charles's career as a politician, so they made a pretence of marital compatibility that may have deceived their friends, but not their servants. Kate was so stupidly immature, and what had seemed amusing in a girl of eighteen, was ridiculous in a middle-aged woman.

Yet, for all her faults, Amelia could see herself in this one particular daughter, for they both enjoyed the company of the opposite sex and the flattery and, of course, the sensual excitement. There were times when she had actually envied Kate, who had the audacity to jilt Basil in favour of Charles, and was not in the least repentant. Her naughty Kate had flirted with every male that crossed her path, and might still be doing so.

'Three outstanding events remain fixed in my memory of that third birthday, Grandmama,' Thomas had told her, some years later. 'I was breeched. You gave me that beautiful rocking-horse. I fell in love with my Auntie Kate.'

Yes, they had taken an instant liking to one another – the adorable little boy, with his golden curls and mischievous blue eyes, and the elegant young woman who had waited till everyone was seated at the tea-table to make her entrance, like an actress who had been waiting in the wings. Fashionably dressed, wearing an expensive French perfume, she had swept into the room, smiling bewitchingly – and every male in the room, including Thomas, had to be kissed! It was an admirable performance, and only the blushing Basil was embarrassed. And wasn't it just like Kate to steal the limelight on her triumphant return to the bosom of her family?

Amelia liked to think she was still the matriarch, holding the reins, directing and controlling her large family, but it was wishful thinking, for they were scattered and lived their separate lives. Even Ellen, who still lived in the house, had gradually adopted the role of visitor rather than resident. As for Bertha, she had Norah.

Once again The Haven would see the family gathered under its fading, hospitable roof. She would put back the clock. And she would wear her best blue gown.

'Who would be the first to arrive?' Amelia asked herself, as she sipped the hot chocolate in the drawing-room that Sunday morning, before they left for church. If she had her way − and she usually had her way − the entire family would be gathered under this roof by noon tomorrow. She had thought of nothing else all the week.

Glancing about the room, her eyes rested approvingly on the polished mahogany, the silver frames, the dainty bric-a-brac on the occasional tables, the shining brass fender and starched antimacassars. The faint smell of beeswax polish still lingered, but it was not unpleasant.

Bertha and Norah had already left for church on foot. She would sit here quietly, waiting for the station cab, contemplating the morrow and the homecoming of her darling boy. She felt as excited as a young girl expecting her sweetheart. For five long years she had waited, living on past memories, seeing him in her mind's eye at every stage, through boyhood into manhood. Only Thomas was hadsome enough, and clever enough, to court the Colonel's daughter. It hadn't surprised her one little bit!

'Expect us short visit Monday. Love, Thomas.' Her lips moved over the magic words. Her daughter Grace would make the long journey from Zurich with her husband, Henry. They could be the first to arrive if they travelled overnight, which was cheaper. The four from London − her daughter, Jane, and Edward, and Thomas's sister, Arabella, with her husband, Roderic − would travel third class and walk from the station. They would not stay overnight. Whenever they came to tea on their free Sunday, once a month, they ate every crumb of the dainty bread and butter, and Norah's cake, and every spoonful of Norah's strawberry jam. They were like children at a Sunday School treat. She supposed they lived on bread and margarine, suet dumplings and Irish stew, but she had no patience with such stupid dedication to an East End Mission. She had never actually visited either of the Missions, but she had heard enough to convince her they were totally unsuited to all four participants. How could

69

they bear it — the poverty, the squalor, the drunken men and blowzy women and squalling babies? Wasting the best years of their lives when they could have been living decently and comfortably in Worthing.

'The cab's here, Mother.' Ellen interrupted her reverie, and she left her own comfortable fireside to shiver in the cold hall. But only for a moment, then Ellen was helping her into her fur coat with its matching cap and muff.

'Have you got a clean handkerchief, Victoria?' she asked her small grand-daughter.

'Yes, Grandmama,' answered the child dutifully, as she followed her down the freshly-scrubbed path.

The cabby was holding open the green gate. Amelia Brent was one of his best customers, since the days when she hired his cab to take her little grandson for a drive along the promenade.

'Morning, Ma'am,' he said, touching his cap.

'Good morning, Harrison,' she answered. When he had settled her in the cab, with a rug over her knees, she confided, with surprising cordiality, 'I am expecting my grandson tomorrow.'

'Back from foreign parts, is it, Ma'am?'

'Yes, indeed. Back from the North West Frontier of India.'

'Fancy that. It don't seem only yesterday you an' 'im was driving along that promenade. Such an 'andsome little fellow, young Master Thomas.'

'Yes, indeed,' she sighed, reflectively. 'Look out for him tomorrow, Harrison, and bring him along.'

'Right you are, Ma'am,' he said.

'Do I get on with the washing, then, same as usual?' Mabel asked anxiously, at 7 o'clock the following morning.

'Why not? Monday is washing day.' Bertha's tongue was even sharper than usual today. It was no use pretending it was a normal Monday, for the house would soon be swarming with the family, but she saw no reason to include Mabel in the celebration. It should all be finished by 10 o'clock, and Mabel would be scrubbing the copper lid and the scullery floor.

But Norah had her breakfast waiting in the oven, and the

70

appetising smell of bacon and eggs and fried bread made Mabel's mouth water. With a good breakfast inside her, she could tackle the big pile of washing and be ready for a nice cup of tea at mid-morning. The worst part in the Winter was hanging it out in the yard. She wore a little knitted cap on her sparse grey hair. Three old jumpers and a heavy tweed skirt that covered her scraggy bones were all cast-offs from one of the Brent sisters. So were the shoes, usually a size too large for her small feet, and slopping up and down as she walked. Her work-roughened hands were blue from poor circulation, and her nails broken. She lived with her cat in the basement bed-sitting room, and counted her blessings. She had a roof over her head, food in her belly, and money enough in the Prudential to pay for her burial. Mabel had never been married. She was too busy charring to give it a thought!

'Best get the brass polished an' them front tiles scrubbed early today. I'll see about it when I've lit the copper fire,' she decided, as she wiped her plate clean with a crust of bread.

'*Before* you light the copper fire, my good woman,' Bertha corrected. 'Who knows what time they will start arriving? We can't have you cluttering up the place with a bucket of soap-suds.'

'That's true. They might 'ave a fit!'

'They might slip on the wet tiles is more to the point.'

'You don't 'ave to worry. I'll get it dried up nice an' proper, an' get me ugly old self out of the way. I knows me place.'

'Do you, I wonder?' Bertha was thinking, spitefully. There wasn't much that escaped Mabel, and the conservatory was a good vantage point from which to view the drawing-room.

Norah took no part in the conversation. She was eagerly looking forward to the invasion. She too knew her place, and would not intrude unless she was invited. They needed her, and to be needed made everything worthwhile. Only Kate gave herself airs. The rest were fond of her. There was no envy or malice in her nature, and she would not have changed places with any one of them.

Last night she had played lady's maid to Amelia, and washed her hair. It was snowy white, and soft as silk. She

71

had carried up rainwater from the butt in the yard. The bedroom must be nicely warm, and two of the best towels kept for her bath – which she took in the morning – and the hair-washing in the evening. It was a kind of ritual, unchanging through the years, and Norah's big, capable hands were gentle. Amelia's fragility was an illusion. She was hard as nails and indestructible.

'Mother will outlive the rest of us, for she takes such good care of herself,' Bertha had predicted.

Only Norah was entrusted with Amelia's washing, and when Mabel saw the dainty crêpe de chine petticoats and drawers and embroidered nightgowns on the clothes line when she scrubbed the back steps one afternoon, she muttered to herself, 'I should like to get them pretty fripperies in me 'ands, jus' once, but the mistress would 'ave a fit, she's that perticler.'

She was the first to hear the station cab pull up at the front gate that Monday morning, and she dumped the heavy basket of washing in the yard, and scuttled up the steps into the conservatory, drying her hands on the sacking apron. She knew that visitors always foregathered in the drawing-room, winter and summer, until Norah announced a meal was ready, when they all trooped into the dining-room. A small pane of glass was missing from the top of the glass-panelled door. Thomas had broken it, years ago, so they said, but that was before her time. Draped in a muslin curtain it did not show, but afforded a good place in which to listen to the excited chatter of new arrivals. A box was kept permanently behind the potted palm, and Mabel mounted her platform with breathless eagerness, twitched the curtain an inch or two, and waited.

A bright fire blazed in the hearth, reflected in the polished silver and brass. An immaculate white carpet covered the floor and the windows were hung with red velvet curtains. It was a room of handsome proportions, much too grand for Mabel who preferred the cosy shabbiness of her basement bed-sitting room, smelling strongly of cats.

The Mistress entered the room like a queen, in her best blue gown. Her small, erect figure, held a dignity that was matched by the woman who followed. Grace, the second daughter, had linked her arm in her sister's, and it was Ellen who was looking so flushed and starry-eyed that she was hardly recognizable. These two sisters had once been inseparable, for only two years divided them, and they had been pushed together in the bassinet by the nursemaid on their daily outings to the park. That was a long time ago, but Mabel had gradually gleaned all the family history from Norah, when Bertha was engaged on her interminable polishing in another part of the house.

'Grace by name and grace by nature. I always thought she was the best looking of the sisters,' Norah had confided.

'Kate was very attractive, with her dark hair and eyes, but Grace had a lasting beauty, as you will see for yourself.'

Norah was right, for here she was, in middle-age, only slightly changed in appearance. The rather self-important little man who followed the sisters into the room, holding Victoria by the hand, was Grace's husband, Henry.

'And that was a story as romantic as you would read in any of those cheap novelettes,' Norah had continued the family saga one morning, while Mabel cleaned the kitchen range. 'She went away to live in London as lady's maid to a banker's wife, and the banker fell in love with her. Grace had always been delicate, and she developed consumption and nearly died. They said she could not stand the strain of being the go-between, for she was a very sensitive young woman. During all this time, it must have been about three years, she never once came home, and Ellen had gone away to India with her husband who was the father of Prue, Bella and Thomas. Do you follow me?'

Mabel had lifted a face smudged with black lead, and nodded assent. It was a lovely story, and as she watched the main characters in the drama that Monday morning she sighed, for the wonder and magic of such abiding love and devotion. For Henry had left his nagging wife and followed his beloved Grace to Switzerland, where she spent two years in a sanatorium. They said he paid for everything, and sent a monthly report to her mother. They said he worked as a bank clerk in Zurich, starting at the bottom of the ladder again in middle-age, and living in lodgings. When his wife died of a heart attack, he bought a little cottage, engaged a

73

housekeeper, and took Grace out of the sanatorium. They were married six months later.

'An' lived 'appily ever after,' Mabel concluded. 'It do look like it, don't it?' she told herself, for Henry had whispered something and Grace smiled and patted his cheek affectionately.

Amelia had seated herself in her favourite chair. 'Now sit down and tell me all your news,' she commanded.

'Yes, Mother.' Grace was the dutiful daughter again, but she had Henry, and it was Amelia, not Grace, who was wishing she could put back the clock.

When the door opened and Bertha came in, followed by Norah in her long white apron carrying a loaded tray, Henry dropped Victoria off his knee, sprang to his feet, and greeted his dour sister-in-law exuberantly. Then he kissed Norah. Grace smiled indulgently. Henry was a lady's man, but it made no difference to their fond relationship. She was his dearest girl and that, for Grace, spelt happiness.

'Silly little man,' Bertha was thinking, but Norah had enjoyed the kiss, partly because Henry had included her in the family, and that would annoy Amelia. There was still a slight constraint in Bertha's manner, as she greeted her sister, Grace, for it was entirely due to Bertha's scolding tongue that Grace had been sent away to London. It was a long time ago, but a guilty conscience is a poor companion.

'Are you not joining us for elevenses, my dear?' Henry asked affably.

'We are not all ladies of leisure. Somebody has to work!' Bertha could have bitten off her tongue, but it was too late.

Amelia frowned disapprovingly, and the heavy silence was broken by the child. 'My cousin Paul is coming to see me today,' she announced, importantly.

Henry scooped her on to his knee again, and kissed the top of her nose. 'Is that why you are looking so pretty, my poppet?' he asked.

'Nana said to wear my Sunday best because it is a very special day.'

'Quite right.' Henry liked little girls sitting on his knee. He would have made a most indulgent Papa, but Grace was not strong enough for motherhood.

'Nana washed my hair and ironed my best Alice band and cleaned my shoes with milk.' Vicky loved an audience, and was making the most of a rare opportunity.

'Cleaned your shoes with milk? Surely not?' Henry was inspecting one small foot.

'Patent leather,' Ellen explained quietly, wishing Henry would not encourage Vicky to be so chatty.

Bertha and Norah had slipped out of the room, and Amelia was glancing at the clock. 'Did I hear another cab? Run and see, Victoria, there's a good child,' she said, with a false smile.

'Yes, Grandmama.'

As she disappeared through the door with a swing of short skirts, Grace reflected, 'I have been wondering who she reminds me of. It's Alice in Wonderland, isn't it?'

'My dearest girl, how clever of you!' gushed Henry.

'Be so good as to close the door, Henry,' Amelia interrupted. And Henry, whose hot chocolate was growing cold, once again sprang to attention. He got no further than the door, however, when Victoria rushed into the hall, dragging her favourite Uncle Edward by the hand.

'It was not a cab. It was all the London aunties and uncles at the front gate!' she squealed excitedly.

'We d-don't take c-cabs. We w-walk,' Edward stammered. And Vicky squeezed his hand. Poor Uncle Edward, he minded so dreadfully about the stammer, and the black patch over his blind eye. It made him look like a pirate, but he was the gentlest of men.

'It was an accident,' Nana had explained. 'Your Uncle Edward tried to stop a fight in a public house at Hoxton, and got slashed with a razor. It was a long time ago, before you were born.'

'Why does everything happen a long time ago before I was born?'

'Not everything, darling. There is something happening every single day.'

'Like Mama having a bad headache, an' you taking me to the park an' helping Mabel polish the letter-box?'

Ellen's dark eyes were soft as velvet as she cuddled the little girl. Is that all she would have to remember of her early childhood? Now she looked at the child's glowing cheek and shining eyes, and listened to her excited chatter with a glad heart, for this was going to be a day to be remembered with nostalgia in later years.

She seemed to be surrounded by happy faces as they swept into the room. Henry was soon claiming kisses from Jane and Bella, and pumping the hands of Edward and Roderic, both a little shy of all the fuss on these visiting days at The Haven, and particularly apprehensive of meeting the formidable elderly lady awaiting them in the drawing-room. She usually made them feel like a couple of naughty school-boys, and nothing was further from the truth, for both were dedicated disciples of Christ, as their respective wives could have told her.

When the sisters had finished their hugging and kissing, and dabbing their wet eyes emotionally, they greeted Amelia rather more sedately, for she was awaiting her turn to be noticed with frowning brows. Where were their manners? The young generation were getting careless. Here she sat, in her best blue gown, totally ignored! So she turned a haughty cheek to be kissed, and refused to smile until Roderic, who came next to Thomas in her affections, laid a small bunch of violets in her lap.

'I saw them in the florists at Victoria Station, Grandmama, and thought of you,' he said, with his shy, disarming smile.

'Dear boy. How kind,' she thanked him prettily, and all was forgiven.

Roderic had spent all his holidays at The Haven from prep school days, because his parents and sisters were in India. Amelia remembered the first Christmas, when Thomas had arrived home with a strange little boy, and she had no option but to make him welcome.

'Thank you, Ma'am. You are very kind,' he told her.

'You may call me Grandmama,' she replied, graciously. For the sake of her own darling boy she would have welcomed half a dozen little strangers! She remembered how little Arabella had mothered him, and when he came again at Easter, they sat on the back stairs sharing their chocolate eggs. So had started another romance, and another young couple had followed Jane and Edward to the Mission at Hoxton, to be trained as wardens. After their marriage, they were put in charge of their own Mission at Stepney.

It was a happy story, and Vicky had listened with absorbed interest to the telling one wet afternoon when they could not walk in the park. Nana had a fund of such stories, for they were a very big family.

Amelia was pinning the violets to the little gold watch on her blue gown. They were much admired.

'Where is Bertha?' Jane was asking. 'Is she not well?'

'There is only one thing amiss with your sister Bertha, and that is her tongue. I do declare she gets sharper. She was complaining about all the extra work, but it does not signify since Mabel is being paid sixpence an hour over and above her usual wages,' Amelia replied.

'Can we help?' Jane and Bella volunteered, automatically, for they were kind souls, and not afraid of work.

'You know the answer to that, do you not?' Amelia retorted.

And they all chorused, '*We can manage!*'

It was true. Norah and Bertha worked as a team, and Bertha resented what she called 'interference', but constantly complained of being 'overworked'. All the sisters, apart from Kate, who never got involved in domestic matters, had offered to help and been rejected, whenever the family gathered together for a special occasion.

It had started when Ellen arrived home from India with her two little girls.

'More work, and more mouths to feed,' Bertha had commented, acidly.

It was a poor sort of welcome for a young woman recently widowed.

'Sit down, Jane, and stop fidgeting,' Amelia told her fourth daughter. And Jane sat down.

'When in Rome, you do as the Romans do,' Henry whispered, and Jane smothered a giggle. She liked Henry. They all liked Henry — apart from Bertha, of course, who disliked every male on principle.

The London contingent were determined to enjoy their free day. Everything was there to be enjoyed. The warmth and comfort – the spacious rooms – the food – and the clean, wholesome smell that pervaded the air once inside that green gate. They all would eat their fill of the roast beef, Yorkshire pudding, roast potatoes and cauliflower, followed by apple pie and cream. It was such a treat to have a cut off the joint, for their limited housekeeping allowance as wardens of the Mission hostels, had to be very carefully managed. Irish stew with dumplings, sausages and mash, suet puddings and treacle tarts, all guaranteed to fill the bellies of their young lodgers. All four were shabbily dressed, with pallid complexions, but it was the cheerfulness of the two women that probably contributed to their popularity. Whether they had caught the spirit of their East End neighbours, or whether it was a natural gift from Above, was a question both husbands would ask themselves. It was doubtful whether Edward orRoderic would have kept their Faith or their sanity without Jane and Bella. Of course they were looking forward to the reunion with Thomas, and he was bringing his small son. Amelia was only pretending to be interested in what they had to say. As if they didn't know she was obviously on tenterhooks, listening for the station cab!

When the door opened and Norah's pleasant face appeared, they all turned towards her. 'How many more for hot chocolate?' she enquired, breezily.

It was Jane who answered. 'Four, please, Norah. Shall I come and fetch them?'

'Stay where you are, Jane. You're a guest today.'

'You're a darling, and I love you.' That was Bella, flying across the room to be enfolded in those strong, warm arms that had so often carried her up three flights of stairs when her short legs found it too much.

Norah's face was flushed, and she smelled of baking. There would be three kinds of cake for tea, and one to take back to London, as well as a jar of home-made jam.

'Let me help,' Bella pleaded.

But Norah shook her head. 'I'll get the hot chocolate. You must be famished after that long journey.' Then she was gone.

Roderic was waiting at the top of the back stairs to take the tray.

'Take good care of that girl, Roderic. She's worth her weight in gold,' she told him.

'I know it, Norah dear. I am a very lucky man,' he said – and kissed her sweating brow.

'What time do you expect Kate and Charles, Mother?' asked Jane as she sipped the delicious hot chocolate.

'Need you ask? Kate has always tried her utmost to steal the limelight. I can forsee she will make an entrance when we are all gathered round the dinner table, so that all the men will be obliged to rise to greet her.'

Amelia was getting more and more agitated, and Vicky was wriggling on Henry's knee.

'You may be excused, Victoria,' Grandmama's bright blue eyes missed nothing.

'Thank you, Grandmama.' Vicky danced away across the room and through the conservatory door.

'I saw you peeping, Mabel,' she whispered, when the door had closed.

Mabel put a finger to her lips. 'There's another cab stoppin' outside. Best 'urry up with that pee, duckie, afore you wet your drawers.'

Vicky flew down the steps and across the yard. It was freezing cold in the outside lavatory, and the seat was uncomfortably damp. She was quickly back.

'I will save you a bon-bon, Mabel,' she promised. Uncle Charles always brought her a beautiful box of bon-bons, but Uncle Edward, who brought nothing because he was so poor, was still her favourite uncle.

This time it was no false alarm for all the family, apart from Amelia, were streaming into the hall, and Henry had flung open the front door to be the first to claim a kiss from the fair Rosalind and a handshake from the gallant Thomas. Here they were at last on the threshold, Thomas resplendent in scarlet uniform, and Rosalind in blue velvet with a white fur tippet and muff. Holding his mother's hand was a very small boy in a serge sailor suit and matching cap. His huge dark eyes swam with tears, and when he saw the crowd of relatives gathered in the hall he buried his face in the blue velvet. Everyone seemed to be talking at once, and Thomas was the centre of attraction.

The charming smile faded from Rosalind's face. 'Darling, pray remove your son!' she cried imperatively.

Thomas spun round, his blue eyes dangerously bright. To be so addressed in the bosom of his family was humiliating.

'Paul! Come here to me!' His voice was stern. The small figure seemed to disappear in the voluminous velvet folds, but Rosalind shook him off, and he was revealed to all his curious relations as a very frightened little boy, and not at all what they had expected.

Ellen started forward, but her son laid a restraining hand on her arm. 'No, Mother. He must learn to obey.'

'He is only a baby,' she protested.

'Paul is four years old. When I was his age I was not clinging to your skirts.'

'No,' she thought, sadly. 'It was your Grandmama's skirts you clung to, not mine.'

'Take off your cap and stand up straight,' the tall, military figure commanded, and the child obeyed. Under the sailor cap his hair was black and shining, his mouth trembled.

'Why, he is like me, the darling,' Ellen was thinking.

'Now come here.' Thomas held out his hand, and Paul walked towards him, hypnotised into obedience. 'That's better. Now shake hands with all your aunties and uncles.' And the child obeyed.

Vicky hovered on the edge of the group, her hands behind her back. 'I shall not shake hands with that horrid new uncle, and I won't be kissed by that swanky new Auntie!' she told herself. 'I hate them both.' It was prompted by their unkind treatment of the little boy, and in that moment of revelation, the first protective instincts were born. This was the little cousin from India that Nana had been telling her about. They would be playmates in the old nursery at the top of the house, and they would bowl their hoops in the park. Then she remembered they were only on a short visit, and she wanted to cry with vexation. Nobody was taking the least notice of her now, not even Nana. That tall, resplendent figure, in his scarlet uniform, with hair the colour of ripe corn and eyes as blue as a Summer sky, was the centre of attraction, and now he led the way into the drawing-room, holding the child by the hand.

Amelia's face was radiant with the joy of his return, and she opened her arms to receive him, ignoring the child. 'My darling boy!' she cried, and gathered him to her breast.

'Dearest Grandmama, you are looking very beautiful in that blue gown that matches your eyes,' he said gallantly.

'Flatterer!' she scolded, playfully, and patted his cheek.

In that brief moment of reunion, they were conscious only of one another. His wife and his son stood waiting to be noticed, and the rest of the family had ceased to exist. It had always been so. Amelia adored him, and Thomas adored Amelia. But Rosalind was not accustomed to being ignored, and she coughed politely. For the second time Thomas spun round to challenge her right to intrude on his moments of glory. Their eyes met and held, and their wills clashed. But it was nothing new. It was happening all the time.

Now the old and the young woman embraced, but it was a sham, without feeling or affection. Then, at last, Amelia's glance fell on the small figure in the sailor suit, standing stiffly to attention, his dark eyes still wet with his tears.

'Well, my little man, have you a kiss to spare for your Grandmama?' she asked.

And he reached out a hand, as he had been trained. 'Boys do not kiss. They shake hands.' He was only obeying his Papa, but it seemed he was still in disgrace.

'You may kiss your Grandmama, Paul,' Papa said.

So Paul kissed her cheek. It was soft and pink, and it smelled nice, but he would sooner have kissed the dark, wrinkled cheek of his beloved Ayah.

'What is the matter with the child? Why has he been crying?' Amelia demanded.

It was Rosalind who answered. 'It has been rather an upsetting day. I do declare we have had nothing but tears all the way. It was saying goodbye to Auntie Millie. I suppose it was a shock. She is retiring at last, poor darling, and going to live with her sister. Paul was quite devoted to her since he lost his Ayah.'

'I want Auntie Millie! I want Ayah!' wailed the child, overcome by the strangeness of everything.

Ellen had seen enough, and she hesitated no longer. Stepping forward, she gathered up the weeping child and carried him out of the room, with Vicky trailing behind carrying the sailor cap. They climbed the stairs to the top of the house. It was quiet and peaceful. The banked-up fire had kept the nursery warm. The clock ticked on the mantelpiece, and a hot cinder fell into the hearth. Ellen sat down, too breathless to speak, and rocked the child in her arms. Vicky knelt on the hearthrug. Paul's heart-rending sobs seemed to be drawn from her own self, and she shared the anguish of parting from his Auntie Millie and his Ayah. She had not met them, but she had heard about them, for it was not fairy stories she asked for on wet Saturday afternoons, but family stories and Bible stories. They got a little mixed up in her mind and her memory, so that she was never quite sure if Samuel was another little cousin and David one of the children Jesus had loved. But there would be no mistaken identity about Paul, for she knew exactly where he belonged — here, with Nana and herself. They would fight for him, because he was too small and too much afraid to fight for himself.

It was Paul who heard the heavy footsteps on the stairs, and clutched Nana with frantic hands. 'Papa!' he gulped, and sobbed afresh.

'Hush, Paulie, hush, darling,' said Nana comfortingly. So she had comforted Vicky, when her Mama had given her a hard slap for wetting her drawers, or spilling her milk, or saying a naughty word.

Then the tall, commanding figure blocked the doorway. He had not expected to find opposition in the gentle mother who had never challenged Grandmama in all the years he had been growing into manhood. Now he saw her dark eyes blazing, and her voice held a new strength and authority, as he reached out his hands to claim the child.

'Take your hands away from the child, Thomas. You are not having him!' said she, fierce in her defence of her small grandson.

Thomas dropped his hands. This was a woman he hardly recognized.

'Sit down and listen to me, *for the first time in your life*. You may be important in your own estimation and in your own sphere but here, in my nursery, you have no more right to lay down the law than poor little Mabel.'

And Thomas, taken completely by surprise, sat down and stared at his mother with frowning brows.

'For years I have wanted to speak my mind, but I have been afraid. Your Grandmama's will was too strong, her personality too dominating. From the moment you were born she claimed you, because you were the male she had been waiting for, and her own six daughters meant nothing in comparison. You were such a beautiful baby. I was your mother, but I was treated like a wet nurse. You fed from my breast for more than a year. You grew strong and healthy, but you sapped my strength. By the time I had fully recovered, it was too late. Your Grandmama was bathing and dressing you, and pushing you out in the park in the new bassinet, dressed like a little prince. Everything had to be new and of the best quality for her adored grandson. She hardly noticed your two little sisters, who were born in India, and Prue was violently jealous. Can you blame her? What do you remember, Thomas, of those early, formative years?'

'I remember nothing at all before my third birthday, when everything seemed to happen at once. I was breeched. I had the big rocking-horse. I fell in love with my Auntie Kate.'

'Quite so. I have heard it told by Grandmama more than once. She was so proud of her grandson that day. With your golden curls and blue eyes, you looked angelic. Your sister Prue was right to call you a horrid, spoilt little boy. So you were. She hated you that day, Thomas, and has never stopped hating you. That is why she is not here today.'

'Is she not? I hadn't noticed. Bella is here, and she was always my favourite.'

'Naturally, because she waited on you hand and foot, like a little slave.'

'Did she? I don't remember.'

'Your memory is conveniently blank, Thomas, when it suits you.'

In the awkward silence that followed, Paul sniffed miserably, not knowing what to expect. Vicky sat back on her heels and glowered at the new Uncle. He smiled disarmingly; but the smile that could charm a bird from a bough held no charm for his small niece. Thomas shifted uncomfortably. It was a strange homecoming, and not at all what he had expected after five years' absence overseas. This unforseen lecture from his gentle mother, the glowering little girl, and his own son shaming him with his baby ways.

But Ellen had not finished speaking her mind. She was determined to settle the matter before Thomas left the room, and to see a smile on that sad little face would be her reward. It was no life for a child in a garrison town. Why should he not be allowed to spend his early years at The Haven?

'What plans have you made for Paul, now that Auntie Millie has retired?' she asked her son.

'We have engaged a housekeeper who will keep an eye on him, and take him for walks. He will have lessons with the Foster-Clarke children, as he did in India. They have a private governess.'

'Is that the best you can do? Is his mother so busy that she has no time for him?'

'Rosalind is very popular with the young set. She has a very pleasant social life. Then she rides, of course. She is a most accomplished horsewoman.'

'Does Paul have a pony?'

'He does, but I am ashamed to watch his poor performance. That a son of mine should be scared of horses is inconceivable.'

'Then why not let the child walk?'

'Mother, you don't understand how important it is for a boy. It is never too early to start disciplinary training. If Paul is to follow in my footsteps, as I fully intend he shall, then riding is an essential part of it.'

'So Paul is to follow in your footsteps, as you followed in the steps of your father? And what did you discover at the end of your journey, my son?' She waited, knowing the answer to that pertinent question, knowing how much his pride had suffered.

'I discovered the truth. I am sorry, Mother.'

'No need to be sorry. I have lived with it for a very long time, and it does not hurt any more. You will not tell your Grandmama what you discovered?'

'Never!'

She sighed. 'That, at least, is something we share — the skeleton in the cupboard.'

'Mother, tell me what you have in mind for Paul. I should be grateful for your advice.'

'*My* advice?'

He nodded.

'Then I would suggest you leave him here with me for the present. He will have Vicky as a playmate, and I could take them both to the kindergarten at the Convent. You could make me a small allowance. When he is seven will be time enough to think about prep school. What do you say?'

'This is uncommonly generous of you, Mother. You will like that, Paul, will you not?'

'Yes please, Papa.'

'Splendid! Then that is settled. Are you coming down to lunch? We still have to meet Auntie Kate and Uncle Charles.'

'Yes, Papa.' He turned to smile at his grandmother, then slid off her lap and took his father's hand. They walked downstairs together.

Ellen's dark eyes were tender with love for the child, as she followed them down the stairs, holding Vicky's hand.

'Ah, here comes my darling boy at last!' The shrill, excited voice could be none other than Kate's, and Thomas looked down on the elegant, fashionably-dressed woman in the hall.

In middle-age she had put on weight, and the whale-bone corset failed to control the spreading lines of the body he had once known intimately. In that moment, when their eyes met, they could see themselves frolicking in the bath, running naked into the bedroom, and making love on the marriage bed Kate shared with her husband, Charles. She had seduced his young, virgin body at the age of fifteen, and they were lovers for almost two years. As a public school boy, with extravagant tastes, Thomas was glad of the money. Charles was often away from home. As a Member of Parliament, he had certain obligations to his constituents. But they became a little too reckless, and servants talk. Charles caught them one afternoon enjoying themselves in such an abandoned attitude, the blood rushed to his head. To be cuckolded by his nephew by marriage was an insult to his own manhood. Mad with jealousy, he could have killed the boy, but he saved his wrath for Kate.

'Get out!' he had yelled.

And Thomas had gathered up his clothes and fled.

Then he had given Kate the hiding she deserved. They had not slept together since that day. Charles had a mistress, and Kate had lovers. There was no scandal and no divorce. It was a long time ago, but for Kate, a memory that often tantalized her demanding sensuality. Never again had she known such exquisite delight. He was so young, so beautiful. The memory tortured her to this day, and seeing him again in his splendid manhood, she would have died for just one more chance to hold him in her arms. If only she could put back the clock!

'Hello, Auntie Kate,' he called back from the top of the stairs.

Auntie Kate? That put her in her place! She had been Kate for that idyllic time they were lovers. The tall, uniformed figure descended the stairs, holding the child by the hand, but she gave the child barely a glance and stood there, reaching up her arms in a girlish gesture that was somewhat ridiculous, for her matronly bosom strained at the tight bodice of the modish gown. When he dropped Paul's hand, he was smothered in a suffocating embrace, and he stiffened involuntarily. The same French perfume, the same scarlet lips and sparkling eyes. More than a decade had passed but it had not changed her. Kate was the eternal sex symbol. Born into another day and age, Charles need not have married her, but Victorian morality and his own career had ordained the conventions.

Now he stood waiting and smiling, to shake the hand of the handsome young officer who once had fled, naked, from his wrath. In the meantime, he shook the hand of the small boy in the sailor suit. 'I am your Uncle Charles,' he said.

'How do you do, Sir,' answered the small boy gravely. 'I am going to live here with Nana and Vicky.'

'Are you, by jove, and what does your Papa have to say?'

'He is going to allow it, is he not, Nana?' He caught at her hand. He felt safe with Nana.

86

'Yes, darling, he is going to allow it,' she echoed, and kissed the top of his dark head.

They could hear Norah and Bertha on the back stairs. There was so much to carry up from the basement kitchen to the dining-room. Such a big family to serve. Savoury smells drifted into the drawing-room, and Bella and Roderic ran to help, expecting to hear the usual 'we can manage' from the dour Auntie Bertha. But, surprisingly, she actually welcomed their offer to help, for she had been feeling a little guilty about the sharp retort she had made soon after their arrival. Bertha never actually admitted that her tongue was sharp, except to Norah who always made excuses for her. Without Norah, she could have developed into a neurotic spinster years ago. So the young ones raced up and down the back stairs, carrying piles of hot plates, Yorkshire pudding, vegetable dishes piled with roast potatoes and cauliflower, and tureens of rich brown gravy, followed by Norah bearing a heavy dish of sizzling roast beef. The table was laid with a starched damask cloth, and the silver cruet and cutlery sparkled in the firelight.

Vicky usually rang the bell to summon them all to the table on these special occasions, but today she handed the bell to a proud little boy, who made the most of the honour till Great-Grandma reminded him sharply, 'We are not deaf!'

Norah was already carving up the beef on the sideboard, Bella and Roderic standing by to serve, thoroughly enjoying their role as waiters.

When Amelia had seated herself at the head of the table, Thomas took a seat beside her. The rest of the family spread out round the long refectory table that had once graced Grandfather Brent's town house in the days of big dinner parties and many servants. Paul stationed himself between Nana and Vicky. Rosalind was much too busy flirting with Henry to notice what her small son was up to. As for Kate, she had eyes only for that handsome officer at the head of the table, while her husband, Charles, gave all his attention to Jane, his favourite sister-in-law, who had a fund of amusing anecdotes from the East End. Grace had seated herself beside Ellen, and they talked quietly together and watched the children, seeing that they ate all their vegetables.

When Norah had finished carving, she covered the meat with a lid, slipped off her long white apron and sat down next to Bertha. Her face was flushed and her brow damp with sweat.

'If only we had a hot plate, we could keep the vegetables hot.' She spoke directly to Amelia, who held the purse-strings.

'We cannot afford such a contraption to use on these special occasions. We are normally such a small family,' she answered haughtily, for she disapproved of Norah making suggestions of that nature. Norah never took offence. She was hungry and ready to enjoy her dinner.

Thomas smiled disarmingly. 'This beef is the best I have tasted since we last sat down at this table,' he declared.

And Norah inclined her head in grateful acknowledgement.

The London contingent all had second helpings, then Bella and Roderic collected the dinner plates and carried them to the basement kitchen, where Mabel was enjoying her own dinner in solitary state.

'Stack 'em up in the scullery, me duckies. I'll be washin' up when I've finished me dinner,' she told them cheerfully.

Three apple pies stood waiting on top of the range, and three jugs of cream on the marble slab in the larder. The young ones loaded the trays and carried them carefully upstairs. It was no hardship. They were more accustomed to serving than to be served. Roderic stole a kiss at the top of the stairs. They were still sweethearts, these two.

The London contingent ate two helpings of apple pie and cream. Their faces glowed, and they sighed with satisfaction as they folded up their starched white napkins.

When all had finished, Amelia bowed her head for grace, and all around the table heads were bowed. 'For what we have received, may the Lord make us truly thankful. Amen.' Her clear, resonant voice echoed to the lofty ceiling. The firelight danced on the bowed heads. Fair and dark and grey heads, all bent for grace. Only the matriarch's head was white, and her daughters hardly remembered the time when her hair was as golden as the grandson's who sat beside her. It had turned white overnight, from the shock of her

88

husband's tragic death. She was still a young woman on that day her beloved Thomas had stopped a frightened carriage horse and got kicked on the head. For years she had worn black, but it suited her, with her snow-white hair, soft as silk, piled on her small, proud head. Everything about her was small and dainty, her hands and feet, her petite figure. Only Lucy, her youngest daughter, had inherited this same daintiness but she had died in childbirth a year after she had married Basil. Because he was now married to Prue — whose bitter hatred of her brother, Thomas, had divided the family — Basil was excluded from all these special occasions at The Haven.

'I will tell you all about the party tomorrow, Papa,' Vicky had promised.

'Yes, you do that, my pet.' His smile was wistful as he watched her running downstairs. Nana was waiting for her at the side door of Thomas Brent & Son. Vicky spent most of the week at The Haven, after attending morning lessons at the convent kindergarten. There was nothing left of that gay young bachelor who had once courted Kate *and* Lucy Brent. Amelia had only contempt for a man who allowed himself to become a martyr to his wife's indisposition. But Amelia was hard, and she had no mercy or compassion for weakness, of either mind or body.

Not one of her daughters had her confidence. She had always kept herself aloof, even when Thomas was master of the house. In her handsome, dark-eyed husband she had found the perfect foil for her fair beauty and capriciousness. Thomas had adored her. Thomas had indulged her. It was a long time ago, and she may have been seeing it through rose-coloured spectacles, now that she was no longer young. Her five daughters admired and respected her. She did not ask or deserve their love. Her three sons-in-law were quite affectionate, especially Charles. She loved the way he kissed her hand. Such a gentleman. Such charming manners. She sometimes had a feeling she would like to lie with him. Such shocking thoughts for a great-grandmother!

Her grandson was standing waiting to escort her back to the drawing-room. She smiled on her assembled family.

'Tea at 4 o'clock,' she announced, and took his arm.

A sigh of relief followed them from the room, then everyone seemed to be speaking at once, and the babble of voices grew louder. Laughter spilled out of Charles and Jane, who were sharing a joke, and Rosalind giggled when Henry whispered a secret.

The children pushed back their chairs, and Paul asked anxiously, 'What do we do now?' He was not yet accustomed to speak or act on his own initiative. Fear of his father's displeasure hung like a threatening cloud since he had lost Ayah. Auntie Millie had done her best to protect him, but she had not always been there. The long journey home from India had been a nightmare from which he had not yet recovered. And England was so cold. He shivered in his unheated bedroom in the new home at Aldershot, where the rain splashed on the windows, and the wind howled down the chimneys. He missed the musky smells of India, the hot sun, the dark faces of the native servants and the gentle voice of Boy. 'Baba Sahib.' It was a nice name. But Papa had told him he would never hear it again. That chapter of his life was finished. All of life was made up of chapters, like a book. When one was finished, you started another.

'Yes, Papa,' he had answered dutifully, not understanding. So now he looked to Vicky for the next step in this big, strange house, filled with strangers called Aunties and Uncles.

She took his hand and smiled at his grave little face. 'We will play in the nursery. Nana has taught me to tell the time. We will come back for tea at 4 o'clock,' she told him.

'Where are you going?' Nana called after them.

'To play in the nursery.' Vicky was very positive. Her fears were small fears that she would outgrow, but Paul would live with fear of his Papa till he was a grown man.

'Take care of Paulie, and do not touch the fire,' Nana called after them.

'A quaint little soul,' Auntie Grace murmured, as they disappeared. She was shy with children. Indeed, she was shy of her own sisters, apart from Ellen, and dumb in the presence of Amelia. That traumatic period of separation from her family had left its mark. The strain of being the go-between in a household where even the servants took sides in the daily squabbles between Master and Mistress. The sickness that sapped her strength. Then the final collapse and the hovering at death's door. The sanatorium in Switzerland, and her slow recovery. In all these memories, only Henry was real and substantial. Only Henry had given her the strength and the will to recover. She loved him with the quiet calm of a woman who had know much suffering. And she recognized suffering in the sad, dark eyes of the little boy.

'What is wrong with that child?' she asked her sister.

'Shall we go into the morning-room? We can talk privately there,' Ellen suggested. And they linked arms and went out of the room.

When Bella and Roderic had helped to clear the table, they joined Norah and Bertha in the breakfast room, and Norah made a pot of tea. The young ones found an interested audience for their tales of life in the East End.

Henry and Charles wandered into the garden to smoke a cigarette, for smoking was not allowed indoors. Edward could not afford to smoke, and his stammer was a drawback to any conversation, so he watched Jane making up the fire with coals from the big scuttle, then he pulled up two chairs, and they sat down.

'Are you enjoying it, my darling?' she asked.

'Very m-much,' he lied to please her.

Kate and Rosalind chattered excitedly about clothes and fashions, and film stars. Kate envied Rosalind her youth and because she was married to Thomas. Rosalind thought Kate rather ridiculous.

'Like two cats, hiding their claws,' Edward was thinking, for he disliked them both.

Paul's eyes widened with fright as he gazed upwards.

'Are you afraid of stairs?' Vicky asked.

'We do not have stairs where we live.' His hand was cold in her warm little fist.

'No stairs? Then how do you get to bed?'

He frowned, trying to explain the difference. 'Our house is called a bungalow.'

'What is a bungalow?'

'It is where we live, in India and in Aldershot.'

They could hear people talking in the drawing-room, the dining-room and the morning-room. Laughter floated up from the basement. The old house was alive again. It only really came to life on these special occasions.

And here they were, at the bottom of the stairs, and nobody bothering with them. Vicky felt very protective towards her little cousin.

'I will go first, and you follow me, then you will not see where you are going. Hold the banister with one hand, and hold my skirt with the other hand,' she explained carefully. Step by step they climbed the first flight of stairs to the landing.

'Are we there?' asked Paul.

'We are halfway. These are the bedrooms for Grandmama and the Aunties, and here is the indoor lavatory. There is an outdoor lavatory I will show you tomorrow. Come and see how grand it is. Look, a seat that is polished, and proper lavatory paper, and a chain to pull. Isn't it exciting? Shall I show you how it works when I have a little pee. Then you can have a turn.'

'All right,' Paul agreed, glad of any diversion to prolong the moment when they must climb more stairs. But Vicky was very brave. He watched her pull up her skirts, unfasten her drawers, and drop them to the floor. Then she hoisted herself onto the high seat, and sat there swinging her legs.

'Sometimes I wet my drawers. It's not my fault. It's my bladder. Nana says it is something I shall outgrow,' she explained, conversationally. 'There, I have finished.' She scrambled down, hitched up her drawers, and fumbled with the buttons. 'When I was a small little girl, Nana or Papa fastened my buttons. Now I do everything my own self.'

'Me, too.'

'Do boys have a bothersome liberty bodice, with buttons?'

'No, I have a vest and pants.'

'Take care not to fall.' Vicky laughed at his fears and pulled the chain. The water gushed into the pan, but only Vicky thought it was a miracle. Paul had never seen any other kind of lavatory in all his short life, but was too polite to say so.

'There, now it's your turn.' She slid off the seat, and watched in fascinated curiosity a performance completely different from her own. Then he lifted the seat with his free hand, and had his little pee standing up!

'That was clever, Paulie,' she told him. 'Do all little boys do it that way?'

He nodded.

'And all little girls do it my way. It's interesting, isn't it?'

'Yes, it's in-tresting,' he agreed gravely, as he fastened his buttons. 'When I lived in India, my Ayah took me to the lavatory. Then she went away, and Papa said I was to take myself. Papa said I must dress myself and eat up all my porridge.' He pulled a face. 'When I had Ayah, she obliged me by eating half of it. Papa said that was cheating. What is cheating?'

'I thought it was when you copied a sum from another child.'

'That's what I thought.'

'Your Papa could be wrong.'

'Papa is never wrong. Papa is always right.'

'Aren't you going to pull the chain?'

'You do it.'

'It's your turn.'

'You can have my turn.'

'Thank you!'

Paul was glad to be excused. Next time he would let Vicky pull the chain after his pee. In their innocence, neither of the children realized they were committing a grave offence, and there would never be a next time.

Ellen had left the gas turned low, and the banked-up fire had burned through. The glowing coals behind the fireguard shed a cheerful glow over the cosy room that had hardly changed since the six sisters had shared it, two by two, with the nursemaid, until they were ready for the governess and the schoolroom.

'I like it best up here. Must we go back downstairs?' Paul asked, already anticipating that fearful descent to the ground floor.

'The clock says ten minutes past two. We have nearly two hours, then we must go back, else Nana will come to fetch us, because Grandmama would be waiting to start tea.'

Paul nodded gravely. Vicky must know best about such things, but it was a pity.

'That is the rocking-horse Grandmama gave your Papa when he was three. Would you care to ride it?' asked Vicky, with the air of a gracious hostess.

'No, thank you.'

'There are boxes and boxes of soldiers in the cupboard. Shall we get them out?'

'No, thank you.'

'We could play mothers and fathers, and you could be father?'

'No, thank you.'

Vicky sighed. Was he going to be difficult? He stood there, staring about the room, his eyes wet with tears.

'What is the matter, Paulie?' she asked kindly.

'I want Teddybear and Elephant. Papa made me leave them behind. He said only babies play with such toys. But I love them.'

'Don't cry. You can have my teddybear. I'll fetch him.' And she ran into the bedroom, scooped him off the bed and brought him back.

'He does not look like my teddybear,' sniffed Paul miserably.

'Take him and give him a cuddle. He is very cuddlesome.'

So he took the teddybear and cuddled it. After a moment or two he smiled through his tears, and the smile was almost as sad as his tears.

'What could you do with such a sad little boy?' Vicky asked herself. Nana would take him on her lap, but Nana was not here, and her own lap was too small.

'I could read you a story? Nana taught me to read.'

'A Bible story?'

'Yes, if you like Bible stories.'

'Auntie Millie read to me every night when I went to bed.'

'Nana will read to you. Her reading is better. I have to miss all the big words. Sit down in front of the fire. I will fetch the book. All the books are in that cupboard. They are very old. Once upon a time they belonged to Nana and the

94

Aunties. Then they belonged to my Mama and Auntie Bella and Uncle Roderic. Your Papa did not care for books, only the soldiers and the rocking-horse. Everything in this house is old. I like it that way.'

'Me, too.'

Sitting on the hearth-rug, cuddling the strange teddybear, Paul felt quite comforted. Vicky came to sit beside him, and spread the book on his knees. They turned over the pages and looked at the pretty coloured pictures. Paul recognized each one.

'That's Samuel. That's David. That's Moses. That's Ruth. That's Joseph. That's Jesus.'

'You know every one. What shall I read?'

'Samuel.' He knew it by heart, but he listened to Vicky stumbling over the familiar words, stared into the fire, and forgot about the fearsome descent to the ground floor. Then Vicky read about Moses in the bulrushes and David killing Goliath.

'Now it's my turn to choose,' she said, and she chose Ruth. 'Where thou goest, I will go,' she read.

'I like that, only it does not happen that way,' said Paul remembering the sadness of parting. 'Ayah went away. She did not take me. Auntie Millie went away. She did not take me.'

'I won't go away, not ever. I promise.'

'Thank you.'

'And Nana won't go away. She is always here. She will take us to the park with our hoops and, when the Summer comes, she will take us to the beach. We shall buy buckets and spades, and dig sand castles. We shall take off our shoes and socks, and paddle in the sea.'

'I don't think I should care to paddle. The sea is so big. I was frightened on the ship that brought us from India.'

'Oh, but it's not the same sea. Our sea at Worthing is small. You can see the end of it when it touches the sky. You can hold my hand if you feel afraid. Nana will take a picnic. Sandwiches and cake and tea in a flask. She has it all planned. We have talked about it a lot, when we heard you were coming home from India. Did you have picnics in India?'

'Yes, in the hills. We had to ride ponies. I was afraid. Papa was angry.'

'The beach picnics will be better, and Nana is never angry. Next to my Papa, she is the bestest person in the whole world. You can share her. I will let you share her.'

'Thank you.'

'Nana will take us to the kindergarten at the convent.'

'What is a kindergarten?'

'A school for little children.'

'Shall I like it?'

'You will like some of it. Nana says you cannot expect everything to suit you in this world. You have to take the bad with the good.'

Paul looked troubled. 'Do they have ponies at kindergarten?'

'No ponies.'

'Do they have boys that pinch and punch?'

'Good gracious, no! The Sisters would never allow it.'

'Can I take your teddybear to kindergarten?'

'Of course you may. I took him once upon a time, when I was only four.'

Paul sighed. Most of the hazards seemed to have been surmounted. There would be others. His small world had always been filled with fear and all kinds of bogies. Even with Vicky's assurance, and the kind Nana to watch over him, he was afraid he would still be afraid.

'Tell me about Uncle Edward. I like Uncle Edward,' he said, surprisingly, for he had had little opportunity to get to know him in such a crowd. But he was Vicky's favourite uncle, and she was pleased to tell the story she had heard from Nana, about the fight in the public house, and the brave Uncle Edward who tried to stop it and got slashed with a razor.

Paul shivered. 'He gave me sixpence. See, I have it in my pocket.'

'He always gives *me* sixpence, but not today. Nana says he could only afford to give away one sixpence today because he is poor. And you had been crying, so you got the sixpence.'

'Next time I won't cry. Cross my heart and hope to die.' He

solemnly crossed his heart. 'That's what I had to say when I fell off my pony in India,' he explained.

Vicky looked puzzled. It seemed a stupid thing to say.

'Your Mama is very pretty,' she said to Paul.

'Yes,' he agreed.

'Do you love your Mama?'

He shook his head.

'No more do I. I was told it was wicked. I had to stand in a corner, and I wet my drawers. I had to write six times, "honour thy father and thy mother".'

'What is honour?'

'I don't know. It was not explained. I love my Papa. Perhaps that is honour.'

'I don't love my Papa.'

'That is bad, Paulie. You must be wicked, like me, but you don't look wicked. You look only sad.'

'I am sad. Auntie Millie told Mama I was born sad.'

'What did she say to that?'

'She said it was nonsense.'

'Does your Mama slap you?'

'No.'

'What then?'

'She says I am a nuisance.'

'That is not kind.'

'My Mama is not kind.'

'She is so very pretty.'

'Yes.'

'Grandmama would say it does not signify.'

'What does it mean?'

'I don't know. I like the sound of it.'

'Me, too.'

'Tell me about your Ayah in India.'

Paul's eyes went soft as velvet when he thought of her, but to describe her was not easy.

'Was she pretty?' Vicky prompted.

He shook his head.

'What did she do?'

'Everything.'

'And?'

'I was her Baba Sahib.'

'Is that a good thing to be?'

He nodded.

'And?'

'She had a nice smell.'

'Like lavender water?'

'No, not like that.'

'What then?'

'Like India.'

'Does India have a smell?'

'Oh, yes, and Boy, too. He had the nice smell of India.'

'Which boy?'

'Just Boy. He was not a boy. He was an old man.'

Vicky looked very puzzled. It all sounded most peculiar, and not at all the kind of place she would care for, but Paul had been happy in India, and now he was unhappy in England. That was something she couldn't bear. Her warm heart ached for this little cousin with the big, sad eyes, and the unkind Mama, and the stern Papa.

He was staring into the fire, cuddling her teddybear. 'I try all the time to please my Papa,' he said gravely.

'But he is not pleased?'

'No.'

'That is like Grandmama. She will tell you that she is much displeased. I am not a favourite with Grandmama because I am a girl. You could be a favourite if you wished, because you are a boy.'

'I don't like her.'

'You must not say that.'

'Why?'

'Because Grandmama is the most important person in this house.'

'She loves my Papa.'

'Yes, she does. Nana says he always was her favourite, and he always will be. She calls him her darling boy, but he is a man.'

'So was Boy in India a man.'

'Grown-ups are funny. They speak in riddles.'

'I know a riddle.'

'Tell me.'

'Why does a chicken cross the road? Go on, say it.'

98

'Why does it cross the road?'

'To get to the other side. Now you have to laugh.'

'But it's not funny.'

'That's what I said. It's not funny.'

'Do you know any more riddles?'

'No, only one.'

'You must tell it to Nana.'

'Will she think it's funny?'

'She may or may not, but she will laugh to oblige you. Nana is so very obliging.'

'Somebody is ringing the bell for tea,' said Vicky, as they sat together in companionable silence on the hearth-rug. The time had passed so quickly and pleasantly, but now they must join the grown-ups.

'I must not take your teddybear downstairs. Papa would be angry,' Paul sighed.

'Leave him sitting in the chair. He will be waiting for you at 6 o'clock,' Vicky suggested kindly.

'All right.' Paul did as he was bid, because he had got into the habit of doing so since he lost Ayah. Everything had changed since his beloved Ayah went away to live with Allah. Her Baba Sahib could decide whether to play in the garden or in the nursery, whether to take Teddybear and Elephant for a ride in the bassinet, whether to wear sandals or to run barefoot on the wet grass after the garden boy had hosed the lawn. Then, of course, Ayah had been so very obliging about the porridge.

'Come along, Paulie. Please do hurry. Grandmama will scold.'

He took her hand and they went out of the room, and there were the stairs, steep and straight, to the bedroom landing, with only a strip of carpet. His hand was cold, and his lips trembled.

'Don't be frightened,' Vicky coaxed. 'After a little while you won't mind at all. You might even slide down the banisters one of these days, like your Papa and your Uncle Roderic when they were boys.'

Paul shook his head. Never could he contemplate such an alarming experience.

From the landing to the hall, the wide stairs curved. They

99

were covered with a thick pile carpet, only slightly worn in the centre from Bertha's vigorous brushing, and hundreds of footsteps through the years. Carpets bought at Thomas Brent & Son were guaranteed to last a lifetime, as Grandmama could have told you. By the time they reached the safety of the hall, with its polished parquet floor, Paul felt quite sick, and not in the least inclined to sample Norah's strawberry jam, or any one of the three kinds of cake usually provided on these special occasions. Hand-in-hand in the doorway they stood for a moment, a little shy and uncertain, then walked slowly towards the two empty chairs next to Nana. At the head of the table two heads did not turn to welcome them – a white head and a golden head, proudly erect. All the rest glanced up and smiled invitingly. Vicky knew they were already in disgrace, for punctuality was a fetish with Grandmama.

'You are late, Paul. You will apologize to your Grandmama,' Thomas admonished sternly.

'Sorry, Grandmama,' Paul muttered, and hung his head.

'What have you been doing, child?' The question was directed at Vicky, who answered truthfully, quite unabashed.

'First of all I showed Paulie the lavatory. I had a little pee, then Paulie had a little pee, standing up. It was ...'

'That will do, Victoria!' Grandmama thundered.

The shocked silence was broken by Kate's smothered giggle. Paul's head sank lower on his chest, but Vicky, stared about the table. 'Were they so very shocked?' she wondered. All the uncles had suddenly developed a cough. Auntie Jane and Auntie Bella fumbled for their handkerchiefs. Auntie Bertha started to hand round cups of tea, and Norah made a dash for the sideboard. Only Auntie Grace looked embarrassed. Nana's dark eyes held no reproach as she explained, 'Not now, darling. Tell me later.'

'Is it wicked?' Vicky asked innocently.

'Not wicked, but not polite.'

Grandmama would have ordered the children to leave the table but for a restraining hand on her arm. 'I do apologize, Grandmama, for my son's lamentable behaviour. I am partly to blame. A father should supervise his son's toilet at a certain age, should he not?'

Amelia changed her mind, and accepted the apology graciously.

'Pass the bread and butter, and help yourself to jam,' she said, with the aplomb of the perfect hostess.

When tea was finished, only one hour was left before the children's bedtime, since the London contingent ate heartily. After the frightening descent of the stairs, and the disgrace, Paul's small stomach could accommodate nothing more than two half-slices of bread and butter, but since all the grown-ups, except Nana, were concerned with their own appetites, it went unnoticed.

Once again Bella and Roderic volunteered to help clear the table and carry everything to the basement, where Mabel was waiting to finish the left-overs, and what she could not eat she would take home.

The prospect of sitting for another hour in the drawing-room was daunting, and Vicky pleaded to be allowed to help.

'A little help is worth a lot of pity,' Norah answered promptly, and gave them each a plate to carry down the back stairs. Bertha would have refused but for the pleading eyes of the sad little boy in the sailor suit. They had hardly exchanged a word on this first day, but she had been sitting opposite the child at the tea-table, and felt a surprising urge to be kind to him. It may have been her intense dislike of her nephew Thomas, that had prompted such an urge. Be that as it may, she followed the children to the basement with unaccustomed patience, and actually invited them to stay until Ellen came to collect them for bed. In a cupboard in the breakfast-room she discovered Ludo and Snakes and Ladders that must have been there for years. Bertha handed round peppermints, and sat watching the young ones with a mixture of envy and guilt. The young generation avoided her. She wished she could put back the clock and start again. Perhaps it was not too late to get to know the two little ones. She would invite them down for a game of Ludo on a wet Saturday afternoon. And Norah would have them down every Saturday morning if she had her way, to make little pastry men with curranty eyes, from the scraps that were left over. The fruit pie was baked on

101

Saturday, and warmed up on Sunday, when they came back from church.

Musing on these friendly overtures for the future, Bertha forgot all her nagging worries, and composed herself to enjoy the young company, so engrossed in the game they had no thought for tomorrow, and no complaints for all the lost yesterdays. She had a new little great-nephew who might like her – he might even love her a little.

Charles had ordered the station cab for 7 o'clock. The London contingent would travel back to Victoria, first class, at his expense. All six of them crowded into the cab, with Roderic nursing Bella.

The children had been piggy-backed upstairs to bed at 6 o'clock, by Edward and Roderic. Bertha and Norah disappeared down the back stairs as soon as the cab had left. Grace and Henry, who were staying overnight, joined Thomas and Rosalind in the drawing-room.

Amelia was flushed and starry-eyed. It had been an exciting day, and her darling boy was staying for three days with his pretty little wife. They were charming to one another, but it was a forced charm. In Amelia's estimation the Colonel's daughter had not improved by her five years' sojourn in India, but it was doubtful whether any young woman would have been considered worthy of the honour of marrying Thomas.

They had talked privately that afternoon about the store, and her income would be increased now that she had agreed to have Paul living at The Haven in the foreseeable future. In the care of Ellen, on the top floor, she would not be bothered with all the tedious routine that surrounds small children. Later on it would be coping with all the childish ailments. Her own girls had rather enjoyed their communal bouts of measles and chicken-pox, far removed from the rest of the household, with the nursemaid in attendance.

Paul was such a puny little fellow and Ellen would be kept busy, but she was obviously in the seventh heaven with the two children in her care. Vicky would go home only on Saturdays, to visit her parents. Ellen was a fool over children. Her husband must often have felt neglected, in Amelia's opinion. Yet she had Ellen to thank for Thomas, the pride and joy of those years that could have been so very dull. In his scarlet uniform he was so very distinguished. There was a subtle change in him, and it was not only that he had matured. She could not put her finger on it. The boy, of course, would be a great disappointment. It was inconceivable that two such handsome parents should produce such a nondescript child.

Thomas would confide in her again during his stay, she told herself. She understood him so well. Neither his wife nor his mother had known him more intimately. But she was wrong. That light-hearted manner hid at least two serious and secretive episodes in his young life of which he was ashamed. Skeletons in the cupboard they would remain to the end of his days — Isabella Foster-Clarke and the grave in the military cemetery.

With the rest of the family on their way to London, the polite conversation in the drawing-room was confined to matters of general interest. The two men had nothing in common, and Grace was too shy and reserved to enjoy the frivolous company of Rosalind.

At 9 o'clock Norah brought cocoa and biscuits, and Amelia retired. Grace, Henry and Rosalind dutifully kissed her cheek. Only Thomas kissed her mouth. It left her feeling very young and desirable. 'Darling boy,' she murmured as she slipped off her best blue gown.

Ellen had Paul sleeping in her room on the comfortable old sofa. He fell asleep as soon as his head touched the pillow. So did Vicky, in the small bedroom that had once been occupied by the nursemaid, and later by Prue and Bella. A third generation of children would be growing up in the dear old house. Its walls had echoed to the laughter of children, and the clattering of small feet on the basement stairs. It was a long way down from the top floor to the basement, but Ellen was in no hurry that first morning. Both children had awakened early and crept into her bed. One on either side, she cuddled their warm little bodies with the joyfulness of a woman born to motherhood. Now she was blessed with a second grandchild, and she loved them both.

This small world on the top floor was her own private

kingdom. Here she could spoil the children as all grand-mothers do, and feel no sense of guilt. They would get all the scolding that was necessary for their welfare when they sat at the table with Grandmama, twice daily, for dinner and tea. And discipline was strict at the Convent kindergarten. Both children needed a mother-figure to compensate for their own self-indulgent mothers.

Norah had brought up cups of tea and *petit-beurre* biscuits at 7 o'clock. Amelia was awake early. She had sponged her face and hands, tidied her hair, and draped her prettiest bed-jacket about her shoulders. Thomas and Rosalind would wish her good-morning on their way down to breakfast.

Ellen and the children had crept past her door for an early breakfast with Norah and Bertha. Both children were served with a small helping of porridge, generously sprinkled with brown sugar. The grown-ups had salt on their porridge. Paul watched his little cousin in silence, but copied her example and cleared the bowl. The rasher of bacon on a small square of crisply fried bread tempted his appetite. It was a good start to the day, and Ellen was pleased. Both children were allowed weak tea because they did not care for milk. Ellen remembered how Grace and Lucy had shuddered over their milk in those early years. A dash of tea would have made it palatable, but Amelia had the last word on everything.

It was cosy in the breakfast room on these chilly winter mornings, and Norah's cheerful face dispelled any reluctance to start a new day. Paul would have liked to spend the entire morning tucked up with Nana in the big bed, but Vicky was eager to be up and about.

'What shall be do? Where shall we go?' she demanded, as soon as she had finished drinking the tea.

'You choose,' said Nana, who liked a little time to enjoy her early morning tea.

'We could take Paulie to the museum. He would like to see all the birds and butterflies. Would you not like that, Paulie?'

'I don't mind,' he agreed sleepily.

Since he had never visited a museum in his short life, he was quite unprepared for *dead* birds in cages, and *dead* butterflies in drawers. They would have to bring him out and take him to Kong's for hot chocolate. Vicky had a lot to learn about the sensitive little cousin she had taken under her wing with such good intentions.

As General Manager of Thomas Brent & Son, Basil was waiting at the front entrance that first morning, to escort the new owner and his wife and mother, round the store. Every department manager and manageress had been advised about the official visit, and every employee, down to the youngest apprentice, warned of the consequences if they dared to disgrace his or her particular department. Instant dismissal was a threat that hung over their heads for most of their working lives.

The General Manager, whom the senior employees remembered as a genial sort of fellow, ready to share a joke and listen sympathetically to a genuine complaint, could no longer be relied upon. He was a dour, impatient person these days, with a balding head and nervous little mannerisms. His wife was blamed for this gradual change in his personality of recent years, but it did not make the situation any easier.

A Board of Directors had been appointed that included Amelia, and Basil had been annoyed that his long service with this flourishing family business had not been suitably recognized by an appointment to the Board. Basil was somewhat of a Jekyll-and-Hyde character, if the truth be known, for his semi-invalid wife, with her tantrums and tears, extracted every ounce of sympathy and patience. It was 'Yes, dear', 'No, dear'. He was no longer his own man, but a worried, embittered husband. The girl he had married with such trusting devotion was even jealous of her own child.

Unfortunately for all the honest and conscientious employees, they saw only Mr Hyde. He left Dr Jekyll behind in the flat that had once been a cosy little nest for a newly married couple. When he had closed the door and left his wife to the cheerful ministrations of a daily housekeeper, his new identity took possession as he slowly descended the stairs. His little daughter had seen both the self-effacing husband and the critical, unsmiling man of authority, but since most normal children accept their parents and their surroundings with unquestioning loyalty, Vicky was not unduly troubled. On their Wednesday afternoons together, her adored Papa was neither a hen-pecked husband, nor a stern employer, but a generous and affectionate parent.

On this particular morning, strutting importantly ahead of his distinguished visitors, his hands clasped under his coat-tails, he was remembering the many occasions when Amelia had brought the golden-haired little boy to the Children's Department for new clothes. Like a little prince, he was measured and fitted. Now here he was, as handsome a man as ever passed through those imposing portals of Thomas Brent & Son, with the same enchanting smile that had all the females twittering and blushing, and all the males hoped for a glance from the ravishing Rosalind. As for Amelia, on the arm of her grandson, she completed the trio in her own inimitable fashion.

'She has such dignity. Such a young, petite figure.' Such compliments followed her from one department to another.

It was an old-established firm, and old-fashioned courtesies were still observed. Bows and curtsies from the heads of departments. Assistants and apprentices standing stiffly to attention. It was like a royal procession, and when they had completed the tour, Basil escorted them to the hired carriage, bowed formally, and retired, exhausted, to his private office. His fists were still clenched. It had taken all his self-control out there on the pavement. To smash his fist into that handsome smiling face would be only a momentary pleasure. The result of such a drastic action would reverberate through the store, and completely disorganize his public and private life. It would be instant dismissal. They would have to move from the flat on the top floor, but whereto? Who would put up with Prue? His own mother was almost a stranger, since Prue begrudged the couple of hours or so he spent in visiting her, one Sunday in the month. She hardly knew her own grandchild. But Vicky was happy with Nana at The Haven.

Back in his office he was once again a man of authority. He had only to ring the bell, and young Simon Jones would hurry to answer it. He was a bright lad, the eldest of a tribe of children of that indomitable little woman who cleaned and cooked for a nagging mistress, and somehow managed to keep cheerful.

'I count me blessings, Sir,' she had told Basil. 'I mean ter say, I got me 'ealth an' strength, an' you paying me more than I would get on any other job. The mistress can't 'elp being the way she is, can she, Sir? It's nerves, an' there ain't much you can do about nerves. Now don't you worry, Sir. I won't let 'er 'arm 'erself in one of them tantrums. They don't last long. Then she'as a good cry, an' I make 'er a nice cup of tea.'

'Mrs Jones, you've a marvel. If there is anything I can do for you at any time, just let me know,' he had answered.

And she lost no time, for a woman with a tribe of kids, and a lazy, good-for-nothing husband, had to grab every offer that came her way.

'There's Simon, what's comin' up to fourteen, an' bright as a button, Sir. I was wondering whether you could find a job for 'im?'

'Fourteen is too young to be apprenticed, but I suppose he could start as a messenger boy. We do employ one lad, but another would be useful. They are rather like the pages at the big hotels. They answer the bells from the various departments. Yes, send him along to me, Mrs Jones. Tomorrow morning, in my office, 8 o'clock prompt.'

It was worth telling a little white lie – for one messenger boy was enough – to see her expression of joy and gratitude.

'You won't regret it, Sir,' she assured him.

That was twelve months ago, and he hadn't regretted it. He was worth every penny of the five shillings weekly wage, plus a good dinner in the staff canteen.

When the boy tapped on the door that morning, and Basil called, 'Come in,' he stepped inside, saluted smartly, and asked, 'You rang, Sir?'

In his neat uniform, his eager, intelligent manner made an instant appeal to the man who had long since forgotten his own youthful aspirations.

'Yes, Simon, I rang. I am utterly exhausted, and feeling very sorry for myself. What do you suggest?'

'Coffee and toast, Sir?'

'A splendid suggestion. A pot of coffee, if you please, black and strong, and two slices of *hot* buttered toast in a muffin dish. Don't let Mrs Stringer palm you off with a cold plate.'

Simon grinned. It was one of the few pleasures of a rather tedious job, getting the better of the canteen manageress.

'Leave it to me, Sir.'

When the door had closed, the General Manager relaxed and lit a cigarette. It was one of the few luxuries he allowed himself.

They went to Kong's for hot chocolate after they left the store, and Rosalind was treated to a lively tale of Amelia's adored grandson, in a sailor suit, driving along the promenade in a hired cab after elevenses at Kong's. Rosalind was already bored with the visit, and too much of an egoist to enjoy such a catalogue of events in the boyhood of her own husband. It was not in her nature to be overlooked, and her sense of resentment had spoilt the harmony of their first day at The Haven. She listened politely, however, because she was clever enough to realize it was a good policy to keep on the right side of Grandmama. To have settled the immediate future of her small son so unexpectedly, was a tremendous relief. Back in Aldershot, her round of social engagements need not be interrupted by the necessity to keep an eye on Paul when the housekeeper was engaged on her normal duties.

He was such an unsociable little boy. She had visualized the faithful Lizzie as their housekeeper on their return to Aldershot, but she had married the gardener, and emigrated to New Zealand. Nothing had gone according to plan, and she missed the native servants.

Her wandering thoughts were interrupted by the arrival of Ellen with the two children, and Ellen's obvious embarrassment when her handsome son leapt to his feet, and Amelia frowned disapprovingly.

'What are you doing here?' she demanded. 'I should have thought a run in the park with their hoops a more healthy pastime for children.'

'We have already been to the park.' The little white lie surprised Vicky, but she made no comment. Both children were fully aware of the strained atmosphere. Ellen quickly recovered from her momentary embarrassment, and felt only annoyance at being scolded in a public place. Paul had removed his sailor cap without any prompting, but his grave little face wore its habitual worried expression in the presence of his stern Papa. A waitress was hovering to show them to a vacant table.

'Excuse me,' said Ellen, with polite dignity, as they turned away.

Thomas sat down and helped himself to another cake. His eyes followed his mother's tall figure with respect and admiration, perhaps for the first time in his life. She had always been over-shadowed by Grandmama – a shy, gentle woman with dark eyes that seldom smiled. Paul had already attached himself to his new Nana, but now Thomas was wondering whether he had made a mistake. A soldier's son should be raised in the environment of the regiment. Why had he allowed himself to be so easily persuaded that The Haven was the best place for a little boy until he was seven?

'I do declare it seems that history is repeating itself with elevenses at Kong's,' Rosalind giggled.

Amelia was not amused by the interruption, and she could not hide her displeasure. 'If you are quite finished, we will go,' she said. And they followed her out with a quick glance at their small son, obviously enjoying his first taste of hot chocolate at Kong's.

Now Thomas, too, was bored. He did not feel the same affection for Grandmama. Five years was a long time, and their relationship had changed. Only two more days, then back to Aldershot and his world of men. It was a world apart in which women had no place.

Amelia had planned their entertainment for the three-day visit. When they left Kong's that first morning, they drove along the promenade in the hired carriage, the hood closed against the wind and rain. The promenade was deserted. The sea was grey. 'Could anything be more depressing than the seaside in Winter?' Thomas was thinking, while Rosalind sat huddled in her fur coat, wishing they had stayed in India.

Amelia was no fool, and she could sense the strained atmosphere between them. Her grandson was making gallant efforts to entertain her with amusing anecdotes of the voyage, but there had been little fun for Rosalind or for young Paul. They both had been ill, and completely dependent on Auntie Millie, for the stewardess was rushed off her feet. Thomas was a good sailor, and had little patience or sympathy for the unfortunate men under his command who spent much of their time hanging over the rails. The violent storm that broke as they left Marseilles followed them all the way to Southamptom. The horses were terrified, and Thomas seemed more concerned for Jason than for his wife and child. The voyage out had been a nightmare; the voyage home, for the majority of the passengers, something best forgotten.

During that depressing drive along the promenade, that winter day, Amelia's small gloved hand was clasped in her grandson's, as she vainly tried to recapture the lost days of his enchanted boyhood, the fond relationship she thought would last a liftetime. She refused to believe it had gone, for ever. Thomas was no longer the light-hearted subaltern who had married the Colonel's daughter. Living in the past was a luxury the old could afford, but not the young. The future beckoned with challenging opportunities of travel and promotion.

'Poor Grandmama, it's pathetic,' he was thinking as he clasped that little gloved hand, and felt nothing but the obligation to be kind because she was old and he was young.

'I have told Norah we shall be lunching at Warnes,' Amelia announced, as they were driving back. Warnes was the biggest and most expensive hotel. They catered for Winter visitors who came south, seeking a milder climate, but this kind of weather would drive them back home.

They were well received in the foyer, for they were quite a distinguished trio, and Amelia was recognized. Her flagging spirits recovered quickly when the manager bowed over her hand, and she proudly presented her handsome grandson and his charming wife. The head waiter was hovering with the menu, and when they had settled themselves, she was once again playing the role of the perfect hostess, with dignity and charm, and Thomas was obliged to change his opinion on 'poor Grandmama'.

110

'You order, dear boy – and don't forget the wine,' she said, in her grandest manner. With her brilliant smile and her flushed cheeks, Amelia was ageless.

'What is the matter, Paulie?' Vicky asked her small cousin, who had not spoken a single word since Nana left to pay her weekly visit to her daughter, Prue.

'I am frightened,' Paul answered, not for the first time, and Vicky asked, kindly, 'What has frightened you?'

'I think my Papa will take me back to Aldershot tomorrow.'

'That is not so. It is all settled, and you are to stay here.'

'Papa can change his mind.'

'Not about this. Nana would not allow it.'

'Papa listens to nobody when his mind is made up.' Paul was quoting Auntie Millie, who had found Thomas a formidable adversary in fighting for the child in her care since the death of Ayah.

'Mama does not want me in Aldershot. She said I would be a nuisance,' Paul reflected, gravely.

'Well, then, that is settled. You are not wanted in Aldershot, but you are wanted here.' Vicky could see no objection to the plan; no doubts clouded her small mind.

'I want you to stay more than anything in the world.'

'You do?'

Vicky nodded emphathically. 'Next to Papa and Nana I love you best. It's lovely to have a little brother. I always wanted a brother.'

'I thought I was your cousin.'

'Cousin or brother. What does it matter? You can be both if you wish. And I will be your cousin and your sister. You do like us, don't you? You do want to stay?'

'Yes.'

'Well then. Why be frightened?'

'If your Papa was like my Papa, you would be frightened.'

'I dare say. He is not a nice man, your Papa.'

'Boy said my Papa was a very brave Sahib.'

'Boy is the old man with the grey beard?'

111

'Yes.'

'My Papa is brave. He is not afraid of my Mama when she has a tantrum.'

'What is a tantrum?'

Vicky frowned thoughtfully. It was difficult to explain.

'Does it hurt?' Paul prompted.

'I don't think it hurts. Papa says Mama is her own worst enemy.'

'I know what an enemy is. We had enemies on the Frontier in India.'

'That must be a different kind of enemy.'

'Yes.'

'After tomorrow we go to school. We have to wear a uniform with an ugly black pinafore to keep our clothes clean.'

'Why?'

'Because it is the custom, so they say. Sister Veronica will measure you for your new uniform.'

'Shall I like it?'

'You may or you may not.'

'Do you like your uniform?'

'No, I like my own clothes best.'

'I like your frock. It's pretty.'

'So do I. It's my favourite. It was a present from Father Christmas.'

'There isn't a Father Christmas.'

'Of course there is! I have heard the sleigh bells on Christmas morning, and he fills my stocking with presents.'

'My Papa says it's a fairy story, and children of the regiment do not believe in fairy stories.'

'Your Papa is hateful. He spoils everything. When you live with us I shall write a letter to Father Christmas and ask him to leave presents for both of us.'

'Does Nana believe in Father Christmas?'

'Of course.'

Paul looked puzzled. His familiar small world was being turned upside down, and everything was strange.

'We shall go to Thomas Brent & Son to buy your new uniform,' said Vicky.

'Why?'

'Because my Papa is General Manager. You will see how important he is.'

'Is your Papa more important than my Papa?'

'Of course.'

'More important than a soldier of the Queen? Boy said it was a great honour to fight for the Queen.'

'I dare say, but I would sooner have a Papa who was General Manager of Thomas Brent & Son. What is honour, anyway?'

'I don't know,' Paul confessed. He was cuddling Vicky's teddybear. It was a great comfort, but he sadly missed his very own Teddybear and Elephant. Vicky had been reading the Bible stories he loved; sitting on the hearth-rug in the fire-light was a good place to be on a winter afternoon. They had promised not to remove the fireguard, or to touch the fire. Nana would be back to tea. They would take turns to toast the bread, and Nana would spread it with butter and honey. Norah would carry up a pot of tea, milk and sugar, and sponge cake.

Grandmama had announced importantly that they would be out for tea as well as lunch that day. There was something called a 'Tea Dance' that Thomas and Rosalind would enjoy, and she would enjoy watching them, for of course they would be the handsomest couple on the floor, and the most accomplished dancers. They had spent the morning in Brighton, and had an excellent lunch at The Old Ship Hotel. Rosalind had bought another pair of shoes. She had some thirty pairs already, but could not resist the tempting display in the shop in King's Road. Thomas was bored with the shops, and Amelia hung heavily on his arm. There were shops in plenty in Worthing, so why go all the way to Brighton to buy a pair of shoes? Thomas argued, and there was good sense in the argument. If the truth be told, Amelia was finding even three days of entertaining quite a strain on her resourcefulness. They were so accustomed to a round of social engagements, so young, so restless, she could not keep pace with them. An outing to Brighton would pass the time agreeably, she had decided.

To please Thomas, after Rosalind had purchased the

shoes — with half the shop turned out for her inspection — they took a cab to the Aquarium. Thomas remembered an outing in prep school days, but it was doubtful whether he had recaptured the same pleasure in those tanks of tropical fish. If Thomas had been bored in the shoe shop, Rosalind was most terribly bored at the Aquarium. They could both be so charming when they chose, but so childishly sulky when things were not to their liking, Amelia was thinking, as they settled themselves in the restaurant. But she was proud of her darling boy in his scarlet uniform, and his elegant little wife in her fashionable clothes.

There was barely time for Amelia to close her eyes in her own drawing-room for her habitual afternoon nap before the cab was back at the green gate to take them to the Assembly Rooms. Not for one moment would she allow herself to wonder why it was necessary to spend so much time and money in the pursuit of pleasure. Had it all been a success? That was also a debatable question. Last evening they had sat for more than two hours watching an uninspired performance of Romeo and Juliet by the amateur dramatic society. Thomas had never been more in need of a stiff chota peg, and had to make do with a glass of warm ale.

Nobody in that house could have been more relieved than Paul when the station cab rattled away from the green gate.

Amelia retired to the drawing-room to have a little weep, Bertha and Norah to the basement to make a fresh pot of tea; Ellen, Vicky and Paul climbed the stairs to play Ludo and Snakes and Ladders.

Chapter Four

Now a new chapter in their young lives had started in earnest for Vicky and Paul. As for Ellen, she had not known such happiness and contentment since her own two girls were small and dependent on her. The long winter days slipped away, and Paul's first term at the convent kindergarten passed without incident, for he was such a good child, and so obedient. The Sisters loved the grave little boy, whose sad dark eyes seemed to reflect an inborn sorrow that could not be explained. They soon discovered, however, that his main interest, and all his attention, could be focused in their religious teaching. His rare smile was touchingly beautiful, but laughter was something he had yet to learn. The atmosphere of the convent suited him. From the very first day he was obviously impressed. It was unlike anything he had known in India. The private governess and her small class of children in the schoolroom had left only hurtful memories of tears and teasing. Here, at the convent, the principles of love and harmony were practised, and the Sisters were living examples of their teaching. The dreaded punishment to be stood in a corner did not apply to Paul. He was the youngest pupil, too sensitive to be punished, and much too good to warrant a punishment in any case.

Under Vicky's protection, the kind guidance of the Sisters, and Nana's loving care, the nervous little boy gradually forgot most of his fears, but not all. He was still frightened of stairs and the dark − Ellen left a night-light burning. He was frightened of horses and dogs − and frightened of Grandmama!

No two children could have been more unlike than those two little cousins, but they suited each other admirably. Paul was timid, Vicky was bold. His shyness was complementary to her challenging self-confidence. Vicky led, Paul followed.

Paul still missed Ayah, Teddybear and Elephant. These three would always be linked together in the happiest memories of those early years. There was also somebody called Uncle David, not a real uncle, but a kind man who had found Teddybear and Elephant in the market waiting for a little boy to love them. They said Uncle David and Papa hated one another, and had been known to fight over his Mama. They said it was jealousy, but nobody had explained what jealousy meant. Vicky had tried, but not succeeded in explaining something so intangible. It could be felt, but not seen. When Nana was asked to explain jealousy, she left the two children still puzzled, and not at all certain how to cope with something that provoked grown-ups into such a state they could no longer control themselves. It was all so contradictory. 'Papa knows best.' 'Grandmama has the last word.' 'You must always obey your parents.' And so on, and so forth, since they first understood the meaning of obedience.

'Did you ever hear of a mother being jealous of her own child?' Nana had asked, and Vicky had answered, 'Why?' She liked to be given a reason. If you had a reason, a good reason, for a person's behaviour, you could understand and forgive, according to Sister Angelica.

'Your Mama is jealous because your Papa loves you best,' said Nana, sadly.

Poor Papa. He was always being blamed for something. It was not fair!

'When we are married, I shall not be jealous of our children. That is a promise. Cross my heart,' Vicky told Paul with great earnestness.

'Are we going to be married then?' asked four-year-old Paul gravely.

'Of course we are.'

116

It seemed that Vicky, like Grandmama, was always to have the last word!

When the Catholic children at the convent kindergarten were taken to Mass, the non-Catholics were taken for a walk by Sister Angelica. Paul was puzzled by this arrangement. He had been allowed to walk around the church, holding the hand of one of the Sisters, and he thought it was a beautiful place. He liked the smell of the incense, and the guttering candles. The Virgin Mary reminded him of Ayah. This might have shocked the Sister, and in his innocent sensitivity, he kept the thought to himself.

'Why am I not allowed to come to Mass? It smells nice. I like it!' he told the Sister.

'Because you were not baptised into the Catholic faith,' she told him gently. 'You attend St Matthew's Church with your family every Sunday, do you not?'

'Yes.'

'That is good. There is only one God, Paul. We worship Him in different ways. We pray to Mary, the Holy Mother of Jesus. If you were a Catholic child, you would be a child of Mary.'

'I should like that.'

'I believe you would, but we must not use persuasion. It is strictly against our principles. Religion is a matter of grave concern, to be decided by the parents.'

'I like Sunday. It is my favourite day.'

'Do you, Paul?'

'Yes. I like our church, but it does not smell nice, like your church. It smells like mice.'

'Mice?'

'Yes, we found mice in our house in Aldershot when we came back from India. Papa set traps to catch them. I cried. They were so small. They only ate a tiny bit of cheese.'

He was beginning to open up, to speak his thoughts aloud, the Sister noticed. It was a good sign. Victoria was helping him to forget his fears and his Nana was a good woman. Children need to feel safe and secure. No child could grow in grace with haunting fears of punishment. It was not the first time a stern parent had broken a child's spirit. But it was not too late. It could be mended, with patience and kindness.

'I do not want to be a soldier,' Paul had told them when questioned on what he would like to be when he was grown up. So there was trouble ahead for this small boy. They taught obedience. 'Honour thy father and thy mother'. It was a fundamental and necessary obligation. But what if a child grew into adulthood strongly opposed to the wishes of a parent? That question would have to be answered one day.

'No sweets are allowed in Lent,' Vicky told Paul, one Saturday morning, when they received their pocket money. Three-pence a week was not very much when a penny had to be saved in the red pillar-box on the nursery mantelpiece. Nana gave them each a penny to put in the collection on Sunday morning. Everyone knew what Grandmama put in the plate. It was a half-sovereign, and it shone and sparkled among the children's coppers. Rows of Sunday School children sat in front of them, and every child dropped a coin in the plate. The older children gave a halfpenny, the little ones a farthing. Sometimes a naughty boy would pass on the plate to his neighbour and keep his half-penny to buy sweets.

Bertha and Norah could spare only a threepenny bit for the Sunday collection, for Bertha received only a small allowance from Amelia, and she was obliged to ask for money to spend on shoes or clothing occasionlly. Shoes were soled and heeled until the uppers were finally worn out. Skirts were turned, woollens re-knitted, dresses dyed, hats re-trimmed.

Ellen was still the family seamstress, and spent one day a week with her sewing-machine in the little morning-room. Sheets were turned sides to middle, towels patched. But Amelia was not included in this frugal 'make do'. Her personal towels were never patched or her linen sheets turned. She was not extravagant with her clothes, but she always managed to look well dressed.

Since the death of her husband – Thomas the Second – she had a dress allowance from the firm, but this courtesy was not extended to her daughters. They lived in a state of genteel poverty. Amelia gave the impression of comfortable affluence.

When Lent had been explained to Paul that Saturday morning, he was badly shocked. Forty days without sweets!

'Jesus had no sweets for forty days in the wilderness,' Vicky reminded him piously. She was going through a stage when she seemed almost to welcome the strict rules of Lent.

'I am going to be a missionary when I grow up,' she had told Sister Angelica, when questioned about her future plans.

'You said we would be married,' Paul reminded her.

'So we shall. You will be a gentleman missionary, and I shall be a lady missionary.'

'Where?'

'In Darkest Africa.' Vicky had all the answers. She knew exactly what they would do and where they would go.

'I do not like the dark,' Paul pointed out, a little fearfully.

'It's not the weather that is dark. It's the heathens. Black all over.'

'Does the black wash off when they have a bath?'

'No, they stay black for ever and ever.'

'Do they like being black?'

'I don't know. We will ask them when we are missionaries.'

'Will Nana come?'

'Nana will stay here and wait. We shall send our children home to live with her.'

'Shall we?'

'That's what missionaries do. Auntie Jane told me. She was going to be a missionary once upon a time. Then she married Uncle Edward and went to live in the Mission at Hoxton.'

'Are there heathens in Hoxton?'

'White heathens, not black.'

'I would like it best in Hoxton.'

'Would you? Then we will go to Hoxton.'

'Thank you.'

Having settled the far distant future, Paul remembered about Lent. 'Would it be wicked for Norah to make us toffee in Lent?' he asked, innocently.

'You ask her when we go down to breakfast,' said Vicky.

119

'No, my pet. Home-made toffee doesn't count,' Norah assured him. 'but don't tell Grandmama!'

'Good Friday is a Holy Day,' Vicky told Mabel, as she polished the brass on the front door. 'We shall go to church and sing 'There is a green hill far away', and there will be no flowers on the altar. When we go to the park with Nana, we shall not be allowed to bowl our hoops or play with a ball. It will be like Sunday only more strict than Sunday.'

'Why is that then, duckie?'

'Because Jesus died on the cross.'

'We don't 'ave a sad time in Chapel on Good Friday. We 'as a tea-party, an' somethink called a Cantata, with 'ymns an' recitations an' such like. Children do sing 'There is a green 'ill far away', but t'ain't sad.'

Vicky looked puzzled. 'Why is your Good Friday not sad?'

'To tell you the truth, duckie, I don't rightly know, but I seem to remember, way back in Sunday School, the Superintendent telling us children we could rejoice because we was saved from our sins. I never took a lot of notice when 'e talked, an' I still don't listen proper to the minister's sermon. If I'm tired, I as' forty winks. It's the singing I like. It's so 'earty. We 'as six 'ymns Sunday morning.'

'We only have three hymns in our church. I think I should like Chapel. Could I come to your Chapel one Sunday and bring Paulie?'

'Your Grandmama would never allow it, duckie.'

Vicky sighed. 'No, she wouldn't. St Matthew's is our church. Paulie's great-grandfather was the vicar once upon a time, and Uncle Edward was a curate. Then he married Auntie Jane and went away to the Mission at Hoxton. That's where me and Paulie are going when we are married.'

Mabel chuckled. 'You is a caution, duckie. You can always cheer me up with your funny stories.'

'It's not meant to be funny. It's true. Cross my heart. When we are married we are going to be missionaries to the white heathen at Hoxton, because Paulie said he would like it better than the black heathen in Darkest Africa.'

'Can't say I blame 'im, duckie. Them black 'eathens would scare the living daylights out of me, an' that's a fact. I seen

120

pictures on the magic lantern at Chapel. We 'as our own missionary in Darkest Africa, an' we 'as missionary boxes for our small change, only I can't always spare me small change for the box. After I paid the rent an' the milkman an' the baker, an' the grocer, an' the coalman, there ain't much left of me wages. Everythink is so 'spensive these days. Would you believe a reel of cotton cost as much as a penny three-farthings? Well it do. Mind jew, duckie, I count me blessings, for I gets a good dinner six days a week, an' Norah slips me all the left-overs, like bits of stale cake, for the Mistress won't eat no stale cake or warmed-up pudding. She's good to me, is Norah.'

'Me, too. She makes us toffee for Lent. Only it's a secret.'

'Your secrets is safe with me, duckie. Wild 'orses wouldn't drag it out of me.'

'What do we do now? They had finished the brass, and had had a nice little gossip.

'It's me day for the flues.'

'Can I help?'

'You'd get soot on that nice clean pinny. Flues is a dirty job, but somebody 'as to do it. That's what I'm paid for, to do the rough.'

'Do you scrub the seat in the outside lavatory?'

'I do.'

'Does Grandmama ever use the outside lavatory?'

''eaven preserve us! She ain't never set foot in the place. She likes 'er comforts. She's 'titled to it, ain't she, for she's the mistress 'ere.'

'I think The Haven is the best house in all the world.'

Mabel smiled affectionately at the small girl. Her bad teeth were ugly, but her smile was sweet.

Paul would always remember his first Easter in England. They had coloured eggs for breakfast on Easter Sunday, and chocolate eggs from Nana and the Aunties. Some came by post. It was exciting to hear the loud rat-tat on the brass knocker, and to hang over the banisters, waiting for Norah to open the door and take in the parcel.

'Is it for us?' Vicky called down.

'Yes, luv. I'm coming up,' Norah would answer.

Auntie Grace sent little chocolate bears from Switzerland The grown-ups had Easter cards. The children had the eggs.

'It's ridiculous. Why don't they send the children something to wear? Much more useful,' Grandmama complained.

'But it wouldn't be Easter without the chocolate eggs,' Nana pointed out.

'Too much chocolate is bad for children. When you and your sisters were young, I always insisted on boiled sweets.'

Yes, Ellen remembered the little shop with the rows of jars, all containing the pure, home-made sweets.

'We shall ration it. A piece each day, after dinner,' she said.

'Mind you put them on the top shelf where they can't be reached when you are out.'

'Mother!' Ellen protested. 'I shall put them on their honour not to touch the eggs.'

'It does not signify,' Grandmama retorted.

There it was again. What did it mean? Vicky was still puzzled. Grandmama was not the only one to speak in riddles. Uncle Charles and Uncle Henry would tell you importantly, 'It does not signify.' Self-importance had something to do with it, Vicky decided. Uncle Charles was a Member of Parliament, and Uncle Henry a banker.

But Easter was memorable in other ways, not only for chocolate eggs. Paul wore his white sailor suit to church on Easter Sunday, and the white sailor cap with a blue band, on which was printed 'H.M.S. Victory'. A whistle was attached to the lanyard, and slipped into the pocket. It was one of Paul's proudest possessions. On the occasion of the Queen's birthday last year, he had been so bored at the military parade, he had actually blown the whistle and caused quite a rumpus. Papa had been furious, and the whistle was confiscated. Now it was back. That would be Auntie Millie who slipped it back in the pocket of the sailor blouse.

'You look nice in the white sailor suit. I like it best,' Vicky told her little cousin.

'You look nice in your new frock,' Paul replied gallantly.

122

'Do you like my hat?'

'I like the daisies.'

'They are not real daisies. Last summer this same hat was trimmed with ribbon. I don't have a new hat every summer, you see, but my gloves are new, and my white socks and shoes.'

'Is it Summer then?'

'Not quite Summer, but we always wear something new for Easter, and the band will play on the promenade for Easter Sunday and Easter Monday, then not again till Whitsun.'

'Why?'

'Because Whitsun is the start of the holiday season at the seaside. You didn't know about that?'

Paul shook his head. There was so much happening all the time that Vicky had to explain. A holiday in India was spent in the hills with ponies and picnics and polo. There were so many strange customs in England. He would be shivering in his white sailor suit in April, but it was the custom to change your clothes for Easter. Vicky would wear a little jacket over her white frock. Her small gloved hand was warm and comforting as they sat with Grandmama and Nana in the hired cab that took them to church. Paul loved the sound of the church bells and the smell of lavender water on Grandmama's handkerchief when she sneezed.

'Have you caught cold, Mother?' asked Ellen, anxiously.

'Of course not! Don't fuss, child!' snapped Amelia.

Vicky and Paul exchanged a puzzled glance. How could a grown-up be a child?

The sea breeze was chilly. 'I am glad I put that long-sleeved spencer on Paulie today, but he still looks frozen,' Ellen was thinking. 'Poor darling, he is missing India.' Her dark eyes were tender with love for the children, and she took their hands and led them into church. Grandmama sailed ahead, her petticoats rustling. Her new Easter gown had a wide flounce that covered her slim ankles. The small hat perched on the up-swept silver hair was trimmed with matching ribbon. She was proud of her tiny feet and hands, and she ate sparingly to keep her slim, girlish figure.

Paul snatched off his sailor cap and followed Grandmama down the aisle. His whole attention was claimed by this special

123

Sunday feeling as soon as he stepped inside the church. He noticed everything, and stored it up in his memory like a squirrel storing nuts. His first Easter Sunday in an English church was filled with light and the scent of flowers. The window-sills were covered in green moss, and bunches of pale yellow flowers. Vicky would tell him later they were primroses. The altar was spread with a cloth of gold, and adorned with tall Madonna lilies in shining brass vases.

He stood back while Grandmama, Nana and Vicky passed into the pew, then he took his place, with grave importance. When he stood on the hassock, he could see the choir and clergy lining up for the processional hymn. Vicky had given up the aisle seat to her little cousin since he came to live at The Heaven. She was two inches taller than Paulie, and did not stand on a hassock. The organ thundered the opening bars of the Easter hymn, 'Jesus Christ is Risen Today, Allelujah!' The volume of voices grew louder, as the choir approached. The boys' voices, high and pure, the men's deep and strong. The clean starched surplices rustled as they passed, and Paul could have reached out a hand and touched them, but he stood there, stiffly to attention, as he had been taught, and did not turn his head. In the choir-stalls they went on singing, the smallest of the boys almost hidden behind the daffodils.

Vicky shared her prayer book, but she knew he could not read. He followed her every move, kneeling on the hassock for prayers, sitting quietly in the pew for the sermon, when she held his hand. He closed his eyes and thought of India. He wondered if he would always be homesick for India. That was something Vicky could not understand, because she had never known the smell of India, or the calm, dark faces of the native servants whose voices were never raised in anger.

'What is the matter?' she whispered anxiously.

He shook his head. How could he explain to anyone in this English church on Easter Day the sadness in his heart when everything about him was touched with a special Easter glory? How could he still feel he was a stranger in an strange land with Vicky holding his hand, and Nana smiling encouragement over Vicky's Easter hat? Would it always be like this, with haunting memories of India to sadden the brightest day?

When they came out of church, the sea breeze tore at his hair, and he crammed on his sailor's cap and shivered as they waited their turn for the hired cab to draw up at the gates. Several carriages had priority, and this annoyed Amelia, who considered herself every bit as superior as those stuck-up carriage folk. The fact remained, they were TRADE and middle-class, no matter that Thomas Brent & Son was the biggest store in town. A hired carriage was a luxury Amelia could not afford every Sunday, and she had to make do with the station cab.

On that Easter Sunday morning, the carriages were filled with well-dressed families from the big houses in Grand Avenue. They had recently moved down from their town houses in Mayfair and Berkeley Square. Wives and children would spend the Summer in Worthing. Husbands would return to Town and join their families at weekends. They brought their servants, governesses for the girls, and nannies for the little ones. Boys were still at prep school or public school, and home for the holidays.

All this Nana explained to Paul as they were driving back to The Haven. Grandmama frowned disapprovingly. Her pride was hurt and her dignity had suffered, watching the carriages take pride of place.

'If we could delve into the archives of their ancestors, we should probably discover some surprising facts concerning their pedigrees. Like as not they inherited their wealth from some Elizabethan favourite of the Queen. It was the custom, in that day and age, to reward those who pleased Her Majesty by some daring enterprise that furthered her Empire overseas. There is nothing to boast about in such acquired wealth in my opinion. My own family were landed gentry, as you well know, Ellen, but when I married your dear father, I automatically found myself in Trade. Love is blind.' Amelia sighed.

'Yes, Mother.' Her eldest daughter had also married for love, and known the loneliness of widowhood.

'Not for one moment do I regret marrying your father,' Amelia hastened to rectify that sigh. 'He was the dearest and most beloved of God's creatures.'

'Yes, Mother.' Ellen wished she could say the same about her own young husband, but that would be hypocrisy. She

looked down on the grandchildren, and wondered what life
had in store for them. The grave little boy, so shy and
sensitive, the eager, intelligent little girl. She loved them
both. Paul was hers to cherish for three short years. When
he was seven, his father would claim him. Perhaps she would
be allowed to have him for the holidays? As for Vicky, it
would depend on her mother's health. If Prue had to be sent
away to a clinic, and it seemed likely, then Basil would want
his daughter to live at home. 'Sufficient unto the day,' Ellen
reminded herself. The pattern of life would be made plain,
one day. Her empty arms had been filled, at long last.

'I can smell roast chicken,' Grandmama pronounced, as
she stepped into the lobby. 'We always have roast chicken
on Easter Sunday,' she told the children. 'And this afternoon
we shall take the cab to the promenade and listen to the band.
Well, what do you say to that?' she prompted.

'Thank you, Grandmama,' they chorused.

Every Sunday evening followed the same pattern. When tea
was finished, they all trooped into the drawing-room, and
Grandmama played hymns. The children stood on either side
of her. Ellen, Bertha and Norah seated themselves on the
sofa. They knew all the hymns by heart, so did Vicky, because
Grandmama played only the familiar ones she had once
played to her own children, and to her three grandchildren,
Prudence, Arabella and Thomas. These two, standing so
obediently by her side, were actually her great-grandchildren,
but she pushed the thought aside, lifted her proud little head,
and touched the keys with a certain delicacy only Grace had
inherited. All her daughters, and her two grand-daughters,
had been obliged to practise on the schoolroom pianoforte
for half an hour each day, apart from the Sabbath. It had
been a laborious task for the girls, and a painful ordeal
for those who listened to those interminable scales and
exercises. Nevertheless, there was no escape, for no young
lady in that day and age could claim to have completed her
education without the rudiments of music, plain needlework
and sketching. It was the custom.

Vicky and Paul enjoyed this last hour of Sunday. They
sang 'Jesus loves me, this I know, for the Bible tells me

126

so. Little ones to Him belong, They are weak but He is strong.' They sang Vicky's favourite, 'All things bright and beautiful, All creatures great and small, All things wise and wonderful, The Lord God made them all.' Then they sang, 'Now the day is over, Night is drawing nigh, Shadows of the evening, Steal across the sky.' Three hymns, no more and no less. That, too, was the custom.

Paul had an ear for music, as Nana had discovered. He liked to pick out nursery rhymes on the schoolroom piano. He missed the regimental band and the singing Welsh voice of Uncle David in the open air concerts. 'Land of my Fathers' and 'The Minstrel Boy' filled his eyes with tears. He could not explain such emotion because he did not know its source, might never know the truth of his birthright. If David Jones had claimed his son, and he had been brought up in Wales, the pattern of his life would have been completely changed. But David loved Rosalind, and she had been spared the scandal. During the following three years, David would send birthday and Christmas presents to the boy who was growing in his likeness, but they would not meet. He was saddened when he discovered Paul had not returned to Aldershot.

It was Vicky who developed measles and passed it on to Paul that first week of the Summer term. Ellen had been expecting it, for it happened to most children in their early years at school. Next year it would probably be chicken-pox. She hoped and prayed they would escape diphtheria, the dreadful scourge that still claimed the lives of so many young children.

Vicky thought it was fun to be tucked up in the same bed as Paul, but she had only a mild attack. He was smothered in a rash and ran a high temperature. He was quite ill, but he made no fuss. Norah squeezed oranges and made jelly, for he had no appetite for food, while Vicky enjoyed such delicacies as minced chicken, poached eggs on creamed potatoes, and grilled plaice. It was quite impossible to keep her in bed for more than a few days, and since she was disturbing Paul with her restlessness, she was allowed to get up at mid-morning; wrapped in a warm dressing-gown, she amused herself with a box of coloured pencils and a copy-book, or curled up in

127

the armchair with a book. A fire burnt in the tiny grate, day and night, and a lamp was turned low to protect their eyes. Strong light was harmful and could cause permanent damage, according to the family doctor, who was called in to diagnose the rash. Not that Ellen needed to be reminded it was measles. She remembered the time when all six sisters had been isolated on the top floor with the nursemaid and the governess, and Kate, who had only a mild attack, had nearly driven them mad with her demands for more attention. When her own two girls had measles, during their first term at the convent, it was Prue who demanded all the attention, and Bella, so accustomed to her sister's domination, who patiently awaited her turn. Fortunately for everyone concerned, Thomas had not caught the measles, or chicken-pox the following year. Ellen was in her true element with a sick child to nurse, and another to keep quietly amused. It was Norah who carried the heavy trays upstairs, and Mabel who struggled up three flights of stairs with scuttles of coal and cans of hot water. As for Amelia, she was not expected to inconveniece herself in any way, and her normal routine was undisturbed.

'Will Vicky's teddybear catch my measles?' Paul asked, anxiously, as he cuddled the bear to his spotty chest.

Ellen smiled, and assured him there was no danger. She was constantly surprised by the sensitive perception of such a young child. From whom did he inherit such qualities? she asked herself. Not from Thomas or Rosalind, and certainly not from Grandmama! It did not occur to Ellen that she could have been the indirect source of such unselfish qualities, for she was much too modest for such thoughts.

When she wrote to inform Thomas that his small son had measles, his only reaction was to send a box of toy soldiers. Paul turned his head away. 'I 'spected Teddybear and Elephant,' he sighed.

'Never mind, darling. You may keep my teddybear for always. I think he loves you best,' Vicky told him, soothingly.

'Thank you.' His weak smile could not hide the tears of disappointment. And the box of soldiers went into the cupboard unopened.

Before they started back to school, Ellen took the children

for walks along the promenade each day. The sea air soon put a flush on Vicky's cheeks, but Paul was pale and languid.

Jane and Edward took a week's holiday from the Mission at Hoxton, and came to stay at The Haven during that period of the children's convalescence. It was Ellen's suggestion, and it did more for Paul than the doctor's tonic. Both children adored Uncle Edward, and Auntie Jane was a great favourite because she was still young at heart, and never too tired or too busy to join in the interminable games of Ludo and Snakes and Ladders. Having no children of her own was her only regret in a very happy marriage. Looking for some new diversion for the children's amusement outdoors, she discovered three bicycles carefully wrapped in old sheets in the shed, and wheeled them into the yard. Memories crowded in as she pumped the tyres and took a trial run on each one in turn, down the lane at the back of the house, watched by the children. 'Perfectly all right. We will make use of them' she announced.

'How? When?' Vicky demanded, excitedly, for she had never seen the bicycles until today, and was much impressed by Auntie Jane's performance.

'Do you remember the bluebell wood?' Jane asked her sister.

Ellen nodded.

'We will take the children on a picnic. You can take Paulie on your carrier, and I will take Vicky. Edward can hire a bike from the shop in Clifton Road. Norah will pack us up some sandwiches, and I will fill the flasks with tea. It will be like old times.' She smiled affectionately at her elder sister, and hurried down the back steps to find Norah most co-operative, as always. They made the sandwiches together while the kettle boiled, reminiscing over the good old days before Ellen's marriage, when the sisters had often spent a day in the woods in the early spring, taking the younger ones on the carriers, and a picnic lunch in the baskets on the handlebars. Those same baskets would be filled with primroses or bluebells on the return journey. The primroses would decorate the church on Easter Sunday, but the bluebells would quickly fade.

'It will be fun,' Vicky told her little cousin as Ellen pulled an extra jersey over his head.

'Will it?' Paul was a little doubtful. He had never been transported by bicycle, and had never seen a bluebell.

'You will en-j-joy it, old chap,' said Uncle Edward, encouragingly, and went off to hire the bicycle.

Grandmama thought it was a most unsuitable expedition for children only recently recovered from measles.

'Nonsense, Mother. It is just what they need,' Jane retorted. An independent married woman for a number of years, Jane was no longer under her mother's thumb.

'Can I take Teddybear?' Paul was asking Nana at the last moment.

'Of course you may. He can sit in my basket with the thermos flasks,' she told him kindly.

'I'll fetch him.' Vicky raced upstairs. Paul smiled his thanks, then they were off.

Edward, Jane and Ellen wore straw boaters, the children wore linen hats stiffly starched by Mabel, who had left her scrubbing to wave them off at the back gate.

Paul clung like a limpet to Nana's waist. Vicky was clutching Auntie Jane's well-padded bottom. Mabel was sceptical about such a dangerous expedition. Shanks's pony was so much safer. And who would want to travel three miles on a bicycle to pick bluebells?'

'What can you do with bluebells?' she had asked Vicky.

'I don't know. I think they would look pretty in a blue jug,' the child answered. Bluebells in a jug? Mabel looked puzzled. In her cluttered bed-sitting-room, smelling strongly of cat, the scent of flowers was something quite alien and quite unnecessary.

'You be careful now. Mind you 'ang on tight,' she admonished her little favourite. Then she closed the gate and went back to her scrubbing.

Having covered the distance with his head tucked into the folds of Nana's jacket and his eyes shut, Paul was lifted down and was instantly transported into Paradise. A million bluebells stretched like a carpet under a canopy of green beech. Birds twittered in the hedgerows, and there was no other sound but the scraping of the bicycles against the fence. Even Vicky was awed into silence, and stared wide-eyed, clutching Paul's hand.

Edward, Jane and Ellen had seen it all before, yet it was new, as everything was born anew at this wondrous season of the year. Jane was the first to speak, her voice husky with emotion.

'We came here on just such a day in April, my darling, and you had my engagement ring in your pocket.' She held out her hand to him, and he took it and touched the ring with his lips. The gesture pleased and surprised her, for Edward was not a demonstrative man. His feelings went deep, and she no longer expected any endearments other than 'my dear girl'. He was her darling, and her best beloved, and she told him so frequently without shyness, and gave herself unsparingly to the way of life he had chosen. When they made love in the marriage bed, it was Jane who straddled his flat belly and kissed his mouth with her wet, warm lips. He was her husband and her child. For his sake she had left the comfortable home in Worthing for the hardship and poverty of Hoxton, and the ever-present threat that the Mission would be closed for lack of funds and public support. The Salvation Army seemed more picturesque, with their uniforms and bands.

On this lovely day of Spring, Jane's thoughts flew back to the familiar world they had left behind − to the drab and dreary tenements, the noisy pub on the corner of the street, the barefoot children and the bare-bottomed babies. If only she could gather them up, all those poor little urchins, and transport them to this beautiful wood. But would they see it with the same eyes as Vicky and Paulie? Would they run amok and trample on that blue carpet with their dirty feet as they trampled in the gutters? It was wishful thinking, and she knew it. Children are best left where they belong.

Vicky had dropped Paul's hand, for he was hanging back, and she was impatient to start picking. Stepping boldly through the gap in the hedge, she skirted the edge of the blue carpet, and bent over, carefully plucking each long juicy stem and so completely absorbed that she did not notice they had left her alone.

Ellen and Jane had wandered off, arm in arm, to explore their old haunts. Edward and Paul sat on the bank, talking earnestly together about the things dearest to their hearts. Edward found he could talk without stammering to this grave little boy, and Paul told of his earliest memories of India, of Ayah and Boy, and the smell of the native market in the hot sun. They had much in common, for the child's understanding and sympathy for the despised natives was similar to the man's love and compassion for his East End neighbours.

'You must come to visit us, Paulie. I will show you a place where no flowers grow, a place as different from this as the India you remember. I will ask your Nana to bring you and Vicky one Sunday. Would you like that?'

Paul nodded, and glanced at the little girl among the bluebells. Her hat had slipped to the back of her head on the loose elastic. The Alice band on her long, straight hair matched her frock. She was not really pretty, not like Mama but he loved Vicky, and he did not love his Mama.

'Is it wicked not to love your Mama?' he asked Uncle Edward.

That was a difficult question to answer, for as a good Christian the Ten Commandments had a significant importance; yet the Fifth Commandment, 'Honour thy father and thy mother', had little meaning to an orphan.

'I cannot answer that question truthfully, old chap, for I have no knowledge of a mother. She died when I was born. I was brought up by my grandmother.'

'Was she like my Grandmama?'

Edward chuckled. 'Not in the least. Gran kept a donkey in the back yard, and a little cart in the shed. We grew a lot of vegetables. Rows and rows of potatoes, carrots, onions, cabbages, peas and beans. We sold them to the gentry. Well, not exactly to the gentry, but their cooks and housekeepers. Gran let me drive the donkey cart in the school holidays. We were happy together, she and I. When I was twelve she passed on.'

'Where did she pass?'

'Heaven.'

'Was it the Jesus Heaven or the Allah Heaven?'

'I am not sure there is more than one Heaven. There is only one God.'

'Is God Jesus?'

'Jesus is the Son of God.'

132

'Like me, the son of my Papa.'

'Well, not quite like that.' Edward was getting into deep water. How much could a four-year-old child assimilate?

'Is Jesus afraid of God?'

'What a question! Why do you ask?'

''Cause I'm afraid of my Papa.'

'That is a pity.'

'He wants me to be a soldier, when I grow up. I don't want to be a soldier. I want to be a missionary.'

'A missionary?'

'Yes. Vicky thought of it. She thinks of everything. We are going to be married when we are grown up. It's a secret. You won't tell?'

'Secrets are safe with me.'

'Vicky said I should be afraid of the black heathen in Darkest Africa. So I would. I am not brave like Vicky. It would be better, she said, to be missionaries to the white heathens in Hoxton.'

Edward exploded with laughter. It echoed through the wood, and Jane stopped in surprise, clutching her sister's arm.

'That was Edward. I have not heard him laugh like that for a very long time.'

'They seem to be getting along famously, those two,' said Ellen, as they went on their way.

Vicky lifted her head and pushed back her hair. The bunch of bluebells hung heavy on her arm. She carried them carefully to the basket on Nana' bicycle, and tucked them in beside the thermos flasks. But they were already wilting, and had lost all their beauty. She sighed with disappointment and went to sit beside Uncle Edward. He put his arm around her.

'Don't they like being picked?' she asked, forlornly.

'Wild flowers d-don't like being p-picked.'

'And bluebells are wild, not tame?'

'Yes.'

'I won't pick any more, not ever. Thank you for telling me. I like to know.'

'So I do,' echoed Paul.

Vicky giggled. 'He gets things back to front. He even gets

133

his jersey back to front. But he is only four years old, you see,' she explained, with careful logic.

And once again that rich, masculine laughter echoed through the wood.

'Them bluebells is dead, duckie,' Mabel asserted, bluntly, from the doorway of the outside lavatory. She often enjoyed a quiet few minutes browsing through old copies of the *Daily News* before cutting them up for toilet paper.

'I know. I shall put them on Jackie's grave,' said Vicky. Jackie had been buried under the yew tree in the front garden.

'Your Papa is waiting to see you, duckie,' said Mabel. ''e looks proper poorly,' she added, as an afterthought.

Part Two

Chapter Five

'Basil never comes to this house these days. Something has happened to Prue. I have been expecting it for some time.' Ellen's voice was calm as she followed Vicky through the conservatory into the drawing-room.

Basil was slumped on the sofa, a stricken look on his haggard face. Vicky ran across the room and perched on his knee.

'Are you not well, Papa?' she asked, anxiously, stroking his face.

He looked at her with tired eyes. He had not slept for two nights, and had relived the nightmare of that last traumatic scene in the bedroom over and over again, since they took Prue away. 'Could it have been avoided if he had gone straight up to the flat when the store closed?' he asked himself. It had been a difficult day, and he had felt the need of a brisk walk along the promenade. When he opened the door of the flat, there was no sound and no light. His heart hammered. Prue had often threatened to take an overdose of the pills the doctor had prescribed. Had she carried out that threat?

'Are you there, Prue,' he called, and pushed open the bedroom door. The street lamp caught the flash of the blade as she stepped out out from behind the door, the knife raised to strike. He caught her wrist in a tight grip as they struggled together.

'Drop it, Prue! Drop it!' he panted. But a maniacal strength possessed her, and her eyes were black as jet in her white face. He lifted his fist, and she caught the full force of the blow on the jaw and slumped to the floor. The knife slipped from her fingers, and she lay there at his feet, spent of her madness, but for how long? He picked her up, laid her gently on the bed, and stood looking down at her with the saddened eyes of a man defeated at last by her tears and tantrums. The girl he had married with such trusting devotion had turned into this querulous, nagging woman, jealous of her own child and the imaginary lovers with whom her husband associated.

When he had telephoned the doctor, he sat beside her, holding her limp hand. This was the end of their life together. It had lasted for little more than six years. The child had separated them still further. For three years his mother-in-law was the go-between. Then she had taken the child to live at The Haven, for there was no peace for anyone in that troubled household. Now she was perched on his knee, her warm little body a comforting reminder he was not alone.

'Are you sick, Papa?' she prompted.

'No, my poppet. Your Mama is sick. The doctor has sent her away for treatment. When she is well, she will come home,' he lied. She would never come back, for that cosy little nest they had planned together had turned into a prison.

'Is it lonely without Mama?' asked the child.

'Very lonely.'

'Then I will come home.'

'Thank you, poppet.'

She kissed his unshaven cheek, and took his hand. 'Come,' she said, and led him away without a backward glance. He was her child now, her dearest Papa.

Paul watched them go. He could not understand what was happening, only that Vicky was going away. First Ayah, then Auntie Millie, now Vicky. And she had not said goodbye.

'That poor man. It would have served him better to remain a bachelor, for marriage has brought nothing but trouble,' Grandmama reflected as the door closed behind them. 'First he lost Lucy in childbirth, with a stillborn child. Now it's Prudence. I could have told him he was making a mistake to marry that daughter of yours, Ellen. You spoilt her. All

138

those silly tantrums. You should have taken your slipper to her bottom!'

'You never understood Prue. She was highly strung.'

'Highly strung fiddlesticks!'

'Prue never recovered from the shock of her father's disappearance. She adored Jonathan. It was a father-figure she saw in Basil from the moment they met.'

'Silly man. He should have married Kate. They were betrothed, were they not, before he married Lucy? Then Kate eloped with Charles, the naughty minx. Wasn't that just like Kate?' she chuckled. Turning her attention to the small boy clinging to her daughter's hand, she demanded, 'Why are you crying, child? I do declare you will never make a man like your Papa. Come now, you may kiss me.'

Paul complied. Her cheek was soft. She smelled of lavender water, and she dried his tears with a lace-edged handkerchief.

'Victoria is only doing her duty.'

'Yes, Grandmama.'

'You know what duty means?'

'Yes, Grandmama.'

'Of course. A soldier's son must be brave.'

He nodded tremulously.

'Run along, then.'

She let him go, and he was glad to get away. Uncle Edward and Auntie Jane were still standing in the yard. The wilted bluebells hung over the basket, a reminder of a place where Spring had been born anew. Now the sadness of parting hung like a threat over this small world that had seemed so safe and secure.

'Vicky has gone away. She did not say goodbye,' said Paul, his voice still choked with his tears.

'She is not far away. Cheer up, old chap. You can visit her, but she cannot visit you,' Uncle Edward reminded him.

'Can I, Nana?' he asked, eagerly.

She nodded. 'There was no time to arrange anything. They left so hurriedly. I will write a letter. Vicky must attend school. I will suggest we collect her in the morning, and take her home. You both could have your dinner at school.

It's only a temporary arrangement. Uncle Basil needs Vicky. We must not be selfish,darling.'

Norah's cheerful face peered over the basement steps. 'What is happening? Has Basil gone?' she asked.

'Yes, and taken Vicky,' Ellen answered.

'What a shame. Come down to the kitchen. The kettle's boiling, and there's a fresh batch of scones just out of the oven. Climb on my back, Paulie,' she invited. He clambered up, and they clattered down the stone steps. He liked Norah. She had a nice, warm smell, and a kind heart.

They climbed the stairs to the flat on the top floor, and Vicky braced herself for the shrill voice and the sharp tongue, but all was quiet. Still holding his hand, she gazed enquiringly at the parent who seemed to have grown old since they last met a week ago. The daily housekeeper had finished her cleaning and gone home, leaving behind a strong smell of beeswax, but no comfort. Basil paid no heed to a comfortless home, but Vicky shivered. The fire was laid in the grate, but Basil stood there, his shoulders slumped, his hat dangling in his limp hand.

Suddenly aware of her new status, Vicky pushed him into a chair and took the box of matches from the mantelpiece. She had never struck a match in her life, but now she did not hesitate. The match flamed and lit the paper. The wood kindled, then the flames licked the coal. She sat back on her heels, waiting for a word of praise, but none came. Poor Papa. He had fallen asleep.

Pulling up a hassock, she sat at his feet, watching the dancing flames. She thought of Paulie, and wondered what he was doing. She remembered she had not said goodbye. She remembered the bunch of wilted bluebells in the bicycle basket, and her thoughts flew back to the lovely wood, with the carpet of blue flowers with the long, sticky stems. She picked and picked alone and undisturbed, till Uncle Edward's laugh echoed through the wood. How could such a happy day end this way? She sighed, and crept on tiptoe to peer into the bedroom. The big bed was empty, and no dark head tossed restlessly on the pillows. Yet the shrill voice seemed to echo with demanding impatience.

'What are you staring at, child? Go away! Go away!'

She ran back to her dearest Papa, knelt on the hassock, and clasped his knees with small, urgent hands, afraid of that echo and her own haunting memories. But he slept on, exhausted and paid no heed to her whispered pleading. 'Wake up, Papa. Please wake up.'

This was her home, she reminded herself, but there was no sense of belonging. Her throat was dry. It was hours ago when she shared a small cup of tea from the thermos flask with Paulie. Could she brew a pot of tea? She had watched Norah in the kitchen, and it seemed simple enough. First you boiled the water. The kitchen was clean as a new pin, as Mabel would say, smelling of yellow soap and faintly of gas that reminded her of the basement stairs at The Haven. The gas stove was a mystery she dare not trust herself to explore, so she filled the kettle, carried it into the sitting-room, and propped it carefully on the flaming coals. Sitting on the hassock, hugging her knees, she waited impatiently for the kettle to boil. What a lovely surprise for Papa! Suddenly the coals shifted, and the kettle toppled with a hiss of steam, spilling water over the hot cinders.

'Papa!' she screamed, and shook him awake. He blinked at her trembling mouth and frightened eyes. Still heavy with sleep, he scrambled to his feet and stared down at the sorry mess.

'What on earth are you doing?' he demanded, irritably.

'I was making you a nice cup of tea,' she answered, and burst into tears.

Then he swung round and wrapped his arms about her, his voice tender with love. 'My darling little poppet. Don't cry. It will be all right. We shall manage, you and I together, shall we not?'

She lifted her head and nodded.

'That's my brave girl. My, what a horrible stink!' He wrinkled his nose.

'Oh, Papa, that was a naughty word,' she chided.

'So it was, and I do apologize.'

'I accept your apology, Papa,' she answered, in the way she had been taught at the Convent Kindergarten. He smiled, and his drawn face was instantly transformed by the smile, like Paul's. 'You are feeling better, Papa?' she asked.

'Much, much better, my darling. It's having you here. I have missed you. Tomorrow I must start work again. My deputy has been acting on my behalf. I went all to pieces. Silly of me, wasn't it? Having you here, my daughter, is like a ray of sunshine. You have no idea what it means to me.'

My daughter? Papa's daughter. She felt very important, quite grown-up. Then she remembered her Mama's scathing accusation. 'You love your daughter more than you love your wife!'

'Does being jealous make you sick?' she asked.

'Sick in the mind.'

'Not sick in the chamber-pot?'

'No, not in the chamber-pot,' he chuckled.

'Paulie was sick in the chamber-pot after we had muffins for tea. He has a weak stomach. Poor Paulie, he is rather delicate because he was born in India.'

'You love Paulie very much, don't you?'

'Next to you, I love Paulie best.'

'So I still come first?'

'Yes, oh yes!'

'Thank you, poppet. Now about that tea. We will boil the kettle on the gas stove. I will clean up this mess later. I dare say there is a floor cloth somewhere. I have never given it a thought − the cleaning, I mean.'

'Mabel keeps her cloth and her scrubbing brush in a bucket under the sink in the scullery.'

'Ah, you know about such things.'

'She lets me help. Not with the scrubbing, with the brass. We polish the knocker and the letter box on the front door, and the brass knob on the green gate. It has to be done every day, but not Sunday.'

'Mabel is going to miss you.'

'Mabel is my friend.'

'Quite so.'

'Did you know about the two lavatories at The Haven, Papa?' Vicky asked, conversationally, as they waited for the kettle to boil.

'Can't say that I remember more than one, and I seldom had occasion to use it.'

142

'Was it indoors or outdoors?'

'Oh, definitely in. On the landing, next door to the front bedroom.'

'That's the one I showed Paulie the first day, and he showed me how he could have a little pee standing up. When we went down to tea, Grandmama scolded, because we were late, and I explained what we had been doing. She was shocked.'

'I am not surprised, my darling. It is hardly a suitable topic for afternoon tea.'

'But it's in-tresting.'

'I dare say.'

'Everybody thought it was funny. Only Grandmama and Paulie's Papa were shocked.'

'All the family there?'

'Yes.'

'I remember now. I was invited, but I could not leave your Mama. Auntie Kate still looking very beautiful, I suppose?'

'Not as beautiful as Auntie Grace.'

'You think not?'

'Auntie Grace smells nice. She washes her face with Pears soap. I don't think Auntie Kate washes her face. Her cheeks are powdered and her lips are red. It's not a nice face to kiss.'

'Out of the mouths of babes,' Basil murmured. Yet there was a time when he would have sold his soul to the devil to share his bed, for just one night, with that tantalising hussy! What an escape! Escape to a future even more troublesome. Gentle little Lucy, saved from suicide only to die in childbirth. Then Prue, tormented by jealousy into a state of madness. He sighed. Such is life. He turned his attention to the homely task of brewing tea. Vicky was laying a tray with cups and saucers, milk and sugar, a pink tongue licking her lips. She had Prue's dark eyes and hair, but none of her mother's temperament, thank God, he was thinking as he poured the tea. He carried the tray into the sitting-room, and Vicky sat on the hassock, sipping the hot tea. She was hungry. A picnic lunch is not the same as a proper dinner.

'Did you know that wild flowers do not like to be picked, Papa?' she asked.

He was surprised by the question, for his own thoughts had no wings. They were tied to this place in the bond of a marriage that had turned sour. 'Wild flowers?' he echoed. 'Who said they don't like to be picked?'

'Uncle Edward.'

'Ah, he would know about such things. He is such a sensitive fellow.'

'He is my favourite uncle.'

'That stammer must be a severe handicap.'

'I have noticed that he does not stammer when he talks to Paulie.'

'Isn't that rather odd?'

She nodded, gravely. 'He was talking to Paulie in the bluebell wood, and when I went to sit with them, I was waiting to help him say the difficult words, the words beginning with B and C and S and W, but he didn't need any help. He spoke to Paulie like you are speaking to me. There is a girl in my class who stammers. She used to sit next to me, and when she had to answer a question, I squeezed her hand. It's awful. I wanted to answer for her because she cannot say these difficult words. Sister Gabrielle moved me because she said I was making her worse. I was only trying to help.'

'Perhaps it made the child more nervous? It is a nervous complaint, is it not? Your Uncle Edward obviously feels at ease with young Paulie. He must have a soothing effect on his nerves. That is the only explanation I can offer. Some things cannot be explained, however. We have to accept there are mysteries beyond our understanding. Do you mind very much that your Uncle Edward finds something in Paulie that he does not find in you, my darling?'

'No, I am glad for him. It must be something very special, like Jesus.'

'Jesus?' Basil was getting into deep water, not for the first time with his small daughter.

'Jesus touched the tongue of the man who was dumb and he spoke.'

'But Uncle Edward is not dumb?'

144

'No, and Paulie did not touch his tongue. He just looked at him with his big, sad eyes.'

'Mind over matter?' Basil asked himself. Could a four-year-old child have the power to communicate confidence to a grown man? To loosen his tongue? It was a solemn thought, but it pleased him that his Vicky had no jealousy in her heart for her little cousin. To change the subject he asked, 'What would you like to do now?'

'Could we make toast? The fire is just right.'

'And the water has dried in the hearth.'

'I make toast with Paulie at The Haven. He likes it. They don't have toast for tea in India. They have cucumber sandwiches and ice-cream. Toast is all right for Paulie's weak stomach, but not muffins, or cabbage, or pea soup, or skin on his rice pudding. Grandmama says he is just being faddy, but she doesn't have to see him being sick in the chamber-pot, does she? Nana understands him better.'

'Your nana is a very understanding person. She could have blamed me, but she didn't.'

Vicky looked puzzled.

'For your Mama's sickness.'

'It was not your fault, Papa.'

He sighed. 'I feel I have failed her, Vicky. I feel guilty. What will she think of me when she wakes up and finds herself in the clinic?'

'I don't know.'

'Neither do I.'

'I like it here without Mama. I was frightened when she shouted.'

'I know. That's why I sent you to live with Nana.'

'Nana never shouts. Shall I go back one day, Papa?'

'Whenever you wish, my darling.'

'Thank you.' She jumped off the hassock to give him a hug. He held her close for a moment, then pushed her away. She must be free to come and go. Only by letting her go could he keep her love and loyalty. That was the paradox.

Three months had passed. Both children were enjoying the long Summer holidays. After an early breakfast, Basil and Vicky walked to The Haven, and Vicky spent the day with

Nana and Paul. He would collect her again in the evening when the store was closed, and they would walk along the promenade together before supper. Summer visitors flocked to this popular seaside resort. Hotels and boarding houses were fully booked for the season, and day trippers arrived by train and charabanc from London's East End.

Basil was busy at the store, and happier than he had been for a very long time. The staff found him agreeable, ready to listen to complaints and suggestions, and surprisingly concerned about their private lives. Apprentices found the Boss approachable and sympathetic. To be called to the office for insubordination or discourtesy to a customer no longer meant the threat of instant dismissal, but an opportunity to apologize, and to improve one's behaviour. Basil's genial manner, as General Manager, was reflected in the changed atmosphere throughout the store, and recognized as the happy result of a man no longer harrassed by a nagging, jealous wife. Indirectly, Prue had been guilty of spreading an atmosphere of discontent and rebellion through that old-established emporium. And it was a small girl, who loved her Papa, who could also claim credit for that spirit of cordiality and contentment among the employees. Trade was booming. It was a time of prosperity for the middle-classes.

Basil's widowed mother was another to benefit from her son's changed circumstances. Every Sunday, after church, he took Vicky to visit the Grannie who was almost a stranger. So different from Nana, but nice and homely. She made the most delicious chocolate cake for tea, and they pored over an album of old photographs in which Basil's first appearance, stark naked on a rug, proved a little embarrassing for poor Papa! Vicky discovered a parent she hardly recognized. 'Was that really Papa in boater and blazer, with a girl on each arm, and a naughty twinkle in his eye?' she asked Grannie.

'Yes, that is your Papa, my dear. A bit of a gay dog in those days, courting both Lucy and Kate,' she answered.

Vicky giggled over the photographs of the bathing belles in long costumes and ugly caps. Grouped about their stern Mama, six young ladies faced the camera, gravely aware of the importance of being photographed for posterity. And there was The Haven, its walls festooned with wisteria, and

146

another little group at the green gate. And a very old lady, in a shawl and beribboned cap, nursing a cat. And a picture of Grandmama, in a deck chair on the beach, wearing *gloves*. Imagine wearing gloves on the beach!

'Your Grandmama is such a very superior little lady, she quite frightens me,' Grannie confessed.

'She frightens Paulie, but then he does not know her very well, and he is only a little boy. When she is in her bed and we wish her good morning, she is really quite gentle, and very pretty. I like her best when she is in bed.'

Grannie chuckled. You get the truth from children, she was thinking as she turned over the pages of the album that recalled the good old days before Vicky was born. Surprisingly, Grandmama contributed a shilling a week to the spending money for both children during that long Summer holiday, and Basil would often dive into his pocket for loose change. There were so many attractions, so many tempting things to buy. Vicky's pocket money simply melted away, but Paul spent his more carefully, and always treated Vicky to a ride in a goat carriage like a little gentleman. The goat carriages were the biggest attraction for small children, and even more popular than the donkey rides on the sands. Tuppence a ride from the pier to the bandstand, and back. They saved this special treat to enjoy when the tide was in, and stayed to watch the patient little animals, with their clean white coats and shining harnesses on their endless trek with their small passengers. Little boys sat importantly on the driver's seat holding the reins, little girls in the carriage. The floor of the carriage was gritty with sand, and the cushions slightly damp from wet drawers, for the majority of the children had been paddling with their frocks tucked in their drawers. Nana was rather reluctant to allow such a liberty the first day of the holidays, but soon discovered Vicky some distance away, on the edge of the incoming tide, being helped by Paul with the interesting performance! Modesty forbade the children to dress and undress in the same bedroom, but it seemed to Nana's prudish observations that modesty was completely discarded on the beach.

Vicky would have liked to bathe, but Paul was frightened

147

of so much water, that seemed to cover the whole world as he stood trembling on the edge, clutching Vicky's hand. To be seen without a hat was asking for sunstroke, over-anxious Nana declared.

'But it's not proper hot,' Paul protested, with memories of India and seeing the haze under the drooping brim of a linen hat that once covered his Papa's golden curls.

Both children had purchased a shrimping net, but caught only baby crabs and let them go. Each had a small tin bucket and a wooden spade, and spent hours building a sand castle that was quickly swept away when the tide came in. Grandmama insisted they went home for dinner, but it was only a short walk, and they were back on the beach in the afternoon, with a picnic tea that Norah prepared. Norah would have liked to join them, but Bertha did not care for the beach, so they stayed at home and sat outside the French windows, behind the high, pebbled wall and the green gate, with the smell of the sea borne on the breeze, a tantalising reminder of childhood.

As for Grandmama, she hired the station cab to take her to the band, where she sat enthroned in a deck chair, holding a pretty parasol in a gloved hand, shielding her fair complexion. Only on Sunday afternoons did she invite her daughter and grandchildren to join her. Dressed in their Sunday best, on their best behaviour, it was more of a duty than a pleasure.

Basil would join them on Wednesday afternoons, bringing a bag of sugar buns from Kong's. Trying to recapture his lost youth, in boater and blazer, was rather a forlorn hope with his tired eyes and greying head. And when he took their hands to run barefoot across the sand, he was panting and breathless when they reached the lapping tide. It was not exactly a restful afternoon for the General Manager of Thomas Brent & Son, for after the paddle, he would be digging a trench round a sandcastle with a small, wooden spade.

On the first day of every month, Ellen received a brief note from Thomas, enclosing the promised allowance for Paul's board and lodging. She called him her 'paying guest'! School

148

fees and clothes were paid for quarterly. It did not occur to Thomas that his small son needed pocket money, and since nobody cared to remind him of the fact, it was left to others to provide it. Various excuses were proffered with regard to visiting – 'Papa was too busy with military affairs', 'Mama had too many social engagements' etc. They need not have bothered with excuses, for Paul received them with a sigh of relief and a whimsical smile. His parents had no place in the happy little world of The Haven and the beach that first Summer. Ellen's feelings were mixed. She was hurt by her son's indifference to the child, but not at all surprised by his selfishness. It was typical of Thomas. Even his beautiful young wife had been forced to accept the humiliating fact that the regiment, and his splendid stallion, Jason, had pride of place in his affections. She could weep and pout and threaten to leave him, but their matrimonial quarrels were invariably settled in bed. Thomas Cartwright was 'Master of his Fate and Captain of his Soul'.

As for Paul, his own quiet acceptance of his parents' self-centredness was not uncommon in that day and age. Few middle- and upper-class parents had their children's confidence and companionship. It was the working-class, in their crowded lives, who often, not always, enjoyed a close relationship with their children. 'What you never 'ave, you never miss,' as Mabel would say. She was not a parent, but her cheerful acceptance of her status was typical of her class of society.

There was one visit, however, that never failed to give pleasure that Summer. Whenever they could get away from the Hoxton Mission, Edward and Jane would spend the day in Worthing. After they had paid their respects to Amelia, and eaten an early dinner, they were off to the beach with a picnic tea. Even Bertha woud put her own feelings aside for one day to join the party, and Norah, as excited as a child, would pick up her skirts and wade into the sea with Vicky hanging on her arm, and Jane splashing happily alongside, while Paul wandered hand-in-hand with Uncle Edward on the edge of the the incoming tide, completely absorbed in a conversation that would have surprised and disturbed his worldly parents. From that early beginning on the seashore, one fine Summer day, a boy's future was decided.

Anyone watching the man, with his shaded, sightless eye, and the grave little boy could have mistaken them for father and son.

'When are you going to bring the children to visit us?' Jane asked, as she stood at the open window, waiting for the train to start.

Ellen had been expecting the question for some time, and dreading it. Remembering her last visit to London, with her own three children, she frowned anxiously. 'They are so young, Jane dear. Could we not wait till next Summer?' she suggested, tentatively.

But Vicky was tugging at her hand. 'Please, Nana, say we can go.'

And Paul echoed, 'Please, Nana.'

Jane smiled affectionately at the two children. 'You see, you cannot refuse. It will be a special treat for the last day of the holiday.'

'Which day would be convenient?'

'Why not Sunday? We have a short service at the Mission in the morning, after Sunday School, and the Salvation Army band playing in the street in the afternoon. Catch an early train and make it a nice long day. The children will love it, and so shall we, shall we not, darling?' She turned her head to include Edward, who was standing beside her.

'Very m-much,' he answered, and smiled at the little group they were leaving behind.

'That's settled then,' said practical Jane, with much satisfaction. 'Let me know the time of arrival at Victoria, and we will meet you.'

'Thank you,' Ellen sighed, resignedly. All her sisters, apart from her gentle Grace, had their way with her. She was the eldest, but could easily be persuaded by a stronger will. It may have been that she still lived under the thumb of Amelia. For a few short years of marriage she had escaped her mother's dominating personality, only to be ruled by her husband.

'No need to mention it to Kate or she will expect you

to visit her. You can do that some other time,' Jane was saying.

Ellen agreed with alacrity, for her first and last visit to Kate, at her imposing residence in Onslow Square, had entailed a programme of lavish entertainment, including a drive to Hyde Park in the carriage, strawberry ices in an open-air refreshment kiosk, and a visit to the circus. Only Thomas had actually enjoyed the treat, but then it had been arranged especially for Kate's 'darling boy'. Prue had been on tenterhooks with nervous apprehension, convinced that something awful would happen and they would never see The Haven again. She herself had arrived back with a blinding sick headache, and gone straight to bed. It was a long time ago, but the memory was fresh. That was the time when her little Bella had decided she would live in the East End of London when she was grown up, for they had also visited Jane and Edward at the Hoxton Mission. Just a childish fancy, Ellen had thought, but it was real enough, for when she had finished her convent education, off she went with Roderic, to whom she was already betrothed. Now they had their own Mission at Stepney; they were devoted to each other, and shared the poverty and privations of their neighbours. No two sisters could be more unlike in every way than Prue and Bella. The one so governed by her emotions, the other happy and content.

Ellen's thoughts had wandered momentarily, but Jane was still busy with her plans. 'I will ask Bella and Roddy to join us. They can leave their deputy wardens in charge at Stepney,' she decided, as the train began to slide slowly away from the platform. 'Goodbye! God bless you!' Her clear, resonant voice was borne away with the guard's shrill whistle.

'Goodbye! God bless you!' echoed the children. Then they were hidden in a cloud of steam.

Few people were travelling at that early hour on Sunday, and Vicky climbed into an empty carriage in breathless excitement, followed by Paul and Nana. While Paul had already travelled thousands of miles in his short life, this was Vicky's first train journey, and a most thrilling adventure.

151

When she had seen Paul kneeling comfortably in a corner seat, she scrambled on to the opposite seat, bright-eyed and eager, and trailed her clean white gloves over the dusty window pane. Dressed in the new Sunday best frock that Nana had made and Auntie Bertha had smocked, with a beribboned straw hat, she looked 'fresh as a daisy', as Mabel would say.

Paul wore his white sailor suit and sailor cap, which he removed and handed to Nana as soon as he stepped into the carriage. Impeccable manners were as natural as breathing for the four-year-old son of Thomas. Both children would be crumpled and grubby on the homeward journey, but that was to be expected.

'Why was Grandmama cross when we said goodbye?' Paul asked, anxiously, as they waited for the train to start.

'I think she was a little disapproving because we were missing church, and a Sunday outing seems most improper. She thinks we are desecrating the Sabbath by travelling on a train to London. But it was Auntie Jane who suggested it, and they do have a service at the Mission, so it seemed harmless enough,' Nana answered quietly.

'We are off!' Vicky squealed excitedly, and Grandmama was forgotten.

'We are off!' echoed Paul, breathing his hot breath on the dusty window.

'You may use your handkerchief, darling. I have clean ones in my reticule,' said Nana, who always came prepared for any emergency, even on the short journey to the beach.

Paul scrubbed at the window with a striped handkerchief that had once served his Papa a number of useful purposes, such as wiping his slate clean of his own spittle, and wrapping a half chewed toffee. Since Thomas had never suffered from a cold in the head, or a fit of weeping, his handkerchiefs had not been regarded as useful for such normal practices. Paul had acquired several of these striped handkerchiefs that had been carefully laundered by Norah, and put away in a drawer where Ellen kept a few mementoes of her small son: his first pair of shoes, the short knickers he wore when he was breeched on his third birthday, one of his golden curls (Grandmama had claimed the rest!), and, tied with

152

blue ribbon, a bundle of letters from his schools that were almost identical in their brevity.

My dear Mama,
    Thank you for the money. I trust you are in the best of health and the weather is seasonable. I have been riding again today.The horses are fabulous. Can you send me an extra shilling in your next letter. One of the masters is getting married, and the boys have to buy him a wedding present.
    Lots of love from your obedient son, Thomas.

Her mouth trembled, and her dark eyes were soft as velvet whenever she untied the ribbon to peruse her son's stilted phrases, for, if the truth be known, Thomas was neither loving nor obedient! As for the masters, they must have been committing bigamy, with all those weddings. A similar epistle would be sent to Grandmama, who never divulged what her 'darling boy' had written. She also kept a drawer of mementoes of boyhood, including the riding crop, with which he had lashed at the beauitful rocking-horse she had bought for his third birthday, his first white sailor suit and sailor hat and, of course, the golden curls. A photograph of Thomas, before he was shorn of his curls, had pride of place on top of the piano in the drawing-room. Other photographs of him in various stages of growth, smiling confidently from the silver frames, to the handsome young subaltern in his scarlet uniform, were on display among the Victorian bric-a-brac on the occasional tables crammed into the drawing-room. Two generations of girls looked out solemnly from their silver frames, but only this one beautiful boy.
    So Ellen took the damp, grubby handkerchief from Paul, and slipped it into her reticule. Then she pushed aside the memories of a careless, unloving son, to enjoy the company of her two affectionate grandchildren.
    When they left the town behind, and steamed through the peaceful countryside, Paul was reminded of the hill station on the Frontier, without the hills. Sheep and cattle were grazing in the green pastures. The harvest had been gathered and only stubble remained where recently the fields had been golden with corn or ripe grasses for hay. Speechless with wonder

153

and delight, he absorbed the scene with dark, reflective eyes, that would always see beauty in God's creation. While Vicky chatted incessantly, and pointed out objects of interest to her little cousin, Paul said nothing, but for his grandmother his silence was more eloquent than words. Thomas's son was already dearer to her heart than his father had ever been. There was an affinity between them that went deeper than the closeness between herself and her grand-daughter. There was something very special in their relationship, and the child responded in a way that was altogether pleasing. She understood his shyness and his fears as his beloved Ayah had understood. It was not his fault, but his misfortune, to be born to parents too absorbed in themselves to notice he was not like other children, or, when they did notice, to scorn his differences.

When Paul turned his head to smile at her, there was no need for words, only an answering smile of such tenderness he was instantly reminded of Ayah. Holding his sailor cap in her gloved hands, she too was reminded of India, and all the little boys dressed like little princes. Their papas had been so proud of their small sons. But she had disappointed Jonathan. Two dear little daughters could not compensate a soldier of the Queen for such a grievous disappointment. If only he had lived to see his beautiful son. If only she could have spared him the shame and the agony he must have suffered in those last few months of his reckless life. Her darling Jonathan! He should have married someone like Kate, who would have coped with his strong personality and devastating charm. As the wheels rattled and the telephone wires tautened and drooped, tautened and drooped, Ellen was back in that far country, nursing her newborn child to her breast, drowsy with sleep, hearing the native bearer announcing the birth to his lord and master.

'You have another daughter, Sahib. It is the Will of Allah.'

And Jonathan had asked for a chota peg. A few minutes later, she heard him ride away, and she knew he had gone to be comforted in the arms of That Woman, while she wept her sad, lonely tears.

Paul turned his head and saw the glistening tears in her

dark eyes. 'I just saw a lot of small little birds on the telephone wires,' he told her, gravely.

'That would be swallows, getting ready to fly away. It is too cold for them here in the winter,' she told her grandson, with a catch in her voice.

'They would like it in India,' he said.

'So they would,' she agreed.

All too soon they were leaving behind that peaceful countryside, and approaching the city. Rows and rows of terraced houses with belching chimneys, and gardens bordering the railway line, where hand-made chicken houses and sheds shared the vegetable patch, and late summer roses trailed over walls and fences. Paul was silent, feeling sorry for the roses. At the hill station, on the Frontier, they were planted about the green lawns and watered every day by the garden boy. There was so much space to grow, and the air was so cool and fresh, it prompted Ayah to pull a warm jersey over his silk shirt.

Soon they were clattering into Victoria Station, a frightening Bedlam of noise and hissing engines. Paul scrambled down from the seat, and went to stand beside Nana, who put a protective arm about his small trembling shoulders.

'Is it not exciting?' Vicky squealed, loving every noisy second.

'Follow me,' Nana instructed, stepping carefully on to the platform. Then she handed them out and they were swept along on a tide of humanity, towards the barrier. They had been picking up passengers at every station en route. Such a lot of people, all desecrating the Sabbath. Grandmama would be most indignant!

'I can see Uncle Edward,' Nana told the children, as they converged on the exit. The tall, gangling figure in the green eye-shade was prominent among the waiting crowd, but Jane's short dumpy figure was completely hidden by a thick-set character in a bowler hat. She popped out like a Jack-in-the-box as soon as Nana had handed over the tickets.

'Here you are at last. We seem to have been waiting for hours,' she said, and both children were hugged and kissed.

155

Edward's greeting was not so exuberant, but his smile was warm, and his fond glance lingered on the small boy. It was Jane who led them to the horse-bus and settled them in their seats, and Jane who pointed out all the interesting landmarks as they clattered through the near-deserted city into the East End. It was a long ride, but for Vicky, who never ceased to exclaim about its wonders, this first visit to London would always remain fresh in her memory. For Jane and Edward, the East End had been home for a number of years. When they alighted from the bus, they were stepping into a familiar world, but for Ellen, who had seen its awful squalor only once, when her children were young, the shock was even more profound than the first time, and she wondered afresh at her sister's capacity for endurance.

Jane had been the first to realize the importance of being practical when their circumstances changed so dramatically after their father's death. She had gone straight from the schoolroom into the kitchen, and Cook had stayed on for a month to teach her the basic rules of plain cooking. She had not known how useful that knowledge would prove when she married Edward. A warden's wife in an East End Mission had to provide good, nourishing meals for a number of young working lads on a limited allowance, and 'making do' had become second nature.

Paul clung to Uncle Edward's hand as they walked down the street, his dark eyes wide with horror. The stench of rotting refuse, horse dung and emptied chamber pots was appalling. He shrank from the close contact of the dirty barefoot urchins who swarmed about them as soon as they were recognized. Toddlers played in the gutter, and blowzy women stood in their doorways, holding puny, bare-bottomed babies.

''ullo, Guv. 'ullo, Missus,' they called cheerfully.

The warden and his wife were liked and respected. Edward smiled his shy, endearing smile, and Jane stopped to admire the babies. Their progress was slow, for Jane twice had to stop to sort out a quarrel in the gutter over a crust of bread. She made the children reply to all the friendly greetings, and they answered politely. 'Good morning, Mrs Harris. Good morning, Mrs Jones.'

'Luverly manners, them kids!' Mrs Harris told her neighbour approvingly.

The gang of dirty, barefoot urchins followed them down the street, and when, at last, they reached the Mission, one cheeky ragamuffin demanded, 'Gie us a penny, Guv.'

'Not today, Alfie. You haven't earned it,' said Jane.

'Fill all the coal buckets, Missus. Peel all the taters. Scrub the floor. Anythink you say, Missus,' cajoled Alfie.

Jane relented. 'A penny to fill the coal buckets.'

Alfie grinned and turned to his gang of devoted disciples. 'Wait artside,' he ordered, ' – an' be'ave yerselves or yer gets nothink!' Then he followed them in.

For Ellen it was putting back the clock. Nothing had changed. She had walked down this same street, disgusted and horrified by the appalling squalor, two decades ago. The same stench stung her nostrils, the same gang of dirty, bare-foot urchins followed them to the door of the Mission. She had to remind herself that young Alfie was probably the son of that boy who had begged for a halfpenny that day, and that Mrs Harris and Mrs Jones could be daughters or daughters-in-law of those blowzy women with their bare-bottomed babies. Their amazing cheerfulness was the same. And Jane's genuine affection for her East End neighbours was the same. Two decades of work and worry had left its mark only on her plump figure and pallid cheeks. Mentally and spiritually she was the same young woman who had promised to serve the poor and needy for the rest of her life. Her earnestness, coupled with her warm heart, made the charity more acceptable, for these people of the East End were poor and proud. They liked the Missus, but they loved the Guv. There was something about his vague shyness and his stammering speech that appealed to them. The women felt protective, the men touched their caps and refrained from foul language in his company. The Guv was a proper gent, to be respected. The story of his courage in trying to stop a fight in the pub on the corner of the street had been handed down from father to son. But it had not stopped the violence or the vice. Guv and his Missus could walk safely through the streets of Hoxton, in daylight or darkness, in their shabby clothes and polished boots. Edward's suits had been sponged and

157

pressed, and the shirt tails cut off to make new collars and cuffs. The jackets of Jane's costumes had been re-lined and the skirts turned. Boots were soled and heeled till the uppers were worn out, underwear patched, socks and stockings neatly darned. The mending basket was never empty, and Jane's busy fingers never idle, as they relaxed in their cosy little parlour at the end of the day.

The Salvation Army lassies they had known in those early days were grey-haired married women now, with growing families. On their monthly visit to The Haven and their week's annual holiday, these same women would take over the running of the Mission with the cheerful aptitude of that splendid band of practising Christians.

Stepping over the whitened doorstep, Ellen was confronted by a familiar little woman in a sacking apron.

'I remember yer, Ma'am. You ain't changed,' beamed Maggie, drying her red, roughened hands on the apron.

'And I remember you,' said Ellen, as they shook hands.

Jane introduced the children. Paul had snatched off his sailor cap.

'Ow are yer, duckie? You ain't much like yer Dad,' she told him. Her new false teeth were very uncomfortable, and she was only wearing them in honour of the visitors. Vicky was surprised to receive a wet kiss. 'I can see the likeness to yer Ma, duckie,' she asserted. 'Seems like only yes'day, Ma'am, you brought them three luverly children on a visit. Now they be all growed up, wiv their own children.' Maggie's garrulous tongue would have gone on wagging indefinitely if Jane had not reminded her they all were dying for a nice cup of tea.

'Kettle's on the boil, Missus, an' bangers an' mash keepin' 'ot in the oven, an' there's treacle tart for afters,' announced that good woman, and bustled away to the kitchen.

'Bangers and mash?' Vicky echoed, looking puzzled.

'Sausages and mashed potatoes,' Jane explained. 'I thought it would be a treat. I know your Grandmama thinks they lack nourishment, but we like them here, and our butcher's sausages are really very tasty.' She was leading the way to the parlour, and the children followed.

Their first impressions of the East End were decidely mixed, and even Vicky would not have dared to walk

158

down that street without the protection of Uncle Edward and Auntie Jane. Paul was frightened and saddened. The native quarters at the garrison in India had been squalid and smelly, but the squalor was acceptable because of Ayah. She belonged to it. All her relations were there. Papa and Mama would have been shocked and disapproving had they know that Ayah had once allowed him to visit the native quarters beyond the compound as a special treat for his third birthday, when she was obliged to obey his commands. A birthday child was granted every wish, like a prince.

When the dirty ragged urchin staggered in with a bucket of coal, Paul shrank away with a sense of guilt, but instinct was too strong, and fastidiousness a natural result of his early environment. Alfie's cheeky grin was friendly and confident, however. He had no inhibitions, and his only fear was his drunken father on Saturday night, but that was a common fear, shared by many of those street urchins.

'That's it, Missus. Two full buckets in kitchen, one in re-cration room, one in 'ere.'

'Thank you, Alfie.' Jane handed over the promised penny. She always kept several pennies in her pocket, and the children knew it, though how she contrived to have anything to spare from that meagre housekeeping allowance was a mystery, even to her own husband.

Fires were not supposed to be lit in the parlour and the other rooms till the first day of October, but the house was damp, and a small coal fire in the Autumn evenings was cosy.

'Thanks, Missus. Ta-ta!' Alfie was off like a shot. Vicky followed him to the front door. Her natural curiosity had to be satisfied. How would he share one penny among six boys? Would there be a fight? The boys crowded round their leader. It was not the first time Alfie had earned a penny filling coal buckets. His hands were smeared with coal dust, and he had bruised his big toe on the cellar steps.

'Come on you lot. Six sherbet bags from 'ole Ma Jackson!' he told them, importantly. And they raced away, whooping excitedly.

Vicky closed the door and went back to the parlour.

'Can he really buy six sherbet bags for a penny?' she asked Auntie Jane.

'Yes, dear, on a stall in the market. Six sherbet bags with a stick of liquorice, or six peppermint humbugs, or a dozen Packers' chocolate drops, or a dozen sweetheart assortment. The sherbet bags are the most popular with the boys, the sweetheart assortment with the girls.' Vicky looked puzzled, so she explained. 'Every sweet is in the shape of a heart, and inscribed with tiny lettering, such as 'Be my sweetheart', 'I love you', 'Will you marry me?' 'I like your blue eyes', 'You are very handsome', 'Give me a kiss' and so on.'

Vicky giggled. 'What fun. They don't have sweetheart assortment in our sweet shop. Do they, Paulie?'

'No, only boiled sweets in jars.'

'But you do have a chocolate bar for a treat,' Nana pointed out, in all fairness. It was Grandmama who insisted that home-made boiled sweets were best for children.

Vicky took off her hat and gloves thoughtfully. She was wondering what it would feel like to have bare feet all the time, instead of only when you paddled. These children were dirty and ragged, but they were happy. It was quite a revelation to discover children could be happy in such a place. 'How can they be happy when they are poor?' she asked.

Auntie Jane knew the answer, as she knew the answer to all her questions that day. 'Children can be happy anywhere. They were born here, and have never known any other way of life, apart from hop-picking, in Kent, but the children you see here today do not go hop-picking. They will grow up here. Some will move away, others will spend their lives in Hoxton, particularly the girls if they marry local boys and have big families. Those boys, and others like them, go hungry to bed every night, yet they have the most amazing energy. The boys have a better life than the girls. Did you notice every one of those girls watching the boys playing football, carried a little brother or sister on her hip?'

Vicky nodded.

'It was not a proper football,' said Paul, who noticed such things.

'No, it was a pig's bladder, and the lamp-post was the goal.

'A pig's bladder?' echoed Paul. Wasn't it a pig's bladder the native boys kicked around their compound? And he had seen little native girls carrying naked babies on their hips, just like these girls. Only the colour of their skins was different, and their smell was different. He began to understand what Auntie Jane meant about children accepting the place and the people without question.

When Maggie carried in the tea tray, he was still standing there, holding his sailor cap, his dark eyes dreamy with memories.

'What are you thinking?' Uncle Edward asked, from the armchair, drawing him close.

'If they had dark faces and another smell, they would be the same as the natives in India,' he said, and wondered why they laughed.

'Fancy 'im thinking o' that. Bless 'is little 'eart,' said Maggie, conversationally.

But Jane was not in the mood just then for Maggie's comments. She had her family to entertain, and the day was all too short. So she made no answer, and Maggie took the hint and shuffled out. Of recent months Jane often felt quite overcome with the waves of heat that swept over her, even in winter. She wanted to snatch off all her clothes, and could hardly breathe. At such times, her temper was short and her tongue sharp, even with Edward. It frightened her, because she did not recognize herself in these ugly moods, and when they had passed, she was quick to apologize. But she need not have worried. ''Tis only the change,' Maggie could have told her. 'We all goes through it, Missus.'

So just when she wanted to feel at her best, in her own parlour, with her sister Ellen and the dear children, Jane was furiously fanning her scarlet face over the teacups. Poor Jane, Ellen was thinking, for she too recognized those distressing symptoms. But the subject was much too embarrassing to discuss, even if they had been alone. It would pass. Everything passes.

'I saw a little boy on crutches,' Paul was saying.

'That was Freddie Partridge. He was born with only one leg. When he is old enough, he will be fitted with an artificial leg,' Jane explained, forgetting her own discomfort in her

161

sympathy for this child. 'He is a plucky little fellow, and the other boys are good to him. When they play football, they put him in charge of the goal, and he stands at the lamp-post. It's surprising how quickly he can move on those crutches.'

'Only one leg. Only one boot and one sock.' Paul shivered with the awfulness of such a predicament.

'No boot and no sock. Freddie is barefoot like the other boys.'

Paul was looking thoughtful. 'If I had only one leg, Papa would not wish me to be a soldier,' he told them, gravely.

'Oh, Paulie! If you had only one leg, you would be a cripple. I couldn't bear it.' Vicky was horrified.

'I couldn't bear it either,' said Ellen, quietly, wondering how Thomas would have coped with a crippled son. It was a solemn thought, too solemn for today.

Edward thought so too, and changed the subject. 'Maggie's b-bangers and m-mash are w-waiting,' he reminded them, with stumbling jollity, and led the way to the kitchen.

Maggie had removed her sacking apron and laid the table with a clean, starched cloth. The stove had been treated to an extra polish, a canary chirped in its cage, and red geraniums made a splash of colour on the window sill. Maggie would eat her own dinner when she had served the young lodgers in the dining-room. They all had attended the short service in the recreation room. It was one of the few rules to be respected on Sunday. Jane played the hymns on the harmonium, and Edward struggled manfully through a short sermon. One of the boys would read a lesson from the Bible. Few of the lads could read or write. The service lasted for no more than half an hour, then they were free to enjoy the day as they pleased. To keep them off the streets, Edward would take them down to the docks, while Jane presided over her Sunday School, and today was no exception. The two children would see them in their normal routine, and first impressions would last a lifetime.

'I suppose you would call it bribery, but every child who attends Sunday School receives an orange and a currant bun. This is strictly between ourselves, and not official,' Jane

162

confessed to her sister as they waited for the children that Sunday afternoon.

Not even the promise of such luxuries as oranges and buns could induce Alfie and his gang, or any of the older boys, to attend Sunday School, however. The girls arrived as expected, carrying babies, with small brothers and sisters clinging to their skirts.

'Their 'ard-workin' Mums likes ter get rid o' the kids Sundie af'noon, jus' ter get a bit o' peace. Can't blame 'em,' said Maggie, as they clattered into the house.

The cripple boy came last, swinging along on his crutches, his pale face alight with eager anticipation, not so much for the promised bun and orange, as for the lesson that followed Sunday School. He was learning to read and write. It was a pleasure to teach a child of such bright intelligence. His sister Maudie had been promised her turn when the baby could walk.

The girls were not encouraged by their families to read and write. It was a waste of time, they were told. They had to mind the kids while their Mums went out to work or they could earn a bob or two in the factory, Maggie pointed out, sensibly enough.

Ellen sat apart with her grandchildren, admiring the way Jane kept the girls interested and the little ones amused with scrap books. The crippled boy watched and listened. They sang 'Jesus loves me' and 'All things bright and beautiful'. Freddie led the thin shrill voices with such unwavering certainty, it brought the tears to Ellen's dark eyes. That a barefoot crippled child, born to poverty and squalor, should sing so fervently of bright and beautiful things was touchingly remarkable. Jane sang too as she thumped the wheezy harmonium, and Vicky and Paul joined in the singing, for they knew every word.

When the children had left the house, clutching their oranges and hungrily devouring the currant buns, Jane pulled up a chair beside Freddie. This was the proudest moment of the whole week, when he had her undivided attention for half an hour. Six days a week he was selling matches outside the pub on the corner of the street. Sunday was a very special day. He played football and went to

Sunday School. He was learning to read and write, had an orange and a currant bun for his dinner, and joined in the hearty singing with the Salvation Army band in the afternoon. It was a fitting climax to a week of patient and cheerful salesmanship. At the age of eight, it was only right and proper that he should earn a few pence to eke out the meagre wages his mother was paid for making the match boxes at home. The smell of glue was a constant reminder of their frugal existence. He loved his mother and hated his father. It was as simple as that.

Now he smiled and relaxed, as the Missus spread his own special copy-book on the table, with his name on the cover. It was a labour of love, to shape the flowing alphabetical letters. Then he read aloud from the *First Grade Grammar Course* and stumbled only once, over the pronounciation of 'constable'.

'The emphasis is on the *first* syllable, dear,' Jane corrected, kindly.

'I shall remember that word. The Missus won't have to tell me a second time,' Freddie reminded himself with grave determination.

When the lesson was finished and the book closed, he sighed. It was all over for another week. They shook hands, and the strange lady smiled as he stumped away on his crutches. The two children from another world stared shyly, embarrassed by his ragged clothes and his bare foot. He was very hungry, and his mouth watered in anticipation of the bun and the orange in his torn pockets as he swung towards home.

It was the children of the upper-class, in their Sunday-best clothes, children who would never know hunger or poverty, who were embarrassed, Jane had noticed − not Freddie, a child of the East End slums − as she tidied the recreation room. This was surprising, but then she was constantly surprised, even after two decades as a warden's wife. None of her children at Hoxton knew the meaning of shyness or embarrassment. They were as natural as little animals, fighting for their existence, from the moment they were pushed away from their mothers' breasts, to make room for the new baby. Only Freddie was different in his approach to life, because of his disability. He stood a little apart from the rest, his fighting spirit undefeated by the cumbersome crutches. He even enjoyed the luxury of a straw pallet under the table, while his brothers and sisters crowded into one big bug-infested bed. He escaped the beatings from a drunken father, and that in itself separated him from the rest, who lived in constant fear of that leather belt and the heavy hand that could knock a child across the room, for no better reason than that he or she got in his way. When there was no money for ale, the children kept out of his way, but there was no escape for his poor wife. Once she had been a pretty girl, with raven black hair and sparkling Irish eyes. Now she was old and grey-haired at forty, her eyes weak with poring over the match boxes. She was expecting her seventh child. She loved all her children, and tried to protect them from a brutal father, but it was a losing battle. He earned good wages as a docker, but the noisy, reeking atmosphere of the pub on the corner of the street attracted him like a magnet. Home was a place where he ate and slept, beat his wife and took her every Saturday night. The children went hungry until he slept in a drunken stupor, and the mother of his children took off his boots and rifled his pockets. Then Freddie and his sister, Maudie, were sent to buy bread, margarine, a penn'orth of jam, a twist of tea, and a twist of sugar, while the kettle boiled. The bread was stale, but it filled their hungry bellies. There was barely a year between the children, and Maudie carried the heavy basket on her skinny arm, and had to run to keep up with his swinging crutches.

On this particular Sunday, back from Sunday School, she sat on the doorstep, peeling the orange for the little ones. The baby sucked the juice from her own orange, and peed in her lap. Her wet frock stuck to her thighs, since she wore no drawers.

'Dirty little bugger!' she scolded, and sat him on the step, where he whined and grizzled for another suck of the orange. She was thinking of Freddie, left behind at the Mission. He was learning to read and write. 'T'aint fair!' she muttered, as she wiped the baby's dribbling chin on his dirty vest. Then she forgot her resentment.

Away in the distance she could hear the drums and cornets,

the marching feet and the singing voices. 'It's the Salvation!' she cried excitedly, snatched up the baby, and ran to meet them. Children swarmed down the street.

'Onward Christian Soldiers, marching as to war, With the Cross of Jesus, going on before.' Like the Pied Piper of Hamelin, the Salvation Army band gathered the children from every doorstep, every pavement and gutter, and swept them along, dancing and prancing on their bare feet, pushing and shoving, and shouting the familiar words in their shrill voices.

'Onward Christian soldiers, marching as to war,' sang Maudie, bouncing the baby on her hip.

'Wait for me! Wait for me!' Little ones were left behind. They would catch up later. The band circled a wide area, and came to rest outside the pub on the corner of the street. It was a popular meeting place on Sunday. Thirsts were quenched, jokes exchanged, and customers stood on the steps, emptying their mugs. Halfpennies were dropped in the tin a bonneted 'lassie' rattled invitingly.

'Cor blimey, they ain't 'arf a lot o' cadgers,' somebody grumbled, but it was not meant to be taken seriously. The Salvation was as much a part of their lives as the poverty and the squalor. They saved souls, but they also fed the hungry and clothed the ragged, scrubbed floors, and brought more babies into the world than the overworked midwife. It was not all drudgery and duty. The band was a tonic to those who followed in the steps of General Booth and those who listened. It coloured their drab lives.

Freddie had finished his lesson. The street was deserted, the doorstep vacant. He could hear the band circling the market, but his thoughts were still with the *First Grade Grammar Course* and the pleasure of reading. It pleased him more than anything he had ever known in his short life. Neither of his parents could read or write. Both had grown up in Hoxton. No letters were written or received. Any relative who had a mind to call did so, without waiting for an invitation.

Freddie was so absorbed in his thoughts, he ate the currant bun and the orange in a day-dream in which he could see himself grown to his full height, and the crutches discarded.

He was walking down the street, on his artificial leg, to catch a bus to the City. He was rather vague about the City, never having been there, but his best friend, Barney, had achieved quite a reputation as a messenger boy. He wore a smart uniform and his first pair of boots with pride, and washed himself every day! They gave him his dinner, and the princely sum of two shillings a week. His exploits in the City held Freddie spellbound. Four years older, fleet of foot and cunning as a little fox, Barney was a hero. Hadn't he got the job in the first place by sheer audacity? Who but Barney would have thought of waylaying the General Manager of the Metropolitan Assurance Company when he stepped out of his cab? It was so daring, it made Freddie ache with admiration and envy.

'Give us a job, Mister,' must have surprised that worthy gentleman, and certainly surprised the uniformed doorman, who stepped forward smartly to grab the precocious urchin by the collar and bid him, 'Get along, or else.'

'Just a moment, Hodges,' interrupted the amused voice, as he was being bustled away. 'What had you in mind, boy?' he asked.

'Messenger boy, Sir,' Barney answered promptly.

'And what makes you think you would suit me, and we should suit you?' The question had an unexpected twist, but Barney was undaunted. He had washed his face, and plastered his unruly mop of red hair with water. His candid blue eyes were eager, and his voice held a determined ring. 'I kin run faster than any of the kids in our street. I knows 'ow ter be'ave meself. I'm 'onest an' I won't ever let you darn, Mister.'

'Fair enough. One could not expect more. In return for such excellent services, we can offer you a wage of two shillings weekly, a free uniform, and a midday meal. What is your name, boy?'

'Barnaby Mason, Mister.'

'Very well, Barnaby. You may consider yourself engaged.'

'I can? Cor blimey, Mister, me Ma won't 'arf be pleased. Me Dad ain't done no work for six weeks, an' me Ma ain't got nufink left ter pawn.'

'Quite so,' readily agreed that august personage. 'See to

it, Hodges,' he commanded, brusquely, and stalked into the building.

The doorman's face was scarlet with righteous indignation, his florid cheeks and bristling moustaches an indication that he once had served in Her Majesty's Royal Fusiliers. In his magnificent uniform, he presented a much more formidable figure than the General Manager in his morning coat and top hat, to a small urchin from the East End, and Barney followed the strutting figure through the portals of the Metropolitan Assurance Company with a quaking heart and shuffling bare feet.

'What had prompted the Guvnor to engage a ragged barefoot brat without even a reference?' Hodges was asking himself. He was seldom in such a good humour, especially at 8 o'clock in the morning. The Guvnor had a reputation as a lady's man. This surprising cordiality could only be the result of bedding a particularly luscious female. The brat was lucky to catch him in such a good mood.

Swinging round to confront the boy, he took him by the ear and pointed up a steep stairway. 'Up you go, you young varmint. First door on the left, an' Gawd 'elp yer, for nobody else is going to in this bloody place!'

'Yes, Sir. No, Sir,' Barney stammered, and fled up the stairs, rubbing his painful ear. Since nobody answered his timid knock, he pushed open the door and stood there, hesitant, staring at some half dozen boys in various stages of undress, sparring playfully. A surly looking individual, sitting behind a desk, looked up to demand, irritiably, 'Where jew spring from?'

'I – – I been took on.'

'What for?'

'Messenger boy.'

The boys hooted with laughter. 'Garn, you're kidding,' jeered the eldest, who could have been a couple of years older than Barney.

'Who took you on? Speak up, boy. We ain't got all day,' muttered his interrogator.

'A genalman what got art of a cab.'

'The Guvnor. Holy Jehosaphat!'

'The Guvnor,' echoed the boys, staring at the newcomer

in wide-eyed curiosity, for he seemed quite unaware of the honour bestowed on him.

'Well, come on in then. Don't just stand there. Me name's Blunt — Blunt by name and Blunt by nature — *Mister* Blunt to you. Lucky for you I always keep a spare uniform and a spare pair of boots. In that locker over there. Get yourself dressed. Make it snappy. We ain't got all day,' he was told in no uncertain manner.

It was intimidating, however, to pull off his ragged jersey and trousers with so many curious eyes staring at his nakedness. But it was an unforgettable moment when he covered his scrawny little body with the smart uniform. It fitted like a glove. The boots were too big, but he made no protest, and lifted his feet carefully. He would get used to them. But could he run fast in boots? He had to, or he would not keep the job.

'Keep an eye on him, Josh, just for today,' Mister Blunt directed the eldest boy, when he had inspected them.

Josh scowled, and gave Barney a push. 'Get along wiv yer, kid, an' keep yer nose clean,' he said, with lordly superiority.

Telling the tale to Freddie on the doorstep at the end of that first gruelling day, Barney was nursing his blistered feet. He seemed to have followed the fleet-of-foot Josh halfway round the city, scared of losing touch with him, and even more scared of the traffic of cabs and carriages. It was unlike anything he had ever known or imagined, for his own small world was crowded but familiar. Darting across the streets in the wake of the older boy, dodging the whips of irate coachmen, his boots flapping uncomfortably on his bare feet, Barney's empty belly rumbled hungrily for a couple of hours or so. Then came a short respite for a cup of weak tea in a basement canteen, and while he sipped the scalding beverage, he gazed about him, trying not to notice that everyone but himself seemed to be eating. Josh was ignoring him, and sharing a thick sandwich with another messenger boy.

'You 'as ter bring somefink from 'ome fer yer elevenses,' another youngster told him, kindly enough.

Barney grinned. 'There ain't nufink ter bring where I come from.'

'You can 'ave 'alf of me slice of bred an' marge if you're 'ungry.'

'Ta.'

'Where jew come from then?'

'Elephant and Castle.'

Barney choked on the bread and margarine. 'Cor blimey. That's a laugh.'

'Where jew come from then?'

''Oxton.'

'Never 'eard of it.'

'Garn, you'r kiddin'. 'Ow long you been a messenger boy then?'

'Six months.'

'Was you took on by the Guvnor?'

'Not bloody likely. Me bruvver got me the job when 'e bettered 'issell.'

'What doing?'

'Clerkin.'

''E were lucky.'

'No 'e weren't. Sitting all day on yer bum on one of them 'igh stools. Call that luck? Rather be a messenger. We gets aht and abaht. Sees a bit o' life. It ain't so dusty once yer gets used to it, an' once you're on yer own. Don't take no notice of that Josh. Thinks 'e's the cat's whiskers 'cause 'e comes from Walthamstow, but 'e don't fool me. Walthamstow kids goes 'oppin' darn in Kent same as kids from the Elephant and Castle.'

'I ain't never bin 'oppin'.'

'Yer ain't missed much, kid. Pickin' 'ops is a mug's game. They calls it a 'oliday. Not wiv our Mum it ain't. "You sit on that bin an' pick them 'ops or you gets no grub," she told me, an' she meant it.'

'Can I sit wiv you for dinner?'

'Sure yer can.'

'What's yer name?'

'Archie − Archie Clark.'

'Ta.'

Archie wiped his mouth on the back of his hand, donned his hat, and hurried away. Barney had to wait for Josh, who was in no hurry. Back on duty, racing after him in

170

breathless haste, his belly still rumbled. Half a slice of bread and marge had not stilled the pangs of hunger, but he had made a friend – from the Elephant and Castle.

Back at the Mission, on that Sunday afternoon, Vicky and Paul stood on the pavement with Nana and Auntie Jane, listening to the band, watching the barefoot children dancing and prancing. Their shrill, excited voices joined in the choruses. Babies squealed and squirmed in the arms of their sisters.

Maudie was there with the rest. Her thin cotton frock still clung to her thin belly as her thin legs trod the dirty cobbles. She sang and she danced in happy abandon, in spite of the child on her hip, for she could see herself on the stage of the old Metropolitan Music Hall in Edgware Road, in a line of chorus girls. She had never actually seen a stage, or a line of chorus girls, but her vivid imagination provided all the glamour and the 'Salvation' all the musical accompaniment. The drums beat the rhythm, the cornets sang of dancing feet, tossing curls and swinging skirts, while her own skirt barely covered her knees, and her uncombed, tangled hair swung about her shoulders.

But they all were thin, these children of the slums, Ellen was thinking, as she held Paul's hand. Nothing had changed. Here she had stood with Thomas, Prue and Bella, twenty years ago. But Thomas had not held her hand, or shrunk from a scene so strange and foreign. Thomas had been bold and arrogant in his Sunday best clothes. Too bold, perhaps, for one of the dirty, ragged urchins had given him a playful push, as though reminding him the 'Salvation' was theirs and he was only a visitor. Those cheeky little street urchins had been poking fun at her beautiful Thomas. To this day he could not bear to be laughed at.

Vicky was holding Jane's hand. Ellen had always thought it such a pity they had no children of their own, Jane and Edward, but now she could see they had adopted all these slum children in their hearts. And not only the children, but the mothers, for many of these young, overburdened mothers had been children themselves when Jane and Edward first came to the Mission. Edward had taken the working

171

lads to the docks. He regarded them as his own particular responsibility. It was not enough to feed and clothe their bodies, he had to interest their minds and kindle in their spirits a Christian belief in the importance of every individual in the eyes of God. These lads had been homeless, sleeping in doorways and alleyways. Edward combed the streets at night, and brought them to the Mission. For many of these lads it was the first home they had known since they ran away from the hovels they had called home, at the age of eight or nine, to live on their wits. Stealing was as natural as breathing. Cunning as little foxes, they evaded the law, and enjoyed their freedom. No more nagging mothers or drunken fathers, no more obligations to earn a few pence to help feed all those hungry mouths. Self-preservation was the only motive.

Edward could not coax them all off the streets, and some stayed only a few weeks under his hospitable roof, and then slipped away.

On this particular Sunday afternoon, which followed the pattern of all the rest, Edward had taken a dozen or so of their young boarders to the docks, where the majority would eventually find work. The Guv was a proper gent, who could pull a few strings. A few short years boarding at the Mission, would build up a puny body and a poor constitution. The Missus would see to that. And for those who had taken advantage of her reading and writing lessons, there would be jobs ashore.

Vicky was puzzled. The Heathen of Hoxton did not seem to need missionaries. They were such happy heathens. Maggie was hanging out of a bedroom window, clapping her work-worn hands. All down the street, windows were flung open, and tousled heads appeared. The doorsteps were crowded with women. Some took their babies from the girls to let them dance unhampered.

Maudie's Mum was one of those who remembered her own childhood, and her own day-dreams, and was quietly determined that Maudie should have her chance. The talent was there, and that indefinable something called personality. Her dancing feet had a natural grace and rhythm, and she sang like a bird. They were a good pair, her Freddie and her

172

Maudie. Bright, intelligent, and the same happy temperament that she herself had known before marriage. She had lost it, but Freddie and Maudie had found it. The rest of her brood were like their Dad, and that was strange. Only in her two eldest could she find a glimmer of hope for the future.

'Your Maudie is a fair caution,' her neighbour declared, for Maudie was seen to be standing beside a Salvation Army lassie, waiting for her cue to sing a verse of a favourite hymn – 'Jesus loves me, this I know, For the Bible tells me so. Little ones to Him belong, They are weak but He is strong.'

'Now children, all together for the chorus.' The band-master waved his arms. The children stopped dancing and shouted the chorus. Then Maudie sang again, then another chorus. Vicky and Paul sang with the rest and clapped with the rest. Were they clapping their own performance? Jane wondered, as she smiled affectionately at her great-niece and-nephew. They stood on the pavement, a little apart from the rest, like two little peacocks in a flock of sparrows. Now three of the boys were being handed the cymbals, and three girls the tambourines. The children had to take their turn for this special privilege. Never a dull moment in the performance. The Salvation knew how to attract an audience, and to bring pleasure and entertainment where it was most needed.

When it was over, and the band marched away to start all over again in a neighbouring area, the little group on the pavement went indoors, and Maggie scuttled down the stairs to brew a pot of tea.

'That was our special hymn Grandmama plays for us on Sunday,' said Paul.

'Yes, it was *our* hymn,' Vicky echoed, more than a little aggrieved at the effrontery.

'It is a favourite hymn of all children everywhere,' Jane reminded them. 'Our children cannot claim it, neither can you.'

'I would like to play the cymbals,' said Paul.

'And I would like to shake a tambourine, but they did not invite us, did they?' Vicky complained. They were guests, and they *should* have been invited.

'We do not belong. We are only visitors.' It was Paul who understood the difference.

'It would not be fair. Those boys and girls had been waiting their turn for several weeks, and I would not suggest it,' Jane told them, with firm conviction. She loved her great-niece and -nephew, but Paul was right. They did not belong, would never belong, unless they gave up their own comfortable little world when they had grown to maturity, like her niece, Bella. A third generation? She looked down at the small boy in the white sailor suit and caught a reflection of something she could not define in that grave little face. He was a strange child – a cuckoo in the nest. 'Where *did* he belong?' Jane asked herself.

'The Salvation do play luverly,' Maggie declared, as she blundered in with a loaded tray. The teapot, milk jug and sugar basin would have served a dozen people. There was a plate of dripping toast, and a plate of fancy cakes (no mention would be made of the market stall from which the cakes had been purchased).

Dripping toast was a treat for the children; Ellen remembered that Prue had been quite ill on the homeward journey on her last visit, so she watched Paul anxiously, and was relieved to see he took only half a slice of the dripping toast, and only one small cake. She hadn't to worry about Vicky, who enjoyed her food, and hadn't a weak stomach.

Paul chewed thoughtfully on the dripping toast. He was not hungry, but he had to eat something for the sake of politeness. Most of the children in the street would go to bed hungry tonight. Auntie Jane had told them so. If only he could feed them, like Jesus fed the five thousand, but he hadn't got five loaves and two fishes like the boy in the story. And they were so ragged, and their feet must be so cold. It was so sad. His heart ached for them, but he could do nothing. How could those children sing and dance so merrily when they were hungry and ragged and had no boots on their feet? He could not understand. The problem was too big for his small mind, but he would never forget this day in the slums. While Vicky would remember only the sunny side – the band, the happy children, dancing and singing, Paul would remember only the shady side – the

174

children who went to bed hungry, the feet without boots, the bare-bottomed babies, and the boy on crutches. Even at this early age he was fully aware of the differences in his world and theirs, of the comforts he enjoyed and the blessings he had received since leaving the garrison town of Aldershot. Ayah would say that Allah had been good to a little boy whose parents did not want him. Whether it was Allah or Jesus was still questionable, but did it matter? He had Nana and his little cousin, kind Norah and a new home at The Haven.

Supposing his Papa had insisted on taking him back to Aldershot? He shivered at the thought of the unhappiness he had escaped only because Nana loved him, and had actually defied his stern Papa. Yet they did not want him at Aldershot. It was no secret. He was a nuisance. Ayah was dead, Auntie Millie had retired, and Uncle David seemed to have disappeared. Gifts for Christmas and birthday could not compensate for his presence.

There was so much sadness, so many partings. Now Vicky had gone back to live with her Papa. He clutched Nana's hand, and pleaded, in a small, choked voice, 'Nana, you won't go away, will you?'

'No, my darling, I shall always be here,' she answered, readily, because she was never surprised by his questions. He was such a strange little boy, and his thoughts would wander. She always knew what Vicky was thinking, but not Paul.

'I shall take you to Victoria and see you safely on the train,' Jane was saying. When they were ready to leave, she bade the children shake hands with Maggie, and when they walked down the street, she bade them wave to the women on their doorsteps and to call out 'Goodbye'.

'Such luverly manners,' Freddie's Mum told her son as they passed.

Freddie snatched up his crutches, hopped off the step, and offered his hand to Ellen. 'So long, Ma'am. Thank you for coming to see us,' he said, with unabashed courtesy.

'It was a pleasure, Freddie,' Ellen took the small thin hand and her eyes were tender.

Then he shook hands with Vicky and Paul. Jane was delighted, and Freddie's Mum as pleased as Punch.

'Trust our Fred ter be'ave like a genalman,' she told her neighbour.

A day to remember through the days and weeks of drudgery, with the smell of glue in her pinched nostrils, and the match-boxes piling up on the table. A day to remember, with Maudie singing like an angel with the Salvation, and Freddie shaking hands with the gentry.

Chapter Six

Three years have passed, three years of peaceful contentment for Ellen, and three years of quiet happiness for Paul. The seasons had come and gone. He had changed from his blue sailor suit into his white sailor suit on Easter Sunday, and back into the blue serge in October.

Another small event in the calendar seemed to take on a certain importance. The first of May marked the day when fires were no longer lit in the drawing-room, the dining-room and the nursery. In place of the glowing coals were fire-screens that remained in position till the first day of October, when they were removed and the fires were lit.

Paul was not the only one to warm his hands as the dancing flames leapt up the chimney. Grandmama would wear a dainty shawl round her shoulders and mittens on her hands on the chilly evenings of early Autumn in the drawing-room, but nothing or nobody would induce her to order the fires to be lit before the first of October. For Paul, the coal fires had a special significance. When he knelt on the hearthrug in the nursery and gazed into the fire, pictures of India were reflected in the dancing flames. Even the musky smell of India could be imagined as his thoughts flew back in time. He could see Ayah's dark, wrinkled face in the fire, and Boy serving his Papa with a chota peg, and the garden boy sprinkling the lawn with water from the hose. He could see the native bazaar, with all the colourful merchandise spread out for their inspection, and the young apprentices squatting on the floor of the dressmaker's small establishment.

Only when he was alone could he see these pictures in

177

the fire, because if Vicky was there beside him, she chatted of this and that, and there were no pictures in the fire. Vicky's imagination was more limited, and her day-dreams more logical. Her dark eyes saw a factual world – to see was to believe. There was a time when they played pretend games together, and Vicky's inventive mind could fill empty cups for a dolls' tea-party, and see a live baby in a bundle of shawls in a game of Mothers and Fathers, but those days had passed. They still played Ludo and Snakes and Ladders with Norah and Bertha in the basement breakfast room on wet Saturday afternoons, and they still bowled their hoops in the park, but this chapter of early childhood was coming to an end; both sailor suits would be packed away in mothballs, and the hoops discarded in the conservatory, together with buckets and spades and shrimping nets.

Paul captured each fleeting moment of happiness that last Summer in a forlorn attempt to delay the approach of *7 September* – the start of the new term at the prep school for which his Papa had entered his name. His name had also been entered for public school. As for Sandhurst, that would depend on whether he passed the entrance examination.

From time to time over the past three years, his stern Papa and his beautiful Mama would arrive from Aldershot to remind him he was still a child of the regiment. There was no escape. Even Nana had spoken of it that last Summer, trying to make it more acceptable, this undisputed fact that a son should follow in his father's footsteps, but Paul was still not ready to start on this fearsome journey from boyhood to manhood. Ayah would say it was the Will of Allah. Sister Angelica reminded him of his duty to 'Honour thy father and thy mother' according to the Scriptures. As for Grandmama, she could not understand how any son could dream of any other way of life. It was the law of the Medes and Persians that a son should follow in his father's footsteps. (Who were the Medes and Persians?)

'I don't want to be a soldier' carried no weight at all, not even with Vicky, who seemed to have forgotten that early pledge of marriage and dedication to the white heathens of Hoxton.

'You will get used to it, my darling,' Ellen told her

178

grandson as she sewed name tapes on all his clothes. But it was wishful thinking, and they both knew it.

The day came at last, as everyone knew it would, and the station cab was waiting outside the green gate. The driver carried out Paul's tin trunk and the tuckbox that Norah had filled with his favourite cakes, mincepies, home-made toffee, and coconut ice. Only Ellen would see Paul on the train, in charge of the guard. The train would be met by a master at Brighton, who would also meet the London train. Everything had been arranged.

Vicky had already started the new term at the convent. She had finished with the kindergarten, and was proud of her uniform in the upper school. No more black pinafores, and no more wet drawers. Her bladder was behaving perfectly.

She was living permanently at the flat with her Papa because her Mama had not come home from the Clinic, and did not want to come home. She was there, at the green gate, to give Paul a hug, then she was gone, racing back along the pavement. She turned to wave at the school gates, and disappeared.

Paul had been choked with tears since he woke to the awful realization that *7 September* was not just a date on the calendar, but an actual fact. He had promised Nana he would not cry, for she too had awakened with an aching heart for the little grandson being pushed out of his comfortable nest into a big, strange world.

'Boys don't cry,' Paul reminded himself, not for the first time that morning. When Norah walked in with the early morning tea and biscuits, like any other morning, she found him tucked up in Nana's bed for the last time, however. When he came home for the holidays, he would be shy of her and very conscious of his new status as a schoolboy. Dressed in his new Eton suit, he felt quite ridiculous and uncomfortably warm in the winter underwear. Eton suits were worn only on Sunday at prep school.

Following Nana down the stairs to the basement breakfast room, the faint smell of gas was as familiar as the warm smell of geraniums in the conservatory. Smells were important to Paul, and The Haven had a number of smells, apart from the gas and the geraniums – beeswax polish in the hall,

Jeyes Fluid in the outside lavatory, hot irons in the sewing room, wet mackintoshes in the lobby, and Grandmama's lavender water in the drawing-room.

Grandmama was remembering that other occasion, so long ago, when her darling boy had departed for the same prep school, wearing an Eton suit, and accompanied by the same tin trunk and tuck box. The same driver and cab had conveyed them both to the station. No two boys could have been more different in every way. Her darling boy had lost his curls, but his hair shone like a cap of gold on his handsome head, and his blue eyes were bold and challenging. Several inches taller than Paul at the same age, he had faced the future with unconcealed impatience, and had long since outgrown the convent kindergarten. Amelia felt no sense of pride in her great-grandson. He was so small and dark, so shy and secretive. In all the three years they had made no close contact, other than what was required for politeness' sake.

So when he walked into the drawing-room that morning, there was no change in her attitude, and no warmth in her manner. It was not her nature to pretend an affection she did not feel.

'Goodbye, Grandmama.' Paul kissed her soft cheek and stood back, waiting to be dismissed.

'Here is a half sovereign,' she said, taking the coin from her little purse.

'Thank you, Grandmama.'

'You will have to hand it over to the master for safe keeping. One shilling, and only one shilling a week for pocket money, I understand, no matter how wealthy your parents. It does not signify.'

'No, Grandmama.'

'How much have you collected from the rest of the family?'

'Eighteen shillings and sixpence.'

'A very lucky boy.'

'Yes, Grandmama.'

'Well, off you go, Paul. Behave yourself. Your Papa will expect to be proud of you.'

'Yes, Grandmama.' He turned and fled from her cold

blue eyes, tears pricking his own eyes, but he blinked them away. She did not love him, and he was still afraid of her. He knew for certain it would never be any different. Some things you could not change.

Nana was already seated in the cab. Auntie Bertha and Norah at the green gate.

'That's my brave boy.' Auntie Bertha's hug was quite frantic. Paul had a special place in the affections of this dour auntie with the sharp tongue, but the kind heart.

'I have put a calendar in the top of the tuck box, luv. You can tick off the weeks. It's only thirteen weeks to Christmas,' said Norah, as she gathered him into her plump bosom.

'Am I coming home for Christmas?' he asked, in a choked voice.

'Why, of course. Your parents are going to Switzerland.'

'I thought I might have to go to Aldershot for Christmas. Thank you for telling me, Norah.'

'You're welcome,' she answered, as always.

'Did you know my Papa and Mama were going to Switzerland, Nana?' he asked, as he settled down beside her.

'Yes, darling. I was keeping it till the last moment, when I saw you on the train.'

'Dear Nana,' he sighed. 'It is only thirteen weeks. That is not long, is it?'

Only thirteen weeks? When that small, frightened face at the window had disappeared in a cloud of steam, Ellen dabbed her wet eyes and walked slowly back down the platform. Her heart was heavy with an anguish she had not known since Prue went away to the Clinic. In three short years, she had enjoyed once again the precious companionship of young children. Now her small domain at the top of the house would be solitary, for Vicky was a visitor, not a resident, and when she came to tea on Saturday, she brought her best friend from whom she could not bear to be parted.

These thirteen weeks would be the longest Paul had ever known. He did not make friends as readily as Vicky, and she could hardly expect him to be popular at a school where sport was so important, since the only game he had played was cricket on the sands with an old tennis ball. The team spirit was encouraged, and Paul was a loner. So much would be demanded of that small boy, in his first term, and she would not be there to comfort him when he was hurt, to encourage him to try again when he failed, to remind him to be brave when he was afraid. There would be no night-light burning in that school dormitory. The stairs would be bare of carpet, but he still would see himself falling from top to bottom. Why? He could not explain. The fear was there in the sub conscious. He was still afraid of horses, yet Thomas had insisted on riding lessons, remembering his own pleasure in the saddle. But Thomas had belonged to the local pony club since the age of three, and did not know the meaning of fear. Compulsory swimming lessons in the public baths were another hazard for a child who had never ventured beyond the paddling stage. And this first term would also see him shivering on the touch line in shorts and jersey, waiting for the football to come his way, and invariably missing an opportunity to score. Healthy bodies and healthy minds. Fresh air was a fetish. Many a small boy would find snow on his bed on a bleak winter morning, and water frozen in ablutions.

Paul was not the only boy to spend a couple of weeks in sick bay with a nasty bout of bronchitis, but it was all part of the hardening process, in preparation for the rigours of public school at the age of thirteen. He shrank from the harshness of the system. It was a frightening initiation for a sensitive little boy. There was no privacy. To share a communal bath, straight off the playing field, and expose his small organ to ridicule, was an embarrassing ordeal. Bombarded with questions, Paul sought refuge in silence that earned him the nickname of Dumbbell.

When the first batch of letters was received at the end of that first interminable week, Paul was surprised and pleased to find a postal order for two shillings tucked inside the letter.

'It's from Nana,' he told the interested spectators, with innocent excitement.

'Cartwright has a nanny! Cartwright has a nanny!' they jeered.

182

'I haven't! She's not a nanny. She's my grandmother,' he retorted defensively. They didn't believe him, but they were glad enough to share the peg-tops and marbles he bought with the two shillings.

When he acknowledged the money, however, he wrote

Dear Gran,
Thank you for the money. Smith Minor says I should call you Gran now I am at prep school. I hope you are well.
Your loving grandson, Paulie.

'You can be my friend if you like, Cartwright,' said Smith Minor magnanimously, as they whipped their peg-tops with blue hands, on a foggy morning in November.

'Thank you. I *should* like,' Paul answered, gravely. Smith Minor had red hair and freckles, and an impish grin with which he faced the world. He had recently suffered a severe caning for climbing the chimney stack, and had to stand up to eat his dinner, his backside was so sore. It was a dare, and Smith Minor could not resist a dare.

'You can call me Carrots, and I shall call you Dumbbell,' said he, as a further concession to friendship.

Paul smiled his pleasure. To have Smith Minor for a friend was a great honour. He would share his triumph when he kicked a goal, swam the length of the bath, or ran a hundred yards in record time. Smith Minor was always breaking records. It probably saved him from more canings, because he did seem to break more rules than he obeyed. Masters and boys alike saw in him a future Olympic champion. For his age, he was practically unbeatable. Why he suddenly chose to befriend young Cartwright was not explained, for Smith Minor simply acted on impulse, and saw no reason to explain himself to anyone.

He had stepped off the London train, that first morning, with careless bravado, his new school cap perched jauntily on his flaming red head, blue eyes twinkling with good humour. The master who was waiting with Paul and three other boys who had boarded the train at Shoreham, recognized a rebel at first glance, and was not amused.

'Hullo!' said redhead, offering a sticky hand – the

London contingent had been sharing a bag of toffees.

'What is your name, boy?' The master was affronted by such casualness.

'Charles Smith.'

'You will oblige me, Smith, by removing your cap and addressing me as Sir.'

Smith obliged, but did not remove the cheeky grin from his freckled face.

'Your brother is head boy, is he not?' the master queried.

'That's right,' Smith agreed.

'Then we shall call you Smith Minor.'

Red head shrugged indifferently.

The bevy of small boys then introduced themselves with polite formality, snatching off their caps, then followed the master to the school bus.

It must be wonderful to have an elder brother already at the school, Paul was thinking enviously. But, as Grandmama would say, it does not signify. Smith Major was a tall, bespectacled 12-year old, who showed not the slightest interest in his young brother. They had nothing in common but the same parents.

From that first moment, when Smith Minor crowded in beside him, Paul was a devoted disciple, who followed his hero's exploits with something akin to worship. Only six months divided them in age, but a wide dimension in confidence and ability. They shared the same dormitory with six others, and shared the four tuck boxes. Smith Minor, Davenport, Hardy-Jones and Foster-Clarke did not bring tuck boxes, but it was considered bad form to enquire into the reason. The two shilling postal order had provided peg-tops and marbles for himself and his seven room-mates. Paul had no thought of bribery. It was doubtful whether he knew the meaning of the word. Smith Minor had shown him how to throw the top with a flick of the wrist. Paul was an apt pupil. They played with the marbles along the trench that collected the rainwater from the playground. It was more often wet than dry, but it was the only place available, and Smith Minor had discovered it. Somebody was always kicking a ball in the playground, or turning cartwheels, or playing Tag. The noise was deafening. They were letting off steam for exactly twenty minutes. When the first whistle blew, the stopped whatever they were doing, and stood like statues, not moving a muscle or blinking an eyelid, till the second whistle. Then they ran to get in line, and marched from the playground like soldiers from the parade ground. This was called 'discipline'. Paul had been acquainted with discipline from his earliest years, so it was no hardship. The Convent kindergarten had continued what the private governess had started. A stern Papa had insisted on it. Then there was Grandmama. Only Nana had spoilt her grandson, but that was a grandmother's privilege, she claimed with gentle persuasion.

Smith Minor was not amenable to discipline. Indeed he resented it. 'I do as I please when I am at home,' he boasted. 'There is nobody to say me nay but a stuffy old guardian who spends all his days in his study, writing the history of Ancient Greece.'

'What are your parents doing?' Paulie enquired tactfully.

'The parents are in Singapore.'

'What are they doing in Singapore?'

'Father is a civil engineer. He travels all over the world. Mother accompanies him everywhere. She says she is a good wife but a poor mother. It could be true, for we have not seen her for three years.'

It was the first time that Smith Minor had mentioned his parents. They were sharing a bar of Cadbury's nut milk chocolate one Saturday morning. Paul nibbled his portion of chocolate thoughtfully. Smith Minor had spoken of 'Father and Mother'. It sounded very sensible and grown up.

'Would you say it was rather childish, I mean, to speak of my Papa and Mama?' he asked, anxious to be worthy of prep school.

'It is a bit soppy, *actually*,' his friend answered. 'My brother and I always have used the more formal address, but then we never heard any baby talk, no nursery or nanny. When we were little, Mother looked after us. My brother was born in Baghdad. I was born in Calcutta, but we were never left to the care of native servants.'

185

'Ayah was a native servant, but I loved her. I still love her.'

'I thought you said she was dead?'

'She is dead.'

'How can you still love somebody who is dead?'

'I don't know, but I do.'

'I wouldn't know about that, for I have never loved anyone who is dead. The grandparents died before I was born. Father and Mother had no brothers and sisters, so we have no aunties or uncles.'

Paul was counting on his fingers. 'I have six aunts and five uncles.'

'You're lucky. You must get a lot of presents for Christmas and birthdays.'

'Yes, I do.'

'It won't be much fun staying here for Christmas,' Smith Minor sighed, gustily.

'Staying at school for Christmas?' Paul could think of no worse punishment.

'No point in going home. The old boy doesn't keep Christmas, anyway.'

'But you can't stay here. I shall ask Nana, I mean Gran, if you can spend Christmas at The Haven.'

'I say, Dumbbell, that's jolly decent of you.'

'That's all right, Carrots.' Paul blushed modestly.

'Would you object, Mother, if Paulie brought a little friend home for Christmas?' Ellen asked, tentatively, over the tea cups.

'It is no more than I expected,' her mother answered, with little enthusiasm. 'We shall think we are putting back the clock, shall we not? How well I remember that first Christmas, when Thomas brought Roderic. Such a dear little boy.'

Ellen refrained from mentioning that Thomas had not asked permission, but had just arrived with the little stranger on Christmas Eve.

'Who is this child?' Amelia asked, in a bored voice. There was no comparison. Her darling boy was entitled to bring a friend home when he so wished. She had felt a tiny bit affronted, but only because she had been so looking forward to her grandson's companionship, and had missed him intolerably during that first term at prep school. Thomas had quickly smoothed her ruffled feelings, however, with that disarming smile, and she found herself welcoming the little stranger with kind words of greeting.

'Paulie refers to his young friend as Smith Minor,' Ellen was saying. 'Such a droll way of speaking, is it not? It would seem this boy's parents are in Singapore, and he would perforce spend the Christmas holiday at school.'

'Quite so. We shall most likely be landed with the child every holiday from henceforth,' Amelia pointed out, reasonably enough.

'It would be unkind not to invite him, and Paulie would be disappointed,' Ellen answered, defensively.

'Paul should be gratified that he hasn't to spend Christmas at Aldershot.'

'But we do know that Thomas and Rosalind have already arranged to spend Christmas in Switzerland.'

'Quite so.'

'Did you expect them here for Christmas, Mother?'

'I did not.' Amelia was too proud to admit that she *had* expected them. They had disappointed her so often in the past three years. She blamed Rosalind, of course. The silly creature was bored in Worthing. Thomas should never have married such a flibberti-gibbet. She hadn't even produced a child her darling boy would be proud to call his son. And then to refuse to bear another. Fiddlesticks! Hadn't she herself borne six children? It was a wife's duty to bear children.

They were happy years, those early years of marriage. Old age was lonely. The days dragged interminably, and the ticking of the little carriage clock kept her awake a night.

'Then may I tell Paulie he can bring his friend home for Christmas?' Ellen interrupted, quietly.

'You may.' Amelia poured herself a second cup of tea and addressed her other daughter. 'I should be obliged, Bertha, if you would call at the Scotch Wool Shop tomorrow morning for another skein of the sage green embroidery cotton, and while you are in the vicinity of

187

Montague Street, more peppermint creams from Luffs, if you please.'

Bertha looked sulky. 'Couldn't it wait till the afternoon, when I have finished the chores?'

'What chores?'

'Tuesday is dining-room day.'

'That can be done on Wednesday.'

'Wednesday is bedroom day.'

'Really, Bertha, you can be so very provoking.'

Bertha would have liked to retaliate. Why couldn't Mother exert herself to take a walk to Montague Street to purchase her own embroidery cotton and peppermint creams? But Norah was pressing her foot under the table, warning her to be careful. Norah had no illusions about her own precarious position in the household, even after so many years of faithful service.

'I will help Bertha with her cleaning, and there will still be time for the shopping. I can do my baking in the afternoon,' she told her mistress.

'Quite so.' Amelia nodded agreement, but Bertha was so incensed, she landed a vicious kicked on Norah's ankle. Norah winced, but bore no malice. It was nothing new to be treated as a whipping post, and she had no pride. She listened to the discussion on the Christmas arrangements, but made no comment.

When they were back in the basement kitchen, she could indulge her happy feelings. 'Hurray! Two little boys for Christmas! And probably Vicky as well.' She hugged Bertha exuberantly.

'Not Vicky. She will be spending Christmas with her other Grandmother – Basil's mother. It's only fair. I dare say Basil will take all three children to the pantomime on Boxing Day, if he is not too tired. Christmas is the busiest season of the year at Thomas Brent & Son.'

'He will make the effort, for Vicky's sake. He dotes on that child, and can you wonder, with Prue still in that Clinic and likely to remain there for the rest of her days? Poor man.'

'*Silly* man, to marry the girl. He knew what she was like. We all knew. From the day Thomas was born, Prue was a trouble-maker. Jealousy can be soul destroying. I should know, my dearest. Until you came into my life, I was so jealous of Ellen and Grace, I could not bear to see them together. They were so pretty, so much admired, the one so dark, the other so fair. I was the odd one, the plain one. I wanted to be loved, but I was too disagreeable. But Vicky and Paulie like me, don't they? Say they do. Tell me the truth.'

'They love you, Bertha.'

'Yes, I believe they do. Have I mellowed, or are they nicer children?'

'You haven't changed very much, dear heart, but they are nice children. Mind you, Bella was a nice child, and quite unspoilt. Prue and Thomas had all the spoiling in that family. I wonder what this little boy will be like? Fancy calling a child Smith Minor. Queer ideas they have in these posh schools for boys. Eton suits for Sunday, and three sets of underwear. We were lucky to have one set in my childhood. When they were in the wash, we stayed home from school!' Norah chuckled at the memory, but Bertha was saddened.

'We always had three sets, Summer and Winter. I wish I had known you then. I would have given you a set of each.'

'Bless you, but it was no hardship to stay away from school. I was a proper dunce, anyway. Never could remember whether they made lace in Birmingham and knives in Nottingham, or vice versa.'

'Oh, my best beloved, what should I do without you?'

'And what should I do without you' Wrapping her arms around Bertha, Norah held her close. Wedded to one another, no man could destroy their life-long devotion.

'Full marks for music and scripture. Other subjects disgracefully low. Paul will have to do better than this.' Thomas was studying the school report for the first term with frowning brows. 'Music and scripture,' he scoffed. 'Two subjects he could well do without. From whom does he inherit such unlikely qualities, my sweet? Mother thinks he is exceptionally clever for his age, and that he plays quite advanced pieces on the piano, but Mother would be prejudiced in his favour, would she not?'

Rosalind agreed, bored with the subject of Paul's education.

The dutiful letter they received Monday morning was a copy of the one they had received the previous week.

Dear Father and Mother,
I hope you are well. I am well. Smith Minor scored two goals at the match. We went to chapel this morning. We had a nice walk on the downs.
Your loving son, Paul.

That Father and Mother was another sore point. Thomas had not expected to be so addressed by a child of such tender years, and had certainly not sanctioned it. Why no mention of the riding lessons?

'Should a child of seven be expected to write a weekly letter to his parents?' Rosalind asked, hiding a yawn. 'I do declare it seems so unnecessary. Why we should rejoice over a strange little boy scoring two goals is quite beyond my comprehension.'

'It would be, my sweet, since you have no experience of boarding school, and have consequently been spared this particular obligation. I can assure you the writer is every bit as bored as the recipient. To compile such a missive to Grandmama every Sunday afternoon required all my ingenuity.'

'Your Grandmama has kept every one of your letters.'

'Has she, by jove?' Thomas exclaimed, with unconcealed pleasure. He also found the subject of Paul's education somewhat boring, but it was a father's duty to show an interest in his son's progress, and nobody could accuse him of shrinking from his duty. As for Rosalind, she was mightily pleased to be spared any further discussion on a subject that could have dangerous repercussions if she spoke her thoughts aloud. *She* knew where Paul's love of music originated. It came from the same source as his religious tendencies. The Welsh are a musical people, and deeply religious. According to David, all their musical festivals had a religious foundation. She sometimes wondered whether he

190

deliberately misled her over his intentions to claim Paul as his son. Could she trust him? 'My word is my bond.' He had sworn to keep her secret, but that was seven years ago. If only Thomas were not so blatantly rude to David whenever their paths crossed. David had a smouldering temper that could erupt one day, and the truth would be told. If only he would marry a daughter of the regiment she could forget her fears of disclosure. Such an appalling scandal, such disgraceful conduct. Yet it pleased her vanity to have David still in love with her. His sultry dark eyes, and his singing Welsh voice, had the same compelling attraction as when they first met.

'The Head wants to see you in his study, Cartwright,' a senior boy announced, gleefully, in the doorway of the recreation room, after supper one evening.

Paul's face blanched. 'Me?' he asked.

'Yes, *you*. Six of the best'

All the younger boys stared as he stumbled to his feet.

'Chin up, Dumbbell,' Carrots whispered.

It was awful, the strong desire to pee in his pants as he hurried down the passage.

'Come in,' a strong voice invited, in answer to his timid knock. Imagination played tricks on a frightened small boy.

Behind his desk, in the lamplight, the familiar grey head seemed grotesquely magnified, the stern features formidable.

'What have I done, Sir?' Paul faltered.

The man's voice was gentle. 'What makes you think you are here to be punished?' he asked. A second generation of boys inhabited the classrooms, dormitories and playing fields. Time and again he recognized the features and the characteristics of that earlier generation, but not with this particular boy. With an astonishing memory of such likenesses, a vivid picture of Thomas Cartwright flashed across his mind − a handsome young scoundrel, taking his punishment for a smashed window with dignity.

'I remember your father, boy. He was not afraid of me.' He chuckled at the memory.

'No, Sir! My father is a soldier of the Queen. He is not afraid of anyone,' Paul ventured, still puzzled by the summons.

'An Army career is a splendid vocation, is it not?'

'Er – yes, Sir.'

'You seem a little doubtful?'

'I do not wish to be a soldier, Sir.'

'Indeed? What had you in mind?'

'A missionary, Sir.'

'Very commendable, Cartwright. Supposing your father withholds his permission?'

'I still want to be a missionary, Sir.'

The Head regarded the determined small boy with kindly grey eyes. 'As man to man, Cartwright, I admire your spirit, but you are making a mistake. In my long experience, I have seen scores of boys follow in their fathers' footsteps to the satisfaction of both parties. Quite a number have chosen Sandhurst, for no better reason than that their fathers, and in some cases, grandfathers, have been military men. Perhaps it is too soon to decide on such an important issue?' Why not wait awhile, and enjoy your schooldays, eh?'

Paul had listened politely, but his mouth was stubborn. He agreed because it would be rude to disagree, but he had known since his third birthday, when the groom sat him on his first pony, that he would never be a soldier.

'Now, are you not wondering why I sent for you?' the Head enquired.

'Yes, Sir,' Paul answered, obediently.

'I have received a note from Lieutenant David Jones. He tells me he is you uncle. He asks if you may be allowed to accompany him to a performance of the 'Messiah' at the Royal Albert Hall on Saturday next, and he suggests you bring a friend. He would meet the 1.50 train from Brighton at Victoria, and see you on the 5.50 train for the return journey. It is somewhat inconvenient on a Saturday to spare a master to put you in charge of the guard on that specific train. However, it *could* be arranged. I am wondering whether your relative is aware of your tender age for such an advanced entertainment?'

'Oh, yes, Sir. I should like it above all things.' Paul's

192

grave little face was suddenly alight with his rare smile.

'Is that so? Then I will reply to your uncle in the affirmative. Who will you take along on this excursion?'

'Smith Minor, Sir.'

'Let us hope his appreciation of the 'Messiah' matches your own, Cartwright.'

'Yes, Sir.'

'Then that is settled. You have my permission to leave.'

'Thank you, Sir.'

As the door closed behind the small figure, the man gazed thoughtfully into the fire. Smith Minor and the 'Messiah'? It seemed the most unlikely choice for that incorrigible young rascal, but of course there would be tea at Slaters, and the train journey, even in charge of the guard quite an adventure for two seven-year-olds. So the son of Thomas Cartwright had decided to be a missionary. Their short acquaintance, on Parents Day, had left an impression of arrogant superiority. That poor child would be up against a formidable opponent if he persisted in such a stubborn act of disobedience. It was unusual for a boy of such tender years to have any original ideas on the subject of a career, other than those already planted in his mind by a parent. A missionary. Now where did that idea originate? It would be interesting to watch developments. A father-son relationship was a fascinating study. Delving into the archives of this particular family, however, he soon discovered that Paul Cartwright's great-grandfather had been Vicar of St Margaret's, Worthing. So there was a connection. The church and the army together could be relied upon to produce an element of courage that soon became evident in these early years at prep school. There was courage as well as fear in that small boy. He was no weakling, and he would survive. It pleased the Head enormously to search the archives of family histories, and discover an answer to that vital question of heredity. But it was wishful thinking, and he would have to delve much deeper to discover the truth about young Paul Cartwright − if he ever did. There was no clue to his identity, for the one person who could have claimed responsibility was sworn to secrecy.

There was no mistaking those two little lads, in their Eton

suits, marching proudly along the platform escorted by the guard, and with a sense of wonder and delight David recognized in Paul, himself at the same age. The guard received the florin and the lieutenant's thanks with a muttered, 'They wasn't no trouble, Sir.'

Both boys sprang to attention, and snatched off their caps. Such a formal occasion demanded a formal salutation. Paul smiled shyly, and took the outstretched hand. 'How do you do, Sir. This is my friend, Smith Minor.'

'How do you do, Smith Minor?'

'How do you do, Sir?' Smith Minor grinned.

'Was it a pleasant journey?' asked the lieutenant.

'Yes, Sir, thank you, Sir,' they chorused.

'Did they give you anything to eat?' he asked, conversationally.

'We had a packet of sandwiches and an apple. It was fun,' Smith Minor answered promptly.

And Paul echoed, 'It was fun.'

The lieutenant nodded. 'Then we will proceed forthwith to the Albert Hall.'

'Yes, Sir,' they chorused.

Pulling on their caps, they followed at a gallop the tall, striding figure to the cab rank. In the closed cab, the lieutenant had no need to search his mind for a suitable topic of conversation. Smith Minor had a fund of tales to relate, and needed no prompting. Paul listened, and nodded approvingly. It was very important that Uncle David should like Smith Minor.

The shyness that he felt in his company could only be explained by their long separation. With a sense of shock and dismay, Paul was reminded he was still a child of the regiment. In the three years that had passed since their last meeting, the scarlet uniform had been seen only on his parents' rare visits, and quickly forgotten in his small world of The Haven and the Convent kindergarten. The glancing dark eyes of the handsome lieutenant searched for a likeness in the clinging child he had last seen and the independent little boy in the Eton suit. The shyness between them was a tangible thing, and the chatter of Smith Minor did nothing to lessen it. Had they been alone in the cab, sitting side by side, making contact, David would have slipped an arm about those narrow shoulders and held him close. This was his son, and they were strangers. The thought was unbearable, yet there was no way to rectify the mistake. And it was a mistake. Only a sentimental fool could be expected to keep such a pledge. Seven years of bitter frustration and envy, with the certain knowledge that his hated rival could claim both a wife and a son.

Had they been alone in the cab, they could have talked of India and Ayah, and those two indestructible creatures – Elephant and Teddybear. A whimsical smile played about his mouth. He could see the child, newly breeched, hoisted on his first pony, and Ayah in the background, clutching the two rejected toys. Papa had given his orders, and Papa had to be obeyed.

'Is that the Albert Hall, Sir?' Smith Minor interrupted, excitedly.

'Albert 'all!' the driver pulled the cab to a halt with careless disregard of the waiting carriage and its distinguished occupants. The boys scrambled out, and gazed, awestruck, at the magnificent memorial to the saintly Albert.

'Gosh!' breathed Smith Minor, visibly impressed.

'It's very ugly, Sir, is it not?' Paul ventured.

David chuckled. 'Out of the mouths of babes. Very ugly,' he agreed, as he pulled a handful of coins from his pocket to pay the driver, then led the way. Even Smith Minor was silenced by the size of the vast auditorium, and Paul's grave little face masked the wonder and delight in such and imposing façade.

There was barely time to take their seats before the gowned ladies of the choir slipped quietly into their places, followed by the men. Row upon row of closely packed figures, matching the vastness of the crowded auditorium. The conductor took his place on the rostrum, turned to bow, then raised his baton. The poignant strains poured over them, and when the voices soared, David shivered involuntarily, and settled down to listen, a boy on either side, each nursing his cap.

The boy on his right was tense and nervous, his senses reeling with the enormity of the sound and his own smallness.

It was frightening. Then his hand was taken in a firm, warm clasp, and the tenseness went out of him. The stranger of the cab was gone. The handsome lieutenant, in the scarlet uniform, reminding him he was still a child of the regiment, was really Uncle David. Spellbound, linked together by an awareness of belonging, of soul reaching out to soul, father and son, no longer separated by distance, by circumstance, by shyness. For the man, the culmination of a dream. For the boy, the strengthening of a bond, hitherto as tenuous as his hold on Ayah, on Auntie Millie, on Elephant and Teddybear.

While the music sobbed and the voices soared, the man and the boy were alone together, alert and sensitive to every vibrant sound, enclosed in a world of dreamlike quality, far removed from the stark reality of their separate lives. The haunting story unfolded with a pathos that caught at the throat, and stirred the imagination of the Welsh idealist and the fruit of his loins. David knew every word, every note of music, for his own voice had been lifted in passionate salute to the Redeemer with the massed choir of his native city. His lips moved in soundless repetition, his dark eyes reflected his innermost thoughts and emotions. The small hand quivered in the warm clasp of his fingers, and the sighing breath of his son held a benediction of a close relationship, still unheralded and secret, but so binding.

Slumped in his seat, Smith Minor chewed a toffee, bored to tears − and wondered if Hopkins had scored a goal. It seemed such a silly waste of time, listening to something he could only describe as an awful noise. It made his head ache. The tedium of the long afternoon was alleviated, however, by the bag of toffees in his pocket. One by one they disappeared into his bulging cheek, as he waited for the end. It was a shattering experience he would not wish to repeat, even with the promise of tea at Slaters.

Startled from a little nap by the crashing chords of the National Anthem, Smith Minor stumbled to his feet and stood to attention beside the tall lieutenant. This was the best part of the performance! As for Cartwright, the poor little devil looked positively dazed, and no wonder.

'Sorry about the toffees. I forgot to share them,

and I have eaten them all,' Smith Minor whispered, as they followed the lieutenant down the crowded aisle.

'Toffees?' Paul echoed, blankly. 'What toffees?'

Chapter Seven

Ellen had seen it all before, and knew exactly how to behave. There would be no kisses, no warm hugs on the station platform. Small boys from prep school were so easily embarrassed. So she stood there, calmly dignified, her dark eyes soft as velvet, watching the two small boys in their Eton suits, stepping off the train the day before Christmas Eve. All the loving tendencies of her maternal nature were held in check as they stood before her, and snatched off their caps. The dark head and the red head, so strikingly different.

Frowning anxiously, Paul reached out a hand and stammered, 'Hel-lo, Gran.'

'Hello, Paul,' she answered dutifully, as they shook hands.

'This is my friend, Smith Minor,' he told her, proudly.

'How do you do, Ma'am,' he said, with a stiff little bow, his hand outstretched.

'How do you do, Smith Minor,' Ellen smiled, but kept her dignity. The little ceremony that she remembered so well had been performed with the same sustained politeness. The difference was in the boys themselves. Neither her grave little grandson, nor the cheeky red head, bore any resemblance to the handsome, self-assured Thomas, or the shy little Roderic of an earlier generation. This regimented system of education for the sons of the upper class could never entirely eliminate individual characteristics. For all the moulding into shape, the communal habits of eating, sleeping and bathing, the playing fields and the spartan hardihood, there they stood,

198

only outwardly changed by the system. Underneath the veneer of manliness, Ellen would find a little boy very like the one who had shared her bed and morning tea in those early days at The Haven, and his freckled companion as ready to enjoy a spoonful of mincemeat as the young Roderic. 'There is a time and a place for everything,' as Grandmama would say, and a station platform was certainly not the place to embrace her small grandson. Dignity must be maintained by both parties. The system had been established too long to be discarded or disrupted by normal behaviour. But Ellen had seen the slight hesitation in Paul, and sensed the struggle to control the urge to fling himself into her arms.

'I will wait here while you find a porter to handle your luggage,' she told the boys, and they ran off obediently, for obedience was second nature now, even for Smith Minor, after only one term at school. For Paul it was as natural as breathing. They were quickly back, with a grinning porter pushing a laden trolley. Two tin trunks and one tuck box. It was happening all over again. She would mother Smith Minor as she had mothered Roderic. Mabel would wash his clothes, and Norah would fill an extra tuck box. As for Amelia, she would soon lose interest in the newcomer for the simple reason he was a friend of Paul's, and she had no affection for her great-grandson.

Ellen led the way to the waiting cab, followed by the boys and the porter. When he had stacked the luggage beside the cabbie, he received his sixpence, touched his cap respectfully, and trundled away to the next passenger. Ellen lifted her long skirts and climbed in. The cab was a luxury, and Grandmama had not offered to pay. The porter could have pushed the luggage on his trolley, for it was only a short distance, but it would please her grandson to drive in state up to the green gate.

The boys sat facing her, and there was hardly time to ask whether Paul had recovered from a recent attack of bronchitis that had kept him in sick bay for two weeks, and to enquire after the health of Smith Minor's parents in Singapore. Nobody was waiting at the green gate, but Norah had hurried up the back stairs to fling open the front door when she heard the rattle of wheels. Her homely face

199

beamed a welcome, and her white starched apron smelled of baking as she enfolded Paul is a warm hug. 'So there you are, my lamb. Just in time for tea,' she said, not giving a thought to his acute embarrassment. It was doubtful if she even knew the meaning of the word.

And when he introduced his friend, she chuckled. 'Smith Minor? Is that what they call you at that posh school? Now isn't that daft? What's your proper name, luv?'

'It's Charles, Ma'am.'

'That's more like it. And you call me Norah. I'm right glad to see you two boys, for Christmas without children is no fun at all,' she told them, as she hung their caps on the pegs in the lobby. 'It's like old times, I told your Auntie Bertha. She's lying down with one of her nasty sick headaches, poor soul. She sent her love.'

'Do you want any help with that?' she called after the cabbie, who was struggling up the stairs with a tin trunk.

'No thanks, Missus,' he called back cheerfully. Ellen had offered him an extra shilling to carry the two trunks to the top floor. He was glad of the money, with a sick wife wasting away with that accursed consumption, and four young children to support on a cabbie's precarious livelihood.

'Best say hello to your Grandmama, Paulie, hadn't you?' Norah nodded at the closed door of the drawing-room.

Paul sighed. This was the moment he had been dreading, and his timid tap on the door only made matters worse, for Grandmama was a little deaf, and he was obliged to tap again. The summons to enter could still frighten him into an urge to pee in his pants, and he pushed open the door, stepped inside and glanced nervously at his great-grandmama. Nothing had changed. There she sat, enthroned in her favourite chair, silvery hair piled becomingly on her proud little head. A tortoiseshell comb glistened in the firelight, and the same cameo brooch fastened the dainty lace fichu at her throat. The tea gown was a pretty shade of blue, and matched her eyes, the gown she had worn for the first time at the homecoming of her darling boy. The colour had faded, like her eyes, but it would do, she had decided. Paul was not a favourite. He was dark when he

200

should have been fair. He was such a big disappointment.

'Well, Paul, have you lost your tongue?' It was her usual greeting. His tongue was not lost, but it cleaved to the roof of his mouth so he could not answer her.

'Excuse me, Ma'am, but Cartwright has been indisposed in sick bay, and is not feeling quite himself,' Smith Minor explained, defensively.

'It does not signify, young man. My grandson is cursed with the poorest constitution. Born in India. And what are you doing here?'

'I was invited, Ma'am.'

'Were you indeed? The first I have heard of it. Nobody tells me anything.'

Norah spread her hands and shook her head in swift denial of such a statement. Grandmama still had the last word on everything, and the deafness was a blind. She heard what she wanted to hear. Of course she had been consulted. Ellen would never have dared to invite a little stranger for Christmas without her consent. Standing outside the half open door, Norah could hear every word, and her heart bled for her poor lamb. He was such a nervous little boy. It would seem that young Charles had no fear of the old lady, for he was answering her questions respectfully, but quite boldly, 'She will like that boy because he is not afraid of her,' Norah was thinking.

'You may kiss me, Charles,' Amelia invited. Then, a moment later. 'Well, Paul have you found your tongue?'

'Yes, Grandmama.'

'Speak up, child. There is no occasion for you to whisper.'

'My throat hurts.'

'Did they not give you anything in sick bay for a sore throat?'

'Matron gave me a drink of lemon and honey.'

'A drop or two of Friar's Balsam on a lump of sugar, much more effective in my opinion. Did she rub your chest with camphorated oil?'

'Yes, Grandmama.'

'All my children had their chests rubbed every night in the winter months. Prevention is better than cure.'

'Yes, Grandmama.'

('And who did the rubbing? Not you, I'll be bound,' Norah was thinking.)

'A soldier's son must learn to put up with a little discomfort without complaining. Your dear Papa will expect to find you showing a little more fortitude, will he not?'

'Yes, Grandmama.'

'Very well, we will not harp on the matter since you do look rather peaked. I should prefer not to be kissed. There is no occasion to spread germs. We will shake hands and have done with it. I do declare you are cold as charity. Kneel down on the rug and warm your hands.'

Paul obeyed.

'And you may ring the bell for tea, young man. The bell is on the hall table.'

'Yes, *Ma'am.*' Smith Minor shot out of the door, his flaming red head colliding with a buxom bosom. Norah put a finger to her lips and pointed at the bell. Then she ran down the back stairs to brew a pot of tea.

Ellen was perched on the edge of the sagging old sofa in the breakfast room. The curtains were drawn, and the gas turned low. Bertha's eyes were closed, and her forehead was covered with a cold compress. Ellen had emptied the basin, but the stench of vomit was sour in the darkened room. She held her sister's limp, clammy hand in a warm clasp, but Bertha wished she would go away. Even Norah had been told 'Leave me alone', but Norah knew her too well to take offence.

Kettles were boiling on the kitchen stove, and when she had filled the big silver teapot and hot water jug, Norah carried the heavy silver tray to the dining-room, and set it down in front of Amelia who was already seated at the head of the table. Without the assistance of Bertha, it had taken nearly an hour to prepare the meal, for everything had to be carried up the back stairs. She was pleased with the appetising display of wafer-thin bread and butter, home-made strawberry jam and blackcurrant jam, a rich fruit cake and a madeira cake, all spread out on a pretty embroidered cloth. It was not such a lavish display as on those special occasions when all the family sat round the table, but for two youngsters from prep school it would seem like a feast. Seated one on either side

202

of Grandmama, they waited for the signal to start. Norah slipped into her place beside Charles, and Ellen sat down next to Paul.

'Why is Bertha not here?' She clucked impatiently when she was told that Bertha was lying down with a sick headache.

'She had one only a couple of weeks ago,' she reminded Norah, as she poured tea into the dainty cups.

'Yes, she seems to be getting them about twice a month now. It must be the change of life, for she gets the hot flushes,' Norah explained, as she handed round the bread and butter.

Amelia frowned. 'There is no occasion to enlarge on the matter in front of the children.'

'You asked what was wrong with Bertha and I was telling you.'

'Don't be impertinent!'

'Sorry.' Norah's homely face was flushed. It was so unlike her to retaliate, Ellen wondered if she was also going through that most uncomfortable process, too delicate to mention at the tea table. The subject was dropped like a hot coal, while the boys helped themselves to strawberry jam. Prep school teas had a sameness five days weekly – thick doorsteps of bread and margarine, *or* bread and jam. On Saturday, being sports day, a high tea of sausages and fried potatoes was served after the communal bath. Sunday it was bread and butter and a slice of cake. Children were not encouraged to talk at Amelia's table, but it was no hardship, for the boys were too busy eating.

Firelight danced on the polished brass fender and on the fire-irons. It was a big room, comfortably furnished, the walls hung with oil paintings in gilt frames. The tall Christmas tree in the window recess would be decorated by Ellen and the boys tomorrow.

Amelia sipped a third cup of tea and waited for the boys to finish eating. Charles had a second slice of the rich fruit cake, and Paul had a second slice of madeira, in order not to lag behind, The fruit cake was too heavy for his weak stomach, and he could always depend on Norah to slice the madeira without explanation.

When they had finished, they bowed their heads while Grandmama said grace. 'For what we have received, may the Lord make us truly thankful.' Then the boys stood up, politely, until she had left the table. Such politeness was practiced every day at school, where the Head presided over meals.

'Come into the drawing-room to collect your pocket money. I dare say you will wish to be away early tomorrow for your Christmas shopping.'

Both boys were surprised and pleased by the summons. Charles had received postal orders from Singapore, and Paul his usual pocket money, but it was not nearly enough for the presents they were expected to buy – on the doubtful principle that it is more pleasant to give than to receive!

When Grandmama took two half-sovereigns from her little purse, Paul could have hugged her he was so grateful, but Grandmama was not a huggable person. They took the coins with a formal little bow, and chorused, 'Thank you very much'.

She patted their heads and smiled benignly. 'There now. Run along and help Norah. She is somewhat fretful. Take care on the back stairs, and close the door if you please. I have letters to write, and do not wish to be disturbed.'

'Gosh!' breathed Charles, as the door closed behind them. 'Am I glad I don't have a grandmother.'

'But she did give us a half-sovereign each,' Paul reminded him.

'True enough. I am not ungrateful. Just stating a fact. Come on, show me those back stairs. Why do we have to be careful?'

'Because it is rather dark, and that makes it dangerous.'

That word 'dangerous' could be said to attract Smith Minor like a red rag to a bull, but had the opposite effect on Paul. Even after three years at The Haven he was still nervous of the back stairs. But he couldn't bear to lose face with his best friend, or to be thought a coward. It was so humiliating. 'Cowardy, cowardy custard!' the boys had chanted when he shrank from the plunge into the swimming bath. And somebody pushed him in.

Ellen was already helping Norah to clear the table, and she smiled encouragingly at the boys as she piled up the plates. Norah disappeared through the little green gate at the top of the back stairs with a loaded tray.

'Give me something to carry down, please, Ma'am,' Charles demanded eagerly, and Ellen handed him a couple of plates.

'Take care,' she called after him, automatically, as he followed Norah down the stairs.

'Oh, *Nana*!' Paul sighed, as she hugged him tightly.

'I have missed you so much, my darling,' she whispered, and kissed the top of his head where his hair lay dark and shining.

When Charles clattered back up the stairs, they broke apart.

'Get a move on, Dumbbell. What are you waiting for?' he said, shattering that precious moment of intimacy.

Paul picked up a couple of plates and led the way down those hateful stairs. Once he had mentioned to Vicky the slight smell of gas on the back stairs. He thought there might be an explosion and they would all be blown to smithereens.

'Don't be silly. It's just one of those smells that belong to The Haven, like the geranium smell in the Conservatory, and the Jeyes Fluid smell in the outside lavatory,' she told him, She was right, of course, for this particular smell was still here, and he had been away for three whole months.

But Smith Minor thought it was fun, and had not even noticed the gas smell. He had to be constantly employed or he got bored. It was not so noticeable at school because they were kept busy all the time, from the moment they opened their eyes at the start of a new day to the moment they closed them again, at lights out. So he followed him up and down the stairs till the table was cleared.

'What shall we do now?' was a question never asked at school because they were told what to do and had no choice in the matter.

Paul looked at Nana for inspiration.

'We will ask Norah if she would like any help with the

washing up,' she said. Mabel had gone home, and the dirty dishes were stacked in the scullery.

But Norah would not hear of it. 'Take the boys upstairs. Their noise will disturb Bertha,' she said, with such unusual sharpness, Ellen stared at her in astonishment. Norah had never complained of noisy children, and her welcome had been so warm.

'Norah is worried about Auntie Bertha,' she explained, as she bustled the boys up the back stairs. Two more flights of stairs to the top of the house, and Smith Minor leaping like a mountain goat.

'Lovely banisters to slide down,' he chuckled. 'It's going to be fun.'

Ellen smiled indulgently. It had been a long time since a boy had slid down these banisters. She remembered Thomas leading the way, yelling like a banshee, and Roderic following with set lips and frightened eyes. It might be good for Paul to have a friend like Charles, but she knew her poor darling would be sick with fright if he was expected to slide down the banisters. She wondered how they were going to keep Charles amused till bedtime. She could not imagine this lively little redhead playing Ludo. While they were changing from the Eton suits into something more comfortable, she turned out the boxes of toy soldiers, the fort and the gun carriages.

Charles fell on them with squeals of delight. They fought mock battles and fired the guns, and the soldiers fell like ninepins. Charles was quite intoxicated with the slaughter. Flat on his stomach, directing operations, his freckled face was flushed with excitement and the heat of the fire.

Ellen sat quietly, watching and listening, busy with her knitting. Paul was only pretending to enjoy the battles and the slaughter. Some of the soldiers had never been out of their boxes. Thomas still sent new ones every Christmas, and Paul still declared, 'I don't want to be a soldier'.

Now here was a boy that Thomas would be proud to call his son, destined for Sandhurst and leadership.

At 7 o'clock she left them to fetch the cocoa from the kitchen, to save Norah climbing all those stairs. She was anxious about Norah. Something was wrong. It was not only that Bertha was indisposed the day before Christmas

206

Eve. Norah could normally cope with any extra work.

The door of the breakfast room was open, and she could see the shapes of the two women in the darkened room. Bertha was drinking a cup of tea, and Norah was sitting on the edge of the sofa. She got up and came to the door.

'Did you want something?' she asked wearily.

'I came down for the cocoa,' Ellen explained quietly.

'Just as well. I had forgotten it.'

'I can make it, if you show me where to find everything.'
The kitchen was Norah's domain. Only Bertha shared it.

'While I'm showing you, I can do it,' Norah grumbled.

Ellen stood waiting, surprised and hurt by the unexpected rebuff. When it was ready, she picked up the three mugs of cocoa on the tin tray, thanked Norah, and went back upstairs. She always kept a tin of sweet biscuits in the cupboard, and the boys could help themselves.

As she climbed the stairs, she wondered afresh about Norah's strange behaviour. Bertha's bad temper was to be expected, but Norah had always been the go-between, softening the edge of that sharp tongue with her unfailing cheerfulness and good humour. 'Neither family nor servant' would be Norah's epitaph if Grandmama had her way. But Ellen could think of a better one – 'Beloved sister of Ellen, Grace, Bertha, Jane, Kate and Lucy.' The Haven would never be the same if ever they lost Norah.

The battles still raged on the nursery floor, but the cocoa was cooling. Charles was reluctant to tear himself away from the battlefield, but Paul sighed with relief. Sitting on the hearth-rug, drinking cocoa and selecting their favourite biscuits from the tin, they made their plans, with Ellen, for Christmas Eve. Shopping in the morning, with hot chocolate and sugar buns at Kong's. Decorating the hall, the dining-room and the nursery with Norah in the afternoon, and the Christmas tree in the evening. There would be presents to wrap and cards to write. It would be a busy, exciting day. Christmas Day would follow the same pattern as other years, with church in the morning, the big Christmas dinner, the children playing with their new toys in the afternoon, the special tea, games – hide-and-seek, blind man's buff, and hunt the thimble. The day would finish with their favourite carols, with Grandmama at the piano.

It was strange without Vicky this year, but Paul had Charles. It was a new chapter. The pantomime was arranged for Boxing Day, when Basil would escort four children, since Vicky's best friend must be included in the invitation. Grandmama and Ellen both wished they could put the clock back to the days when all the family forgathered at The Haven. Now they made their excuses and their own arrangements.

Amelia had at last to accept the fact that her summons would not be obeyed. Christmas without her darling boy was a travesty. 'I do declare I have no heart for it,' she told Ellen, as she unwrapped the fourth bottle of lavender water.

Basil presided over tea at Mitchell's like a father-figure. It was the customary conclusion to the Boxing Day matinée, and he had reserved a table. The restaurant hummed with the excited chatter of happy children, and Basil liked to think that other patrons of this popular rendezvous were speculating on the relationship of his family – a red-head, brown, fair and dark. There was the family likeness, so it was assumed he was a favourite uncle indulging his young nieces and nephews. It was a jolly tea-party, with three of the children arguing good-humouredly on the sex of the principal boy and the riddles posed by the 'funny man'. Paul sat quietly. The excitement had given him a headache, and his weak stomach was still a little queasy after the Christmas Day feasting. He envied Smith Minor his amazing digestion. Yesterday he had hardly stopped eating all day. Now he was helping himself to a third chocolate éclair. It had been a shock to discover his best friend gave no thought to the true meaning of Christmas, or the birth of the Christ child. He had been brought up with the belief that Christmas was a pagan festival, and the tree, the holly, the ivy, and the mistletoe were symbols of that festival. His parents were not Christians, but for their son at an English prep school attendance at church or chapel was an obligation. It had no more meaning than his attendance at the gymnasium or the swimming bath. He did not say his prayers, and the Bible stories that Paul had loved were coupled with nursery rhymes

208

for the amusement of infants. There was a kind of honesty about his unchristianlike belief and behaviour, for he made no secret of the fact.

Uncle David had written to Paul to ask what he would like for Christmas, and Paul had asked for a Bible. It was his favourite present, and he examined its coloured pictures of the Holy Land with the same intent interest as Smith Minor examined every intricate part of his new Meccano set. It was a revelation, this discovery, on their first Christmas together. It made no difference to their friendship, but it saddened Paul because Jesus was a very real person. The Sisters at the Convent kindergarten had nourished the seed planted by Auntie Millie in India.

To have a friend like Smith Minor was both a privilege and a problem, for they did not think the same thoughts. As for Vicky, she had changed so much since September he hardly recognized her. She was still giggling with her best friend when Uncle Basil announced, 'I am sending you two boys home by cab. It is too far for you to walk.'

'Thank you, Sir,' they chorused.

The Haven was like a ship at sea, ablaze with lights. Not a curtain was drawn on this cold December night, and that was surprising, for Grandmama always had the curtains pulled by 4 o'clock on winter afternoons.

The boys stood for a moment inside the green gate, admiring the Christmas tree, framed in the French windows. Tinsel and baubles sparkled in the gaslight, and the silver star atop the tree shone as brightly as a star in the sky.

'Come on, let's get inside. We can fight another battle before supper,' Smith Minor urged, and rapped loudly on the brass knocker.

They waited and waited, but nobody answered the knock. Paul tapped on the dining-room window, but he could not see beyond the spreading branches of the tree. He shivered in the cold night air. Something was wrong. Something had happened.

Smith Minor rapped impatiently on the brass knocker, grumbling at the tardiness of people who did not open their doors.

'I'm frightened,' Paul whispered, hugging himself on the

209

doorstep. Then, at last, the door opened, and Grandmama stood there – Grandmama, who never opened doors, was standing there, and she seemed to have shrunk since they last saw her.

'Where have you been?' she demanded, irritably.

'To the pantomime, Ma'am, with Uncle Basil and the girls, and we had tea at Mitchell's,' Smith Minor told her.

'I had forgotten. So much has happened. I feel quite faint. Somebody has hidden my smelling salts. You had better come in. It's draughty standing here.'

They stepped inside, and closed the door. Even Smith Minor was worried now. The old lady looked so strange. There was an eerie silence in the house, and no other sound but her shuffling feet as she pottered back across the hall. In the open door of the drawing-room, she seemed to remember she had not explained why she had answered the door, and she turned to confront them.

'We have had no tea. Norah is dead. It does not signify,' she said, with weary resignation, and went inside and closed the door.

'Norah – dead?' breathed Paul.

'She can't be,' Smith Minor contradicted. 'She was shovelling coal on that fire when we left, and she told me she had made another nice trifle for supper. So she can't be dead, can she?'

'I don't know.' Paul was trembling with shock.

Where was Nana? Why didn't she come? He was so frightened. In the silent house the two small boys waited, for what? Then they heard somebody moving about in the basement, and footsteps on the back stairs – slow, dragging footsteps. They crept forward till a tall figure emerged through the little green gate, and they saw the tears on her stricken face. So it was true.

Speechless, she opened her arms and gathered them close. The dining-room fire had burned out. Tea was laid, but untouched. Ellen sank on to a chair and stared at them with anguished eyes.

'I can't believe she has gone. It was so sudden. She was brewing a pot of tea in the kitchen. She just collapsed and died.' She covered her face and wept, distraught.

210

The silver star on the top of the tree had lost its brightness. There was no warmth in the room, no sound but the weeping of a woman who never wept. It was the end of an era. Without that bright spirit, the house seemed to close in on itself, like the lonely old woman who had shut herself in the drawing-room.

'Nana', Paul gulped. 'Please don't cry.'

She lifted her head, her dark eyes drowned in tears, and shivered involuntarily.

'Shall we go upstairs? She asked. 'It's cold in here.'

'Yes,' they nodded, and followed her stooped figure. On the first landing, she put a finger to her lips and whispered, 'Auntie Bertha is sleeping. The doctor gave her a sleeping draught.'

Then they climbed the stairs to the top floor. Ellen dropped to her knees to poke the damped down fire into a blaze. Still dazed with shock, she seemed to forget the boys as she knelt there.

'I feel sick,' Paul whispered.

Then she was all maternal again, forgetting self in her anxiety over the child.

'Excuse me, Charles,' she said, and hurried him into the bedroom.

Smith Minor pulled a face at the unpleasant noises in the adjoining room. A healthy little animal, he had never been sick in his short life, and was consequently impatient with other sufferers. Standing on the hearthrug, hands thrust into his pockets, he wondered if they would be sent back to school tomorrow. It had not taken him long to realize it was Norah who did most of the work. He liked Norah. Who would fill their tuck boxes if Norah was dead? And where *was* Norah? Pondering on these important issues, he looked around for some kind of amusement and spotted the old rocking-horse. Climbing on its back, he rocked to and fro, wishing he had a toffee to suck. Imagine Cartwright being sick when he had nothing more than one toasted muffin for tea? Those chocolate éclairs were scrumptious.

He was hungry again. He was always hungry. Such a waste that nice tea laid out in the dining-room and nobody had touched it. Who would carry everything down the back stairs if Norah was dead? They were going to help her make more mincepies. She had promised they could eat the sugar in the candied peel. He sighed and went on rocking.

'So you have found the old rocking-horse, Charles.' Ellen was standing in the doorway. She was very pale. 'I have put Paul to bed,' she said. 'Can you amuse yourself with the soldiers, or shall we play a game of Ludo?'

'I can amuse myself with the soldiers, thank you, Ma'am.'

'I do wish you would call me Gran. After all, you are one of the family now.'

'Am I?'

'Of course. I am so very grieved this had to happen on your first visit. You must come again at Easter. We always go to the Goring Woods to pick primroses to decorate the church for Easter Sunday. Once upon a time we all rode our bicycles, all six sisters, and we took a picnic lunch. It was such a happy occasion.' She seemed to be talking more to herself than the child, her dark eyes reflecting nostalgic memories.

Smith Minor stopped rocking, slid off the horse, and wandered back across the room to kneel on the hearthrug.

'Where is Norah?' he asked, looking up at her with frank curiosity.

'She is lying on the sofa in the breakfast room. We carried her there, the doctor and I.'

'Does she know she is dead?'

'That is a question I cannot answer.'

'Shall we be sent back to school?'

'Not if I have my way.'

'We shouldn't be a nuisance.'

She smiled, tremulously. 'It all depends on Grandmama.'

'I understand.'

'Will you excuse me if I leave you again to amuse yourself? Grandmama is so very distressed, I think I should sit with her for a while. Then I will make her cocoa, and our cocoa. Paul can give his stomach a rest until tomorrow. You know where to find the soldiers?'

'Yes, Ma'am – Gran.'

'Bless you, Charles.' She squeezed his small shoulders. He

was such a little fellow, but he had the looks and the manner of a much older boy. He was so good for her Paulie. She turned away, with a swish of her long skirts, and vanished through the door.

Now he was alone. The thought of her making cocoa in that basement kitchen, with Norah lying dead in the breakfast room, sent a cold shiver down his spine. It was altogether beyond the scope of his limited imagination – the dead Norah. He could see her alive in his mind's eye, quite clearly. A big, jolly woman in a white apron. Her sudden death frightened him, and fear was an unfamiliar element. To be so alive in the morning, and to be dead in the afternoon. How was it possible?

To be alone with his fear in the silent house was an alarming experience, but he had to put up with it till that nice Gran person came back with the cocoa. Fetching the boxes of soldiers and the fort from the toy cupboard, he made a pretence of forming the columns of artillery and infantry that would storm the fort. The few brave survivors of the siege were at their posts, standing over the dead bodies of their comrades. They would fight to the last man and never surrender. He knew all the rules and all the manoeuvres of such a siege, but something was missing today, and there was no sense of reality. It was just a game to pass the time. Toy soldiers. The shock of Norah's death had blunted his imagination. It was his first encounter with death. Cartwright was sick in his stomach because Norah had died, and the nice Gran had put him to bed. His own stomach was never sick, and he certainly had no desire to be put to bed. But he wanted company. Someone to share the confusion of his thoughts, to explain the meaning of her death in a language he could understand.

Restlessly, he scrambled to his feet and went back to the rocking-horse. Closing his eyes, he pretended he was riding his favourite pony, Jess, at the riding school.

When Ellen came in with the hot cocoa, she was pleased to see he was not moping, but she could not know that Norah's sudden death had badly disturbed his normal, carefree attitude to life, and that it would be a very long time before he stopped worrying that he could suffer the same fate.

213

'Grandmama did not wish for my company, so I cleared the tea table and put everything away, then I made the cocoa. She says she has a headache, and will retire early. I brought you a slice of cake, Charles, and a few of Norah's ginger biscuits.'

'Thank you very much,' he said, and came to sit beside her on the sofa. 'Did she say if we had to be sent back to school?' he asked, taking a bite from a generous slice of cake.

'She did not mention it, so I think we can assume it will be all right for you to stay till the end of the week. I would suggest you both keep out of her way as far as possible, then she may forget you are here. In her present state of mind, she is concerned only with the inconvenience. Norah's death will mean changes, and Grandmama cannot abide changes of any kind. You see, Charles, she has been so spoilt, she resents any alteration in her own comfortable routine, and I cannot conceive how this household can continue to function in the same way without Norah. For one thing, we do not know how my sister, Bertha, will react when she awakes. I must keep an eye on her during the night. She has always suffered with her nerves, and she is not an easy person to live with. They were so devoted to one another, and shared the work of the house, with Mabel to do the rough. Consequently, the household seemed to run on oiled wheels, so to speak. Bertha is very house proud. Perhaps I should say she *was* house proud while she had Norah's affection and companionship to keep her reasonably happy. Not one of her sisters meant as much to her as her dear friend. Bertha was always the odd one, and when we were children, we were a little afraid of her black moods. Norah joined the household when my sister Grace went away to live and work in London. She and Bertha had already formed an attachment, and it was a happy day for The Haven when Norah set foot inside the green gate.'

He nodded, and she continued the story while he drank the cocoa and ate the cake and biscuits.

'We sisters all accepted Norah as one of the family, but Grandmama never did. When Norah sat down to the meals she had cooked and carried up the back stairs, she removed her apron but she felt uncomfortable in the drawing-room, so they used the breakfast room as a sitting-room, and shared a bedroom. Norah was always most respectful to Grandmama without being subservient. It was quite a shock to hear her answer Grandmama so rudely the day you arrived. She may have been feeling unwell, for she was very flushed, I remember. Poor darling. We shall never know. As soon as the funeral has been arranged, telegrams must be sent to my sisters, and to Paul's father. They will all wish to attend. Norah was such a favourite. Who could help loving her? Vicky will be sad. I must get in touch with her father. Perhaps you and Paul could spend the day of the funeral with Vicky? I am sure her other grandmother would be delighted to have you. She is such a very agreeable person, and would take you to the Museum and the Lifeboat, if you were to suggest it. Both of considerable interest to boys. I have been thinking, since I shall be expected to take over the cooking, we three will eat all our meals in the breakfast room – Norah will not be there after today. Grandmama can have her meals in the little morning-room, where I do the ironing and the sewing. She will not care for it, but I shall insist. It is not my nature to insist on anything, Charles. I have been too easily persuaded in the past, but I must assert myself from tomorrow on this question of meals. The dining-room can be used for the funeral tea, then I shall close the door. Mabel cannot be expected to take on any extra work, so we shall have to employ a daily woman. I know I shall have a tussle with Grandmama over this. She holds the purse strings very tightly.' Ellen sighed. 'Thank you for listening, Charles.' She smiled whimsically, and he was reminded of his mother. When she kissed him goodnight, he lay awake for some time, thinking of Norah, lying dead in the breakfast room. The nice Gran had said she would not be there on the morrow. Where was she going, and would she know that she was leaving The Haven for ever?

When he fell asleep at last, he dreamed that Norah had turned into the school matron, and Cartwright was sitting on his bed, covered in spots. But when he woke, Cartwright was sitting on his bed, looking very solemn.

'Gran said to tell you we are having breakfast in the

morning-room today. Grandmama always has her breakfast in bed.'

Smith Minor nodded. Yesterday Norah had brought them mugs of tea and biscuits while they were still in bed. Now Norah was dead, so they washed and dressed and went downstairs. Yesterday Smith Minor slid down the banisters, but it would be unseemly to do so today. Paul followed him downstairs, fighting back the tears. Breakfast was laid in the little morning-room, but it was uncomfortably chilly without a fire. They sat down to wait, shy of one another in this house of death.

After a few minutes, they heard Gran climbing the back stairs, and when she stood in the doorway with a loaded tray, they stood up and stared at her ashen face. She had been weeping, and the tears were still wet on her lashes, though she greeted them with a tremulous smile as she unloaded mugs of tea, boiled eggs, a loaf of bread and a dish of butter.

'It's chilly in here, but we shall not take long over our breakfast. Mabel will light this fire and the drawing-room fire. There is no hurry for Grandmama's breakfast. She has had her morning tea and biscuits.'

The boys ate their boiled eggs and bread and butter. Yesterday they had had a proper breakfast of bacon and eggs, with crisp fried bread, toast and honey. Yesterday Norah had cooked the breakfast.

'You boys can help carry up the wood and coal, and I will light the nursery fire. It is too much for Mabel to climb all those stairs with her poor legs,' Ellen was saying.

So Mabel carried up the scuttles of coal and the wood baskets, and dumped them noisily on the floor outside the little green gate. Her face was streaked with tears and coal dust. 'Ain't it terrible? Can't believe she's gorn. One of the best. Never did no 'arm to nobody. Always bright as a button. Wore 'erself out I reckon, poor soul, but never a word of complaint, not 'er.' She sniffed miserably, and stumped back to the basement.

The days that followed till the day of the funeral were long and uneventful, for Ellen was busy, and the boys had to amuse themselves. They played football in the park with the new ball Smith Minor had bought with some of the money his parents had sent for Christmas. Paul had no heart for it. His heart ached for Norah, and his eyes burned with the hot tears he was not allowed to shed. 'Boys do not cry,' Thomas had instilled this stern principle in his son on his third birthday.

Remembering Nana's advice about avoiding Grandmama, the boys used the back gate and the basement steps when coming and going about their outdoor activities. A bag of toffees from the sweet shop on the corner of the street helped the morning along, for there were no elevenses. They took turns to enquire the time of an old man, smoking his pipe in the shelter. A dejected little dog sat at his feet and wagged its tail expectantly when one of the boys approached.

'Would you like me to take your dog for a walk, Sir?'

The question surprised the old man, but the boy looked respectable and spoke politely, so he agreed.

'What's his name, Sir?' Smith Minor patted the shaggy head.

'Just Dog. Never got around to giving him a name.'

They ran off across the grass, Dog barking excitedly, chasing the ball. Norah was forgotten. It was fun to have a dog. And when Smith Minor kicked the ball too hard, and it flew across the park, all three went in search of it, scrambling in the bushes. They played with the dog till the old man came out of the shelter and whistled. Dog hesitated, with lolling tongue and limpid eyes, till a second whistle sent him racing back to his master.

'Twelve o'clock. Dinner time,' said the old man, as he fastened the leash to the dog's collar.

'Will you be here tomorrow, Sir?' Smith Minor asked eagerly.

'Aye, we shall be here. The Missus turns us out. Says we get under her feet. Good-day to you, boys.'

'Good-day, Sir,' they chorused.

It was Irish stew for dinner that first day, with prunes and custard for pudding. Smith Minor could have told the nice Gran it was exactly the sort of dinner they served up at prep school, but he was too polite, and he felt sorry for her.

Auntie Bertha stayed in bed for the rest of the week, and

217

wanted nothing more than cups of tea and bread and butter. On the day of the funeral, with all the family gathered at The Haven, she still refused to get up. One by one, her sisters went in to see her with their respective husbands, but they stayed for only a few minutes.

'Poor dear, she is suffering from shock.'

'Time will heal,' they said.

'But not to attend the funeral. This is scandalous!' Grandmama asserted irritably. She had no patience with Bertha.

The boys were packed off to Vicky's other grandmother soon after breakfast, and did not see the station cab depositing all the relatives in their sombre clothes.

This was no time for Kate to wear one of her pretty gowns, or a huge, feathered hat, or for Bella's bright scarlet cap and matching scarf that Jane had knitted so laboriously with her chilblained fingers. It was no time for Henry's jokes or for Charles to discuss the Bill for Reforming the Licensing Laws.

There was no Norah to serve them with hot chocolate and biscuits for their elevenses, and the glass of sherry was a poor substitute. No Norah to cook a delicious roast followed by fruit pies made from her bottled gooseberries, plums and damsons.

It was a buffet lunch, prepared by Ellen as soon as the boys had left the house. Jane and Bella helped her with the funeral tea and the washing up. The baker had delivered fresh bread and cakes.

They spoke of Norah in hushed voices, as though she had been a saint. It would have amused her. Only Grandmama was sparing in her praise. 'Certainly one must give credit where credit is due, and Norah was a good cook,' she said, glancing reproachfully at Ellen, who was obviously a very poor cook.

Quietly and sadly they went their separate ways. Bertha was sleeping — or pretending to sleep, and Ellen would not have her disturbed. Nobody asked to stay the night. Grandmama was so obviously expecting her darling boy to stay for several days, but he excused himself on the grounds of duty, after his Swiss holiday. By 7 o'clock the station cab had collected the last of the family, and Ellen closed the green gate for the last time. It had been a long , exhausting day. They had paid their respects to Norah.   Back in the old, silent house, Grandmama sat alone in her drawing-room, dabbing her eyes with a scented handkerchief, while Ellen went to sit beside the dying embers of the fire in the little morning-room, to await the return of the boys.

The future was bleak. Tomorrow she would see the boys on the train with their tin trunks, and the one tuck box they must share. She had ordered cakes and mincepies from the baker, and the boys could choose their favourite sweets in the shop on the corner.

She was worried about Paul, who was still complaining of stomach-ache, but she would write a little note to Matron.

Supposing Bertha refused to get up? Without Norah, she would drift like a ship without a rudder. And Grandmama would expect hot chocolate and *petit beurre* biscuits if the heavens were falling! Ellen sighed, and closed her eyes.

Chapter Eight

Five years had passed. A rather superior daily help had taken over the housework at The Haven. Her name was Elfreda, but Amelia always referred to her as 'that person'. She had no time or inclination to gossip with Mabel, and had a poor opinion of that courageous little woman who did 'the rough'.

At precisely 10 o'clock, Elfreda sat down to her elevenses, and at 12 o'clock to her dinner. Then she was gone, leaving behind a strong smell of Mansion Polish.

Ellen's cooking had improved over the years, but could not compare with Norah's, She ate her meals with Grandmama in the morning-room.

As for Bertha, she had never recovered from the shock of Norah's death. The day following the funeral, she had dressed and crept downstairs to sit on the sofa in the breakfast room. There she had stayed – a strange, silent ghost of her former self, with idle hands and dull eyes. She ate the meals that Ellen served on a tray, but made no comment. After a month of such idleness, the doctor was called to examine her, but his diagnosis was too vague to be helpful. Bertha was not ill. It was a state of acute depression that time would heal.

'But how much time? My daughter has always been such a busy person. Now she does nothing,' Grandmama pointed out, reasonably enough.

To which he replied, patiently, 'That I cannot say, Ma'am. I am not a doctor of the mind. In my opinion, your daughter has lost the will to live.'

'Fiddlesticks! She has lost a *friend*, not even a husband or a child. It does not signify.'

'Be that as it may, a shock to the nervous system can have far-reaching results.'

'If she is unbalanced, should she not have treatment in a clinic?'

'To be quite candid, Ma'am, I'm not at all sure what she needs, apart from rest.'

'But she has been resting for a whole month.'

'Does she complain of headaches?'

'Not to my knowledge, but then I do not see her. She has buried herself in the basement. She knows where to find me, if she wishes to see me. She is not neglected. My daughter Ellen, attends to her needs. You have talked to Ellen?'

'Yes. She is very worried about her sister.'

'Ellen always worries about someone. It is her nature. Then you do not advise a course of treatment in a clinic?'

'Not at this stage. I will keep an eye on her.'

Amelia sighed. 'Very well. Help yourself to a sherry, doctor.'

He thanked her, sat down for a few minutes, then bowed himself out. Amelia Brent was a wonderful old lady, but not very sympathetic to a daughter suffering with acute depression, he was thinking as he let himself out. He had attended the family for many years, but was never at ease with that formidable lady. With a shrewd idea of the strange, unnatural relationship between the daughter, Bertha, and her friend, the doctor was not surprised at his patient's condition. Unnatural human relationships were responsible for so much that baffled the doctors. Poor woman, and she had not cried. That was a bad sign.

Five years later, there was no change in Bertha. The doctor no longer called, and Ellen had given up hoping for a miracle. Without the will to live, Bertha went on living. Only Paul could get close to her, during the school holidays, but she shrank from Smith Minor's breezy familiarity. With Paul she would play a quiet game of Ludo, or help to fit the pieces of a simple jigsaw puzzle. She would listen to his tales of prep school and a wan smile would touch her lips, but would not reach her eyes. Paul's gentleness had a soothing effect on

221

the poor woman, and his deep sense of compassion for the suffering of God's creatures, both human and animal, had grown with the years. He often brought home a maimed bird or small animal, to be left in Ellen's care when he returned to school. The conservatory at The Haven no longer smelled of geraniums, but the hot, musky smell of furry bodies and droppings. Food and water and clean straw were provided for the inmates in the big cages, and when broken limbs and wings were mended. Ellen would open the door to freedom.

Since the conservatory was an extension of the drawing-room, Grandmama complained of noisy squeaks and squawks, but Ellen was adamant in her refusal to get rid of the small menagerie.

It was an interesting pastime for a woman who had little enough enjoyment during the long terms when the boys were away at school, and Vicky was a weekly boarder at the Convent. Jane and Edward spent their annual holiday at The Haven. So also did Bella and Roderic. These holidays would be arranged during the Summer vacation, when the old house came to life and the dining-room once again echoed to the clatter of dishes, Jane's shrill excited laughter, and the lively conversation of Bella and Roderic. Even Grandmama seemed to enjoy these brief periods when the London contingent arrived to enliven her homely routine, when she dipped into her purse for extra housekeeping money.

Vicky and Charles had formed an attachment that often excluded Paul. They were two of a kind, and Vicky's readiness to accept a challenge appealed to Charles. They were strong swimmers, while Paul still played around in the shallows and watched them diving off the high breakwater, and surfacing like seals from the waves.

When Vicky's bosom friend had joined her parents in South Africa, she had turned to Charles rather than Paul in adolescence. She still adored her young cousin, but Charles amused her. Puberty was a time of conflicting loyalties and emotions for both the girl and the boy, but Paul was not affected, and there was no jealousy in his nature. Their relationship had not changed and their feelings were those of brother and sister. With Charles it was different. The wet

222

bathing costume, clinging to her little pointed breasts, teased his senses, and provoked a disturbing sensation in his loins. She was not pretty, but her lively intelligence matched his own, and he was constantly aware of her during that Summer holiday at the end of their last term at prep school.

To spend a day with Uncle David was one of the highlights of Paul's school holidays. Every Good Friday, they travelled to London to share with a vast audience the emotional experience of a superb performance of 'The Crucifixion'. The same choral society would perform the 'Messiah' at Christmas. Not for Paul a visit to the circus. He was much too tender-hearted. That was left to Vicky and Charles, who enjoyed a day in London in the company of the irrepressible Auntie Kate, who still saw herself as the bewitching young woman with whom her lover had eloped. Nevertheless, she was an amusing companion, and generous with her treats. Lunch at Slaters before the matinee, and tea at Fullers, with a half sovereign apiece as a parting gift She liked the young Charles, not that he reminded her in any way of her husband, Charles, but she had always liked the opposite sex, and, according to her disillusioned husband, would flirt with any male between eight and eighty. They still lived under the same roof, in the house at Onslow Square, but went their separate ways. A divorce might have ruined his political career, and Kate was a good actress. Only the servants and the family were aware of the disloyalties that divided them.

Kate was not entirely to blame, for her husband had kept a mistress for years. But he could never forget of forgive that affair with the young Thomas.

If Paul had resembled his handsome Papa in any way, then Kate would have adored him, but she had no affection for her great-nephew, and did not invite him to London.

Ellen had to wait two years to see her favourite sister. Grace, and her husband, Henry, for they could not afford an annual holiday. On the occasion of Norah's funeral, Grace had pawned her wedding ring. Their circumstances, on the day they received Amelia's telegram, were so sadly reduced, they could hardly have covered their train fare to Berne. Henry had only a bank clerk's salary, and was often tempted to accompany a friend to a stag party at the nearest tavern. Grace never nagged. She loved him dearly, and put him to bed like a mother with a wayward child. It was his only weakness, and it was forgivable in a man who had once lived so extravagantly.

On their two-yearly visits to Worthing, Henry would spend many pleasant hours in a hired sailing boat, while his 'dearest girl' sat quietly content in a deck chair on the promenade with Ellen for company. To be parted from Ellen was her only regret in a happy marriage. The years that divided the two sisters had only strengthened their devotion, and their frequent letters contained all the intimate details of their separate lives.

It irked Amelia to see them setting out for a walk in the park, with arms linked and their trim figures still girlishly slender, but Amelia had never been close to her daughters. It was too late to bridge the gap that divided them. Her own self-indulgence had always taken priority over everything, and her daughters had long since accepted the obvious fact that maternal love was not a quality a mother automatically acquired at the birth of her first child. Only Ellen had produced grand-children, and only Thomas had found a way to Amelia's heart. Even that was self-indulgent and possessive. For reasons best known to themselves, Grace, Jane and Kate were childless. Lucy had died in childbirth. Watching her two elder daughters in such close harmony during the holidays had been a thorn in the flesh, and a guilty conscience reminded her of her own part in their prolonged separation. She had Henry to thank for saving her daughter's life, but she did not care for the pompous little man, or the scandal of the divorce.

Looking back on that unhappy period, Amelia had reluctantly to admit it had been a mistake to listen to Bertha's complaints that Grace was lazy, and an even bigger mistake to entrust her young, innocent daughter to be housekeeper to a couple she had not even met, and whose marriage was already on the rocks. Only to herself, in old age, had she admitted her mistakes, for it would never do to apologize to her daughters. To have the last word on all family matters was her prerogative, or *had* been her prerogative. She could no longer claim to hold the reins for married daughters.

They did not consult her, and the diminished household at The Haven was a poor substitute for the days when she saw herself as the Matriarch, with six daughters, a cook, a governess, a nursemaid, and a housemaid, all obedient to her wishes. To cling to her familiar routine, and to insist on such small privileges as breakfast in bed and a fire in the drawing-room on Summer evenings had given her a small measure of satisfaction, but Ellen had her way about closing up the dining-room, and had over-ruled her decision to send Bertha away for treatment. Ellen was not so amenable these days, and that Elfreda person barely acknowledged her existence. To sit in the drawing-room and reflect on the changes that had been introduced since Norah's death was a sad reflection on her dominant personality, for the reins had gradually slipped away from her grasp, her objections over-ruled. Who would have supposed, for instance, that she would be expected to eat the baker's buns for her tea, when all her married life she had enjoyed madeira cake? But Ellen was the cook now, and had no time or inclination to bake madeira cake.

The three children avoided her in the school holidays, but then she had never been fond of children. Looking back over the years was her main occupation in old age, and always it was Thomas, her darling boy, who claimed the biggest share of happy memories. Since his regiment had been posted to Singapore, however, she was denied the pleasure of his company at The Haven. He never came for more than three of four days, but she always had such joy in their reunion. The anticipation and the aftermath occupied her thoughts during the long, lonely hours in her drawing-room. She always wore her most becoming gowns, and he played up to her with charming gallantry.

Rosalind was nothing more than a sulky 'go-between'. It was a duty that Thomas insisted on, but she could not bear to watch them appraising each other with loving glances and compliments. In Aldershot, Rosalind's self-importance was never threatened. She was the Colonel's daughter. In Singapore, she would be enjoying much the same round of social engagements as she had so enjoyed in India. An idle, pleasure-loving way of life, with native servants and only one ever-present danger – the excess of whisky and soda in the Officers' Mess. Marital relationships had a way of deteriorating in a hot climate, and Thomas and Rosalind were no exception.

Captain David Jones had been left behind when the regiment sailed for Singapore. He was recuperating from a fall from his horse in the final round of the Open Championship at the annual Gymkhana. As always, his rival for the coveted trophy, and the favourite of the majority, was the handsome Captain Thomas Cartwright.

They had raced neck and neck, with the cheers of the crowd in their ears, and the thirst for victory in every pore of their strong, virile bodies. David's horse had refused the last hurdle, and he had been thrown heavily over its head, while Thomas's horse flew over like a bird. Poor David. It was a cruel blow.

He would have recovered from the concussion in a matter of days, but there was a back injury, and he was still confined to bed at his home in the Welsh mining village when the troop-ship sailed from Tilbury.

That was the Summer when Paul travelled to Wales. That was the Summer when Charles was left behind at The Haven for two weeks. That was the Summer when Charles discovered Vicky as the perfect foil to his own disregard of danger, and she narrowly escaped drowning.

As the holiday came to an end, Paul was wishing he could spend the rest of his life with Uncle David, and never again have to face the stern displeasure of an irate parent. It was wishful thinking to hope the regiment would be kept in Singapore at the end of their five-year term of duty, Uncle David reminded him, with a whimsical smile, from his chair in the open window, where the doctor allowed him to sit for an hour or two each day.

'Sure to goodness, there is time enough to start fretting,' his uncle also reminded him in his singing Welsh voice. Back in his home environment, stripped of the scarlet uniform, the accent was more pronounced. For a man in constant pain, he was determinedly cheerful and optimistic, and was already badgering the doctor for a couple of sticks.

'This is one issue on which we must disagree, for I cannot

wait to hear they are back in Aldershot, while you would have them stuck for ever in Singapore.' He shook his head.

'Life is not made to suit us, but what we ourselves make of it. To fret about tomorrow, next week, or next year, is a waste of time. "Sufficient unto the day is the evil thereof." That is a biblical quotation, and worth remembering.'

'But I cannot help myself. Nana tells me I am a born worrier.'

'Your Nana is a dear woman, but I cannot agree to that particular sentiment. No child is born to worry, or any other restrictive influence. A new-born child has no thoughts, only the natural urge to satisfy its hunger. Thoughts come later, much later. I wonder when that particular thought entered your mind, and who put it there? Was it your Ayah? Was she, perhaps, over-protective in her constant anxiety for your welfare?'

'I loved her very much.'

'Of course you loved her, because hers were the arms that first cradled you, and hers the voice you first recognized. But she made you afraid of so many things. Fear is contagious, Paulie, and a young child the most vulnerable of all God's creatures. If you had been born in England, and had had no Ayah to cosset you, it might have been a good thing. In this respect I am inclined to agree with your father, that Ayah babied you. A boy-child should cut his teeth on his father's shoulder, and girl-child on her mother's breast. If I had a son, I would not stand aside until he was three years of age. I would have him with me as often as was reasonably possible, from the day he was born. That may be a revolutionary attitude, but then I am a queer sort of fellow, as your esteemed Papa has taken pains to point out, on more than one occasion.'

'I wish you had been my Papa, Uncle David.'

'Thank you, Paulie. That is a very nice compliment.'

'Mama calls me a cuckoo in the nest.'

'She doesn't mean it unkindly. She loves you.'

'Does she? Then why has she never told me so?'

He parried the boy's question with one of his own. 'Have you ever told her you love her?'

'N – no.'

'Why not?'

'I don't know'

'You could try.'

'Yes.'

'In your next letter.'

'Yes.'

It was a dangerous subject for David. Wild horses would never drag the truth from him. He had sworn a solemn oath on the Holy Book.

'Let's talk about you, Uncle David,' the boy was saying.

Looking into those dark, sombre eyes, so like his own, he asked, 'What would you like to know?'

'What did you do when you were a boy like me?'

'When I was your age, I was walking five miles to the Grammar School, mark you.'

'Five miles?'

'Yes, indeed, bach. There was no transport, so it had to be Shanks's pony. But I had Lloyd Watts for company. We two boys had sat for the examination together in the village school. We were pleased with ourselves, and our families were proud, when we passed. Only the two of us in the village, mark you. Yes, it was a long trudge, but we sang hymns, and hunted for birds' nests, and took our time, for we left home early. We carried our books and a dinner box in a haversack on our back. The winters were hard. Sometimes the roads were impassable, with deep snow drifts, then we had to stay at home until the snow plough had cleared a way in to town. But we always had homework, and were not expected to be idle when we could not get to school. In the school holidays, we earned a few shillings as delivery boys. Lloyd delivered telegrams for the postmistress, and I delivered groceries. The money we earned we gave to our mothers, who gave us back sixpence a week for spending. On summer evenings, we went fishing. It was a good life. A mining village is like a family. The pits our natural habitat. My father and my two elder brothers are miners, as you know, and my three sisters married miners. They had no option, my brothers. I was fortunate in being the youngest. The money was there to pay for my education. Grammar School was a step towards college, then came the entrance examination to Sandhurst. I have Mam to thank for pushing me in the right direction. She was very ambitious for her youngest son. The army attracted me, Paulie, or it could have been the scarlet uniform. You say your Mama calls you a cuckoo in the nest. They say the same about me, but they are only teasing. My roots are here, and the sense of belonging is so strong, I can be away with the regiment for five years, and come back to find it almost unchanged. Da had grey hair, and his shoulders are stooping now, but Mam is as sprightly as ever, and would pass for a sister to her eldest daughter, Megwynn.'

'You love your Mother very much?'

'Aye, that I do.'

'Perhaps I shall love my Mama when I am a grown man?'

'You will, bach, you will.'

'Tell me more about Lloyd and you, when you were boys.'

'There is nothing much more to tell. We were busy all the week, and we went to chapel twice on Sunday. Everyone goes to chapel. Religion is part of our culture and our heritage, and we live to sing. The miners have their own choir. They sing at all the festivals all over the country, and once they sang in the Albert Hall.'

'You sang to Mama in India, when Papa was away at the Frontier.'

David had the grace to blush.

'And you played croquet with Mama.'

'With Auntie Millie as our chaperone.'

'She was kind to me when Ayah died.' Paul sighed nostalgically.

'Fetch the chess board. There's time for our return match before supper.'

'Yes, Uncle David.' To beat his uncle, who was the family champion, would be quite an achievement, and only two more days in which to do it.

'Mam's frying onions.' David sniffed the savoury smell appreciatively. There was nothing wrong with his appetite, and a savoury supper, eaten to the accompaniment of a new recording of Gigli, or Clara Butt, was as good a way as any to end the day.

The gramophone was a novelty for Paul, and a taste for opera was cultivated on that first holiday in Wales. So was a taste for the classics. The glass-fronted bookcase in the parlour was crammed with books.

'Da was a great collector of books in his younger days, second-hand books. He bought them at auctions. We were all encouraged to read on winter evenings, and there was no trash on those shelves, so we read the classics,' David had explained. 'My brother, Frank — you have not met him — had no time for books. Frank was a rebel. There is one in every family, mark you. He would sneak out of that little window over the porch when the rest of the family were asleep, to meet his sweetheart. Poor Frank. He got her in the family way and had to marry her. The naughty Clara was the minister's daughter, and the minister is a most respected member of the community.'

'What does it mean, Uncle David, to get a girl in the family way?' Paul asked innocently.

Surprised at the question, he answered, 'She was expecting his child.' Then he went on the explain the facts of life, without embarrassment. There is little that escapes a growing boy or girl in a crowded miner's cottage. Birth and death hold no mystery. Two children had died in infancy, and taken their toll of a mother's grief, but life went on. For a boy of twelve, shortly to be catapulted into the rigours of public school, a lesson in sex was a necessary preparation.

Paul was shocked. The communal bath at prep school had still not prepared him for such an intimate relationship with the opposite sex. Should he warn Smith Minor? Could it happen to Vicky?

'There is no need to look so startled, bach. Is it such a shattering revelation?' David asked, kindly.

Paul nodded.

'It would have been far more shattering to learn the facts of life at public school. Boys can be cruel, and ignorance is a poor substitute for knowledge. Sex can be a very disturbing element in adolescence, for boys and girls are emotionally immature. It can be dangerous if it is not controlled, but then you could say the same of jealousy, greed, envy and lust. Without sex between a man and a woman, there can be

230

no love, and love is of God. The word sex has been misused, Paul, in this day and age. It has become a dirty word, bandied about by those who seek to satisfy the demands of the flesh. It is a pity it has become so ugly and distorted. I was lucky. The facts of life were not suddenly disclosed at puberty, but already accepted as a natural part of living. Nothing was taboo. There was no mystery about any function of the human body, not in our family. As a small boy, I watched my sisters stripped to the waist, bathing their breasts, and there was no embarrassment. Why should there be? Modesty was just a word in the dictionary, but it had no personal significance for my sisters.'

Paul had listened to these disclosures with something akin to panic. Why had Smith Minor never mentioned these disturbing facts? They had shared everything for nearly six years. Now they shared Vicky. Should Vicky be warned to be careful – careful of Smith Minor?

Part Three

she hadn't really expected him to accompany them on such a frivolous outing.

'We will take good care of her, Sir,' said Charles gallantly. 'And it's my treat,' he added. 'It will be a pleasure, Auntie J.'

Her sigh of relief was echoed by Edward, who would have to dig into petty cash for such an outing, and there were other more essential needs. Whitewash, for instance. The kitchen, parlour and dining-room walls were damp, with dark patches. A fresh coat of whitewash hid all the defects, and a couple of their young boarders would do the job.

The Hoxton Mission was still run on a shoe-string, but Jane was a wonderful manager, and always so cheerful, bless her. She would enjoy the outing with Vicky and Charles, and he would hold the fort till her return.

'I will just check on the dinner. There's a casserole in the oven, and Maggie should be preparing the vegetables,' Jane was saying, as she collected cups and saucers on to the tin tray. Charles took the tray and followed her to the kitchen, where Maggie sat on a high stool at the kitchen sink for much of the day.

'It's me varicose veins, duckie. I 'as to get orf me feet,' she told Charles. ''ave a look at this.' And she lifted her skirts to display the ugly, knotted veins on her swollen legs.

'Gosh!' said he. 'I never knew veins could swell to that size.'

Vicky had followed him into the kitchen. 'Poor Maggie,' she said, as she slipped an arm round her neck and kissed her wrinkled cheek.

'She always was a kind-'earted little soul,' Maggie told Charles.

'A kind-hearted little soul! Well! Well!' he teased.

Vicky blushed. She used not to mind his teasing. There was a time when she teased him back and gave him a playful slap, but not any more. His teasing hurt. If *only* he would treat her like a grown-up! She *was* grown-up.

'What can I do to help, Auntie J?' he demanded, turning his back on her with apparent disinterest.

'You could go to the market for me. We shall need more vegetables and bread for the weekend. Here is the list. Take a basket, and take Vicky with you. Thank you, Charles.'

Vicky opened her mouth to say she would sooner stay with Uncle Edward, but closed it again, for Charles was grinning and holding out his hand. She took his hand, smiling tremulously. It was going to be all right. He was only teasing.

Jane watched them go. 'That poor child is going to be hurt, Maggie. She wears her heart on her sleeve, and it's such a mistake. That boy is not ready to be tied down. But we all have to learn the hard way. I hoped it would be Paulie. They were inseparable at one time, but there is something about Charles that is quite irresistible. He is so lively and amusing. But Paulie is such a dear. Whenever we visit The Haven and he is there, I find him so very kind and thoughtful. And kindness is a quality so often overlooked when a girl sets her heart on a certain person and loves him with all his faults. What is forgivable in a boy, however, could be quite objectionable in a husband. Vicky has changed. With Paulie she was always the dominant partner, but seeing her with Charles, her own personality seems to shrink. He is so forceful. I like him, but he is not right for Vicky.'

Maggie sliced another cabbage and wondered if there was any tea left in the pot. When the Missus got on her pet hobby horse, there was no stopping her. What will be will be. They called it Fate. They said the stars had something to do with it. That was just a lot of poppycock. Any bloody fool could have told you it was SEX! Only you couldn't put it so bluntly to the Missus. The Missus was a LADY.

The Metropolitan Music Hall was ablaze with lights. Patrons were stepping from their cabs at the kerbside, and a noisy group surrounded the box office.

Charles took command of the situation, steered his companions to a safe corner and went off to purchase tickets and a box of chocolates. The chocolates he presented to Auntie Jane with a courtly little bow. His man-of-the-world air impressed Vicky enormously, for she was ready to be impressed, and she followed him into the auditorium, hoping to sit beside him. Would he hold her hand when the lights were dimmed? The touch of his hand had become for her, of recent months, a thrilling contact that sent all her pulses

238

tingling, and her heart racing. She could not understand what had happened between them, for Charles seemed quite unconscious of the change in her, and still treated her with the casualness of a brother to a sister.

When they reached their seats in the dress circle, Charles gave her a little push and she went in first, followed by Auntie Jane, and Charles took the aisle seat. It was silly to feel so disappointed, she told herself. There would be lots of time on the homeward journey when she would have him all to herself.

'This is most exciting, Charles. Do you know this is the very first time I have set foot in a music hall, and I feel quite daring,' Auntie Jane confided, as she settled herself comfortably between them. 'But I do hope you have not spent too much money, dear? The best seats *and* the chocolates. Such extravagance!' she added.

'Think nothing of it, Auntie J. The Pater increased my allowance this year,' Charles whispered, confidentially.

'Will you kindly remove your hat, Madam?' A man was leaning over Jane's shoulder. 'You too, Miss,' he asked Vicky. His breath smelled strongly of garlic, and his voice held a foreign accent. The Metropolitan attracted patrons from all walks of life, all parts of London, and visitors from abroad. The noisy anticipation of the audience gave Charles his first taste of an entertainment that would soon become familiar.

They hadn't long to wait. The orchestra sprang into life with a lively rendering of a Strauss polka, and the patrons in the gallery beat time with their feet on the floorboards. Then curtain went up, and a roar of applause greeted the line of chorus girls, high stepping in the CanCan. Charles leaned forward, bright-eyed and eager to catch his first glimpse of Maudie.

'The girl in the centre,' Jane whispered.   He caught his breath. They all were beautiful, alternating blondes and brunettes, along the line, but there was something very special about Maudie, and he followed her every movement in hypnotised fascination. Her petticoats swirled provocatively in the rhythm of the dance, and a feathered hat clung precariously to her chestnut curls. The audience loved the

239

girls. Whistles and cat-calls indicated their enjoyment of the billowing petticoats and the long, slender legs. They sparkled with glittering magnetism, like creatures from another world, far removed from the women who stared at them so enviously and from the fascinated males.

'She's lovely,' Charles whispered hoarsely.

Vicky leaned forward and caught his enraptured glance with a shiver of premonition. A future bereft of Charles would be unbearable, yet how could she compete with that gorgeous creature if he had already lost his heart? Love at first sight was a threatening possibility. It *could* happen. It happened in the romantic novels she liked to read in bed. But to read about it was on thing and to have it happen here, before her eyes, was a very different matter. For the first time in her life, Vicky knew the meaning of jealousy. It was an overwhelming emotion that frightened her. She remembered the terrible tantrums when her mother had seemed quite mad, and her dear Papa a helpless victim of her lashing tongue. Vicky's memories of early childhood held no recollection of a mother's loving arms, only of Nana.

Her wandering thoughts were interrupted by a change in the rhythm of the music. The girls had stopped dancing, and Maudie had stepped out from the chorus to stand alone. She had dropped her petticoats and removed her feathered hat. It swung on a ribbon as she stood there, poised and smiling, waiting for her cue. She sang like a choirboy, a pure, high treble, and the complete contrast to the noisy introduction surprised and silenced the audience into a stillness that was, in itself, a compliment to the singer. She sang 'Ave Maria', and when the last note died away, the audience seemed to sigh, and then to explode into thunderous applause.

'Bravo!' Charles shouted.

'Encore!' yelled the man whose breath stank of garlic.

Maudie curtsied prettily and sang 'Greensleeves'. Still the audience wanted more, but they had to wait till the finale. As she stepped back into line and the girls moved away to the wings, tossing their petticoats, Maudie was swept away with the rest; only her auburn curls distinguished her, but *she* knew, and *they* knew, she was different. Maudie had star quality. The little girl from Hoxton, who had sung so naturally and delightfully to the accompaniment of the Salvation Army band, had been discovered by a talent scout searching London for a troupe of children to dance and sing in a Christmas pantomime. Hundreds of little girls had been auditioned, but only twelve engaged. Maudie was one of the lucky twelve, and she was over the moon with excitement.

She had taken to the stage like a duck to water. Starry-eyed and intelligent, she learned the routine quickly, and grasped the importance of saying 'The show must go on' at an early age. When puberty and monthly periods had a way of afflicting a girl when she most wanted to look her best, grease-paint covered her pallid cheeks, and determination kept her from fainting. Born and bred in the East End, and lacking proper nourishment, it was not stamina that kept Maudie on her toes, but the indefatigable spirit and good humour she had inherited. The twelve little girls had lived together in lodgings, supervised by a stern martinet. They had no freedom and no time for anything other than rehearsals and the twice-daily variety shows in which they appeared in the Midlands and the North. An agent was responsible for the bookings, and theatrical digs were seldom comfortable, and always overcrowded. But to sleep four in a bed was no hardship to Maudie. They kept each other warm in winter under the thin blankets. They travelled on Sundays, third class, packing into one compartment like sardines in a tin, always accompanied by the martinet.

Yet it was fun. They were young, and they had achieved something they had always wanted. Hard work and discomfort were the price they paid most willingly to be part of the exciting world of show business.

Maudie had joined a troupe of older girls at the age of fourteen, for she had outgrown the juveniles, but there was little change in their circumstances, with travelling and touring, rehearsals and variety shows a way of life. There was one important objective – London. The Metropolitan Music Hall had a reputation, and only the best was good enough. The majority never reached it in a lifetime of touring, and the privileged few were quite outstanding in their own particular sphere. Maudie could have spent years on tour with second-rate variety artistes but for her voice and her personality. 'She's a natural,' they said of her, and it was true. There was no other life for her. If her many admirers took her flirting too seriously, it was their mistake, and she accepted their homage and their presents with easy informality. Her heart was fancy-free, and she wanted it to stay that way. When she fell in love would be time enough to think of lasting attachment, but she could not see herself being faithful to a lover. The stage was her first love. No man could compete for her favours with this all-embracing career she had chosen. So Charles was doomed to disappointment if he thought to claim her. Maudie was already a young woman of worldly experience while he was still a schoolboy. But it would be a challenge, and Charles could never resist a challenge.

So he sat back in his seat when the last of the frothy petticoats had disappeared, and made plans for the future with precocious egoism. He saw himself escorting the lovely Maudie in the vacation to the best restaurants, dining and dancing at the Ritz, driving in Hyde Park. It would cost more than he could afford, but Mother would increase his personal allowance. It was a secret between them. Now that he was at public school, she understood his need to entertain his friends. Smoking and drinking and escorting a pretty girl to the cinema, with supper at Frascati's, used up Father's allowance, so he would need more.

In an atmosphere of hilarious enjoyment, punctuated by Auntie J's infectious laugh, Charles watched the acrobats, the juggler, the magician, and the ventriloquist with scant interest in their clever performances. A Russian baritone made quite a hit with his rendering of 'The Volga Boat Song', and a tiny Japanese geisha girl, with a fluted voice, fanned her way through an intricate dance, bowed ceremoniously, and shuffled away. Every act deserved the enthusiastic applause. Vicky almost forgot Charles in the excitement of her first variety show, and she shared her enjoyment and the chocolates with Auntie Jane.

Not until the finale did Charles lean forward with the same eager anticipation he had shown at the start. The chorus girls, dressed as rabbits in the scantiest of costumes with furry tails and paws and enormous erect ears, were greeted with shouts of laughter and piercing whistles as they circled the stage, with their little furry tails bobbing enticingly on a dozen little bottoms. But when they stood in line for their dance routine, Maudie was missing. Charles felt his heart plunge with disappointment. Love at first sight is a very emotional experience for a boy who had hitherto seen in a pretty face nothing more than a pretty face.

But it was only a momentary disappointment. As the last of the bobbing tails disappeared on the left of the stage, a small figure emerged from the right – a girl in a print dress with an Alice band on her auburn curls, and slippers on her feet. She looked very young and childish standing there in the centre of the stage, and not at all the same person who had danced the CanCan in frothy petticoats. But Charles had yet to learn that Maudie Partridge was full of surprises, and her moods as variable as the wind. Whatever she wore, and whatever she sang, the audience would love her. She sang 'The Minstrel Boy' for the Welsh in the audience, and 'When Irish Eyes are Smiling' for the Irish, and 'Loch Lomond' for the Scots. It pleased them enormously. She smiled and curtsied, then spread her arms in a gesture that included everyone.

'All together!' she cried invitingly, to the opening strains of 'Land of Hope and Glory'.

Charles sang as he had never sung before, his eyes hot with tears, for over and above the massed voices of the audience, the voice of the girl rose pure and high and beautiful. She had dropped her arms and she stood there, singing with the effortless voice of a lark.

'Wider still and wider, Shall thy bounds be set, God who made thee mighty, Make thee mightier yet.'

They were on their feet, clapping and cheering, as the rest of the cast poured on to the stage from the wings, and the applause swelled to a roar of approval that must have warmed the hearts of each one of the artistes.

Then it was over, and the opening bars of the National Anthem brought everyone to attention.

'Auntie J, can we go backstage? Will you introduce me to Maudie?' Charles asked eagerly, as soon as the last note had died away.

'Yes, can we?' Vicky echoed.

'That was wonderful,' breathed Auntie Jane, ecstatically, still in the realms of 'Land of Hope and Glory'. 'Backstage? Yes, why not? Maudie belongs to Hoxton and we are very proud of her.'

The backstage dressing-room for the chorus girls was a lively place, smelling of greasepaint, powder and sweat, and crowded with girls in various stages of undress. Maudie was perched on the edge of a dressing-table, hugging a bouquet of red roses. Still in the print dress and satin slippers, she was kissing the cheek of a tall, distinguished gentleman in morning dress. The girls were chatting and giggling. It was pandemonium and unlike anything Charles had expected.

Grouped in the doorway, the three visitors waited to be noticed, reluctant to intrude on a scene in which they played no part. A wave of jealousy swept over Charles, and his cheeks burned with the blush that so often bothered him in adolescence. Why hadn't he thought of flowers?

Then Maudie saw them. 'The Missus!' she shrieked excitedly, dropped the bouquet, pushed her way to the door, and flung herself on Auntie Jane. 'Where did you spring from then?' she demanded. 'Did you like the show?'

'I enjoyed every moment, Maudie, and you sang like an angel'.

'Thanks.'

'You remember Vicky?'

''Course I remember Vicky. Hello, duckie. You haven't changed a bit. Would have known you if I met you in the street, and that's a fact. Where's Paulie? Who's this?' She hardly paused to take breath. The vivid little face was still the face of the child who had danced and sung in the streets of Hoxton. Her eyes twinkled mischievously as she turned her attention to the blushing youth.

'This is Charles, a friend of Paulie. He wanted an introduction,' said Auntie Jane.

'Pleased to meet you, Charles.' Maudie proffered a hand.

He took it and raised it to his lips in a gallant gesture that surprised Vicky, but did not surprise Maudie. In fact, it was doubtful if anything surprised Maudie Partridge these days. She reached up to kiss his mouth.

'Excuse me, my dear. I must be on my way,' the distinguished gentleman interrupted, ponderously.

'Ta-ta, Bunty, darling. Thanks for the lovely roses,' chirped Maudie, with an enchanting smile.

'My pleasure.' He bowed to Maudie and Jane, and lifted his silk hat in salute of the girls, who chorused, 'Ta-ta, darling.' Then he was gone.

In the meantime, Charles had found his voice. It was not often that he lost it, but it was not every day he was kissed by a music hall star.

'I wanted to congratulate you. I loved all your songs, especially the 'Ave Maria'. My mother used to sing it when I was a small boy and lived with my parents in Singapore. Mother had a lovely voice, but not as good as yours.'

'Go on with you, flatterer!'

'No, I mean it. I agree with Auntie J. You sing like an angel.'

Maudie shrugged, and asked, 'Why didn't you bring Paulie?'

'He was not feeling too good, so we left him at home.'

'He was such a shy little boy.'

'He is still shy.'

'Not like you!'

'Not like me,' he grinned.

'Are you just up for the day?'

'Yes.'

'How's the Guvnor?'

'Fairly well, thank you, Maudie,' Auntie Jane answered.

'Give him my love.'

'I will.'

She had so much love to give away, she scattered it like rose petals. Charles would adore her, slavishly, but Maudie got bored with too much adoration. She was her own person, yet she belonged to everyone. It was a paradox.

'Could you come and have tea with us, Maudie? Charles and Vicky are catching the 6 o'clock train from Victoria. We thought to have tea in the station buffet,' Auntie Jane invited.

''Fraid not, Missus. The evening performance starts at

7.30. It's been nice seeing you. You too, Vicky. Give my love to Paulie. You engaged of anything?'

'No.' It was Vicky's turn to blush.

'Bags of time for that. She's only a kid,' said Charles, disparagingly, as a brother might speak of a sister.

'Come along, you two,' said Auntie Jane, who could see the sparks flying between them.

'Ta-ta, Missus.' Maudie watched them walk away. At the end of the passage Charles turned to wave, and she waved back. They would meet again.

'Did you see her home?' Paul asked.

'Who?'

'Vicky.'

'I put her in a cab and paid the cabby. Satisfied?'

'Yes, thank you.' Paul wondered what had happened to upset Charles. Like a bear with a sore head, as Mabel would have said.

Hunched over the fire in the nursery with a mug of cocoa, he had answered Gran's questions absentmindedly. Now she had excused herself and retired to bed. It had been a busy day, and she liked to read in bed for an hour or so. She found it relaxing.

Now they were alone, perhaps Charles would talk, Paul was thinking, as he sipped the hot drink of lemon and honey. Gran had rubbed his chest with camphorated oil. The vapour still clung to his clothes, but the smell was not unpleasant.

'Fabulous,' muttered Charles, staring into the fire.

'Who?'

'Maudie Partridge.'

'You liked her then?'

'*Liked* her? I damn well nearly made a fool of myself! I've got to see her again.'

'When?'

'Soon.'

'How?'

'When? How? Don't ask such bloody silly questions!'

'Sorry.'

Charles placed his mug in the hearth. When you had met and fallen in love with a girl like Maudie Partridge, you

246

should be drinking champagne, not cocoa! He lifted his head and stared at his friend with frowning brows. The firelight played on his red head. Tense with suppressed emotion, his normal light-hearted attitude to the opposite sex had completely deserted him.

'She sings like an angel, but there's devilment in her eyes. I had a feeling she was laughing at me,' he told Paul. 'We went backstage after the show. Auntie J said she would introduce me. The dressing-room was crowded with girls. It smelled pretty awful. A smart looking gent had just presented Maudie with a bouquet of roses. When she kissed him, I could have bashed his silly face. Heaven knows what came over me. She knew him pretty well. That was obvious. Called him Bunty, silly old fool. Old enough to be her father! But when she spotted Auntie J in the doorway, she left him standing there. You could tell she was pleased to see her. As for Auntie J, she greeted Maudie like a daughter.'

'She would. She calls them all her children, and tries to get them in off the street. I like Auntie J. She doesn't preach, but she's a good Christian. So is Uncle Edward. They are a wonderful couple. They run that Mission on a shoe-string. I would like to join them, if they will have me, when I've finished at Winchester.'

'What about Sandhurst?'

'I am not going to Sandhurst.'

'But it's expected. Your name's down for Sandhurst, like mine.'

'I know, but I am not going.'

'My dear chap, since when have you arrived at this momentous decision?'

'Ages ago.'

'You're a dark horse. What's the parent going to say?'

'"You will do as you are told, my son".'

'But you won't?'

'No.'

Charles chuckled. It had taken his mind off Maudie. If Paul intended to fight his father over this question of Sandhurst, then he had more guts than he had given him credit for, and he had supposed there were no secrets between them. Years ago, of course, when Cartwright and

Smith Minor shared everything, including the tuck box, at prep school, there had been some mention of his best friend not wanting to be a soldier, but that was natural. A chap changed his mind, was expected to change his mind. Hudson Minor was set on being an engine driver, and was persuaded to take up chemistry because his father was a pharmacist. But Charles could foresee a battle between this father and son. There would be no persuasion with that arrogant, self-opinionated parent. And Paul was frightened of his father, so what chance had he of getting his own way? Looking at that pale, ascetic face in the firelight, Charles had to admit it was not the face of a man of action. It was the face of a scholar.

'Have you told anyone else about this decision of yours?' he asked, striking a match to light a cigarette.

'Yes, Uncle David.'

'The officer who was thrown from his horse, whom you went to visit in Wales?'

'Yes.'

'What did he advise?'

'To go my own way.'

'And disobey your father?'

'Yes.'

'That seems hardly in keeping with a fellow officer.'

'They are sworn enemies.'

'Why?'

Paul smiled reflectively. 'Because they were both in love with my mother.'

'And she chose your father?'

'Yes.'

'Poor fellow. What a shame. And he is still a bachelor?'

'Yes, and likely to remain so.'

'The faithful swain. But rather pointless, don't you think?'

'No, I admire him tremendously.'

'You're a romantic, my dear fellow. I am a realist.'

'What about Maudie?'

'Maudie will be the one exception.'

'And Vicky?'

'I will leave Vicky to you.'

'But it's you she loves.'

'She is so young, so naive. She has been so sheltered.'

'Not entirely. With her mother a patient in that Clinic, Vicky looks after her father. They are very devoted.'

'She never mentions her mother.'

'Only to Gran. They go together, once a month, to visit Vicky's mother. It upsets them both. There is no cure, so she stays in the Clinic. It's a mental condition.'

'That's bad.'

'Your Grandmama is not going to approve of your decision. Isn't she expecting you to follow in your father's footsteps?'

'It's taken for granted.'

'How do you propose to wear down all the family opposition? I don't envy you.'

'Gran will support me, when the time is ripe.'

'Have you made any plans?'

'Uncle David has suggested a theological course at University. I think I shall follow up that suggestion. I shall have to enrol in the New Year to get a place. He has offered to meet the cost of fees and expenses. It's very good of him. I thought of asking Auntie Jane and Uncle Edward if I could work at the Hoxton Mission during the vacations. It would be useful experience, and they are bound to approve of my decision. They couldn't afford to pay me, but I should get free board and lodging, so I could manage. There won't be a penny piece from Father. He will be furious,' Paul sighed. 'I'm sorry I have to deceive my parents, but the army is not for me, Charles.'

'A pity. I was looking forward to Sandhurst in your company, but it seems we have to go our separate ways next year. We must keep in touch. I shall often be dashing up to Town if Maudie is still at the Metropolitan. I have just got to see her. Saturday will be the only day to get away without too many questions being asked.'

'What about rugger and cricket, and all the other sports you are so keen on?'

Charles grinned. 'I have a very strong feeling that sport will be relegated to second place!'

'I never thought to hear you say that. Maudie must be very special.'

'She is.'

On the landing below, a door closed.

'Grandmama is going to bed,' said Paul. 'She clings to the drawing-room fire till her bedroom is nicely warm. Gran lit her fire a couple of hours ago. I keep the coal buckets filled when I am at home, but it's Freda's job when I am away. It offends her dignity, but Mabel is too old and too breathless to climb all those stairs. Every time Freda hands in her notice she had to be offered more money, and Grandmama has reluctantly to open her purse.'

'What age is your Grandmama?'

'I have no idea. I suppose Gran would know, but it seems rather an impertinent question. She is actually my great-grandmother, of course, but she does not care to be reminded of the fact. It makes her feel old.'

'But she *is* old.'

'Yes, but she takes such good care of herself, she does not give the impression of a very elderly lady. I have never got close to her and cannot pretend to know her intimately, but one has to admire the trouble she takes with her appearance. You wouldn't catch Grandmama in dressing-gown and slippers outside her bedroom. I still find her rather formidable.'

'That's because you are still a little afraid of her. I have never found her formidable, but then I was not so easily scared as a small boy, and I had the advantage over you, with a guardian who took very little notice of my brother and myself, provided we kept out of his way. I may have found your parent somewhat formidable. He does rather tend to dominate, doesn't he?'

'Yes, he does.'

'It will be interesting to see his reaction when he discovers his son to be a rebel.'

'You make it sound so disgraceful.'

'Your fond Papa will see it as such.'

'You sound as though you were on his side.'

'Only because I can appreciate his disappointment. The regiment is a proud tradition. So is Sandhurst. How would

250

you feel if your only son rejected it for the priesthood?'

'I hope I should understand, and to understand is to forgive.'

'It's not as simple as that, my dear fellow. It's a question of heredity. What is in the blood will out, they say, and where does the priesthood come into it?'

'My paternal great-grandfather was Vicar of St Matthew's when Uncle Edward was curate.'

'Go on.'

'This army tradition, as you call it, dates back only two generations. That is not long. Not long enough to claim priority over the priesthood. And what about trade? Three generations in trade on the maternal side of the family. I could just as easily have decided on being a draper. Even Grandmama would find it difficult to disapprove of trade. After all, Father was nicknamed Thomas the Third, and he did inherit Thomas Brent & Son. With a private income he is not obliged to live on his army pay. Grandmama, by that time, may have been a little ashamed of the trade connection. To see her favourite grandson in scarlet uniform would be more to her liking. No, Charles, I am not convinced I am behaving disgracefully.'

'Point taken,' said Charles with a grin. It was not often that Paul was so articulate, but if he was determined on the priesthood, it would be a necessary part of a profession that depended largely on the personality of the preacher. Could this shy, delicate boy, on the verge of manhood, have the courage and the endurance for such a demanding profession? Those dark, expressive eyes, so like kind Gran's, held a depth of feeling and steadfastness. They did not smile readily, and often reflected a sadness that seemed irrelevant to those who were not acquainted with Paul's history. But he had survived prep school with creditable success in the classroom, if poor on the playing field. Public school had continued the sound policy. The individual was tailored to the system. Yet here was Paul, in the last year, already rejecting the system in his search for the truth and purpose of the individual.

In the adjoining room, Ellen listened to their voices with a sad heart. The voices had changed, as everything else had changed. The boys' voices had broken in adolescence, when

251

they had grown and developed so quickly she was shocked into realization of their impending manhood. Now they both had topped her own height, and she was the tallest of the sisters.

Propped against the pillows, she turned the pages of *David Copperfield* with only a desultory interest, for the voices in the next room claimed her attention from the printed page. Charles Dickens could usually be relied upon to take her mind off her worries at the end of the day, but not tonight. She was worried about Vicky. That poor child would break her heart if Charles was serious about this showgirl. And he had talked of nothing else but Maudie Partridge since he arrived back. It had seemed so natural for Vicky to fall in love with Charles, since he had spent every holiday at The Haven since he was seven. Roderic had grown up with Bella in much the same way, like brother and sister, then sweethearts. She could remember them sitting on the back stairs, holding hands, when they were supposed to be taking part in a game of hide-and-seek, the Christmas they announced their engagement. But Charles was not Roderic. It was wishful thinking to make plans for someone as casual and carefree as Paulie's funny old Smith Minor. He was a dear boy, but she couldn't forgive him if he made Vicky unhappy. Growing up was a painful process at any time, and when you fell in love with the wrong person, and that love was not reciprocated, then it could be disastrous.

Shivering at the remembrance of her own love story, all those years ago on the North West Frontier, Ellen closed her eyes against a memory that still could hurt and haunt a guilty conscience. The years had left their mark on two of her children. Only Bella had escaped. And now, history and heredity were repeating themselves. It was Vicky's turn to be rejected for a bright new personality, and Charles was too fascinated to notice what he was doing to a young and innocent girl. First love was so very precious, and so fragile. It could be shattered by an unkind word or a broken promise. And Vicky wore her heart on her sleeve. She adored Charles.

Now Paul was the go-between, forfeiting a relationship that had seemed so promising, so permanent. It was not in his nature to be jealous of Charles, or to criticize his best friend. Ten years was a long time, and Paul was still a loyal disciple. In this new, unexpected development, however, Ellen could foresee these loyalties threatened if Vicky's happiness was at stake. To stand aside for Charles was natural, but to see Vicky rejected for Maudie Partridge would be unforgivable.

Listening to the voices in the next room, her own feelings were mixed, and she was saddened by the changes that seemed inevitable in the near future. All three would go their separate ways. This would be the last Christmas they would spend together, for Vicky would start her training at St Thomas's Hospital in the New Year. Basil was an unselfish father, and had agreed to the separation, though he wished there was a teaching hospital locally. It had to be London. And Charles would be at Sandhurst. As for Paul, he had not yet decided − or had he?

Paul was a dark horse these days. Surely he could confide in her and trust her not to divulge his aspirations to Thomas? She would not probe. She knew him too well. They were two of a kind. She knew only that he was not going to Sandhurst. The regiment would soon be posted overseas again, and Thomas naturally assumed that Charles and Paul would be starting their military training together. Sandhurst, for his father, was a foregone conclusion. It would never occur to him that a son of his could actually refuse to enrol. How would he react to the letter he would receive? Ellen shrank from the angry scene she could visualize in this very house. Would Paul have the courage to withstand the onslaught of such parental authority? Would he succumb to that domineering influence? Was he still afraid of his father? Such questions must soon be answered, and she feared for the future of her darling grandson.

Chapter Ten

The old house seemed to tremble to the vibration of that loud, rasping voice. The dining-room door had closed on Thomas and his son. It had closed with a slam, for the irate father had kicked it shut with a booted foot.

He had arrived from Aldershot in mid-afternoon, taken a cab from the station, pushed open the green gate, and strode down the tiled path. The clatter of the brass knocker had brought Ellen hurrying up the back stairs. The visit was not unexpected, for Paul's letter had been posted the previous day.

When she opened the door to the tall, distinguished figure in the scarlet uniform, he barely acknowledged her greeting.

'Where is he?'

'Upstairs,' she answered, quietly, and stood aside.

Paul was standing on the landing. He looked very young and vulnerable in a grey flannel suit and school tie. There was no escape. As he slowly descended the stairs, his dark eyes met the hostile glance of cold blue eyes and were held captive in their magnetism. As far back as he could remember, riding on Ayah's hip, those cold blue eyes had made him tremble. 'Put him down' had been his very first memory of that stern commanding presence. And Ayah had put him down, but had not let go of his hand. To remember it now, as he descended the stairs, was like a caress. He could feel her hand, small and bony as a bird's claw, and his fingers closed round it. This was not the first time he had felt the old woman's presence at a moment of acute sadness or fear.

Not a word had been passed between father and son as Paul descended the stairs, but when he had stepped into the hall, Thomas turned on his heel and marched smartly towards the dining-room. A brief glance at Nana in passing showed her white-faced and anxious. The drawing-room door was closed, but Grandmama was listening.

'Now!' thundered Thomas, 'let us hear no more of this nonsense! You will take back every word of that letter, and I shall personally escort you to Sandhurst.'

'No, Sir. I am not going to Sandhurst.'

'How dare you contradict me! You will do as you are bid, and no two ways about it. Have you taken leave of your senses?'

'No, Sir.'

'Well, then?'

'I have no heart for it, Sir.'

'Who is talking of heart? This is a question of duty and obedience to your parents and to the regiment. Have you no pride, no ambition?'

'Not for the army, Sir.'

'No, it is too dangerous, is it not? I always knew you were a coward. Well, you are going to Sandhurst if I have to drag you there!'

'No, Sir, I am not going to Sandhurst.'

A stinging blow across the face sent Paul sprawling. It was not unexpected, but his slight, boyish frame had small resilience.

'Get up on your feet and take your punishment like a man!' growled Thomas, standing over him.

Paul staggered to his feet and was instantly felled to the floor. His head swam and blood trickled from his ear.

'On your feet!' roared Thomas in a fine fury.

And Paul went down with a crash, striking his head on the leg of the table, and lay still.

When Ellen burst into the room, Thomas was gazing down at the boy with a pitying glance.

'Aren't you ashamed of yourself?' she demanded, bending over the prostrate form. Taking Paul's head on her lap, she could feel the swelling bruise. His nose was bleeding, his teeth had cut through his lower lip, and a trickle of blood from his ear had soiled his collar. But he was breathing, and he was only stunned.

'You could have killed him!' she accused her son, with blazing eyes.

'A coward is better dead. I wash my hands of him,' he said, and stalked away.

Paul opened his eyes. 'I heard what he said,' he whispered. 'I'm sorry, Nana.'

'Lie still,' she coaxed, cradling his head. 'And stop reproaching yourself. I am proud of you, Paul. You stood up to him in spirit for the first time, and he did not expect it.'

'It's strange, but I am no longer afraid of him.'

Ellen's dark eyes were soft as velvet now as she dabbed at the bleeding nose and lip with a clean handkerchief. 'That's something I have been waiting to hear for a very long time, my darling,' she said, and kissed the swelling bruise on his head.

The drawing-room door opened and closed. Thomas strode across the room, fell on his knees and laid his proud head in the waiting lap.

'My darling boy, that was rather brutal.' Grandmama smoothed his blond hair. Her faded blue eyes were tender with love for this man. He was breathing heavily. She could smell his sweat. That violent temper should have been curbed when he was a little boy, but she would not have him restrained in any way, and he was never punished, not until he went away to prep school.

'Was it deserved, the punishment?' she asked, quietly.

He lifted his head. His eyes were anguished. 'That a son of mine should reject the regiment. It is inconceivable. He is not going to Sandhurst.'

'Where is he going?'

'To London University.'

'That is not such a bad thing.'

'Dearest Grandmama, how can you condone such deceit? Paul is taking a course in theology. He wants to be a priest!'

'*He wants to be a priest? My God!*'

'Exactly,' said Thomas, with a groan.

'What would you like to do?' The question had been asked a

score of times by a score of admirers in all classes of society since she made such a hit at the Metropolitan. It was fun. Everything was fun. Variety was the spice of life. Charlie was not the youngest of her admirers, but he was the only red-head and cheeky as a Cockney sparrow. In his blazer and boater he cut quite a dash, and he doffed his boater with a flourish, and proffered his arm with a man-of-the-world air. She knew by the blazer and the school tie that he could not be more than eighteen.

This was their second date. She had much enjoyed the first, at the fair in Battersea Park. They had sampled everything, like a couple of kids, and deserved to be sick, but they both had strong stomachs. Charlie was taking French leave again from that posh school. It was Sunday, and they were not the only couple meeting under the clock at Victoria station. It had not taken long to get acquainted. Well, he could hardly carry on calling her Miss Partridge when they were practically standing on their heads on the switchback railway! There was no better place to get acquainted with a young beau than Battersea Park. The old codgers liked to drive out to Richmond or Kew Gardens, and the romantic foreigners had a preference for dinner by candlelight in some stuffy little restaurant in Soho. It was all experience, and she enjoyed their company.

Charlie was a scream. At the end of the day in Battersea Park he had taken her back to her lodgings by hansom cab, and kissed her goodnight with such passion he had knocked off her hat! And that was the signal for a good laugh. Anyway, she was not looking for a serious attachment. 'Take me as you find me,' she would say, and 'So far and no farther'.

Maudie Partridge, from Hoxton, was still, surprisingly, a virgin. She had seen too many babies born on the wrong side of the blanket to be landed with one. So she smiled, enchantingly, at Charlie's question and took his arm.

'What about the river? We could take one of them ferry boats from Westminster Pier and go as far as Hampton Court.'

'Your servant, Ma'am,' said he.

257

'With the greatest pleasure,' she giggled happily, and they walked away together.

Heads turned to look back at them. 'That's Maudie Partridge,' they said. And young Charles Smith, proud as Lucifer to be seen escorting a star of the Music Hall, saw himself as her special favourite, destined to become her lover. In his scarlet uniform, as a Sandhurst cadet, he would court her in the old gallant tradition. The cheers of his supporters on the rugby field faded into insignificance when Maudie hung on his arm, and he caught a glimpse of auburn curls under the brim of her wide, leghorn hat.

Taking a cab to Westminster Pier, and getting an appreciative *'Thank you, Sir!'* for the handsome tip, was a further boost to Charlie's morale. The cabby's broad grin followed the young couple as they ran down the steps and jumped aboard. There was barely room for two more on deck, but Maudie smiled, and obliging passengers moved along to make room for them. With his arm about her slim waist, and the scent of 'Ashes of Roses' in his nostrils, Charlie considered himself the luckiest of fellows. The memory would linger long after their brief acquaintance was broken, for first love was particularly nostalgic.

He had no need to ask if Maudie was enjoying it, for she made no secret of the fact. It was one of her most endearing qualities that she abandoned herself to the pleasure of the moment, so that each and every beau imagined himself the be the favourite. She snatched off her hat, the breeze tossed her curls, and her sparkling eyes invited a kiss. But it was a laughing mouth and it was fun to tease.

'This is the life, Charlie boy!' said she, as though she had no other thought in her head than sailing down the river on a Sunday afternoon. Then, as suddenly as she had laughed, she was serious. 'I wish we had all those kids from Hoxton aboard. They wouldn't half enjoy theirselves.'

'One of these days, when I make a lot of money, we will hire one of these boats and fill it up with your kids from Hoxton,' he promised, recklessly.

'Are you expecting to make a lot of money, then?' she asked, eagerly.

'When my ship comes home.'

'That's what Freddie says.'

'Who's Freddie?'

'My brother. You'd like him.'

'Should I?'

'Freddie's got guts. You should have seen him hopping around on his crutches when he was a kid. Only one leg, see? Now he's got an artificial one, and a job in the City. Proud as Punch. The Missus at the Mission taught us both to read and write and grammar. That's important, grammar, ain't it, Charlie?'

'Very important,' he agreed, wishing they could get back to a more personal topic.

'The Missus from the Mission is Paulie's Auntie Jane, isn't she?'

'Yes.'

'I like her.'

'Everyone likes the Missus. Mind jew, she don't stand no nonsense from the kids, and you don't get a penny for nothing. You has to earn it.'

'How?'

'How?' Maudie shrugged. 'Filling the coal buckets, peeling the spuds, fetching the bread, cleaning the steps. It's like I said, you has to earn it afore you can spend it.'

'Quite right, too,' a jocular individual in a check suit and bowler hat agreed heartily.

'You come from Hoxton, Mister?' Maudie asked.

'Elephant and Castle,' he answered with a chuckle.

'Makes you laugh, don't it?' she giggled, and turned her attention back to Charlie whose arm had tightened possessively about her waist.

'This is the first time I been down the river on one of these boats. I seen 'em passing, but that's not the same as being on board. Trust you to think of it Charlie.' She squeezed his hand affectionately, and he blushed at the compliment.

Had he thought of it? Did it matter if Maudie had given him the credit for this trip down the river?

'What's it like at Hampton Court?' she was asking. 'I know there's a maze and people get in and can't get out.'

'I only know what I've read in the history books, and history is not one of my best subjects. To tell you the truth,

259

I'm a pretty poor scholar. Paul's the brainy one. There's sure to be a booklet we can buy and read all about it.'

'Do it matter about the history book, I mean, if we can see it for ourselves?'

'Not really.'

'Let's get lost in the maze and have something nice to eat. With all this lot, and all the other visitors, it should be a good old crowd.'

'You like to be with people, don't you?'

'Why, of course. I ain't never been on me own, not ever.'

'Not with one other person, like me, for instance?'

She shook her head. 'I still like to see people all about the place. Is that being queer? I guess it's because I'm a Cockney, born and bred. That's what matters, Charlie. It's where you was born and bred, not what you do when you grow up. That's me. I won't never be no different. Take me or leave me.'

'I'll take you, Maudie,' he grinned.

'That's settled then.' She kissed his mouth, for the second time, and her curls brushed his cheek. All his pulses raced. Her nearness was a tantalizing reminder of the shapely legs under the long skirts. He had seen them on the stage, and again at the Battersea Park fun fair. There would be no opportunity for showing off lovely legs at Hampton Court.

He sighed, and Maudie asked, innocently, 'You all right then?'

'Fine,' he lied. If only they could be alone together. But he knew now they would always be together in a crowd. For the first time in his life he wanted to be serious, and Maudie was light-hearted and carefree.

It was pandemonium on board. Children were racing round the deck, passengers laughing and shouting, and a dark little man, with a sad little monkey in a red jacket, played a hurdy-gurdy. Three tunes, over and over. 'Rule Britannia', 'Soldiers of the Queen' and 'The Blue Danube'. Maudie was entranced with the sad little monkey.

'Give me a penny,' she demanded, and ran off to drop it in the bag.

'Poor little bugger. It's wet itself,' she announced,

compassionately. And Charlie joined in the shout of laughter from their near neighbours.

Loud-voiced and vulgar, Maudie was soon the centre of attraction.

'We seen you in the show at the Metro, luv,' said one of her admirers.

'Give us a song, duckie,' said another.

'Wait a tick. Give the hurdy-gurdy man a chance,' she told them, like a good trouper.

So they waited, till the last note had died away.

'What would you like?' she asked. Since they all shouted something different, she sang her own particular favourite — 'Onward Christian Soldiers' because it reminded her of Hoxton and the Salvation Army band. It was a surprising choice for such an occasion, but it had a good chorus and they all joined in.

Charles would always remember that trip down the river, and the sudden hush on board when that pure, angelic voice floated across the water. She had slipped out of his embrace, and stood there, unadorned, and unaffected, while he cradled her hat on his knees.

They would not let her stop till she sang several old favourites, and had promised more for the homeward journey.

'You Maudie's sweetheart, Mister?' asked one small girl, seeing the hat on his knees.

He was pleased and proud to answer in the affirmative. If loving Maudie meant sharing her, then he would do so, for as long as he was privileged to enjoy her favours.

But he did get her alone in the maze at Hampton Court.

Student nurses were not encouraged to dream. 'Life is real, life is earnest' was obviously the maxim on which Sister Tutor based her training. She was a sturdy, forthright Scotswoman, and Vicky was not the only one to feel the lash of a sharp tongue if her thoughts wandered during a lecture. A flaming red head and a cheeky freckled face sometimes intruded on the grim reality of anatomy that first year at St Thomas's.

She had seen Charles only once since that day at the Metropolitan Music Hall when young Maudie Partridge had cast her spell over his unsuspecting red head. On that

261

occasion, she had been enjoying a brief spell of off-duty with her new friend, Connie Marshall. The ferry boat at Westminster Pier was already crowded and ready to cast off when the young couple leapt out of the cab and ran down the steps.

Under the tight bodice of the uniform dress, Vicky's heart missed a beat. Choked with emotion, she followed Connie's pointing finger.

'I know that girl. Her name's Maudie Partridge. She used to live in Hoxton, next door to my Auntie Flo. She made quite a hit with her voice, so they say, but I wouldn't call it all that remarkable.'

Vicky made no answer. The Charles who had swung the girl from the cab and run with her down the steps was not the Charles she had known in Worthing. Her Charles had never helped her out of the station cab, nor taken her hand over the steep, shingled beach. He had led the way with long, loping strides, and she followed in breathless haste. She was his slave, his willing, adoring slave, while he treated her with the rough affection of a brother.

As the ferry boat moved slowly away from the pier, she could see them seated, close together, on a crowded bench. Maudie was laughing up at him, and Charles had an arm about her waist. Their happiness was so natural, so spontaneous, she felt no envy, only a great sadness. He had fallen in love with Maudie as she danced and sang on the stage of the Metropolitan that Saturday afternoon, and who could blame him? She was so lovely, so vivacious, she cast a spell over her audience, and Charles had been entranced by her vivid personality. Maudie was his first love, but not the first girl he had teased and kissed. Maudie was different.

He had told Paul he was in love with her and wanted to marry her, but first he must serve his time at Sandhurst. That was a year ago, and Vicky had seen her smile driving in the park with the elderly admirer she called Bunty. If she was flirting with Charles, he would be hurt, and she didn't want him to be hurt.

'She's got what it takes, that Maudie Partridge, and she knows it,' Connie was saying, spitefully.

'What's that?' Vicky asked, in a choked voice.

262

'Sex appeal. It stands out a mile. Can't mistake it. You and me have missed out on sex appeal, Vic, and we haven't got the looks, neither. Well, you're not bad. You've got nice eyes, but look at me – plain Jane and no nonsense! That's why we haven't got a regular fellow. Men are all alike. It's sex appeal and a pretty face.'

'Not *all* men, Con.' She was thinking of Paul.

'All we are likely to meet for the next three years or so. Haven't you noticed how those young students hang around in the canteen whenever Margery is in our company? It's not us they're waiting for.'

'I know. She *is* pretty.'

'But dumb. She won't even pass the first year exam, you'll see.'

'You don't need to be clever when you're as pretty as Margery.'

'I wonder why she took up nursing in the first place? I bet she thought a nurse had only to bathe fevered brows and feed the patients chicken broth!' Connie giggled. 'She wouldn't be the first one to be sadly disillusioned, would she, Vic?'

Vicky had the grace to blush. It *had* been a shock to discover a first year probationer spent her days rushed off her feet, emptying bed pans, scrubbing lockers, and mopping out the sluice. There were so many rules and regulations to remember, so many superior beings entitled to give orders. Vicky's head was in a whirl, her feet ached, and her hands were permanently red from the hot soda water. Yet, for all the hard work and strict discipline, she would not have changed it for any other job. It suited her mentality. She liked looking after people. She liked the good fellowship among the probationers, all struggling with the same conditions. And she liked being called Nurse. Many of the elderly patients could not discriminate between the uniforms and called everyone Nurse. They were so pathetically grateful for the smallest service. '*Thank you, Nurse,*' and a brave smile. Vicky loved the old ones, and would have liked to have a little friendly chat, but it was a crime to linger at the bedside, and if you were caught giggling in the sluice with a fellow student, your life would not be worth living for the rest of the day. Staff Nurse could be even more dictatorial than Sister. It was 'Yes, Sister', 'No, Sister' from morning till night.

'They say if you can stick it for the first year, you may eventually find yourself qualified,' Connie had observed, but several girls had already left.

'It's like boarding school, only more so,' Selina Bartley pointed out in her upper-class voice. They came from all classes of society, with the same determination, but not all had the stamina or the humility to subject themselves to such gruelling discipline.

Connie only just managed to escape instant dismissal when she answered back Sister Tutor in an unguarded moment. 'Count ten before you answer' was a good maxim in normal circumstances, but not as a trainee nurse. There was no time! From the moment you opened your eyes in the dormitory till you closed them again at the end of the day, not a single moment was wasted. A rigid timetable had to be observed. Solid, nourishing meals were eaten with an eye on the clock. Punctuality was a fetish.

Vicky seldom got though the day without a reprimand, but she was not deliberately lazy, disobedient or disruptive — all crimes of which you could be accused in a single day if you were not careful. There was no time to write letters, but it was comforting to hear a familiar voice on the telephone once a week. A telephone had been installed at The Haven, and the General Manager of Thomas Brent & Son had a connection between his office and the flat.

As for Paul, he was also enduring the rigours of a first year student with the same determination. A weekly letter from Nana and another from Uncle David were all he could expect, and neither could afford to enclose more than a florin, which he spent on the bare necessities.

To accept money as an adult was humiliating, and he soon decided to follow the example of other students lacking private means in the long vacation. Washing up in the steaming basement of a hotel kitchen was not an easy way to earn a few shillings, but it eased his conscience — and a conscience was a very active and disturbing element in a student of theology.

He had not seen Vicky since she left for London. A whole year had passed since their last meeting at The Haven, and he missed her intolerably. There was no way of knowing whether Charles was still courting Maudie, for they had lost touch since he enrolled at Sandhurst. Another chapter had closed, and the three who had seemed inseparable in those early years at The Haven had drifted apart. New careers and new interests claimed their time and attention. In three separate worlds Vicky, Paul and Charles were discovering fresh limits to their energy and enthusiasm for their chosen careers. Vicky and Charles enjoyed a healthy, gregarious attachment to their surroundings and their new friends. Paul was a loner. For the first time in his young life he could enjoy the privacy his soul craved in an atmosphere of intellectual inspiration. His small study was a haven of quiet contemplation of the Scriptures, and the thoughtful searching of his mind and heart. Poor health still dogged his footsteps, however, and he knew for certain now that he would never pass the medical for the Mission field. It was a sad disappointment, but there were other ways of serving God, and it was Nana, in one of her weekly letters, who suggested an alternative. Why not apply to the Vicar of St Matthew's in Worthing towards the end of his three years of study at the University? There might be a vacancy for a curate after his ordination. This new trend of thought was welcome to both, for Ellen would know the great satisfaction of having her beloved grandson living locally, and the long association with St Matthew's would enjoy a fresh impetus. Cartwright was a name to be remembered and revered in the annals of St Matthew's.

The future that had seemed so bleak had suddenly acquired an optimistic outlook. The letters they now exchanged had a definite purpose and direction, and they both would be spared the long separation that missionaries suffered.

Paul spent most of his free time at the Hoxton Mission, where he was encouraged in the new project by his Uncle Edward, a curate at St Matthew's in his younger days. It was discussed long and earnestly until it seemed to be a foregone conclusion, but then the practical Auntie Jane reminded them they were counting their chickens before they were hatched. A disciple of Christ had a long road to travel towards priesthood. She was not at all enamoured at the prospect of her great-nephew under the autocratic thumb of the Vicar of St Matthew's, who would probably work the poor boy to death. Vicars were all alike in Auntie Jane's honest estimation, and she could not forget or forgive the misery her darling Edward had endured. Paul was just such another – shy, nervous, and easily persuaded to overtax his strength.

'You must not allow yourself to be pushed into a situation for which you have no particular bent, dear boy,' she argued.

To meet Vicky, face to face, on the Embankment one Sunday afternoon in late Autumn would be the quickest way to heal the breach between them. Staring at the familiar little figure in the neat uniform, with a leaping heart, he smiled that shy, enchanting smile and snatched off his hat.

'Vicky!'

'Paul!'

The cry of recognition was simultaneous. They met and hugged as though they had never been parted.

'What are you doing here?' Vicky demanded, breathlessly.

'Looking for you.' His dark eyes were tender as he searched her face. 'It's true. I often walk this way on Sunday afternoon on the principle that if I come here often enough, I am certain to run into you one of these days.'

'Oh, *Paulie*.' She shook her head at him. 'Why didn't you write?'

'I thought ...'

'You thought I was still in love with Charles?'   'Yes.'

'It's all over. He doesn't want me. It was all my fault,' she sighed.

'Shall we sit down?' he suggested.

They sat on a bench overlooking the river. It was grey and sluggish. A fresh wind tossed a scrap of paper across their feet. Their eyes dropped, then lifted, and locked together.

'I've missed you,' he said.

'I've missed you,' she echoed.

266

They sat there, holding hands, in companionable silence, till Paul shivered.

'Where is your overcoat?' she asked.

'I don't possess one,' he confessed.

Then she was all maternal, wrapping her cloak about his thin shoulders, holding him in a close embrace. The years slipped away and they were children again at The Haven, huddled under the blankets, waiting for Norah to bring the mugs of early morning tea and the *petit beurre* biscuits. Their thoughts were matched in nostalgic memories as they sat there. Putting back the clock was a natural process now they were together again, clinging to the threads of childhood to soften the harshness of their separate adult lives. Growing up had been hurtful, for they had lost the trusting intimacy of those early years, the shared relationship. Only by going back in time could they find their way to a better understanding, a new awakening of the senses. Nana had bridged the gap that divided them since they left The Haven with her weekly letters, but being together under the cloak, with their arms entwined about each other's waist's, their breaths mingling, their two hearts beating as one, was to reach forward as well as to reach back.

Vicky was the first to speak. 'Why did you change your mind about training for the Mission field? Nana says you will apply for the curacy at St Matthew's after your ordination.'

'Yes. Are you very disappointed in me?'

'Only because we had talked about it so often.'

'I know I would not have passed the medical with a bronchial chest, and to tell you the truth, I did lose interest when I thought you were getting betrothed to Charles.'

'There was never any likelihood of that.'

'I'm sorry. I thought you were ideally suited, so compatible.'

'So did I, until he met Maudie.'

'But Maudie is just a butterfly. According to Auntie Jane, who has known her since she was a little girl, Maudie will marry for money, not for love, and certainly not a young army man, liable to be posted overseas.'

'Then I am sorry for Charles.'

'I think you will find he will get over it. Sandhurst and the regiment will claim his loyalty, for Charles is a born leader, and a man's man for all his philandering.'

'You are probably right. You know him better than I.'

In the thoughtful silence the breach was finally healed, and a deep sense of belonging established between them. They both felt it, and turned their heads in wonder. Dark, searching eyes answered all their questions.

It was Paul who recovered first from that moment of revelation. Cupping her face in his hands, he whispered, 'I love you.'

'I love you,' she echoed.

It was such a tender kiss, that first kiss, unlike any other kiss they had exchanged since that first day when a tearful little boy, homesick for Ayah and India, had been kissed by his little cousin. They were sweethearts now, but they still were cousins, and Paul would be afraid of the consequences. For Vicky, who had wanted Charles so desperately, it was indeed a revelation, for now there seemed to be all the time in the world to love and be loved by Paul. His gentleness was a contradiction of the arrogance and bossiness she had known with Charles. 'Do this – do that – come here!' Looking back on those years when Charles had spent all his holidays at The Haven, it was easy now to see that he had regarded her with the casual affection of a brother, and she herself had invented deeper feelings and emotions, and given his words a meaning that was not intended. The boisterous games, the teasing, the rough hugs were those of a carefree boy. Only when he saw Maudie, even before he had spoken or held her hand, he had fallen in love.

'What a lot of time we have wasted, darling. I must have been blind. I'm sorry,' she said.

'Time is not wasted if we discover the truth about ourselves, my dearest.'

'Am I your dearest?'

'Now and for ever.'

'Shall we tell them?'

'Only Nana and your father, Uncle Edward and Auntie Jane. Not Grandmama. She will disapprove most strongly of cousins getting betrothed.'

268

'It's an old wives' tale. Are you afraid?'

'When I'm with you I am not afraid of anything. You give me courage, sweetheart! I am rather a weak character, as you surely must know.'

'How dare you call yourself a weak character when you defied your father and refused Sandhurst?'

He smiled at her vehemence. 'That was just being stubborn.'

'It was *not*. It was courage, and I was so proud of you.'

'Were you?'

'Of course.'

They kissed again and sighed, rapturously. They were convinced their happiness was unique.

'How soon can we get married?' Paul asked, with boyish eagerness.

Vicky smoothed the lock of hair from his forehead and answered, reluctantly, 'When we have finished our training.'

'I suppose we have to be sensible?'

'Yes, we must. Student nurses are not permitted to marry, and you have to finish your course at the University.'

'Two years seems and eternity.'

'It will pass, and we shall have the rest of our lives together.'

'Shall you mind being poor? A curate's salary is somewhat meagre.'

'My darling, need you ask? I shall manage – until such times as you are promoted to Vicar!'

'Bless you,' said he, with a grateful hug.

The traffic of the river was slow-moving today – barges laden with coal and timber, and small craft piloted by sturdy helmsmen wearing reefer coats against the chilly breeze. The holiday season was over for another year, and the ferry-boats tied up at the pier. For many working-class Londoners, the holiday had consisted of a day on the river to Hampton Court or Greenwich. Some had taken day trips to Epping Forest by charabanc. Only the middle-class could afford to stay in a seaside boarding house for the two weeks annual holiday, but since the working-class were unaware of such privileges, they were not envious, on the principle that what you never have you never miss.

Huddled together under the cape, Vicky and Paul watched the traffic on the river in starry-eyed wonder at their own amazing good fortune. Could anything in the world compare with their sublime contentment? Would they ever forget this chilly Autumn day, when the warmth of their hearts warmed the atmosphere, and each other, with a glowing sense of well-being? The future was bright with the promise of everlasting togetherness, and the present could be tolerated because it was only a temporary separation. Once a week they would meet again, if only for a brief hour, for Vicky's hours of duty were changeable.

'It will be such fun, darling,' Vicky promised, as they scrambled out from under the cape. The little watch pinned to her uniform dress had reminded them she had barely twenty minutes to get back on duty, but she would run all the way. They clung together for a final hug and a kiss before they were torn apart, and Paul stood there, shivering and forsaken, watching the billowing cape that covered his beloved float away into the distance. At the top of the steps she turned to wave, and he waved back. Then she was gone, and his heart sank, for now it all seemed like a dream.

He hadn't Vicky's capacity to visualize a future in which they would live happily ever after. Only in her company could such a miracle be seen to be believable. Now she was gone, his doubts returned, and he was beset by worry. Supposing, just supposing, it was not God's will? Hadn't he been a little presumptuous? To be so occupied with the physical aspect of loving could be detrimental to the spiritual. It was a solemn thought. First and foremost, even before his love for Vicky, his love for and duty to God must take priority. Would Vicky understand this? In a sense, he had forsaken the regiment for God. The dedication and devotion that claimed his father was equally demanding, he supposed, and he wished they might have agreed on the principle of their differences. To serve the regiment, or to serve God. He had chosen God. But he had not looked ahead to marriage and the desires and demands of a wife.

Walking slowly back along the deserted Embankment,

his doubts increased. Had he made a mistake? Then he remembered Uncle Edward, that saintly man, whose living example of love and duty was an inspiration to a humble novice. Hadn't he taken for a wife a young woman of courage and determination, to share his life at the Hoxton Mission? And wasn't his Vicky a similar personality?

Pushing aside his gloomy thoughts, he stepped out briskly. He would take a bus to Hoxton, and be just in time to join them for the Sunday high tea.

Chapter Eleven

In the lonely flat over Thomas Brent & Son, Vicky's father sat dozing before an empty grate one evening in Christmas week. The store had remained open till 8 o'clock, and tomorrow, Christmas Eve, it would be 9 o'clock when they closed the doors on the last customer.

He was exhausted and depressed, and utterly out of sorts with everything and everybody, including Vicky, who had telephoned to say she was on the duty rota for Christmas Day, but he could expect her on Boxing Day. This was the second Christmas he had been disappointed, and his mother had found him poor company without his lively young daughter. The traditional merry Christmas had been sadly lacking in the festive spirit last year, and this year could only be a dreary repetition of last.

Looking back over the two years since Vicky had left home to start her training at St Thomas's, Basil knew he had slipped into the old habits and the black moods he had known before Prue was taken to the Clinic. The staff were once again wary of his temper and his sarcastic tongue. Work and sleep were a poor substitute for those few happy years when Vicky had been here to play the little mother with such loving concern for his health and comfort. When she went away, his home became merely a place to eat his breakfast and supper – his main meal was served in his office, but he had not appetite – and to sleep, exhausted.

The future seemed bleak. 'What had he done to deserve such misery?' he asked himself. Fate had dealt the cards unfairly. Twice married, and both wives lost to him, for

Prue would never come home. In a sense he had also lost Vicky, for when she had finished her training, she would marry Paul. One Sunday in the month they spent together, when he tried to recapture that sweet intimacy they had once enjoyed. But it was gone. Her heart was given to Paul, and her thoughts wandered. It was a relief to see her on the train at the end of the day.

His separation from his dearly loved daughter was a much deeper emotion than the separation from Prue. Had he been selfish in his desire to keep Vicky at home? He could have found her a much more congenial position in the store. Nursing was such a hard life. Indeed, she could have chosen any department, and they would have made room for her.

'No thank you, Daddy.' Vicky knew what she wanted. She was a very determined young woman.

He sighed, found a more comfortable place for his balding head, and drifted away into a dream world in which he was young and carefree, walking on the promenade with a girl on each arm. He recognized Lucy and Kate, as they used to be, in their pretty muslins and picture hats. They were laughing and teasing him. He was wearing a blazer and a boater. It was a hot Summer day, and the promenade was crowded with visitors. Then they were gone, Lucy and Kate, and on his arm – he could see her quite clearly when he turned his head – was the plump, jolly, manageress of Baby Wear. Her name was Rose Jackson. She had started as an apprentice in Haberdashery and had worked her way, by gradual stages, to be in charge of the department that had never given him a moment's anxiety in the past decade.

Rose, in middle-age, was still unmarried. She declared she was in love with Thomas Brent & Son, but to find her hanging on his arm on a crowded promenade was strangely suggestive. Could she be in love with the General Manager?

When the dream faded and he opened his eyes to the chilly room and the empty grate, Rose Jackson was still with him, in spirit if not in the flesh, and that blithe spirit had the power to lighten his heavy heart.

'Rose Jackson. Rose,' He whispered her name again, and liked the sound of it on his tongue. She was like a full-blown rose, with her flushed cheeks and fluttering hands.

Although he hoped to recapture the dream when he slept that night, it evaded him, but he slept soundly and woke refreshed to a new day a little after 7 o'clock. Undismayed by the thought of Christmas Eve – one of the busiest days in the year of Thomas Brent & Son – he took a leisurely bath, and dressed with meticulous care to every detail. So many of their regular customers liked to do their Christmas shopping till Christmas Eve, and the children were handed gifts by Father Christmas – blue for a boy, pink for a girl – in the fairy grotto. He remembered taking Vicky as a tiny tot to receive her gift, and her delight in the picture book, though she already had half a dozen in her toy cupboard. Opening her stocking on Christmas morning, she had exclaimed with lisping innocence, 'Isn't Father Kismas kind, Papa?'

Reflecting on such nostalgic memories, he drank two cups of tea, ate his boiled egg and two slices of toast and marmalade, and went downstairs. It was his custom to walk through every department before the store opened. With a feeling of self-importance, his hands tucked under his coat-tails, he watched the apprentices scurrying about with dusters, and received the homage that was his due – little bows and bobs from the lesser fry, and a respectful 'Good morning, Sir' from the heads of departments. This was his little world, his one absorbing occupation. All his working life had been spent here, and here he would remain till his retirement at seventy. But that day was still so far distant, he dare not reflect on the emptiness of his days without Thomas Brent & Son.

Shortly before 9 o'clock, he stood in the doorway of Baby Wear, his keen eyes observing the festive decorations and the pretty display of tiny garments on the counters. The young apprentice was putting her duster away, and a sales assistant arranging a bonnet on a pedestal.

Rose Jackson was standing on a step ladder, reaching up to a top drawer, displaying surprisingly slim ankles beneath the hem of her long black dress, uplifted breasts strained against the tight-fitting bodice. The posture was seductive, innocently so, but his senses were aroused, and his heart missed a beat. Suddenly aware of his scrutiny, she turned her head. Their eyes met, and held, for a long moment.

She blushed like a schoolgirl, confused by his penetrating glance. But she recovered quickly, stepped down the ladder, and greeted her superior with a warm smile.

'Good morning, Sir,' she said.

'Good morning, Miss Jackson,' he answered, and added, as an afterthought, 'Come to my office, if you please, in the coffee break.'

A startled expression troubled her grey eyes, then it was gone, and she was smiling again. 'Certainly, Sir.' She inclined her head, wondering why he should send for her on this particular day, when all heads of department met in his office for a glass of sherry and a mincepie when the store was closed, and received a bonus in a sealed envelope.

'Come in,' he called, in answer to the timid tap on the door at precisely 11 o'clock.

He was sitting behind his desk when she pushed open the door, but he stood up to greet her, grave-faced, as always.

'So there you are, Miss Jackson. Take a seat, if you please.' He indicated the chair facing the desk.

She sat on the edge of the chair and folded her hands in her lap. She tried not to worry. If, for any reason, she had given offence to a customer, she would apologize. What other reason could there be to invite her here? Her assistant was quite capable of taking charge in her absence, but she liked to be there for it was such a happy atmosphere in Baby Wear on Christmas Eve, with fond grandmothers and aunties choosing gifts for young relatives, and mothers standing their offspring on the counters to be measured.

'You will join me in a cup of coffee, will you not?' he asked.

'Thank you, Sir.'

'Cream?'

'Yes, please.'

'Sugar?'

'Yes, please.'

'One spoon or two?'

'Two please, Sir.'

'Ah, a sweet tooth?'

'I'm afraid so, Sir.'

275

'Why should you apologize? There is nothing untoward in liking your coffee sweet.'

'Oh, but it's not only coffee, Sir. It's everything. I even sprinkle sugar on the rice pudding, and it's quite adequately sweetened, and I can't resist cream buns or sweet biscuits.'

His glance swept over her comely figure. It did not surprise him that she was overfond of sweet things. What matter? He liked her that way, and would not wish to change her.

'My biscuits are plain. You will not care for them.' He handed her the plate, and she took one with a shy smile.

Sipping the hot coffee, Basil was wondering how to approach the subject of the interview. He had rehearsed his little speech in the bath. Confronted by the object of his dream, he was as tongue-tied as a schoolboy.

'Was there something you wished to discuss, Sir?' Rose prompted.

He put down his cup, leaned on the desk, and asked, quietly, 'What do you do on Christmas Day? I mean, do you spend the day with friends or relatives?'

Surprised by the question, she answered frankly, 'I have no relatives that I know of, Sir. I was brought up in an orphanage. As for friends, they have their own families at Christmas. It's a family time, isn't it? I go to church in the morning, and take a walk along the promenade in the afternoon. My landlady usually invites me to share their Christmas dinner. She lives in the basement with her husband.'

'You live in lodgings?'

'Yes, Sir.'

'That must be unquestionably dreary.'

'Not really, Sir. I read a lot, and I go to bed early.'

'What kind of reading? Do you like Dickens?'

'Too heavy going for me, Sir. I like something light and, well, romantic.' She was blushing again.

'To take your mind off work?'

She shook her head.

'To pass the time?'

'Yes.'

'You like it here?'

276

'I love it. Thomas Brent & Son is my life, and working here is my only pleasure.'

'Me too.'

'I know.' Her grey eyes were thoughtful, and she had forgotten to call him 'Sir'.

'I wondered whether you would care to join me tomorrow. I shall be spending Christmas Day with my mother. My daughter will be on duty at the hospital. I could call for you at 12 noon, if that would suit you?'

'I should like it very much.'

'That's settled then. Where do you live?'

'Number 8, West Buildings. Will your mother mind? I mean, she hasn't invited me.'

'*I* have invited you. Mother never questions my motives.'

He came round from behind the desk and took her hand in a warm, firm clasp. 'Just one thing I must emphasize, Miss Jackson. This is strictly confidential. You do understand?' He grinned boyishly.

'Yes, Sir. Thank you very much, Sir!' She bobbed a mock curtsey, her eyes dancing with mischief.

'Till tomorrow, then.' He opened the door and she slipped past, leaving behind a faint odour of perspiration.

If Christmas Eve had always been a happy day in Baby Wear, this year it was charged with such merriment, such mutual understanding between staff and customers, it would long be remembered. The beaming countenance of the manageress, and the excited dashing to and fro of the young apprentice, both contrived to add a quota of goodwill. Babies squealed and small children ran about, tossing coloured balloons, and stood on chairs to watch the cash box rattle across the ceiling.

Sustained by short breaks for meals, and occasional cups of tea delivered to the cubby-hole, known officially as Miss Jackson's office, these three willing servants of the public survived the last hectic hour before closing, then sank thankfully on to the little gilt chairs when the last customer had been escorted to the door. The young apprentice could hardly keep her head from nodding, she was so exhausted, and the twenty-year old assistant was suffering from a nagging head.

'You poor dears. Have I worked you too hard?' asked Rose, sympathetically.

Her assistant smiled weakly, and the young apprentice murmured, 'It's all right, thank you, Miss Jackson.'

'Well, off you go and thank you both. You've been simply splendid. You will find your Christmas bonus in my office, and my own little present. Bless you both. Have a happy Christmas.'

'Thank you, Miss Jackson. Have a happy Christmas,' they echoed. With wan smiles and weary feet, they walked away.

And Rose sat there, her plump body sagging with fatigue, but her thoughts were jubilant. Never in her wildest dreams had she imagined such a surprising climax to that interview. She was choked with emotion, remembering that teasing tone of his voice as he held her hand. 'This is strictly confidential, Miss Jackson. You do understand?' She *did* understand and she would be most discreet, but now she wished she could share the secret with someone. She had loved him dearly and devotedly since he first appointed her to be manageress of Baby Wear.

'Coming, Miss Jackson?' a brusque voice demanded from the open door.

She looked up to see the tall, regal figure of Grace Pearson, the manageress of Gowns. They had little in common, save the fact they both had started as apprentices. But this was Christmas Eve, and Rose was reminded the long day was not yet over.

In the crowded office, the General Manager was playing host to a dozen or so heads of departments, men and women, as varied in appearance and temperament as any group of people gathered to celebrate the eve of Christmas. The General Manager was obviously in a genial mood, pouring sherry, and handing round mincepies with smiling bonhomie. They laughed at jokes he repeated every Christmas Eve, and drank his health, but they did not linger for more than the half-hour that politeness demanded, for homes and families were waiting. Each and every one was willing to forget the several occasions in the past year when their genial host had seen fit to criticise their methods or contradict their opinions.

The General Manager was not such a bad fellow, they agreed. And who could blame him for his black moods when his home life was so sad and so lonely?

To a chorus of 'Happy Christmas, Sir!' they departed, clutching their sealed envelopes. The Christmas bonus was a godsend at this expensive season of the year. His short speech of thanks and appreciation was sincerely rendered, and his firm hand-clasp made amends for any misunderstanding.

And Rose Jackson was not the only one to feel the warmth of his personality that night.

When the cab stopped outside the terrace house in West Buildings, more than one pair of eyes peered out from behind the muslin curtains. The other lodgers had been informed that Miss Jackson would not be joining them for the traditional Christmas dinner in the parlour. The landlady stood on the basement steps to get a better view of the gentleman who had stepped out of the cab. Her romantic heart fluttered as she witnessed the meeting of her favourite lodger and the well-set-up gentleman on her doorstep.

Doffing his hat, he took Miss Jackson's hand with the warmest cordiality. In her Sunday best, smiling and blushing, she was assisted into the cab. The door closed, the cabby tugged on the reins, and they moved away.

In all the years that Miss Jackson had occupied the small back room on the second floor, her daily routine had followed the same pattern, year after year. She paid her rent regularly, had a pleasant manner, no gentleman callers, and in every respect could have earned a diploma as the perfect lodger.

The couple were much too occupied with each other to notice the landlady hovering on the basement steps, and she stood there watching the cab drive away with a sense of loss and disappointment. Christmas dinner would not be the same without her jovial company, and the parlour games in the evening, in which all her lodgers would participate, would be sadly lacking in laughter. She sighed as she closed the door of her basement apartment, filled with the savoury smells of roasting beef and boiling Christmas pudding.

'I've got a feeling she won't be with us much longer,' she told her husband.

'Who?' he asked blandly, lifting his eyes from the sports page of yesterday's '*Daily News*'.

'Miss Jackson.'

'Why? What's she done?'

'Just gone off in a cab with a gentleman friend. I told you, Fred, she'd been invited out for the day, only you don't listen.'

'Sorry, gal.' He grinned apologetically. And since she still could see in his balding head and drooping moustache a semblance of the dapper young man who had courted her some forty years ago, she forgave him.

In the meantime, the object of her thoughts was enjoying the close proximity of her gentleman friend in a ladylike manner. Her flushed cheeks and shining eyes contradicted her stiff posture and folded hands, however, and Basil was not unaware of her suppressed excitement. It pleased his ego. Four gaily wrapped packages, to be exchanged later in the day, were piled on the seat between them.

'Happy, Rose?' he asked, after a long companionable silence.

'Yes, Sir,' she answered, demurely.

'*Basil*,' he corrected. And her blush deepened as she spoke his name aloud for the first time.

His mother had the door open as the cab drew to a halt, and she hid her disappointment in a stiff smile of welcome. She had been hoping to see her grand-daughter, though she had been warned that she might be on duty. When a strange woman was handed out of the cab, she knew instinctively, with a mother's intuition, that this was not just any woman, but someone special.

'Mother, may I introduce Miss Jackson?' her son enquired politely, when he had kissed her cheek.

'How do you do, Miss Jackson.' She liked what she saw — a happy face, with a wide, generous mouth and kind grey eyes.

'Pleased to meet you, Ma'am,' said Rose, with a little bob.

Basil was carrying the packages as they followed his mother

into the house. It was going to be all right. Mother liked Rose. She had not liked Prue, but she had loved Lucy. Everyone had loved Lucy.

'Will you pour the sherry, dear, while I take Miss Jackson upstairs.'

Basil's mother led the way, the perfect hostess, as always, while he hung his coat and hat in the lobby, and smoothed his thinning hair with hands that were not quite steady.

'This is my son's room,' his mother was saying. 'He often sleeps here Sunday night since my grand-daughter went away to London. Leave your coat and hat on the bed. Come down when you are ready.'

'Thank you.' Rose was so anxious to please – too anxious, perhaps? And Basil's mother would be questioning her son, at this very moment, on her pedigree. She was a rather superior lady.

Removing the hat pins from her Sunday best hat she laid them carefully on the dressing table between the hair brushes. Then she took off her hat and slipped off her coat. It was beginning to look shabby, but she hadn't noticed it till today. Looking about the room, she could see, in her mind's eye, the boy who had grown into a man – a studious boy, for the tall bookcase was crowded with books – a boy who loved the sea, for a beautiful model of the Cutty Sark graced the chest of drawers – a boy who collected china cats; they were lined up on the mantelpiece – a boy who had covered one wall with autographed photographs of his favourite actors and actresses. This glimpse into the boyhood of the man she loved and admired was a moving experience. She felt she knew him better now, and she closed the door on the boy and went downstairs to find the man waiting in the hall.

'You have been admiring my cats!' he teased.

She nodded tremulously.

'Come along. Mother is waiting.' He took her arm. It was then that she knew there was still something of the boy in this middle-aged man, the only adored son, still influenced by his mother's strong personality. Today was a testing period. He had invited her here to meet his mother's approval or disapproval. Twice married he could not bear to upset her.

The General Manager of Thomas Brent & Son had no place

281

in his mother's house, yet his status had influenced her taste, and the middle-class lounge had replaced the working-class 'front room', and a comfortable settee had replaced the old horse-hair sofa. The parlour had been converted into a pleasant dining-room, and a small Christmas tree in the bay window was laden with all the baubles and the silver star that Basil remembered from his earliest childhood. Only the tinsel had tarnished and been replaced. The packages he had brought had been placed around the tub with several others. There was a time and a place for everything in this house, and they would be opened after they had eaten the Christmas dinner and washed the dishes.

There had been a stocking to open on Christmas morning in those early years, and small toys and books to help pass the time. Mother was right to keep the big presents till after dinner. Mother was always right. They smiled at each other with perfect understanding over the glass of sherry. That Mother had not liked Prue was unfortunate but understandable, for Prue was her own worst enemy. Now it did not matter any more, for they hadn't to meet or pretend a fondness they did not feel.

'Prue is in the best place. She should have been there years ago,' was his mother's only comment on the tragic situation.

She had already discovered that her guest was manageress of Baby Wear, that she lived in lodgings, and that she was unmarried. It was enough. She had been right in her intuition. Rose Jackson was not just any woman. She would fill the role of her son's mistress.

It was a solemn thought that kept intruding. She thought she knew her son, but she was mistaken, as every mother is mistaken, sooner of later. It saddened her, on this Christmas Day, when she had expected to be surrounded by the loving attention of a devoted son and affectionate grand-daughter. Not even with Lucy had she seen Basil so besotted. His amorous glances all but undressed the woman as he sipped his third glass of wine. As for Rose, her loud laughter was rather vulgar. Could she be jealous of this woman? she asked herself.

Rose was not a lady. She was not even ladylike. Two glasses

of wine was all she needed to tell a funny story and have Basil chuckling in a rare good humour. His mother thought it was a silly story, but then she was tired after all her exertions in the kitchen. One small glass of wine was all she allowed herself, because it went to her head.

That they were both deliberately covering up their nervousness did not occur to Basil's mother. Basil had carved the plump chicken while she carried in roast potatoes, brussel sprouts, bread sauce and gravy. She would not allow her guest to help, and Rose felt embarrassed watching the older woman, so obviously overwrought.

The Christmas pudding, served with brandy butter, was made from an old recipe handed down from mother to daughter.

'The best I've tasted, Ma'am,' said Rose, holding up her plate for a second slice. She ate with the enjoyment of a person whose healthy appetite is seldom satisfied. Her wages had to be carefully spent.

'That was a marvellous meal, Mother,' her son declared, folding his dinner napkin. 'Now you sit down. I will do the washing-up as usual, and Rose will dry.'

She was glad to leave them to clear the table, for she really was exhausted, not only with her culinary efforts, but with the strain of pretending all was well with their normal routine. She could hear them giggling together in the kitchen, and reminded herself that her son would not embarrass her a second time. A mistress is not like a wife, and Basil would never marry Rose while Prue was alive.

So the long day passed, with Rose as flushed and excited as a child over her presents, hurriedly assembled by Basil's mother: a box of lavender soap − she always used Wright's Coal Tar; embroidered Swiss handkerchiefs − she liked a man-sized handkerchief; a bottle of scent − she didn't care for scent. But Basil's box of chocolates was a welcome gift, and she smiled her thanks.

When Basil had received his usual socks and ties, and his mother her usual twin set, they opened Rose's gifts of handkerchiefs. It was all she could afford, and it seemed a safe choice since she did not know their tastes.

Then came the tedious business of cutting down all the

little packages on the tree, so lovingly wrapped by a mother and a grandmother who still expected the same delight and appreciation.

'There is no hurry, dear,' she reminded her impatient son, as he tore off the wrapping.

'Another china cat! Oh, *Mother!*' he grinned, and kissed her cheek.

One by one the little packages were opened, in strict rotation, and Basil's mother exclaimed, 'Isn't that pretty, Basil?' 'Isn't that a useful gift?' 'I do declare it is just what I need,' and so on and so forth, as though she had never seen them until the moment they were unwrapped.

Rose had collected a tablet of soap, a single handkerchief, a face flannel, a hair-tidy and a lavender bag. It did seem rather a silly idea, but when you are in Rome you do as the Romans do, she reminded herself.

Basil had found it even more tedious than usual this year, and was glad to get it over. 'Sit still, Mother. I will make a pot of tea,' he said, like a dutiful son, and he was quickly back with a loaded tray.

The gramophone provided light entertainment till a high tea was served at 6 o'clock, when they sat down to a second substantial meal of ham and tongue, salad, sherry trifle and rich fruit cake.

The evening was enlivened with childish card games, and Hunt the Thimble. Vicky had long since grown up, but her fond grandmother could think of no alternative amusement.

Sustained by frequent pickings at the good things on the sideboard, even Rose was feeling a bit squeamish after emptying the box of Turkish Delight.

Basil had ordered the cab for 9 o'clock. It was a relief to all three when the grandfather clock struck the hour. Basil's mother offered her cheek and Rose kissed it, tentatively.

'Thank you ever so much, Ma'am. It's been a lovely day,' she said, and was ushered into the cab.

'Many thanks, Mother dear.' Basil's lips brushed her cheek, then he was climbing in after Rose. The cabby touched his whip to the mare's flanks, and they moved away. The rattle of the wheels echoed down the silent street, and the woman they had left behind was choked with tears as she went inside and closed the door.

In the semi-darkness under the closed hood, Basil clutched Rose in a fierce embrace. His heart was pounding, his loins aching.

'I want you, Rose. I need you.' His voice held a desperate urgency he had not known since the days when the haughty Kate had teased him into buying her an engagement ring. Her soft, plump body held no resistance. She was hot and sweaty, and infinitely desirable.

'You can have me, love, just as soon as we get back to your place,' she answered. And nearly drove the breath from his body in a bear-hug. Her hat rolled on the floor. She laughed. What did it matter? She would remember this Christmas Day as long as she lived. She was his woman, and he was her man. She hadn't expected him to declare his love, but she had love enough for the two. 'I want you, I need you.' What woman could ask more of a man?

The cabby was not unduly surprised by the size of the tip. It was Christmas Day, and most men were generous with their tips in the company of wives and sweethearts.

'Thank you, Sir!' he said, saluting smartly. 'Goodnight, Sir. Goodnight Madam.'

'Nighty-night,' Rose chirped happily, swinging her hat.

They climbed the stairs. Once inside the flat, Basil seemed to think it was the duty of a gentleman to explain his position before taking advantage of such a trusting nature.

'I can't marry you, Rose, and can't afford to pay you. Prue's private clinic takes most of my salary,' he explained.

'Who said anything about payment?' Rose demanded indignantly, brushing aside his apology. As for marriage, there was no need to mention it. She wasn't a fool.

Dead ashes in the grate did nothing to dispel the cheerlessness of the room. 'Come into the bedroom. I will light the gas fire,' Basil invited, taking her hand.

Rose smiled. 'Sounds cosy.' It *was* cosy. She undressed in front of the fire and Basil undressed in the bathroom. Rose was waiting in the marriage bed. He dropped his bathrobe on the floor and climbed in beside her.

Her warm arms enfolded him, and her plump bosom received him as though he was born to lie there. Lucy and Prue had no substance, no reality, in this overwhelming embrace of Rose.

'Take me then. I am all yours, love. What are we waiting for?'

To wake on Rose's bosom, suckling her breast, was the nearest thing to Paradise Basil had ever known.

'But it's Boxing Day, love, and it's 7 o'clock, and you've ordered the cab for 8 to meet Vicky's train,' Rose reminded him with exasperating calmness.

'My sainted aunt!' he shouted, and sprang into action. He washed, shaved and dressed in record time. Rose was quicker. She had the kettle boiling and had brewed a pot of tea, and made toast without being asked. The early morning is not a man's best time. 'Like a bear with a sore head,' she thought, not unkindly, still enjoying the aftermath of intercourse.

'Never eat anything in the morning,' Basil growled, and drank a second cup of tea standing up, dabbing at a bleeding spot on his chin.

'You need cotton wool for that,' she said. He told her not to fuss. It was quite a revelation that a wonderful lover, who had awakened suckling her breast, could reveal himself as an irritable husband within the short space of half an hour. But she was still a novice and had much to learn of the strange and unpredictable behaviour of the opposite sex.

So she left him, to make the bed and tidy the bathroom. She changed the sheet that was stained with her virgin blood for a clean sheet that she found in the linen cupboard. What would the daily housekeeper make of a blood-stained sheet in the dirty clothes basket? Rose was too happy to worry about a woman she was never likely to meet. It was the daughter for whom she must be careful to leave no trace, so she washed the two cups and saucers under the tap, and hung them back on the dresser. Shortly before 8 o'clock, she put on her hat and coat, and kissed Basil's cheek.

'Where are you going?' he asked.

'Home,' she said.

286

'How are you getting there?'

'Walking.'

He frowned, but could think of no alternative. The cab would be taking him in the opposite direction.

'Goodbye, Basil.' Her smile was warm, and her eyes were kind.

'Rose — you will ...?' he stammered.

'Of course.' She patted his cheek affectionately. Then she was gone.

Chapter Twelve

'Daddy!' She sped down the platform into his outstretched arms. She hadn't changed. She was still his little girl, bubbling over with excitement.

'Hello, pet.' He kissed her tenderly, and they inspected each other with the frankness they had always known in the past.

'You are looking tired, Daddy,' Vicky was quick to see the pouches under his eyes and to smell his stale breath.

'Christmas Eve,' was all he said.

'Of course. That explains it. Poor darling. But you did have a restful day with Granny yesterday?'

He nodded.

'How was Granny?'

'Very well. She sent her love and the present.'

'What is it?'

'Wait and see!'

'You're and old tease.' Her luminous dark eyes were so like her mother's, but there was nothing of Prue in this lively warm-hearted daughter of his. No angry tears or violent tantrums, and no jealousy. Vicky was a normal, affectionate young woman, and he loved her dearly.

She greeted the cabby with a cheery 'Happy Boxing Day!'

'Same to you, Miss,' he grinned. They had known each other since Paul's first Christmas at The Haven, when he had taken both children to the pantomime on Boxing Day.

'I've booked seats for the matinée. It's Mother Goose,' he told Vicky, as they settled in their seats.

'It should be fun,' she said, wishing she could put back the clock. Paul would be working in that hotel kitchen all over the Christmas vacation. Poor darling. She sighed.

'Why the sigh? Is anything wrong?' Basil asked, anxiously.

'Just thinking of Paulie. Washing up all those pots and pans.'

'It won't do him any harm. We all have to shoulder our own burdens and swallow our pride if we want to keep our self-respect.'

'But he's not strong. Coming out from a steaming hot kitchen into the cold air could be harmful to his weak chest.'

'He must wear a muffler.'

'Daddy, don't you care?'

'For Paulie? Of course I do. I think he is a splendid fellow to stick to his guns. Never thought he would have the nerve to defy that arrogant bastard of a parent.'

'Daddy!'

'Sorry, pet. He gets my goat. And just to ignore his own son for no better reason than he discovered Paulie had a will of his own and no taste for the army is absolutely monstrous. Who *did* pay Paul's fees, and who is paying his lodgings?'

'Uncle David.'

'Very decent of him, considering he has no love for Thomas.'

'But he is very fond of Paulie.'

'So I believe.'

'Daddy.'

'Yes?'

'You won't mind if I marry Paulie after we both have finished our training? I love him so very much.'

'This time last year you were in love with Charles.'

'I *thought* I was in love with Charles, but now I know it has always been Paulie.'

'Then you have my blessing.'

'Thank you, Daddy.'

Kissing his daughter reminded him of Rose. They had always shared everything, but not any more. A mistress and a daughter must be kept apart. No trace of Rose remained in the empty flat, no lingering scent, no garment, no unwashed cups or glasses. Basil sighed with relief as he followed Vicky into the bedroom, and watched her drop her cape and hat on the bed.

'I'm starving, Daddy. I missed breakfast,' she told him.

'Then you must make toast,' he said indulgently.

They sat in the kitchen. It was warmer. The dead ashes in the sitting-room would not be cleared till the morrow, when everything was back to normal.

'Why don't you have a gas fire installed? It would save a lot of work and mess,' Vicky suggested.

'That's not such a bad idea. I'll think about it.'

Vicky was facing him across the kitchen table with a plate of toast. She poured him a cup of tea from the fresh brew, and he listened to her chatter about the hospital with only half his mind. He was never likely to meet any of the doctors and sisters of such supreme importance to a young probationer.

'I am taking you out to lunch,' he said, when she paused for breath. 'I thought we would go to Warnes. Give ourselves a treat. What do you think?'

'I think it would be super.'

'How about a brisk walk along the promenade to work up an appetite?'

She giggled. 'I don't need to work at it, darling. I'm always hungry, and heaven knows the hospital food is pretty ghastly. But a breath of a sea sir would be lovely. How was Mummy the last time you visited?' It was a duty question, for the answer seldom varied.

'About the same.'

'Was she expecting you today?'

'She won't know it's Christmas. Matron told me not to worry if I couldn't get there. She said it made no difference, and I was forgotten as soon as I walked out of the house.'

'It's sad, Daddy.'

'It's very sad.'

'Does she mention me?'

'No.'

'Perhaps she has forgotten she has a daughter?'

'Perhaps?'

'Don't look so sad, Daddy. You still have me. It won't

always be like this. When I have finished my training we shall be married and living here in Worthing. Paulie has been promised the curacy at St Matthew's.'

'That's splendid news. I'm glad you won't be staying in London. I did wonder whether you would apply to train as wardens for one of the East End Missions. You and Paulie have always got along so well with your Uncle Edward and Auntie Jane.'

Vicky shook her head. 'Paulie wouldn't last six months. The spirit is willing, but the flesh is weak.'

'You know best.'

'I think so, I hope so.'

'Does Paulie ever hear from Charles?'

'No, not since he left for Sandhurst.'

'Will he marry that girl in show business?'

'I don't think either of them wants marriage, and Auntie Jane told us that Maudie would be going to America.'

'She must be good.'

'Maudie is super. Quite fantastic. Charles adored her.' A fleeting shadow darkened the lively grey eyes, then it was gone.

'Shall we go, Daddy?' she asked, with a tremulous smile.

Thomas was overseas with his regiment, so could not attend his son's ordination or his wedding, but the rest of the family supported him. Both occasions attracted a big congregation to St Matthew's.

The wedding was arranged for a Wednesday afternoon, when the store was closed and the staff of Thomas Brent & Son filled a dozen pews in the side aisle. Resplendent in scarlet uniform, Charles played his role of best man with light-hearted gallantry, flirting with the pretty bridesmaids and kissing the bride with obvious enjoyment.

The Haven was once again echoing to the happy voices and excited laughter, and the clatter of feet on the basement stairs. The green gate stood invitingly open all day, and Grandmama had surprised everyone by offering to pay for outside caterers.

There was no better place for a wedding reception, and the old nursery suite at the top of the house provided just

291

the right nostalgic setting for a honeymoon. Few changes had been made on the top floor since the days when Ellen and her five sisters, with a governess and a nursemaid, had occupied the nursery suite. Old fashioned wash-stands, with rose-patterned jugs and basins, were still considered adequate for the bedrooms, but Grandmama had reluctantly agreed to the conversion into a bathroom of the small bedroom adjoining her own room, soon after the death of Norah, since the superior Elfreda had bluntly refused to carry up cans of hot water for Amelia's hip bath. And who could blame her? She was not a chambermaid.

Ellen had paid for a gas fire to be installed in the old nursery, but she missed the lively company of a coal fire. Three generations of little girls had curled up on the hearthrug to read their books.

Ellen had put fresh flowers in all the rooms, clean towels smelling faintly of lavender, and a new tablet of lavender soap in the soap dish. The rocking-horse still occupied the window recess, and dozens of toy soldiers, packed neatly away in the toy cupboard, had not been taken out of their boxes since the young Smith Minor came to stay. The same sofa, resprung and re-covered, had rested the sick bodies of so many little girls with measles and chicken pox, toothache and earache. To the familiar haven of childhood came Vicky and Paul on their wedding night, when the last of the family had driven away in the station cab, and Grandmama had retired to bed.

The dear old house was silent again, but for the quiet movements of Ellen, tidying the drawing-room. She would be sleeping in Bertha's old room for a week, when the young couple would be moving into the furnished annexe at the Vicarage, and Paul taking up his parochial duties as curate. It was the end of another chapter, and Ellen was sad as she moved about the room, with its lingering scent of lavender water. She could make no plans for herself while Grandmama was alive, and everyone seemed to think she would live to a great age. But there could be a baby this time next year, another child to call her Nana. Now her dark eyes reflected the deep maternity of a woman born to motherhood. When one chapter closed, another opened.

292

'You may use my bathroom, Victoria and Paul,' Grandmama called after them, as they climbed the second flight of stairs.

'Thank you, Grandmama,' they chorused, much surprised by the invitation.

She closed the door on a strong smell of the Wintergreen ointment she rubbed on her aching joints. Her heart was still young enough to envy her two great-grandchildren, and when she was settled in the big marriage bed, she wept a little for her own adored husband, who seemed to be closer in spirit in her old age than in all the long intervening years, since he left her with a family of six girls. She often found herself in tears, in the privacy of her bedroom, tears she was too proud to shed in public. Memories, always memories, and her senses so alert to the tenderness of that long-departed lover, she could actually feel the touch of his bearded face on her breast. He had loved her swollen belly in pregnancy. There was no shyness between them, no Victorian modesty. She must have been rather a naughty little puss!

It had been an exciting day, and she fell asleep with the tears wet on her cheeks.

As for Vicky, she had seen too many naked bodies to be embarrassed by a newly-wed husband. But Paul was shy, and their wedding night might easily have been the prelude to impotency but for her understanding of his natural reluctance to take the initiative. His lean young body, still damp from the bath, trembled under the clean night-shirt as he climbed in beside her. She was wearing her prettiest nightgown, and her skin smelled faintly of the lavender soap.

'I do love you so very much, my darling,' she whispered, stroking his cheek. His dark eyes were anguished. 'We could wait, Paulie. It doesn't have to be tonight. We have all the time in the world now we are married.' It was the voice of a mother soothing a child. She could be his mother or she could be his wife, on their wedding night. She was all woman, all maternal, and she held him close. He could feel her heart racing, her breath was sweet. Her hair tickled his cheek. This was Vicky, and she was no stranger. They had shared this same bed with Nana in the early morning, one on either side, waiting for Norah to bring the mugs of tea and the *petit beurre* biscuits. They had opened their stockings on Christmas morning in this same bed.

His thoughts flew back to the very first day he had met his little cousin. She had taken his hand and they had climbed the stairs.

'We have an indoor lavatory and an outdoor lavatory,' she had explained, with great seriousness. 'The indoor lavatory is more comfortable. It smells of Mansion Polish and it has proper toilet paper. The outdoor lavatory smells of Jeyes Fluid, and it has little squares of newspaper tied to a string.'

So they used the indoor lavatory after they had climbed the stairs to the first floor. It was all part of the conducted tour while the grown-ups were chatting in the drawing-room.

'Ladies first,' said Vicky. The seat was high. She dropped her drawers and climbed up, swinging her legs.

He was a very grave little boy and very obedient. Being a soldier's son, obedience was second nature. So when she slid off the seat, pulled up her drawers, and invited, 'Your turn, Paul', he raised the seat, unfastened the buttons, and took out his little dickie. Vicky was obviously impressed.

'Aren't you clever. You can pee standing up!' she cried. 'Do all little boys pee standing up?'

'I don't know. Ayah showed me when I was three.'

In all the years they had shared this bed with Nana, he had not seen her drawers or her bottom.

'Cover yourself, dear,' Nana would say, as Vicky climbed into bed.

Now she was holding him close, the same Vicky, in the same bed.

'Why are you smiling, darling?' she asked.

He told her. She hugged him tight, and shouted with laughter. It was shared laughter that cured his shyness, and warm young bodies clung together in a ecstasy of naked fulfilment.

Paul Cartwright climbed the stairs to the pulpit to preach his first sermon. Here, in the Church of St Matthew's, his great-grandfather had preached, and his spirit was here. 'Courage, my boy, and Faith. All is well,' he was saying.

So when he looked down on the packed congregation that Easter Sunday morning, he was not afraid. The sweet scent of lilies on the altar took him back in time for a brief moment, to the grave of his beloved Ayah, in the cemetery some distance from the North West Frontier.

The verger was showing a couple of late-comers into a back pew, and he waited for them to be seated, a tall, distinguished figure, in scarlet uniform, and a fashionably dressed little lady – *his parents*! He had not seen them for four years. His throat went dry, and his mind was a blank. Then Vicky coughed discreetly in the front pew, and he glanced down. She smiled, her dark eyes tender with love. All the family was here, to honour his ordination to the ministry – Grandmama, nodding energetically, Nana, Auntie Jane and Uncle Edward, Auntie Kate and Uncle Charles, Auntie Grace and Uncle Henry, Auntie Bella and Uncle Roderic and Uncle Basil. Uncle David, inconspicuous in civilian dress, sat alone in the side aisle. It was a proud moment.

Paul lifted his head. His voice was clear and confident. His young face exultant. 'I have taken my text for today from the Sermon on the Mount – "Take, therefore, no thought for the morrow, for the morrow shall take thought for the things of itself. Sufficient unto the day is the evil thereof".'

Major Thomas Cartwright was impressed. Here was courage of a different kind. He would congratulate his son after the service, and they would have lunch together at The Haven.

'He is rather sweet, is he not, my darling?' Rosalind whispered, as he clasped her little gloved hand.